TILL DEATH

TILL DEATH

A HAVE BRIDES, WILL TRAVEL WESTERN

WILLIAM W. JOHNSTONE

AND J.A. JOHNSTONE

PINNACLE BOOKS
Kensington Publishing Corp.
www.kensingtonbooks.com

PINNACLE BOOKS are published by

Kensington Publishing Corp.
119 West 40th Street
New York, NY 10018

Copyright © 2021 by J. A. Johnstone

PUBLISHER'S NOTE
Following the death of William W. Johnstone, the Johnstone family is working with a carefully selected writer to organize and complete Mr. Johnstone's outlines and many unfinished manuscripts to create additional novels in all of his series like The Last Gunfighter, Mountain Man, and Eagles, among others. This novel was inspired by Mr. Johnstone's superb storytelling.

All Kensington titles, imprints, and distributed lines are available at special quantity discounts for bulk purchases for sales promotion, premiums, fundraising, educational, or institutional use.

Special book excerpts or customized printings can also be created to fit specific needs. For details, write or phone the office of the Kensington Sales Manager: Attn.: Sales Department. Kensington Publishing Corp., 119 West 40th Street, New York, NY 10018. Phone: 1-800-221-2647.

PINNACLE BOOKS, the Pinnacle logo, and the WWJ steer head logo are Reg. U.S. Pat. & TM Off.

First Kensington Books Hardcover Printing: April 2021
First Pinnacle Books Mass-Market Paperback Printing: September 2021
ISBN-13: 978-0-7860-4735-2
ISBN-10: 0-7860-4735-6

ISBN-13: 978-0-7860-4736-9 (eBook)
ISBN-10: 0-7860-4736-4 (eBook)

10 9 8 7 6 5 4 3 2 1

Printed in the United States of America

Chapter 1

"How is it that with all the roamin' around we've done for more'n forty years, we never made it up into this part of the country?" Scratch Morton asked as he peered out the railroad car window at the heavily timbered slopes rolling past. The hillsides came up fairly close to the roadbed on both sides.

"I don't know," Bo Creel replied from where he sat on the hard wooden bench next to his old friend. Bo stretched his legs into the aisle that ran down the middle of the car and crossed them at the ankles. "I reckon we just never had a good enough reason to drift up this way."

Washington State was a long way from Texas, that was for sure, and was where Bo and Scratch hailed from. Not that they had spent most of their time there over the years, as Scratch had indicated.

They had grown up in the Lone Star State and had, in fact, taken part in the fight for Texas's independence from Mexico when they were in their middle teens. In those days, that had been considered being a man "full-growed," especially if a fella was big enough to pick up a rifle and take part in the fight against the dictator Santa Anna's army. Bo and Scratch had done just that at San Jacinto, back on that warm April day in 1836.

Since then the two of them had been through a lot together: triumph and tragedy, dreams fulfilled and hopes lost, and restless natures that wouldn't be denied as they drifted fiddle-footed around the frontier, not searching for trouble but inevitably finding it.

In recent months they had taken to working for a matrimonial agency, of all things. Cyrus Keegan, who ran the business out of Fort Worth, provided mail-order brides for lonely bachelors all over the West, from the Rio Grande to the Milk River, from the Mississippi to the Pacific. Those brides often needed protection when they were traveling to meet their new husbands, and Bo and Scratch provided it. At their semi-advanced age, Bo and Scratch were considered safe enough chaperones and guards for young ladies.

This trip was just getting started, but already it had been quite a journey for Bo and Scratch, all the way up here to the Pacific Northwest from New Mexico, where their previous chore had resulted in a surprising number of powder-burning ruckuses.

That was all right, though; neither of the Texans enjoyed being bored, and flying lead broke up the monotony just fine as long as it didn't come too close.

At the moment they were on their way to Seattle. Cyrus Keegan had given them the job in person, once things were squared away down in Silverhill. Bo and Scratch never could have made it up here in time if they hadn't been able to make connections on several different railroads.

Now they were rocking along in a passenger car belonging to the Northern Pacific, which had only recently completed its route through this part of the country and become the nation's second transcontinental railroad. Farther back in the train, Bo's and Scratch's horses rode in one of the livestock cars.

More than likely, the horses would have to be stabled once they reached Seattle, because the next leg of the journey would be by ship.

"Alaska," Scratch mused as he thumbed his cream-colored Stetson back on his thick silvery hair. "I swear, until mighty recent, if somebody had asked me, I would've said it was part of Roosha."

"Not since 1867. And I'm sure you heard of Seward's Folly back then, because we talked about it. You've just forgotten."

"I never forgot a thing! My mind's like a steel trap."

"Rusted shut?" Bo asked with an innocent look.

"I thought Seward's Folly was when Pancho Seward up and bought that house of ill repute down in Laredo—"

Scratch didn't get any further than that, because the train suddenly lurched violently and both Texans were thrown forward against the back of the bench seat in front of them. The adventurous lives they'd led had allowed them to retain the reflexes and reactions of younger men, and they were able to catch themselves against the seatback and push to their feet.

"What in blazes!" Scratch said.

The train was still moving, but a lot slower now. Wheels screeched loudly on the steel rails. Other men in the car stood up and asked questions, and some of the women let out frightened cries because obviously something was wrong.

"The engineer's trying to stop in a hurry," Bo said. He

raised his voice so the other passengers in the car could hear him as he called, "Everybody grab on to something!"

Another jolt rocked the car, so heavy this time that, for a second, Bo thought the train might derail. The cars stayed upright, though, as the train finally shuddered to a halt.

Bo and Scratch had braced themselves on the seat and were able to keep their feet. Some of the other men hadn't been as quick to react and spilled to the floor in the aisle.

From somewhere outside came sudden, booming reports of gunfire. Scratch said, "You folks stay where you are and keep your heads down!" He looked at Bo. "I reckon we're gonna see what this is all about?"

"What do you think?" Bo said as he drew the walnut-butted Colt on his hip and stepped over one of the fallen passengers. He hurried toward the vestibule at the front of the car.

Scratch was right behind him. The silver-haired Texan carried two long-barreled Remington revolvers with ivory grips, and they were in his hands as he emerged onto the car's front platform.

A shot blasted somewhere not far away. Bo heard the wind rip of the bullet as it passed close beside his ear. He pivoted toward the sound and saw a man on horseback about twenty feet away, thrusting a gun at him for a second try at murder.

Bo's Colt snapped up and spewed flame. The would-be killer, who had a red bandanna pulled up over the lower half of his face, rocked back in the saddle as the .45 slug ripped through his upper right arm. His gun flew out of his hand before he could get another shot off. His horse began to dance around skittishly, and the wounded man quickly lost his grip and toppled off his mount.

On the other side of the platform, Scratch crouched at the railing and leveled both Remingtons at a handful of masked riders charging up that side of the train. The men fired their guns into the windows of the cars they passed, shattering glass and prompting terrified screams from the passengers inside.

They didn't notice Scratch until they came alongside the platform, so he took them by surprise as he began triggering both Remingtons. Lead scythed through the group of riders, knocking two of them out of their saddles. A couple more twisted and cried out under the slugs' impact.

They concentrated their fire on the platform then, as they realized that a deadly threat lurked there. Scratch ducked back, grabbed Bo, and dived to the floor as a storm of bullets ripped through the air just above them.

Farther up the train, toward the engine, an explosion roared and a cloud of smoke billowed up. "They've blown the door to the express car!" Bo said as the riders on both sides of the train abandoned their attack and charged forward along the railbed.

Scratch raised his head to look around. "Appears they ain't gonna bother robbin' the passengers. Must be something in the express car safe they're more interested in."

Shots continued to come from up ahead. Bo said, "The express messengers are putting up a fight."

"Want to go give 'em a hand?"

"I was thinking about it," Bo said.

As Bo stood up, he glanced toward the spot where the man he'd shot had fallen. The hombre wasn't there anymore. Bo figured one of the other outlaws had picked him up.

Holstering his Colt, Bo stepped across to the rear platform on the next car and gripped the iron grab bars on the side. He climbed to the roof with a speed and agility that belied his years. Scratch came up behind him.

The Texans drew their guns again and started forward, sticking to the middle of the roof and crouching as they hurried so they wouldn't be spotted as easily from the ground.

There were two more passenger cars ahead of the one in which Bo and Scratch had been riding, then the express car. A thinning cloud of smoke from the dynamite that had gone off hung over that car. The outlaws on that side of the train had dismounted and scattered, taking cover in nearby brush and behind rocks as they fired at the express car.

The ones on the other side had galloped ahead, no doubt to take over the engine and keep the engineer and fireman from causing any trouble. Bo spotted them up there around the cab.

That was a problem to be dealt with later, if at all. It was more important right now to keep those robbers from looting the express car.

Not that he and Scratch had any stake in whatever was in the safe. Nobody was paying them to fight off these owlhoots. They were doing it because they had a deep and abiding dislike of lawbreakers, despite the fact that they themselves had been accused of being outlaws over the years and had wound up behind bars a few times because of it.

They leaped the gap between the next two passenger cars, then dropped to their knees and stretched out behind the shallow raised area in the center of the roof. It wouldn't provide much cover but was better than nothing. From where they were, they had a good angle to open fire on the robbers.

Before they did that, they thumbed fresh rounds into the cylinders of their guns so they had full wheels when they started shooting. They didn't blast away indiscriminately, either, but aimed their shots where they caught a glimpse of the outlaws or at least the spurts of powder smoke from their guns.

The steady, lethal fire raked through the brush and among the rocks. One of the outlaws toppled into the open after Scratch drilled a .44 bullet through his head. An arm snaked out from behind the same boulder, caught hold of the man's foot, and dragged him back out of sight, but it was too late to help him. Scratch's shot had killed him instantly.

Below them in the express car, a rifle cracked frequently, interspersed with dull booms from a shotgun. The shotgun wasn't going to be very effective at this range, Bo thought, but in a fight, it never hurt to have some buckshot flying around at your enemies. Might make them keep their heads down a little more, anyway.

Some of the men who had taken cover in the rocks and brush raised their sights and returned the fire from Bo and Scratch. The Texans had to scoot backward and keep their own heads down as bullets whipped through the air above them. They took advantage of the opportunity to reload again, and then when the gun thunder let up, they poked their revolvers over the crest of the railroad car's roof and slammed more rounds in the outlaws' direction.

Between the stubborn defenders inside the express car and the two Texans atop the train, the robbers were meeting much stiffer resistance than they had expected. That was what Bo figured a minute later when a harsh voice yelled, "Let's get out of here!"

"What about the boys up at the engine?" another man shouted.

"They're on their own, damn it!"

Several men leaped to their feet and retreated, firing as they fled deeper into the brush where they had left their horses. Bo and Scratch sent more slugs after them to hurry them on their way. A moment later they heard the swift rat-aplan of hoofbeats and caught glimpses through the undergrowth of men and horses moving fast in flight.

Bo turned his head to look toward the engine and saw that the members of the gang up there were abandoning the robbery attempt as well. Four horses raced away from the rails, one of the mounts carrying double. More than likely that extra rider was the man Bo had shot through the arm.

As the shooting died away but echoes continued to roll around in the hills on both sides of the tracks, Scratch said, "Looks like they're takin' off for the tall and uncut, Bo. You want to grab our horses out of the stock car and go after 'em?"

"I reckon that's more than anybody could expect of us," Bo replied as he reloaded the Colt yet again with fresh cartridges from the loops on his shell belt. "Anyway, by the time we could do that, they'd have a big enough lead, we couldn't catch them. Let's climb down from here and see if anybody's hurt bad."

"And find out how they got the dang train to stop in the first place," Scratch added.

Bo was a mite curious about that himself.

Chapter 2

They clambered down from the train on the same side as the blown-open sliding door on the express car. The dynamite had blasted the door right off, Bo saw, but he couldn't tell how much damage it had done inside. He didn't want to spook the men in the car, so as he and Scratch approached the jagged opening, he called, "Hello, in the express car! Hold your fire. We're friends."

Now that the echoes from the gunfire had finally faded, the sound of shotgun hammers being cocked inside the car could be heard.

"How do we know that?" a man demanded. "You could be some o' them no-good snake-in-the-grass train robbers!"

"We're no train robbers," Scratch responded. "We're the ones who ran 'em off, you old codger!"

The shotgun's twin barrels poked out of the opening, and a leathery white-whiskered face appeared above them.

"Old codger, is it? You look to be ever' bit as old as I am, you fancy-dressed skalleyhooter!"

It was true that Scratch's outfit was a little on the fancy side. In addition to the cream-colored Stetson and ivory-handled guns, he favored a fringed buckskin jacket over a white shirt, brown whipcord trousers, and high-topped darker brown boots into which the trousers were tucked.

Bo, in contrast, wore a long dark coat and trousers, and with his white shirt, string tie, and flat-crowned black hat, he resembled a circuit-riding preacher more than anything else. Not many preachers carried a Colt with a butt so well worn from long usage, though.

"My friend's telling the truth," Bo assured the fierce old-timer. "When the train stopped so short, we knew there had to be trouble brewing, so we decided to take a hand. My name's Bo Creel, and this is Scratch Morton."

"Never heard of ye!" the old-timer snorted. "Keep them guns leathered and don't reach for 'em, or I'll touch off both barrels!"

Bo made sure to keep his hands in plain sight as he said, "Don't worry about that, mister. We're peaceable men."

"You just claimed you shot up that bunch o' train robbers! You can't have it both ways."

"Well," Scratch said, "we're peaceable men until some owlhoot comes along and forces our hand."

A moan came from somewhere else in the express car. The old-timer withdrew the shotgun abruptly and said, "Josh! What's wrong, boy?"

"I . . . I'm all right, Smitty," the voice of a younger man answered. "A bullet nicked me. It's not bad, but it hurts like blazes!"

Scratch said, "Reckon Bo or me could tend to it. We've had a heap of experience patchin' up bullet wounds."

Smitty stuck his head back out of the opening and said, "All right, come on in if you want. I suppose you fellas'll do to trust. I seen some of those desperadoes get ventilated, and I could tell it wasn't Josh or me doin' it."

Bo said to Scratch, "I'll deal with this. You go on up ahead and check on the engineer and fireman. Give me a boost before you go, though."

"Yeah, we ain't quite as spry as we once were, are we?"

Bo could have pointed out that just a few minutes earlier they had been running around on top of a train and shooting it out with a gang of robbers . . . but that had been in the heat of battle. A fella was capable of a lot more when bullets were zipping past his head. That tended to make him forget how old he really was.

Scratch made a stirrup with his hands and helped Bo pull himself up into the express car, then trotted off toward the engine. Bo looked around and saw that the force of the blast had knocked over the two chairs inside the car, but the sturdy desk and even sturdier safe didn't appear to have been affected.

The old-timer Smitty set one of the chairs upright and helped a younger man sit down on it. Josh wasn't exactly young, probably in his early forties, with dark hair so thinned that only a few strands of it ventured from one side of his scalp to the other. Both he and Smitty wore pin-striped trousers, gray wool vests, and white shirts with garters on the sleeves. It was standard garb for employees of Wells Fargo who rode these express cars. They functioned more as clerks than guards, but as today's events had proven, in times of trouble they were expected to fight back.

Josh had blood on his vest and shirt. Bo knelt in front of him and said, "Let me take a look." He moved the bloody garments aside and revealed a small hole low on Josh's right side, just above his waist. Bo reached around and felt more blood on the back of the man's shirt where the bullet had come out.

"You're lucky," he said. "Through and through. It's messy and I'm sure it hurts like blazes, like you said, but where the holes are located, I doubt if it did any real damage. I can clean it up and bandage it, but you'll need some real medical attention when you get to Seattle." He turned his head to ask Smitty, "Do you have any whiskey in here?"

"We ain't allowed to have liquor in the express car."

Bo just looked at him for a couple of seconds.

"All right, all right, I might have a little flask cached somewheres."

"Pour some of it on a clean rag," Bo told him.

While Bo was cleaning the entrance and exit wounds, a stocky man wearing a blue uniform and black cap hurried up to the blown-out door and said, "Josh, Smitty, are you boys all right in there?"

"We're alive," Smitty answered. "Josh got drilled, but this fella don't seem to think it's too bad." The old-timer paused. "Claims he and a pard of his are the ones who helped drive off them robbers."

"It's true," the conductor said. "I saw you up there from the caboose, mister. Who are you? Are you and your friend railroad detectives?"

"No," said Bo, "we're in the mail-order bride business."

He had to admit, he kind of got a kick out of how the other three men stared goggle-eyed at him.

A short time later, Bo and Scratch stood alongside the cowcatcher at the front of the engine with the conductor, the engineer, and the fireman and looked at the pile of logs haphazardly blocking the tracks. Some of them had been scattered by the collision with the cowcatcher.

The fireman had a bloodstained rag tied around his left arm where he had been grazed by a bullet. He raised his right arm and pointed at a steep slope to the left.

"They rolled 'em down from there," he said. "I saw the last couple of logs comin' down the hill at the same time as Roy spotted the ones already on the tracks, and I threw on the brakes."

"We almost got stopped in time, too," the engineer said. "It gave the train a pretty good jolt when we plowed into the pile, but it would've been worse if we'd been going faster. Might have even been enough to derail us."

The conductor sighed and nodded. "I'll go through the passenger cars and see if I can get some volunteers to move those logs. Hope we've got some big, strong men on board today. That'll be faster than climbing a pole and cutting in on a telegraph line to call for a work train out of Seattle."

"How far out are we?" Bo asked.

"Not all that far, really. We'll be there in a couple of hours. Or I should say, we would have been. It'll take a while to get these tracks cleared." The conductor stuck out his hand. "Thanks for pitching in like you did, both of you. I reckon they would have killed Josh and Smitty, and there's no telling who else they might have hurt. As far as I know, nobody else was wounded, just shaken up some when the train had to stop so short."

Bo and Scratch shook hands with the conductor, and then the engineer and fireman wanted to shake, too. While that was going on, Scratch asked, "Have you been havin' trouble with holdups on this run?"

The conductor shrugged. "Some. Today's the first time they ever dynamited the express car, though. The other times they just robbed the passengers."

"Same bunch?"

"Who in Hades knows? One outlaw with a mask on looks just like every other one." The conductor shook his head and went on. "Somehow they must have known—"

The abrupt way the man stopped made Bo think. He said, "The express car was carrying a bigger load of money than usual, wasn't it?"

"If you were a lawman, friend, I might answer that."

"Lawman, hell," the engineer said. "I don't care who these fellas are, they done us a favor, and when they get to Seattle, Rollin Kemp ought to give them a reward, if you ask me. Or at least stand 'em to some drinks in his saloon!"

Bo said, "I take it that money shipment is going to this fella Kemp?"

The conductor sighed and then said, "You didn't hear it from me, but . . . yeah, that's right. He owns one of the biggest saloons in Seattle."

"Seems like he'd be more likely to be shippin' money out instead of in," Scratch commented.

"Don't ask me about Kemp's business. He's a good man not to get too curious about, if you know what I mean."

While the conductor went to round up more help, Bo, Scratch, and the engineer got busy moving logs. The fireman, with his wounded arm, had to stand aside from that chore. Most of the logs were too heavy to lift, even for four men, but they were able to roll some of the thick trunks out of the way.

With the help of a dozen more passengers, the track was cleared in about an hour. Everyone climbed back aboard, the engineer got up steam, and the train rolled on toward Seattle.

Once Bo and Scratch were settled in their seats again, the silver-haired Texan took off his hat and said, "I could practically see the wheels turnin' in your head, Bo, while we were talkin' to the conductor. He got you wonderin' about the gang that's been holdin' up trains in these parts, didn't he?"

"We don't know it's always the same gang," Bo said.

"Could be, though. And you were curious, too, about how they knew about that pile of money in the express car safe."

Bo nodded slowly. "Yeah, those thoughts crossed my mind. It's going to be up to somebody else to poke around and get to the bottom of it, though, if that ever happens. We have responsibilities of our own, remember?"

"I ain't likely to forget, especially when those responsibilities are named Beatrice, Martha, Sally, and Caroline."

Chapter 3

Seattle's Occidental Hotel was a grand, two-and-a-half-story, whitewashed wooden building at the foot of a hill covered with fine homes, although the residences were less ostentatious as the slope went higher. Beyond the hill, the snowcapped peak of one of the mountains east of the city was visible.

Looking the other direction from the second-floor balcony on the front of the hotel, as she was doing this moment, Beatrice O'Rourke could see Puget Sound and Elliott Bay, as well as Bainbridge Island on the opposite side of the wide stretch of water. Beatrice rested her hands on the railing and thought, not for the first time, what a beautiful place this was.

She had no interest in remaining in Seattle, however. Not with what she hoped was waiting for her in Alaska.

Beatrice was an attractive dark-haired woman in her late thirties. A small beauty mark near her mouth gave her face character rather than detracting from her looks. Her brown eyes displayed intelligence and determination as she peered toward the waterfront, where the tall masts of numerous ships stood out against the sweep of water in the sound.

A soft footstep behind her made Beatrice turn away from the railing. Her niece Caroline DeHerries stood there, her hands clasped together and a nervous look on her lovely face. Caroline was twenty years old, in the full flower of young beauty. Fluffy blond hair surrounded her face.

"He's downstairs again, Aunt Beatrice," Caroline said. "I spotted him waiting in the lobby and ducked back upstairs before he noticed me. At least, I hope so."

"Kemp, you mean?"

"Yes, Mr. Kemp."

Beatrice's lips tightened in anger. "I've had one talk with the man already. It appears I shall have to have another one."

"Perhaps I can just avoid him until it's time to leave Seattle," Caroline said. "Surely it won't be much longer before the escorts employed by the agency arrive and we can book our passage to Alaska."

"Yes, they should be here any day now," Beatrice agreed, "but any time spent enduring the unwanted attentions of a boor such as Rollin Kemp is too long."

She moved past Caroline and went into one of the two adjoining rooms where the mail-order brides were staying.

Martha Rousseau and Sally Bechdolt sat at a table in the room, playing cribbage. They were younger than Beatrice, in their early thirties, but like Beatrice and Caroline, they were quite attractive. Martha had auburn curls piled on her head, while Sally's blond hair was darker than Caroline's, more like the color of honey. Both women looked up from their cards as Beatrice stalked into the room.

"You look like you're about to march off to war," Sally said. "What's wrong?"

"Caroline just told me we have a snake lurking downstairs," Beatrice replied.

"And you're going to go chop his head off?" Martha asked.

"It may come to that," Beatrice said.

The three women followed her as she left the room and headed for the stairs. Caroline hung back, staying behind Martha and Sally.

When Beatrice reached the bottom of the staircase, she stopped and looked around the lobby, which, while hardly as ornate as the hotel lobbies to be found back east in the big cities, was furnished comfortably and had a few potted plants here and there. Beatrice's gaze focused on a man wearing a gray tweed suit and sitting in a wing chair next to one of those plants.

He was reading a newspaper, or at least pretending to. He kept shifting his gaze to look over its top. A black derby hat rested on a small round table on the other side of the chair from the plant.

With a frown on her face, Beatrice strode determinedly toward him.

The man saw her coming, of course. The lobby wasn't busy enough that he could fail to notice her approach. He lowered the paper and stood up, then folded the paper and tossed it onto the table next to the derby.

"Mrs. O'Rourke," he said with a smile. "It's nice to see you again."

When they first met, he had referred to her as Miss O'Rourke, but she had set him straight immediately, informing him that she was a widow, as were Martha and

Sally. Caroline was the only one among them who had never been married.

"I wish I could say the same about seeing *you*, Mr. Kemp," Beatrice responded coolly. "I thought I made it plain in our previous conversation that Miss DeHerries has no interest in being courted by you."

Kemp didn't know that Caroline was actually her niece, and she didn't see any reason to explain it to the lout.

"Well, that's what *you* said, ma'am." Rollin Kemp took a cigar from his vest pocket and clamped it between his teeth so it stuck up at a jaunty angle. Around the fat unlit cylinder of tobacco, he went on, "I haven't actually heard that sentiment expressed by Miss DeHerries."

Kemp was a burly man of medium height with oily dark hair and a thin mustache. Some women might consider him handsome in a coarse, earthy way. Beatrice just considered him crude.

She knew that he was a successful businessman who owned a large saloon called the Timber Treasure, and there were rumors that he was involved with a number of even less savory enterprises. He had been in the Occidental Hotel's lobby when Beatrice and the others had arrived from the railroad station almost a week earlier, and as soon as he'd laid eyes on Caroline DeHerries, he had decided that he wanted her, even though he was close to twice her age. He had approached her and invited her to have dinner with him.

Caroline had refused him in a sweet and polite fashion— because Caroline never did things any other way—but Kemp didn't want to take no for an answer. He had been hanging around the hotel every day since then, trying to catch Caroline so he could speak to her and plead his case, to the point that Beatrice had been forced to step in and have a talk with him.

Beatrice was the one who had come up with the plan to seek husbands through Cyrus Keegan's matrimonial agency. She considered herself the leader of their little group and felt some responsibility for the others' safety and comfort.

Since Alaska was considered an untamed frontier, Mr. Keegan had promised to provide two men to escort them from Seattle on the rest of their journey, but Beatrice didn't know anything about them except their names— Creel and Morton—and the fact that they hadn't arrived yet. She supposed they were trustworthy, or else Mr. Keegan wouldn't have hired them.

Kemp stood there with a challenging look on his face. Beatrice lifted her chin and said, "I believe Miss DeHerries *did* express her feelings to you, but if you insist on having them repeated . . ."

She turned and gestured for Caroline to come out from behind Martha and Sally. She had to repeat the motion, a little more curtly this time, before Caroline finally stepped around the other women and approached, looking like a terrified fawn about to bolt.

Kemp took the cigar out of his mouth and said, "Miss DeHerries, I'm very pleased to see you again. I apologize if I've caused you any discomfort. It's just that in a place like Seattle, a fellow never runs across such a rare gem as yourself."

Caroline looked down at her toes. Beatrice frowned at her until she looked up, and then Beatrice nodded for her to go ahead and speak up. Caroline cleared her throat and said, "Thank you for the compliment, Mr. Kemp, but I . . .

I must insist that you abandon your . . . your quest to woo me. You see, as has been explained to you, I am already betrothed and have a husband waiting for me."

"In Alaska," Kemp said, sounding as if he thought that was the most insane thing he had ever heard. "And a gent you've never even met, at that. It seems to me, Miss DeHerries, that you're under no obligation to honor such a dubious arrangement, especially if a better opportunity were to come along—"

"Which it has not," Beatrice interrupted him.

Kemp had the cigar between his fingers. As Beatrice saw anger flare in his eyes, she thought he might close his hand and crumple it. Instead he blurted out, "I didn't ask for your opinion, you witch."

Beatrice stepped closer and slapped him. Her hand came up and cracked across his face so rapidly that he didn't have time to avoid the blow. In fact, he looked so surprised as he took a step back that it appeared he hadn't even seen it coming.

Caroline gasped and hopped backward a couple of steps. Martha and Sally moved forward, closer to Beatrice if she needed their help.

Kemp threw the cigar aside. He had been making an effort to speak in a polite manner, but that disappeared as he rasped, "Why, you old bat! No woman's gonna do that to me and get away with—"

He took a step toward Beatrice and raised a fist as he spoke, but she didn't retreat. She wore an angry, defiant expression and seemed to be daring him to do his worst.

Kemp didn't get a chance to do anything other than stop in his tracks, because at that moment the muzzle of a rifle barrel pressed against the side of his head and a voice drawled, "That ain't no way to treat a lady, mister. You best stand right where you are, or I'll blow your brains out."

Behind Beatrice, Caroline sighed and swooned, falling to the floor in a dead faint.

Chapter 4

Bo stepped around Scratch, nodded, and pinched the brim of his hat as he said to the nice-looking dark-haired woman, "Ma'am, are you all right?"

Amusement twinkled in her brown eyes as she said, "Why are you asking me? I'm not the one who got slapped."

"Considering the way he was talking to you, ma'am, I'd say he got what was coming to him."

"I agree with you, sir. I'm fine, although I don't believe this . . . gentleman . . . would have dared to lay a finger on me. However, I appreciate your assistance."

The ugly fella with Scratch's Winchester held to his head said, "You stupid cowboy, do you have any idea who I am?"

"Can't say as I do," Scratch replied, "and I can't say as I give a darn. All I know is you're an hombre who don't know how to talk to womenfolks, or how to treat 'em, neither."

"I'm an important man in this town. I'm Rollin Kemp!"

"Is that so? Well, now that I know that, I'm a mite sorry we saved that money o' yours from those train robbers."

Despite the threat of Scratch's rifle, Kemp turned his head slightly, enough to stare at the Texans and exclaim, "What!"

"Outlaws stopped the train we just came into Seattle on," Bo explained coolly. "They were after the money in the express car that we were told belongs to you. We helped run them off before they were able to grab the loot."

"And if we'd known you were the sort of hombre to mistreat a lady," Scratch said, "we wouldn't have risked our hides to do it!"

By now the tense confrontation had drawn quite a bit of attention. Other guests of the hotel, as well as the desk clerk, were staring at the group of people not far from the bottom of the staircase. Nobody stepped forward to get involved, but Bo thought it was likely somebody had slipped out to fetch the local law.

It might be a good idea, he decided, to bring this to an end so they wouldn't have to spend a lot of time standing around talking to some badge-toter. Lawmen tended to blame him and Scratch any time there was trouble, whether it was their fault or not.

"I don't reckon Mr. Kemp will be trying anything else," he said. "Why don't we let him be on his way?"

Scratch pulled the Winchester's muzzle away from Kemp's head. He'd been standing there holding the rifle one-handed, not an easy thing to do, especially for an extended time. But the Winchester had never wavered in Scratch's grip.

"You heard the fella, Kemp. Light a shuck outta here."

The man glared at both of them and said, "You'll be sorry you ever meddled in my business."

"People have been telling us we're going to be sorry for

one thing or another for more than forty years now," Bo said. "Are you sorry, Scratch?"

"Not one dang bit," the silver-haired Texan replied. He lowered the rifle but kept it ready to lift again if he needed to.

Kemp grabbed his derby from the table, turned on his heel, and stalked toward the door, slowing down only long enough to bark, "Get out of the damn way!" at a man who was standing there. The man stepped hurriedly aside and Kemp slammed out.

Bo and Scratch turned toward the group of women. Bo had taken note of it when one of them—a young, pretty blonde—had fainted, but a statuesque, auburn-haired beauty and a smaller woman with honey-colored hair pulled behind her head had been tending to her. The woman—little more than a girl, really—who had swooned was back on her feet now but looked none too steady as the other two supported her.

Bo took off his hat and held it in front of him as he said to the blonde, "I'm sorry if we frightened you, miss. When you're dealing with varmints like that fella Kemp, you have to speak a language they understand."

"And .44 caliber's sort of a . . . what do you call it . . . universal language," Scratch added.

The dark-haired woman put a hand on the young blonde's shoulder and asked, "Are you all right, Caroline?"

"Yes, Aunt Beatrice, I . . . I suppose I'm just not used to seeing guns being waved around." She summoned up a weak smile for Bo and Scratch and went on. "Thank you, gentlemen. Mr. Kemp has been quite a . . . a vexation."

Scratch grunted and said, "That's a good word for it, I reckon. I can think of some others that—"

"Would you happen to be Mrs. O'Rourke, ma'am?"

Bo had heard what the young blonde and the dark-haired woman called each other when he and Scratch had walked into the Occidental's lobby, so he interrupted Scratch to get everyone back on track. When Bo had noticed the four women standing together, he'd wondered if they might not be the ones that he and Scratch were looking for. It would be quite a coincidence if it turned out that way, but life was full of coincidences, after all.

Beatrice looked a little surprised. "Why, yes, I am. And you are . . . ?"

"Bo Creel, ma'am. And this is Scratch Morton."

Scratch took his hat off, too, and said, "It's a plumb honor, Miz O'Rourke."

"You mean, you're the men Mr. Keegan promised would meet us here in Seattle and accompany us to Alaska?"

"That's right," Bo said.

"Hope you're not plumb disappointed," Scratch added with a grin.

"Not at all. We've been expecting you."

"I'm sorry we couldn't make it here sooner," Bo said. "We were down in New Mexico Territory when Cyrus told us to come on up here as quickly as we could, and it took a considerable amount of switching trains along the way."

"Well, you're here now, and I'm glad. I think all of us are ready to depart from Seattle as soon as it's practical to do so."

"Yes, ma'am. And these other ladies are Mrs. Rousseau, Mrs. Bechdolt, and Miss DeHerries?"

"That's right. I suppose we can take care of the formal introductions later, perhaps at supper. Caroline looks as if she needs to go upstairs and lie down for a while."

"Sure, that'll be fine. Scratch and I will get a room and see you later."

"We're in rooms seven and nine," Beatrice O'Rourke said.

She ushered the others upstairs.

"Mighty fine-lookin' bunch of ladies," Scratch commented quietly as he watched them ascend the staircase. "Ol' Cyrus seems to know how to come up with 'em. But you wouldn't think gals who look like that, and the others we've dealt with, would need help findin' fellas who'd want to marry up with 'em."

"You never know what somebody else's story is," Bo said.

"Shoot, half the time I don't know what mine is."

Bo nodded toward the desk and said, "Let's get checked in before the law gets here and starts asking questions."

The crowd had broken up, and the slick-haired desk clerk no longer looked worried that blood and brains were about to be splattered around the lobby. He wasn't too friendly, though, as the Texans came up to the desk.

"The Occidental's guests are not in the habit of brandishing weapons in the lobby," he said. "The authorities have been summoned." He added peevishly, "I'm not sure why they haven't arrived yet."

"When they do, be sure and tell them that Rollin Kemp spoke harshly to a lady and threatened her physically," Bo said. "And anybody who was in here can back that up."

With a surly scowl on his face, the clerk asked, "What do you want?"

"A room for my friend and me."

"We don't have any—"

"Now, son, don't try to tell me you don't have any

vacancies," Bo interrupted him. "Because I can see from that key board on the wall behind you that it's not true. You wouldn't want to lie to me, would you?"

The clerk sighed and turned the register around. "Go ahead and sign in."

"We'll take a room somewhere close to number seven and number nine," Bo said as he plucked a pen from an inkwell.

"Fourteen is the best I can do. On the other side of the hall but only a few doors away."

Bo nodded and said, "That'll be fine."

"How many nights will you be staying?"

"Now, that I don't know. It depends."

Bo didn't explain what it depended on, which was how long it would take to arrange passage for him, Scratch, and the four ladies on a ship bound for Alaska. He figured they would go down to the waterfront the next morning, since it was fairly late in the day today, and find out what the situation was.

He paid for two nights, since it was likely to be at least that long before they left Seattle. Anyway, Cyrus Keegan had advanced them some money for expenses, and there was still plenty of that cash left in the money belt Bo wore under his shirt.

They had already stabled their horses and left their saddles at the livery, so all they had to take upstairs were their rifles and saddlebags. Years of drifting had taught them how to travel light.

Sailing off to Alaska was going to be a brand-new experience for them, however, and at their age they didn't get too many of those, Bo reflected.

There was a basin and a pitcher of water in the room.

By the time Bo and Scratch washed up, shaved, and put on clean shirts, dusk was settling over the city. They wore their handguns but left the Winchesters in their room when they went down the hall to knock on the door of room nine. Their bootheels didn't make much noise on the carpet runner in the center of the corridor.

Auburn-haired Martha Rousseau answered Bo's knock. She stood so that Bo could see into the room. He noted that all four of the mail-order brides were there, and the door between the adjoining rooms was open.

"You're Mr. Creel," Martha said with a smile. She extended her hand to him. "Martha Rousseau."

Her palm was cool and smooth. She shook hands with Scratch as well, and by then the other ladies were on their feet and coming toward the door.

"Beatrice said we're going to have dinner together," Martha commented as she stepped out into the hallway. She looked very nice in a bottle-green gown. The others had changed clothes for dinner, too. Bo figured there wouldn't be a prettier bunch of women in the Occidental Hotel's dining room this evening.

He was right about that. Over steaks and potatoes, everyone introduced themselves and filled in a little of their backgrounds. The women were all from Pennsylvania.

"Our late husbands were friends, and so are we," Beatrice said, indicating herself, Martha, and Sally. "There was another couple in our circle, somewhat older, who both passed away." She drew in a breath. "My dear sister and her husband."

"My parents," Caroline said. "But the shock of their deaths was eased by such good friends who took me under their wings."

"Like you had three aunts instead of just one," Sally said.

"Or older sisters," Caroline said, although considering their ages, Martha and Sally easily could have been her aunts, too.

Regardless of how they thought of it, they were all obviously good friends, so Bo wasn't surprised that they had decided to embark on this adventure together.

With his typical plainspokenness, Scratch asked, "How'd you ladies wind up headed for Alaska as mail-order brides?"

"I'm afraid that was my idea," Beatrice said with a laugh. "You see, my late husband spent some time in that part of the world when he was a young man. He was from Canada, originally, and served as a constable in the North-West Mounted Police."

"A Mountie," Scratch said.

"That's right. He crossed the border into Alaska on occasion, and he always talked about what a magnificent land it was and how he wished he could have explored more of it. So I suppose . . . in a way . . . I'm continuing my husband's dream. Unfortunately, I can't share it with him, and I knew that it would be impossible for me to reach Alaska any other way . . ."

Sally Bechdolt smiled and said, "Why don't you just tell these gentlemen the truth, Beatrice? We all have a yearning for adventure, and with the exception of Caroline, we're not as young as we used to be."

"And I wasn't about to let Aunt Beatrice go off on such an exciting jaunt without me," Caroline put in. Although she still seemed rather shy, she appeared to have recovered from the shock that had made her faint earlier.

If the sight of a Winchester being held to an hombre's head was enough to make her swoon, though, Bo wasn't sure how good an idea it was for her to go traipsing off to a wild territory like Alaska.

Still, it wasn't his business to approve or disapprove of the arrangements these ladies had made through Cyrus Keegan's agency. The only job he and Scratch had was to get them safe and sound to where they were going.

"Where exactly are we headed?" he asked.

"A settlement called Cushman," Beatrice said. "Have you heard of it?"

"Ma'am, we've barely heard of Alaska," Scratch said.

"It's located on the Yukon River, some miles inland from the coast. I have a map and detailed directions. I'm sure we won't have any difficulty finding it."

Considering how big and untamed Alaska was, according to what Bo understood, he thought that finding Cushman might turn out to be a bigger challenge than Beatrice O'Rourke believed it would be. But they would give it their best shot. He and Scratch had never stayed lost for very long.

The meal was a pleasant one. The ladies were good company, and Bo and Scratch instinctively liked them. They might not know much about the frontier, but the Texans could tell that except for Caroline, maybe, they were made of pretty strong stuff.

Given where they were headed, they would need to be.

Bo and Scratch discussed that, briefly, after they walked the ladies back upstairs and saw them safely inside their rooms for the night.

"You reckon they'll be all right up yonder in Alaska?"

Scratch asked as he and Bo walked along the corridor to room fourteen.

"I think so. They seem pretty determined."

"And that Miss Beatrice ain't the sort to back down from anything," Scratch said with a chuckle. "If we hadn't got to the hotel when we did and that varmint Kemp actually took a swing at her, I've got a hunch she would've belted him right in the mush."

"I think you're right," Bo said as he turned the key in their door. He grasped the knob and started to turn it, then stopped suddenly.

Out of habit, he had wedged a small piece of a broken matchstick between the door and the jamb when they'd left the room for dinner. That sliver of wood now lay on the floor, just outside the door.

Somebody had been in their room while they were gone. . . .

Or was still in there, waiting to ambush them.

Chapter 5

Bo went on talking, saying, "Well, I reckon we'll find out in the morning," as he caught Scratch's eye and pointed at the telltale piece of matchstick on the floor.

Scratch nodded and noiselessly slipped his right-hand Remington out of its holster. He looped his thumb over the hammer.

Bo drew his Colt. He moved to the right of the doorway, and Scratch went to the left. Stretching out his left arm, Bo grasped the knob again, gave it a sudden twist, and shoved the door open. He and Scratch stepped back even farther and trained their guns on the opening.

For a long moment, nothing happened.

Then, from inside the room, a man said, "I expect you boys are out there pointin' guns at the door, all fierce-like. But there's no need, because I ain't lookin' for trouble."

Bo heard the rasp of a match being struck, and a moment later yellow light welled up inside the room and fell through the open door. Whoever was in there had just lit the lamp that sat on the table with the pitcher and basin.

"Come on in," the unknown man invited.

"And walk right into a shotgun blast?" Scratch said. "I don't reckon I cotton much to that idea."

"All right. I'll step out so you can see I don't mean any harm."

"Do it slow and easy," Bo warned.

Footsteps sounded. A lean figure eased into the doorway. The man had his empty hands half raised so they were in plain sight. He was twenty-five or so, wore range clothes, and had a battered hat thumbed back on sandy hair. A gunbelt with a holstered Colt was strapped around his hips.

"Name's Chick Ferguson," he drawled. "I work for Rollin Kemp."

"Knowin' that don't make me any less inclined to shoot you," Scratch said.

"Did Kemp send you here?" Bo asked.

"He sure did."

"To ambush us?"

Chick Ferguson shook his head, not in denial of the accusation, necessarily, but more of a rueful gesture.

"You boys are just too suspicious," he said. "The boss sent me to convey his apologies, and to deliver an invitation."

"Kemp wants to apologize to us?" Scratch said.

"It's Mrs. O'Rourke and Miss DeHerries he should be apologizing to," Bo added. "They're the ones he treated badly."

Ferguson said, "I expect he wants to ask you fellas to talk to the ladies on his behalf, but I really hadn't ought to be speakin' for the boss."

"What's this invitation you mentioned?"

"He wants you to come down to the Timber Treasure

and have a drink with him. Reckon it's his way of makin' peace. A, uh, goodwill gesture, I reckon you'd call it."

Bo hadn't seen any signs of goodwill from Rollin Kemp, nor did he believe completely in the idea that every man deserved a second chance. Some were such sorry varmints that one chance was more than enough for them.

"Why would Kemp want to make peace with us?"

"Because he found out more about how you boys saved that money shipment comin' in on the train earlier today. He's grateful to you, doggone it. Feels like y'all got off on the wrong foot when you first ran into each other."

With a slight frown, Scratch asked, "Are you from Texas?"

"Hail from Arkansas, originally. But I've spent a lot of time in Texas."

"Thought I heard it in your voice. But that don't mean we believe what you're sayin'."

Ferguson's shoulders rose and then fell in a shrug as he said, "Believe it or don't. All the boss done was give me a message to deliver, and I've delivered it. But I can tell you he's plumb grateful and he'd like to show his appreciation. Just have a drink with him. He'd feel a heap better about things if you would."

Bo lowered his gun and nodded for Scratch to do likewise. He pouched the iron and said, "He wants us to come down to the Timber Treasure, eh?"

"That's right."

"I suppose we could do that."

"I don't know, Bo," Scratch said. "It's gettin' late, and we've had a long day."

"That's true. We're not as young as we used to be, and we need our sleep."

"It wouldn't take long just to have a drink and accept Kemp's apology," Ferguson said.

"All right," Bo told the young man. "But you're going to be walking right between us."

Ferguson grinned. "Afraid you're gonna be amblin' into an ambush, are you? Sure, I'll walk along with you. Nothin' to be scared of."

"We'll see. Let us get our hats."

Ferguson waved a hand casually toward the open door and said, "Help yourself."

A minute later, the three men walked out of the Occidental Hotel. The same clerk was behind the desk. He gave Bo and Scratch a baleful glare as they went through the lobby.

Seattle was a busy town, with a lot of activity from shipping and the timber industry. On one side of the hotel was the wide street known as Skid Road, where the loggers brought down the felled trees on giant skids. Chick Ferguson turned at the corner and led the Texans along that street.

Bo was sure it had another name, but everybody would just call it Skid Road. Now, after dark, nobody was bringing in logs bound for the mill at the far end of the street, but it was a busy thoroughfare anyway because of the saloons, hash houses, gambling dens, dance halls, cheap hotels, and out-and-out brothels that lined both sides of it, clamoring for the attention of the loggers and bullwhackers who traveled up and down it during the day.

There were other, more reputable businesses scattered along Skid Road, but they were all closed and dark at this hour. Respectable folks didn't venture much onto Skid Road after nightfall.

The Timber Treasure Saloon and Gambling Hall took

up an entire block. A sign proclaiming that name ran along the second-floor balcony and could be read easily in the light from the gas lamps on poles spaced along the street. More light came from the windows, the garish illumination spilling out onto the boardwalk in front of the place. The saloon was big enough to have two entrances. Those openings with their swinging batwings broke the front wall into thirds.

Bo and Scratch could hear the uproarious tumult of tinny piano music, shrill female laughter, men's shouts and curses, and stomping feet shod in hobnail boots while they were still almost a block away.

"Sounds like the boys are havin' themselves a good time in there tonight," Scratch commented.

Ferguson grinned. "The boys in the Timber Treasure always have a good time. The boss sees to that. He's got the best booze in Seattle, along with the prettiest gals in the skimpiest outfits. The games are even halfway honest, most of the time."

He pushed through the batwings in the right-hand entrance and motioned for Bo and Scratch to follow him. When they were inside, Bo saw bars against both the right and left walls; tables and gambling apparatus between the long stretches of polished hardwood; and in the rear, a piano where a slick-haired "professor" tickled the ivories next to a dance floor and a raised area where more musicians could play. Against the back wall was a stage that was empty at the moment, like the bandstand.

Men were lined up at both bars, two or three deep in places. All the tables were full, with chairs crowded around them. The poker tables, roulette wheels, and faro layouts were doing a booming business.

About three-fourths of the customers were brawny men in flannel shirts, suspenders, thick canvas trousers, work boots, and fur or cloth caps. Bo and Scratch had seen enough loggers to recognize the breed. Most of the other men in the place wore sailors' garb and came from the ships docked along the waterfront. Here and there were a few cowboys in range clothes like Chick Ferguson. The eastern part of the state had some big ranches, but Seattle wasn't really a cowtown.

Ferguson angled through the crowd toward the bar on the right. Bo and Scratch followed, and as they came closer Bo spotted Rollin Kemp standing at the bar with a drink in his right hand and a cigar in his left. He saw Ferguson approaching with the Texans and threw the drink back, then thumped the empty glass down on the hardwood.

"Welcome, gentlemen, welcome!" he said as he turned toward them, sweeping the hand holding the cigar in an expansive wave. "I'm happy to see that you accepted my invitation, and I hope you accept my apology as well. Please, have a drink with me."

"It ain't often I'm holdin' a Winchester to a fella's head in the afternoon and havin' a drink with him that night," Scratch said.

"Well, these aren't normal circumstances," Kemp replied with a chuckle. "And Seattle isn't a normal place. Everything is bigger than life here, my friends. Passions run higher. Blood runs hotter. That's why I wanted to say that I'm sorry I let my emotions run away with me earlier."

Bo said, "It seems to me it'd be more fitting for you to apologize to Mrs. O'Rourke and Miss DeHerries."

"You're absolutely right, my friend. And that's exactly what I'm going to do. I hope you'll convey my sentiments to them, but I also plan to write them each a letter of apology, since I don't believe they really want to see my face again."

"That wouldn't be a bad start," Bo admitted.

"I'm glad you agree. Now, how about that drink?"

Bo shrugged and said, "That'll be all right."

"Reckon I could stand it," Scratch added.

Kemp half turned and signaled to a man behind the bar. "Bring one of my private bottles, Dex."

The man nodded. The other bartenders wore short scarlet jackets over white shirts and bow ties. The man called Dex wore a brown tweed suit. The jacket's right sleeve hung empty because Dex's right arm rested in a black silk sling fastened around his neck. He was a lean man with an angular, lantern-jawed face and close-cropped, tightly curled brown hair. He used his left hand to reach under the bar and bring out a bottle of whiskey, which he held by the neck as he brought it over.

"Here you go, boss," he said. He reached under the bar again to get two more shot glasses.

"Hey, don't I get a drink?" Chick Ferguson asked.

"You did your job," Kemp said, his affability vanishing for a second. "Go on down the bar and tell Thompson I said to give you a bottle. But *not* from my private stock."

That put a grin on Ferguson's face. "Thanks, boss."

Kemp pulled the cork from the bottle and splashed amber liquid in his own glass and in the two that Dex had just placed on the bar. Bo didn't trust the man, so he watched closely. At times in the past, hombres who couldn't be trusted had slipped knockout drops into his and Scratch's drinks, or at least tried to.

The glasses Dex had set on the bar were clean and dry,

though, and Bo would have bet his hat that Kemp didn't drop anything into the drinks when he poured them. Chances were, the bottle wasn't doped, since Kemp obviously intended to drink from it as well.

Kemp pushed the glasses toward the Texans and picked up his. "Now," he said, "here's the other reason I wanted you fellas to have a drink with me tonight. I want to say thanks. I owe you for keeping those bandits from looting that express car. I had a significant amount of cash in the safe. You're probably wondering what it was for."

"No," Bo said, shaking his head. "It's none of our business."

"Maybe not, but you need to understand how important it is to me. As you can see by looking around, the Timber Treasure is a pretty lucrative business. There's a bank here in Seattle, but I prefer to send my profits back to my bank in Chicago. That's where I'm from, you know."

Bo didn't know that and didn't care, but he wasn't rude enough to say that.

"At any rate," Kemp went on, "I had the bank send me a sizable amount of cash that I'm going to use to buy an interest in one of the timber companies that operate here. I reckon I was born to be a saloonkeeper, but there's no harm in having a hand in some more respectable businesses, too." He chuckled. "Maybe if I did, respectable young ladies like Miss DeHerries might be more inclined to give me the time of day."

Scratch said, "Money usually does seem to make a fella more attractive to gals, all right."

"So you can see why I said I owe you a debt." Kemp raised his glass. "Thank you, gentlemen."

Bo and Scratch nodded, and all three of them downed

their drinks, although Bo waited half a second just to make sure Kemp was going to swallow his.

Kemp said, "Ah," and reached for the bottle. "Another?"

"No, I reckon not," Bo said. "We're obliged to you, Mr. Kemp, and glad that we can all be on more friendly footing, but Scratch and I ought to get back to the hotel. We have things to take care of in the morning."

He didn't go into detail about needing to find a ship to take them and the ladies to Alaska. No point in rubbing Kemp's face in the fact that Caroline DeHerries was going off to marry somebody else.

"I thought maybe you'd enjoy some of the games we offer here at the Timber Treasure," Kemp suggested.

"We're not really the gambling sort," Bo said, with a quick glance at Scratch to make sure his friend wouldn't contradict that statement. Actually, Bo was an excellent poker player and sometimes supported their drifting with his skill in handling the pasteboards.

"There are plenty of women who work for me, if you're interested—"

"We're a mite long in the tooth for that."

"Well, you're not *dead*, are you?" Kemp sounded a little exasperated, but he held up his hands, palms out, and went on quickly, "No, no, my apologies again, fellas. I don't mean to be pushy. Like you said, I just want us to be on friendly footing."

"No need to worry about that," Bo assured him.

"And you're welcome here in the Timber Treasure anytime, as long as you're in Seattle."

"Don't know how long that'll be, but if we're here for a while, I'm sure we'll drop in again."

"I'm glad to hear it." Kemp clapped a hand on Bo's

shoulder, then on Scratch's. "Thank you again, and I'm sincerely sorry for the trouble I caused."

"That's all right," Bo said. "Reckon we'll be going now."

Kemp looked around the room. "I'll have Chick walk you back to the hotel—"

"That's not necessary. It's not that far, and we can find our way back just fine."

"You're sure? Skid Road can be a pretty rough place."

Bo nodded and said, "We're used to taking care of ourselves."

"All right," Kemp said. "Good night."

Bo and Scratch said their farewells and left the saloon. As they walked away, Scratch said under his breath, "You reckon any of what that fella was spoutin' was true?"

"He might be planning to buy an interest in a timber company," Bo said. "Other than that, not one damned thing that came out of his mouth wasn't a lie."

"How you figure?"

"Well, for one thing, that fellow Dex is one of the train robbers I shot this afternoon."

Chapter 6

"How do you figure that?" Scratch asked. "All those fellas were wearin' masks, at least the ones that I saw."

"Dex was, too," Bo said, "but his general build is the same as the man I drilled through the arm—"

"And he's got *his* arm in a sling," Scratch finished, nodding slowly in understanding now.

"Yeah. I watched the way he carried himself. He didn't just sprain his arm or anything like that. It was hurting him, despite the act he put on. I've seen plenty of hombres who've been shot through the arm, and he was acting just like them."

"But that don't make any sense, unless he was tryin' to double-cross his boss by stealin' Kemp's money."

"It wouldn't be a double-cross if he was trying to steal it *for* Kemp."

Scratch thought about it for a moment, then said, "Yeah, I get you. Kemp has the money shipped with Wells Fargo, so they're responsible for it. If Dex and those other fellas steal the cash, the company's got to make good on it. Then

Kemp has the original shipment, *plus* what he gets from Wells Fargo."

"We don't have a bit of proof, but that's the way it looks to me. It's certainly possible, anyway."

"Yeah, from what we've seen of Kemp, I sure wouldn't put a tricky scheme like that past him," Scratch agreed. "Those two express messengers, Josh and Smitty, likely would've died just so Kemp could double his money. That's so low Kemp'd need to climb a ladder just to kiss a snake's belly."

"That's one more reason to get Miss DeHerries and the other ladies out of Seattle and on their way to their new husbands in Alaska as soon as possible."

"Yep, I sure—" Scratch stopped what he was about to say and asked quietly, "Bo, do you see what I see?"

"I see them," Bo replied as he looked at the four men who had just drifted out of an alley mouth ahead of them. "I'm not surprised, either."

"Kemp's men?"

"That'd be my guess."

The Texans hadn't stopped, but they slowed down as the four men sauntered toward them. One of the men said in a jeering tone, "Say, aren't you old-timers out past your bed-time?"

Bo and Scratch came to a halt. Bo said, "We're on our way back to our hotel right now."

"What are you doing here on Skid Road? Don't you know this is a place for young men? Real men?"

"Didn't know there was any sort of age limit," Scratch said.

"We've been to the Timber Treasure Saloon," Bo added. "Rollin Kemp invited us to have a drink with him."

Bo added that last statement on the off chance that

Kemp *hadn't* sent these men to waylay him and Scratch. Kemp was a powerful man here on Skid Road. If they were just ordinary would-be robbers, they might decide to move on rather than risk angering Kemp by attacking a couple of his friends.

Of course, if Kemp *had* sent them, as Bo strongly suspected, such a ploy wouldn't do a damned bit of good.

The men laughed and swaggered closer, confirming Bo's suspicion. Kemp had just pretended to be friendly, and now he was going to have the men who had defied him robbed and beaten, maybe worse. It was entirely possible that Kemp intended for their bodies to be found in that alley in the morning.

Bo lifted his left hand and held it out as if to stop the advance. He said, "Here's the thing, fellas. There are four of you and only two of us. Not only are we outnumbered, but even in this light I can tell that you're all a lot younger than us. So if you're looking for a fight, there's no way it'll be a fair one."

"What in the hell makes you think we're lookin' for a fair fight, you old geezer?"

"What my friend's tryin' to say," Scratch said, "is that if you boys come a step closer, we're gonna pull our guns and get to work . . . and then it's devil take the hindmost, you sons o'—"

"Kill them!" rasped the man who'd been doing the talking.

Bo and Scratch had been in so many situations like this, where lives depended on hair-trigger reflexes and ice-cold nerves, that they didn't have to say anything or even glance at each other to know what to do. Hands dipped to holsters and flashed up filled with flame-spitting guns. Bo took the two men on the right, Scratch the pair on the left.

Bo shot the outside man first, while the hombre was still clawing at his gun and hadn't cleared leather yet. The slug smashed into the left side of the man's chest, spun him around, and dropped him on his face.

The next man in got his gun out, but a slug punched into his belly before he could level the weapon and pull the trigger. He doubled over and came up on his toes. Agony made his finger clench spasmodically on the trigger. His gun thundered, but the shot went into the planks of the boardwalk at his feet. He crumpled and lay curled in a ball around the pain in his midsection.

Meanwhile, Scratch's Remingtons roared simultaneously. The outside man on the left went over backward as if he'd been slapped down by a giant hand. The remaining man staggered but stayed on his feet and fired. The bullet narrowly missed Scratch and plowed a furrow in the wall of the building next to him. Scratch lifted his right-hand gun, didn't rush the shot, and coolly drilled the last man through the forehead. That dropped him into a limp heap.

Seven shots had been fired in four seconds. Maybe a hair less. The booming racket echoed from the buildings on both sides of the street. The acrid tang of burned powder stung the noses of both Texans, but they were used to it. The never-ending breeze from the water quickly dispersed the gun smoke.

Bo and Scratch stood still, guns leveled and ready, and watched the four sprawled bodies for any sign of movement. Seeing none, Bo said, "We'd better move on while we can. We've managed to duck the law in this town so far, and I'd like to continue that."

"They ain't gonna be too quick to respond to reports of shootin' in this neighborhood," Scratch said. "I expect it happens pretty regular-like."

They leathered their guns and stepped over the bodies, rather than venturing into the street. It rained so much in these parts that Skid Road was pretty slick and muddy.

In fact, it had started to drizzle by the time Bo and Scratch rounded the corner and headed for the Occidental Hotel.

Beatrice and Caroline shared one of the adjoining rooms, Martha and Sally the other. Beatrice was on the verge of retiring for the night, while Caroline had already turned in and was lying in bed with the covers pulled over her.

The door between the rooms was open a few inches, so Beatrice could hear Sally and Martha talking quietly, although she couldn't make out any of the words. The two of them had played cribbage for a while after returning to their room. Beatrice didn't know if they were in bed or still sitting up. Their lamp wasn't out, but it was turned low, like the one in her room.

Beatrice sat at the dressing table, brushing her thick dark hair as she always did before she went to bed. If the light had been brighter, she could have looked in the mirror and picked out a few strands of gray, but she didn't have to do that. She knew they were there.

Anyway, she had earned them. Life with her late husband, Daniel, had never been easy. . . .

A faint noise drew her attention and made her frown slightly. She turned her head toward the door that opened onto the balcony as she heard it again.

Someone was out there.

There was no good reason for anyone to be skulking around outside their rooms. She thought about rousing Caroline, alerting Martha and Sally, and then herding them all down to the room occupied by Mr. Creel and Mr. Morton. Those two had been hired to protect the women, after all.

However, a fiercely independent streak ran through Beatrice O'Rourke. During some of their arguments, Daniel had been known to call her stubborn, even mule-headed. *And* reckless. Beatrice knew there was at least a small element of truth to those accusations, even though she never would have admitted it, especially to him.

She set the hairbrush aside and turned the little knob on the lamp that cut off the supply of oil. The flame burned for a moment longer, then guttered out.

Wearing only her nightdress, Beatrice rose from the chair in the darkness and turned toward the balcony door. She reached back and picked up the pitcher of water on the dressing table. She moved to a spot beside the door and stood there, waiting. It was so quiet that she heard Caroline's deep, regular breathing from the bed. In the next room, Martha and Sally were silent now, too, and probably had dozed off.

A few tense minutes went by before a tiny clicking sound came to Beatrice's ears. She knew it was the knob on the balcony door turning. Since it had been rather dim in the room to start with, her eyes had adjusted quickly to the darkness. She was able to make out the door easing open.

Where Beatrice stood, the door swung toward her, so she was behind it and the man who stepped silently through the opening wouldn't have any idea she was there. She waited for him to move farther into the room. As soon as he cat-footed past the door and she had a clear shot at him, she raised the pitcher and swung it at his head.

With a crash of crockery, the pitcher knocked the man's hat off and shattered against the back of his head. The blow made him grunt in pain and surprise and stagger forward a couple of steps. Beatrice held just the pitcher's broken handle now, and that wasn't going to do her any good, so she dropped it and lunged at the man, planting both hands in the middle of his back and shoving as hard as she could.

Beatrice O'Rourke was a beautiful, elegant woman, but she wasn't a lightweight. She was able to put enough force behind the shove to make the intruder stumble wildly across the room as he waved his arms and tried to catch his balance. His feet tangled in a throw rug, and he went down hard enough that Beatrice felt the floor shiver under the thin soles of the slippers she wore.

The crash of the breaking pitcher, followed by the thud as the intruder hit the floor, woke Caroline and made her sit up sharply in bed with a cry of alarm.

"Aunt Beatrice! What—"

"Caroline, stay there!" Beatrice said. She swung around toward the dressing table again. One of her small bags sat on the table, and inside that bag was a two-shot over-under derringer. She fumbled for it in the darkness.

A heavy footstep behind her made her realize something she had forgotten.

The intruder wasn't necessarily *alone*. . . .

At that instant, an arm went around her waist from behind and jerked her away from the table. A rough hand clapped over her mouth and choked off the outcry she tried to make. She felt herself pressed tightly against a man's body.

"Aunt Beatrice, what's wrong?" Caroline asked from the bed. "What's happening?" She sounded completely disoriented, and having been jolted out of a sound sleep, that was probably the case.

Beatrice writhed in the man's grip, but he was large and strong and she couldn't get loose. She smelled tobacco and whiskey on his breath as he leaned his head close to hers and said in a low voice, "Stop fightin', you wildcat. We ain't after you."

That meant they were after Caroline. Beatrice had never had any children, but since her sister's death she had felt a fierce maternal instinct toward her niece. Both arms were free, so she reached back, grabbed the man's crotch, and twisted as hard as she could.

He howled in pain and let go of her. The way he had been holding her, her feet were almost off the floor, so she stumbled a little as he released her. She caught her balance in a split-second, though, and laced her fingers together. As she whirled around, she swung her clubbed hands where she thought the man's head might be.

Instinct did a good job of guiding her. The two-handed blow landed solidly against a bearded jaw. The man grunted and staggered and then with a curse swung a wild backhand.

He was lucky, too. His forearm crashed against the side of Beatrice's head and knocked her to the floor. For a second, all reason fled from her brain. She recovered her wits quickly, but when she tried to scramble up, she realized she was too stunned to make her muscles work.

"You loco little hellcat!" the second intruder grated. "I'm gonna kick the stuffin' outta—"

At that moment, Caroline screamed at the top of her lungs.

Chapter 7

Bo and Scratch were halfway down the hall from the landing when they heard the scream from room nine. Neither Texan hesitated for even a fraction of a second. They charged forward, filling their hands with their guns as they ran. Scratch reached the door first, raised his right foot, and crashed his bootheel against the panel just below the knob.

With a splintering of wood as the lock tore out, the door flew open. Bo dashed into the room first while Scratch caught his balance after the kick. The hall had a couple of lamps mounted in wall sconces, and the light from them slanted into the room enough for him to see a large burly, bearded man standing over Beatrice O'Rourke, who had fallen to the floor or been knocked down.

Unfortunately, Bo didn't spot the man lying not far inside the door until one of his feet caught on the obstacle and robbed him of his balance. His hat flew off as he fell forward.

The man he had just tripped over rolled and grabbed him.

Scratch surged into the doorway with a Remington in

each hand. With the light from the hall behind him, he was silhouetted and made a good target. The man standing over Beatrice yanked out a gun and snapped a shot at him. The bullet sang past Scratch's ear.

Scratch crouched slightly and thrust out both revolvers as he squeezed the triggers. The double blast was like a huge clap of thunder in the small confines of the hotel room. The man who had no business being here reeled backward. Scratch didn't know if one or both of his bullets had found their target, but the varmint was hit, no doubt about that.

The man caught himself in the doorway and tried to lift his gun for another shot. Scratch didn't wait. He slammed two more rounds into the man's already bloody chest. This time the intruder did a jittering dance backward until he came to the railing along the front of the balcony. His momentum made him flip up and over it and plummet out of sight.

A few feet away, Bo was still wrestling on the floor with the other intruder. He had lost his gun in the struggle. His opponent was wiry and writhed like a snake. Fists hammered Bo's face, and a knee dug sharply for his groin. Luck twisted Bo's body so what could have been a devastating blow landed on his hip instead.

Bo shot a short but powerful punch upward and landed it under the man's chin. His teeth clicked together and he let out a strangled cry of pain. He must have been panting for breath, because as he shook his head and blood spattered on Bo's face, Bo realized the punch had caused the man to bite through his tongue.

The pain of that blunted the man's attack enough for Bo to clamp a hand around his throat. Bo bucked up from the floor and threw himself to the side. That forced the man underneath him. Bo got another hand on his throat, lifted him a little, and banged the back of his head on the floor.

He did that a couple more times before the man got a leg up, jerked it around in front of Bo's chest, and used it to lever him off. They sprawled apart, and as they came up on their knees, the man scooped Bo's fallen gun from the floor and raised it.

The roar of Scratch's Remington and the much smaller pop of a derringer blended together. The man went over backward as Bo's gun fell unfired from his hand.

Bo scrambled to his feet. He saw his old friend standing there, smoke curling from the muzzle of the gun he held.

The other way, Beatrice stood holding a derringer and staring at the man on the floor. Her face was drained of color and seemed white as milk, framed by the dark wings of her hair. Her pallor made the beauty mark near her mouth stand out even more. She was breathing heavily, a fact that was uncomfortably obvious in the thin nightdress she wore.

In the bed, Caroline DeHerries sat huddled against the headboard, clutching her bedclothes around her as she looked on in horror.

Scratch stepped over to the man who had just been shot, who now lay on his back with both legs doubled under him at the knees. The silver-haired Texan prodded him with a boot toe and said, "He's dead, Bo. Looks like one of us hit him right in the throat."

"I . . . I killed him," Beatrice said.

"No, ma'am, I don't reckon you did," Scratch told her. "He's got a hole in his arm, too, and judgin' by the looks of the wounds, you winged him there while I done for him with that shot to the throat."

"Oh. I . . . I . . ."

Bo gently wrapped his hand around the derringer and said, "Better let me have that for now, ma'am."

Beatrice let go of the little gun and turned toward him. She pressed herself against him and buried her face in his chest. Bo cleared his throat and put his other arm around her shoulders in a comforting embrace. Even under the circumstances, the fact that she was hardly dressed wasn't lost on him. He would have had to be dead not to notice that.

The door between the rooms creaked a little as it opened more. "Is . . . is everybody all right in there?" Martha Rousseau asked. "Beatrice? Caroline?"

"They're fine, ma'am," Scratch replied. "You ladies best just stay in there for now. The air in here's a mite full of gun smoke."

Bo looked at the open balcony door and said, "Scratch, maybe you'd better go in the other room, light the lamp, and sit with Mrs. Rousseau and Mrs. Bechdolt for a spell. We don't want any varmints trying to sneak in over there, like they did here."

"Good idea," Scratch said. He went to the connecting door. "Make yourselves decent, ladies. I'm comin' in."

Bo didn't think it was likely anybody would try to invade Martha and Sally's room. He had a hunch these two men had been after Caroline DeHerries—and an even stronger hunch that they worked for Rollin Kemp.

But with both of the intruders dead, they couldn't be questioned, which was a stroke of bad luck. Under the circumstances, though, he was willing to accept that as long as Beatrice and Caroline were safe.

"It's all right," he murmured as he clumsily patted Beatrice on the back. "The trouble's over now."

Actually, it probably wasn't, he thought. And more than likely it wouldn't be until they had left Seattle behind and were on their way to Alaska.

There was no avoiding the authorities this time. A gun battle in a hotel room and a couple of dead men attracted too much attention for that to be possible.

The four mail-order brides were dressed now and sitting together in room seven, since a considerable amount of blood had been splashed on the floor in room nine. Bo and Scratch were there, too, standing and talking to a short stocky man in a brown tweed suit and brown bowler hat. His jowly face reminded Bo of a bulldog. Incongruously, he had a flower stuck in the top buttonhole of his suit coat.

He had introduced himself as Detective Oblinger. The blue-uniformed policeman who stood just inside the door was Officer Tench. Both men looked tired and not happy about being dragged out at this time of night.

"I've heard about you two," Oblinger said as he pointed a blunt finger at Bo and Scratch. "You got in a ruckus with Rollin Kemp down in the lobby of this hotel earlier today."

"And now we've been forced to kill two of his men," Bo said. The body of the man Scratch had shot had been found lying facedown in the mud in front of the hotel, after he'd fallen over the balcony railing.

Oblinger shook his head. "Those two don't work for

Kemp. Didn't work for Kemp. They don't work for anybody anymore."

"Are you sure about that?" Scratch asked.

"Their names are Bishop and Hagen. Were Bishop and Hagen. They've been in trouble before for robbery. They probably just snuck in here figurin' on stealing something."

Beatrice spoke up, saying, "Excuse me, sir, but that's not what happened. They came here to steal Caroline away. One of them said as much to me." Her voice got icy as she added, "And we all know perfectly well who has made it clear he has his eye on my niece."

Oblinger's shaggy eyebrows drew down in a frown. He said, "Now, ma'am, did the fella come right out and *say* he intended to kidnap Miss DeHerries? What were his exact words?"

"He told me to stop fighting and said they weren't after me—"

"Well, there you go," Oblinger interrupted her. "They weren't after you because all they wanted was money or jewels or anything else of value they could find to steal." He turned to Bo and Scratch. "Of course, it's all right that you fellas went ahead and killed those two, even if they weren't tryin' to hurt these women. You didn't know that, and anyway, Bishop and Hagen ain't any great loss to anybody. I'll write it all up when I get back to the station house. Won't be any need for any of you folks to be bothered no more."

"What about the inquest?" Bo asked.

"For the likes of those two?" Oblinger shook his head. "Coroner'll read my report, mark 'em down as death by self-defense brought on by the decedents' own criminal activities, and that'll be the end of it." He looked around at the people in the room. "You're welcome. Come on, Tench. After that shootin' we were called out on a while ago and now this, I'm tired." The detective paused and looked at Bo and Scratch. "You two wouldn't know anything about some fellas bein' gunned down over on Skid Road earlier tonight, would you?"

"First we've heard about it," Bo said.

"Uh-huh."

The two policemen left with Beatrice glaring at them as they departed. When they were gone, she said, "That man was absolutely and utterly mistaken."

"Maybe not," Bo said.

She stared daggers at him. "Do you really think those men were just common thieves?"

"Not hardly. But there's a good chance that Oblinger knows the truth, only he's in Kemp's pocket so he can't acknowledge it. Fellas mixed up in crooked business, like Kemp's rumored to be, usually spread some money around to make sure the local law doesn't bother them."

Understanding dawned on Beatrice's face. "Or to keep from being embarrassed when the men they hire to kidnap young women fail and wind up being killed instead."

"Now you're gettin' it," Scratch said.

Caroline said in a voice that shook a little, "Kemp is never going to leave me alone, is he?"

"A man like that maintains his hold on power because people are afraid of him," Bo said. "That's why, any time somebody stands up to him, he has to act swiftly and decisively to crush them. That keeps other people from wanting to risk it."

"Then what are we going to do?"

"We need to go ahead and get out of Seattle as soon as

we can. Scratch and I will see about booking passage first thing in the morning. I'd suggest that all of you be packed and ready to leave on short notice, just in case we can get a ship right away."

"We can do that," Martha said. "Honestly, I'd pack up and leave right now if we could."

"So would I," Sally added.

"I figure we'll be lucky if we can sail tomorrow," Bo said, "but until we do, Scratch and I are going to be careful not to let anything like this happen again. It'll be crowded, but I want you four ladies to stay together in this room if you can. Lock that connecting door, too. We'll put a chair out on the balcony, and one of us will stay there all night while the other sits out in the hall."

"But you won't get any sleep that way," Beatrice objected.

"Sure we will," Scratch told her. "We've slept in a heap worse places, let me tell you. The important thing is fixin' it so no more varmints can get to you ladies."

"Well . . . all right," Beatrice said.

"But we'll worry about you," Sally said.

"No need for that," Bo assured her. "Just try to get some rest."

Scratch said, "I'll take the balcony. I'd rather be sittin' out in the fresh air."

"I don't know how fresh it'll be. You're liable to get rained on."

"Well, it won't be the first time, will it?" Scratch asked with a grin. "We've spent some mighty wet nights on the trail."

"That's true."

"Let me get my Winchester and slicker from our room."

Bo set a ladderback chair just outside the balcony door, then took the room's other chair and positioned it in the hallway beside that door.

"You ladies go ahead and settle down for the night," he told them. "Scratch can go out onto the balcony through the other room, and I'll be right outside this door all night."

Beatrice came up to him and rested a hand on his forearm. "Thank you, Mr. Creel," she said. "I realize we haven't known you and Mr. Morton for long, but believe me when I tell you that we already have a great deal of confidence in you."

Caroline came up behind her and said, "I feel a lot better just knowing that you're here, Mr. Creel."

"Glad to hear it," Bo said with a nod. "Good night, ladies."

All four of them chorused, "Good night."

By the time Scratch returned with his Winchester tucked under his arm, Bo was waiting for him in the hall and said, "I told them you'd go out to the balcony through room nine so they won't have to be disturbed anymore."

"Good idea."

"Before you go, though . . . let me ask you a question."

The silver-haired Texan eyed his old friend warily and said, "All right, but I got one to ask you, too. You go first."

Bo kept his voice low enough that it couldn't be overheard through the door as he said, "That second intruder, the one you claimed you shot in the throat . . . that was your bullet in his arm, wasn't it?"

Scratch shrugged. "I figured you might want to ask the varmint a few questions and find out who sent him, not that there's any doubt it was Kemp. So yeah, I just winged him."

"But you said you killed him so Mrs. O'Rourke wouldn't know it was her who actually did it."

"Well, hell, Bo, you'd have done the same thing. Ain't no need for a fine lady like that to have to live with knowin' she took a man's life, even though he was a no-good kidnappin' skunk."

Bo nodded slowly and said, "You're a good man, Scratch Morton."

"Shoot, you've known that for more than forty years."

"Yeah. Now, what was the question you wanted to ask me."

Scratch grinned. "Just how much did you enjoy havin' your arm wrapped around a fine-lookin' woman like Miz O'Rourke when she was all upset and barely dressed?"

"None of your blasted business," Bo said. Then he grinned, too, and went on, "Now go sit on the balcony."

Chapter 8

As Bo expected, nothing else happened that night.

Kemp had tried to have him and Scratch killed not only because of their run-in with him in the hotel lobby but also because they had ruined his plans to have his own money shipment stolen from the train—assuming Bo's theory about that was correct, and he was confident that it was.

On top of that, Bo was also sure Kemp had hired those two men to kidnap Caroline, and *that* effort had failed as well. That was plenty of villainy for one day. More than likely, Kemp would want to think things over before he tried anything else.

But he *would* try something. Bo was equally sure of that. So it was important for him and Scratch to get the ladies on their way as soon as possible.

After they had all eaten breakfast together in the hotel dining room, Bo said to Scratch, "You stay here and keep an eye on the ladies. I'll go down to the waterfront and see about getting passage on a ship."

"Sounds good to me," Scratch agreed. "Sally and Martha

like to play cards, so I thought I might see if I can talk one of the other gals into gettin' up a poker game with 'em."

"You behave yourself," Bo warned him.

"Why, sure," Scratch said with a grin. "I'm just talkin' about a friendly game to pass the time."

Bo gave him a dubious look but left the hotel and headed for the waterfront.

He and Scratch had been to port cities before, including New Orleans and San Francisco. Seattle's waterfront district wasn't as large as the ones in those cities, but Bo had no trouble finding it because the tall masts of the ships docked there were visible even over the cavernous warehouses lining the streets. Bo made his way through the busy streets, and once he reached the long row of wharves stretching out into the water, he asked a passerby where the harbormaster's office was.

A harried-looking clerk in that office responded to Bo's questions by saying, "A lot of people want to get to Alaska these days, mister. Ever since they started finding gold up the Yukon, folks figure they can go up there and get rich."

"I'm not looking for gold," Bo said, "but I need to get to Cushman anyway."

The clerk picked up a piece of paper and shoved it in front of Bo. "Here's a list of the ships sailing today and where they're bound for. You can look it over, but you can't take it with you."

"So I'll have to just go to each ship and ask if I can book passage?"

"That's the way it works. I'm not a ticket agent, mister."

Bo studied the list for several minutes and committed several names and pier numbers to memory. Luckily, he still had good recall for such things.

"Thanks," he said as he gave the paper back to the sourfaced clerk.

He left the office and walked along the wharf that seemed to stretch for a mile or more along the shore of Elliott Bay. He checked the names of the ships he passed, as well as the pier numbers, looking for some he recognized from the list the clerk had showed him.

For the next hour, Bo walked up and down gangplanks, stood on ship decks, and asked captains or first mates about booking passage to Alaska. Each time he got a curt shake of the head and an apology that varied in sincerity. He was about to decide he would have to start searching for available berths on ships sailing in the next few days when he came to a vessel with the name *John Starr* painted on the bow.

That was one of the ships on the list, he recalled. Maybe the last one he hadn't checked already. Bo didn't know much about boats. This one had a couple of masts with furled sails and looked to be in decent shape, although there was nothing fancy about it. As he walked up the gangplank, one of the sailors noticed him and moved along the deck to greet him.

"Help you with something, mister?" the young man said. He was tall and broad-shouldered, with a shock of tawny hair under a pushed-back cap with a short, stiff bill.

"I'm looking for the captain, or the first mate if he's not available," Bo said. "I need to see about booking passage to Alaska for myself and five other people."

"Six folks?" The young sailor let out a whistle. "I don't know about that. I was about to say that you might be in luck until I found out how many passengers you're talking about. We had a party cancel on us, but there were only four men in it."

"We don't mind some crowding," Bo said. This was really the first sign of hope he had come across on the waterfront, so he wasn't going to give up easily. "There's just me and another fella, and four ladies—"

"Ladies?" a gravelly voice bellowed behind him. "You want to bring *women* aboard my ship?" The man who had spoken didn't wait for an answer before continuing, "Kelly, get back to work!"

"Aye, Cap'n," the young sailor said. He gave Bo a look of sympathy and then hurried off along the deck.

Bo turned around, then lowered his eyes to look at a man who stood a head shorter than him. The man in the blue jacket and black cap was almost as wide as he was tall, though, or at least gave that appearance. His jaw was like a slab of rock, and his nose bore a resemblance to a potato. Curly gray hair stuck out from under the cap.

"What are you doin' on my ship, cowboy?" he demanded as he glared at Bo.

"Trying to book passage to Alaska," Bo replied. He wasn't going to be buffaloed. He had run into plenty of hombres like this before, who tried to get their way through bluster, yelling, and intimidation.

"For *women*."

"That's right. Four ladies bound for Cushman, Alaska."

The captain of the *John Starr* waved a hand with short stubby fingers as fat as sausages. "Cushman's a good ways inland. This is a sea-goin' ship."

"Inland or not, you still have to travel over the sea to reach the mouth of the Yukon River." Bo knew from looking at Beatrice's map that they had to follow the river until they reached one of its tributaries called Finbar Creek, then proceed a short distance up the smaller stream to Cushman.

"Aye, that's true, but females on board a ship are bad luck. I won't have it." The captain crossed his arms over his barrel chest. "I won't have it, I tell you."

"You just lost some passengers," Bo pointed out. "We'll replace them, and pay for six passages instead of four."

"That lad's got too big a mouth." The captain leaned to the side to point past Bo and yelled, "You! Chart Kelly! You've got a big mouth, boy!" He turned his attention back to Bo and went on, "You're talkin' about cash?"

"How else would we pay?"

The captain snorted. "You wouldn't believe how many fellas want me to carry 'em to Alaska and promise they'll pay me for the trip when they strike it rich."

"No, we'll pay cash," Bo assured the man. "As long as the price is reasonable."

The captain got a shrewd look on his beefy face. "If you're in a hurry to get somewhere," he said, "that gives reasonable a whole new meanin', don't it?"

"No," Bo said flatly. "It doesn't."

The two men looked at each other for a long moment. The captain scowled, but Bo's expression was calm and impassive. Finally, the captain shrugged burly shoulders and said, "All right, but we're leavin' in less than an hour." He stuck out his hand and named an amount. "Pay up."

"Half now," Bo said. "Half when we get there."

"That's robbery! What if we sink and never get there?"

"Then you won't need the other half, will you?"

The man's scowl deepened, but he blew out an exasperated breath and said, "I wouldn't do it if you'd haggled over the price. And I still don't like the fact that I'll be haulin' females. But you drive a tough bargain, mister."

Bo sensed that all the objections were an act, for the most part. Like most sailors, the captain might be superstitious about having women on board his vessel, but he was glad for the passengers to replace the ones he'd lost.

"We have a deal?" Bo said as he extended his hand.

"We do." The captain clasped Bo's hand in a hard grip, then added, "I make no promises about how comfortable these *ladies* of yours will be, though. This ain't no luxury ship!"

"I'm sure the accommodations will be fine." Bo had taken some cash from the money belt before he came down to the waterfront. He brought out what he needed from his pocket and handed it over. "You sail in less than an hour, you said?"

The captain took out a pocket watch and flipped it open. "I'll give you an hour from right now, no longer, and only because I'm in a generous mood!"

"I'm obliged to you. My name's Bo Creel, by the way."

"Cap'n Jedediah Saunders."

"I'm pleased to meet you, Captain."

Saunders just snorted as he turned and stalked off toward the stern.

Bo headed for the gangplank. The young sailor named Chart Kelly drifted over to intercept him and said quietly, "Don't worry too much about the cap'n, mister. He makes a lot of racket, but he ain't really a bad sort."

"As long as he can get us to the Yukon River, I reckon we can put up with some racket."

"St. Michael."

"What?" Bo said.

"St. Michael. That's the name of the settlement at the mouth of the Yukon. That's where you'll start if you're headed upriver."

"Oh. Thanks." Bo started to step onto the gangplank, then paused. "Have you been up the Yukon? My friends and I are headed for a place called Cushman."

"Heard of it, never been there. I'm a sailor, not a prospector. Although the idea of finding gold and striking it rich *does* have some appeal. Is that what you're after?"

"Not exactly," Bo said.

Since going to work for Cyrus Keegan, he and Scratch were dealing in a whole different sort of treasure.

"An *hour*?" Beatrice said.

"Less than that, by now," Bo said. He refrained from pointing out that he had warned them to be packed and ready to travel on short notice. He figured a comment along those lines wouldn't go over well.

"All right, all right, we can manage, I suppose." Beatrice looked around the room at the others. "Ladies?"

"Let's get busy," Sally said.

"We'll leave you to it," Bo said. "Come on, Scratch."

All the Texans had to do to prepare was fetch their saddlebags from their room. Bo went to do that while Scratch stood guard right outside room seven.

When Bo rejoined him, Scratch had a worried frown on his face. "I've been thinkin'," he said. "I knew we'd have to take a boat to get where we're goin', but I don't reckon it really sunk in on me until now."

"Don't use the word *sunk* when you're talking about a ship," Bo said.

"Don't get me started on that. I was thinkin' more about how it makes you feel to ride on one of those blasted things. I've been on plenty of riverboats and they never bothered me, but you remember that time we sailed from New Orleans down to Vera Cruz?"

"You mean when we got mixed up with that gun-runner who called himself the Macaw and had folks shooting at us from one end of Yucatán to the other?"

"Yeah, that little dustup," Scratch said. "But that ain't the part I'm talkin' about. I just remembered how sick it made me to ride on that ship. You think it's gonna do that this time, too?"

"I honestly don't know. I hope not."

"Yeah, you and me both. I don't reckon I ever felt so puny in my life—"

Scratch stopped short as the door opened and Beatrice said, "All right, we're ready to go. Someone's going to have to deal with our bags, though."

Bo looked past her, saw the pile of baggage in the center of the room, and said, "I'll go see if I can rent a wagon."

Chapter 9

Almost an hour had passed by the time the wagon with the ladies' bags loaded into the back and the rented buggy carrying the ladies themselves came to a stop on the wharf near the gangplank leading up to the John Starr. Bo had worried a little that Captain Saunders might have jumped the gun and sailed away already, so he was glad to see that the ship was still there.

Saunders was pacing back and forth on the deck, though, with his arms crossed and a stormy glare on his face. "It's about time!" he called down to Bo. "I suppose those are the women?"

That seemed so obvious, Bo thought it really didn't deserve an answer, but not wanting to get any further on the captain's bad side, he said, "That's right."

"Lots of frills and frippery, I see!" Saunders turned to several sailors who stood on the deck nearby, including Chart Kelly. "Well, don't just stand there. Get all those bags full of geegaws loaded!"

Bo had figured that he and Scratch would have to tote all the bags up the gangplank themselves, so he was glad for the help. Kelly grinned at him again as he led the other sailors down to the wharf. They got busy hauling the bags onto the ship.

The gangplank was wide enough for two people and had rope railings along its sides. Bo took Beatrice's arm and went up the sloping passage with her. Scratch followed with Caroline, then they went back to accompany Sally and Martha. The ship was barely bobbing, so the chances of anybody falling off into the water alongside the gangplank were pretty slim, but Bo didn't want to run any risks he didn't have to.

Once all the ladies were on board, Captain Saunders looked them up and down in a brazen manner and then said to Bo, "When you told me you were takin' women to Alaska, I figured they'd be whores."

Before Bo could respond, Beatrice said in a voice cold enough to freeze a man's blood in his veins, "Your ridiculous assumption was incorrect, sir."

"Yeah, I reckon I can see that now," Saunders admitted. He raised a finger to the bill of his cap. "Even an old sea dog like me knows ladies when he sees 'em. My apologies."

That was more graciousness than Bo expected from the captain.

"Thank you," Beatrice said, her tone still cool. "Where are our cabins?"

"Only have two empty, so you'll have to double up."

"That's all right. That was what we anticipated. What about Mr. Creel and Mr. Morton?"

"They'll sleep belowdecks with the crew, wherever they can find a spot."

"That's not acceptable—" Beatrice began.

"For now it'll be all right," Bo said. "We'll still be close by, and there shouldn't be any more trouble once we're out of Seattle."

Saunders's eyes, set deep in pits of gristle, widened as he looked at Bo. "Wait just a blasted minute!" he said. "You never said anything about any trouble—"

"Cap'n," Chart Kelly said with an urgent edge in his voice, "look yonder on the wharf."

The others all looked where Kelly was pointing. Bo's hand tightened on the Winchester he held as he saw, about a hundred yards away, Rollin Kemp striding toward the *John Starr*, backed by a couple of dozen rough-looking men, many of whom carried clubs.

"Kemp!" Captain Saunders said, making the name sound like the most obscene curse possible. He jerked around toward Bo and Scratch. "Is Rollin Kemp out to make trouble for you?"

"He set his sights on Miss DeHerries," Bo said as he nodded toward the young blonde, "and he won't take no for an answer."

"No, he ain't the sort who would." Saunders turned and roared, "Cast off! Raise those sails! Cast off, you devils!"

"You and Kemp don't get along either?" Scratch said.

Saunders's face twisted with anger. "He's hated me ever since me and the boys busted up his place one night. 'Twasn't our fault. Some of those blasted loggers tried to cheat us at cards, and then Kemp's boys pitched in on their side. Whatever happened, he had it comin'! Cast off!"

Men were running all over the deck now, hustling to complete all the tasks needed for the ship to depart. Bo and Scratch didn't know much about that, but they recognized urgency when they saw it. Sailors grabbed ropes and hauled on them. Seemingly endless yards of sails rose along the masts and snapped as the breeze filled them. Men with long poles used them to push the ship away from the dock. A sailor on the raised quarterdeck stood at the big wheel and grasped the handles of the spokes to turn it steadily.

Caroline watched anxiously as Kemp and the men with him broke into a run toward the *John Starr*. "He's seen us!" she said. "He's going to stop us from leaving!"

"I don't think so," Bo told her. "We're already pulling away."

It was true. The gangplank had been raised, and the stretch of water between the ship and the dock steadily widened. Kemp was yelling, Bo could tell that by the way his open mouth worked, but in the general hubbub of the waterfront, he couldn't tell what the saloonkeeper was saying.

Nothing good, Bo was sure of that.

Kemp stopped short as he neared the pier where the *John Starr* had been docked. He reached under his coat and yanked out a pistol. He didn't raise it, though, because as soon as Bo and Scratch saw the gun, they lifted the Winchesters smoothly and swiftly to their shoulders and drew beads on Kemp's chest.

"Mrs. O'Rourke, you and the other ladies get somewhere inside," Bo said sharply without looking around.

"I'll show you where to go," Chart Kelly volunteered.

"Go ahead and shoot the scoundrel," Saunders urged the Texans.

"If we did, we'd probably have murder charges waiting for us when we get back to Seattle," Bo said. "We'd just as soon not do that."

Kemp still held the gun, but he kept it pointed toward the wharf as he lifted his other fist and shook it vehemently at the departing ship. He shouted something. Scratch said, "I can make out a few words. I think he's tellin' us that we won't get away with this."

"I reckon we already have," Bo said. He kept his cheek nestled against the smooth wood of the rifle's stock until the *John Starr* was out of pistol range. Even then, he didn't lower the Winchester, because Kemp might have one of his men try a rifle shot at them.

Scratch expressed the same thought. "If I hear any bullets whistlin' around us, I'm gonna blow a hole in that varmint no matter who pulls the trigger."

"No need for that," Saunders said. "I've got a three-inch swivel gun that'll reach the dock just fine from here." He sighed. "But on the other hand, I might blow up some friends of mine, and I don't want that."

The wind had caught the sails even better now, and the ship was picking up speed as it angled out into the deeper water. Bo finally lowered his rifle and said, "I reckon we're safe enough. Kemp will just have to learn that he can't get everything he wants in this life." He looked around and saw that Beatrice and the others were nowhere in sight. "I appreciate that sailor of yours getting the ladies out of harm's way like that."

"Kelly's a good lad," Saunders said. "He's third mate right now. Might work his way up to first mate someday."

"How about cap'n?" Scratch asked.

"No, he's too damned nice for that. Something I've never had to worry about." Saunders jammed his fists against his waist and went on, "Now tell me why are you takin' those women to Alaska?"

Bo and Scratch spent a few minutes telling the captain about their job with Cyrus Keegan's matrimonial agency and how the ladies were on their way to Cushman to meet their prospective bridegrooms.

Saunders shook his head in amazement and said, "I never have understood why some blasted fool would send off for a wife like that. There are enough females in this world already who are just lookin' to trap a man into getting hitched."

"Probably not in the middle of Alaska," Bo said.

"Well, maybe not. 'Tis a harsh land, from what I've seen of it. One of the few places in the world that *doesn't* suffer from an overabundance of women, I'll wager!"

They told him as well about the various run-ins with Kemp and men who worked for him, going back to the train robbery that the Texans had spoiled the day before.

"Aye, such a devious plan sounds like something Kemp would come up with," Saunders agreed. "So you were on his bad side even before you ever held a gun to his head, he just didn't know who you were yet. He'll never forgive that, by the way. You made him look weak, and he can't stand that."

"Well, we don't plan on spending a lot of time in Seattle when we get back, so maybe we won't run into him again," Bo said.

"Just long enough to get our horses and start driftin' to wherever Cyrus needs us to go next," Scratch added.

"You'd best have eyes in the back of your head while you're there," Saunders warned.

Bo said, "We're in the habit of that, anyway."

"Folks tend to try shootin' us now and then," Scratch said.

"I can believe that," Saunders said. "Some men attract trouble, and I've a hunch you two fall into that category!"

After a few more minutes of talking with the captain, Bo said that he wanted to make sure the ladies were all right.

"I'll take you to their cabins," Saunders said.

"How many passengers do you have on this ship?" Scratch asked.

"Ten, not countin' the ladies. Our normal complement is fourteen, which is why you gents are extra and get to bunk wherever you can find a place."

"All men?" Bo asked.

"Aye, and all bound for St. Michael, too, just like you. The lure of gold is mighty powerful."

Scratch said, "You don't have to tell us about that. We were in California in '49."

"And you didn't get rich, did you?"

Bo chuckled. "Just about broke our backs is more like it. We found some color, but not enough to last long."

"And then we got to feelin' like it was time to pull up stakes again," Scratch said. "Never did like to stay in one place for too long."

"Have they found much gold in Alaska?" Bo asked.

"Quite a bit down around Juneau," the captain replied. "Old Joe Juneau, the fella they named the place after, was a prospector, you know. Man named John Treadwell has a big mine not far from there, and it's a good, steady producer, so they say. Hasn't been near as much found up the Yukon from St. Michael, but enough to get folks interested. Cushman, the place you're bound for, is supposed to have several good claims up the gulch where Finbar Creek runs. Must be some truth to it, because Cushman is sort of a boomtown these days. But everything I'm tellin' you is just what I've heard. I don't know any of it for a fact and never will, because I've no interest in bustin' rocks all day."

Scratch smiled. "Even if it was to make you rich?"

Saunders waved a hand at the water all around them and the heavily timbered slopes of the hilly landscape through which the sound ran.

"How much richer could I be when I'm surrounded by such beauty?"

"I reckon that's a good way to look at it," Bo said. "And speaking of surrounded by beauty . . . let's go check on the ladies."

Chapter 10

The four mail-order brides were together in one of the cabins. Beatrice answered Bo's knock with "Come in."

When the Texans stepped into the cabin, Caroline said, "Thank goodness you're all right. When we didn't hear any shooting, we hoped the ship had gotten away before Mr. Kemp and his men could come on board."

"They didn't miss their chance by much," Bo said, "but it was enough."

"And they'd have had a tough time gettin' anywhere with this ship's crew," Scratch added. "They look like a mighty salty bunch to me, from the cap'n on down."

Beatrice said, "We could tell the ship was underway. There's no turning back now, is there?"

Bo shook his head. "No, ma'am. But you didn't want to turn back, did you?"

"Not at all," Beatrice replied with a smile. "But you have to admit, setting off for the wilds of Alaska to marry men we've never even met is quite a large undertaking."

"You've sent letters back and forth with those fellas,

haven't you?" Scratch asked. "Your intendeds, I mean. That's usually the way it works."

"Of course. They're not *complete* strangers."

Martha said, "Although all we really know about them is their names and what they've chosen to tell us. Still, it should be a splendid adventure."

"I hope so," Bo said, and meant it. He couldn't imagine being in the position the ladies were in—but he supposed there was plenty about being a woman that he couldn't imagine.

Beatrice went on, "I do hope the two of you will be able to find comfortable berths. It didn't occur to me that we might be taking the last cabins."

"That's all right," Bo assured her.

"Yeah, like we've told you before, we're used to roughin' it," Scratch added. "As long as the water don't get too rough, I reckon we'll be fine."

"Are you prone to seasickness, Mr. Morton?" Sally asked.

Scratch's voice had a grim note in it as he said, "I reckon we'll find out."

The water in the sound was fairly calm, so Scratch didn't have any problems as the *John Starr* navigated north from Seattle and then turned west into the Strait of Juan de Fuca. It became choppier then, causing Scratch to turn a little green, but he discovered that if he stood at the railing and kept his gaze fixed on one point on the horizon, it helped.

"And if my belly decides to act up, I'm already at the railin', so that's handy," he told Bo.

"Maybe it won't be too long before you get your sea legs, I think the sailors call 'em."

Scratch looked over at his old friend. "You ain't the least bit sick, are you?"

"Not so far," Bo admitted. "And I'm grateful for that, too."

Chart Kelly came up to them where they stood at the railing and asked, "Are you fellas doing all right?"

"I am," Bo said. "And I'm sure Scratch will be soon."

"I sure hope so. You're doing the right thing, Mr. Morton. Just keep it up until you get used to the ship's motion."

"It don't bother you?" Scratch asked the young man.

Kelly grinned. "Not a bit. I was practically raised on a ship. I was born in Maine, and my pa ran fishing boats. I started helping out on them when I was mighty young. I wanted to see more of the world, though, so as soon as I was old enough, I went to sea. I've been 'most everywhere, from Madagascar to China."

"How'd you manage to do that, no older than you are?"

"Like I said, I started young," Kelly replied with a grin. "The past couple of years, I've been sailing with Cap'n Saunders up and down the Pacific coast. The *John Starr* is a good ship, and he's a good captain. One of these days I'll probably head back around the world again, but for now I'm happy to be here."

Bo said, "A man's lucky to be happy in what he does. Too many folks work at a job just to have something to do that makes them a living."

"I've got a hunch you and Mr. Morton aren't like that, though."

Scratch said, "Not hardly! Bo and me are too fiddle-footed for that."

"Some would say shiftless and lazy," Bo added dryly.

Kelly stood there quietly for a moment, and Bo sensed he was getting around to the real purpose of this conversation. Finally, the young sailor said, "I noticed when we were loading the ladies' bags that you didn't bring any supplies with you. Passengers are expected to, uh, furnish their own rations on this voyage."

"Nobody told us that," Bo said.

Scratch groaned and said, "Don't go talkin' about food right now. Anyway, we had to get out of Seattle so quick-like that there probably wouldn't have been time to round any up."

Kelly nodded. "I know, and I intend to point that out to Cap'n Saunders. Luckily, we carry enough extra supplies that we'll be all right until we dock at Juneau, and we can pick up more provisions there. I just wanted you to know that the captain's probably going to charge you extra, though."

"I suppose that's understandable," Bo said. "We won't object, as long as he's not unreasonable."

"You'll find that Cap'n Saunders is an honest man. Plenty rough around the edges, but honest as the day is long."

Kelly fell silent again but continued to stand there. After a moment, Bo said, "You seem to have something else on your mind, son. What is it?"

"Well . . . is it true those ladies are going to Alaska to get married?" After the initial hesitation, the words came out of Kelly in a rush.

"That's right. They have prospective husbands waiting for them."

"But only prospective, right? They could, uh, change their minds?"

Scratch said, "Boy, what are you thinkin'? Sounds to me like you've got your eye on one of those gals."

Kelly swallowed hard and then blurted out, "I've never seen a prettier girl in my whole life than Miss DeHerries! I mean, looking at her is like . . . like watching the sun come up over the ocean. It just sort of blinds you with how pretty a sight it is."

"I won't argue with you about Miss DeHerries's looks," Bo said. "But she's betrothed to a fella in Alaska, and it's our job to deliver her to Cushman, safe and sound, and we wouldn't appreciate anybody trying to interfere with that."

"Anyway," Scratch said, "if you're hankerin' to roam around the seven seas again, you don't need a wife tyin' you down, now, do you?"

"When I was a boy in Maine, I saw a lot of men sail off and leave their wives behind."

"And what is it they call those little platforms on houses along the coast?" Bo asked. "Widow's walks? There's a good reason for that, isn't there?"

"Are you saying that the chance of leaving a woman a widow is worse than making her suffer through an Alaskan winter? Spending her days helping her husband chip away at rocks and her nights in a cabin hardly fit for a bear to live in? You don't really think that's going to be a good life for those ladies, do you?"

It had crossed Bo's mind that Beatrice and the others didn't really know what they were letting themselves in for, so he couldn't argue with Chart Kelly about *that*, either. Caroline, especially, seemed too delicate for such a hard-scrabble existence. But like the others, Caroline was a grown woman and could make up her own mind about what she wanted to do. Such decisions were none of the Texans' business.

"All I'm saying, son, is that I'd take it kindly if you'd keep your interest to yourself. Miss DeHerries and the other ladies are all committed to going on to Cushman and meeting the men they've agreed to marry. You don't have any right to interfere in that."

A stubborn look came over Kelly's face. "Are you saying you'll stop me if I try to talk to Miss DeHerries?"

"Talk to her? No, I reckon you can do that."

"Start tryin' to court her and it'll be a different story," Scratch said.

Kelly frowned at them for a moment longer, then turned and walked away. Scratch watched him go and said quietly, "That boy's gonna be trouble."

"Maybe, maybe not," Bo said. "I get the feeling that he's actually a pretty decent sort. Maybe he'll see that it would be a mistake to try to get Caroline all mixed up."

Scratch shook his head. "This is the part of the whole business I don't like. But at least talkin' to that youngster, even if he's bound to make trouble, kept my mind off how my belly's feelin' for a few minutes."

"Starting to act up again, is it?"

Scratch groaned again and tightened his grip on the rail. "I'll let you know," he said, "but I got a hunch it ain't gonna be good!"

Chapter 11

As it turned out, Scratch got his sea legs in less than forty-eight hours—but before that, the silver-haired Texan was pretty miserable a lot of that time. When Bo saw him on the morning of their third day at sea, he could tell right away that Scratch felt better.

"You reckon maybe you won't die after all?" Bo asked with a wry smile.

"Not right away," Scratch replied. "Although as many times as we've dodged that old boy with the scythe, he's bound to catch up to us sooner or later."

All the crew's bunks in the forecastle were taken, and although someone was always on watch so at least one bunk stayed empty, none of the sailors wanted to share. Bo and Scratch had pitched their bedrolls in a storage compartment instead. The quarters were very cramped but better than nothing.

They had gotten to know the other passengers, men ranging in age from twenty to forty-five, from all over the United States, who had their minds made up they were going to Alaska to find gold and make their fortunes. A couple of them were married and had left wives and children behind, but the rest were single and regarded this journey as a great adventure.

Most of them—probably all of them—were destined for failure, Bo knew, but if they survived . . . if they made it back home safely . . . they would know that at least they had tried to strike it rich, and the younger ones especially would look back on this part of their life with fondness, forgetting all the misery and hardship they had endured along the way. That was the nature of things, and Bo had lived long enough for such bittersweet knowledge to sink in on him.

Scratch wasn't the only one who had been sick. Beatrice, Martha, and Sally had all been struck low by the ship's constant motion at one time or another. Caroline was the only lady who had come through unscathed so far.

She and Bo spent some time walking on deck while the others were in their cabins. Anytime Bo spotted Chart Kelly in the vicinity of where they were walking, he steered Caroline in a different direction.

She was observant enough that she finally noticed, and she asked him, "Why are you trying to avoid that young sailor Mr. Kelly, Bo?"

By now, all the ladies were calling the Texans by their first names, because, as Sally explained it, "You're like friendly uncles to all of us."

"I'm not necessarily trying to avoid him," he said to Caroline.

"Indeed you are," she insisted, "and if he doesn't bother *you*, then you must be trying to keep *me* away from him."

"Don't you worry about it, Miss Caroline. It's nothing for you to be concerned with."

"I've seen the way he looks at me when he thinks I'm not watching. I'm not a babe in the woods, you know. He's got a . . . How would Scratch say it? He's got a hankering for me, doesn't he?"

Bo had to laugh at that. "Yeah, I reckon he does. Can't blame him. If I was his age, I'd have noticed how good-looking you are, too."

"I know it's immodest to ask . . . but are you saying you *haven't* noticed?"

"No, ma'am," Bo admitted. "I'm old, but my eyesight's still pretty good."

Caroline blushed and said, "Thank you."

"How much do you know about this fella you're supposed to marry when you get to Cushman?" Bo asked, changing the subject.

"His name is Eli Byrne. He sent me a small tintype of himself. He's a very handsome young man of twenty-four."

"A prospector?"

"He told me in his letters that he's done some prospecting, but he also works for one of the local businessmen in the settlement, a man named Amos Lawson." Caroline paused, then added, "Mr. Lawson is Aunt Beatrice's intended."

"I see," Bo said. Until now, he hadn't talked to any of the ladies about the men they were supposed to marry.

"I believe all the gentlemen we're betrothed to are affiliated with Mr. Lawson," Caroline went on. "Evidently he's quite successful. I'm sure his enterprises will only grow more so once he's married to Aunt Beatrice. She's a very canny person, you know. Mr. Lawson will do well to take heed of any advice she cares to give him."

Bo nodded. From what he had seen of her, he didn't expect Beatrice to be shy about offering advice to this fella Lawson, either. But Caroline was right; Beatrice was smart as a whip.

They were strolling along the deck when Chart Kelly stepped right in front of them, seemingly out of nowhere. He must have noticed that Bo was trying to steer Caroline clear of him, and he knew the ship well enough to slip up on them.

Bo stopped short, and so did Caroline.

"Good day to you, Miss DeHerries," Kelly said as he snatched his cap off and held it one-handed in front of his chest. "Beautiful day, isn't it?"

As a matter of fact, the day was overcast, with thick gray clouds hanging over the waves. There was enough wind to ruffle Kelly's tawny hair, but the water wasn't too choppy. The coastline was visible as a low, dark line several miles to the east. Bo wouldn't call the day beautiful, but he supposed it could be a lot worse.

"If you say so, Mr. Kelly," Caroline responded with cool but polite reserve. "Do I call you Mr. Kelly? I believe I heard mention that you're the third mate on this ship, but Third Mate Kelly seems rather awkward."

"Mister is fine," he said with a grin. "Or even better, just call me Chart. My real name is Charles, but my father dubbed me Chart when I was a boy, and it stuck. He was a fisherman, you know, so he always had charts around the house and on board his boats."

"It's an interesting name, and it suits you, but using it would be much too familiar in my case, Mr. Kelly. I'm a betrothed woman, as you know."

"Betrothed to a fellow who's all the way up in Alaska," Kelly said with a knowing look.

"That's enough, Kelly," Bo said. Caroline's right arm

was looped through his left one. He tightened his grip slightly and went on, "We'll finish our walk now."

"Don't let me disturb you," Kelly said as he stepped aside. "I just wanted to say hello to you, Miss DeHerries."

"And so you have," Caroline murmured. "Good day, Mr. Kelly."

They moved on past the young sailor. Caroline started to turn her head, but Bo said from the corner of his mouth, "Don't look back at him. He's just waiting for you to do that."

Caroline fixed her gaze straight ahead and said, "Perhaps you're right. I have a feeling that if I were to give him the least bit of encouragement, he could become quite persistent."

"Yeah. So you're not going to encourage him, are you?"

"Of course not," Caroline said.

Bo wished he could believe her fully, but somehow he just couldn't quite do that.

The *John Starr* sailed on northward, staying fairly close to the mainland for this first part of the journey. Bo knew from talking to Captain Saunders about their route that after stopping at Juneau, the ship would swing far to the west in the northern Pacific, circling the Aleutian Islands before beating back to the east toward St. Michael at the mouth of the Yukon. The whole trip would take approximately three weeks.

After several days, Beatrice recovered from her bout of seasickness, although Martha and Sally were still suffering, as were at least half of the would-be prospectors. Most of the time, Beatrice had stayed in the cabin she shared with Caroline, but as she began to feel steadier, she emerged on deck more often.

Bo found her standing at the railing one day, with her right hand resting on the smooth wood as she peered out over the tossing blue-gray water. The sky was like iron, as it usually was in these northern latitudes.

He nodded to her and said, "How are you doing today, Miss Beatrice?"

"Much better, thank you, Bo," she replied. A faint smile curved her lips. "To put it bluntly, I suppose I look like hell, don't I?"

"No, ma'am. You look just fine. A little pale, maybe . . ."

"Positively wan, and bordering on haggard. I have a mirror among my things, you know. I made myself as presentable as possible before emerging into the light of day again."

Bo had to laugh at the dramatic way she put that.

She gave him a quizzical look. "Did I say something amusing?"

"No, ma'am. But you don't have to worry about the way you look, I can promise you that."

"Well . . . thank you. I'll take compliments wherever I can get them."

"I reckon your late husband must have complimented you all the time," Bo said.

She cocked a finely plucked eyebrow at him. "You think so? You'd be wrong."

"I find that hard to believe."

"Oh, don't misunderstand. Daniel O'Rourke was full of smooth talk and flattery at one time in his life. I suppose that's part of the reason I married him. That and the fact that he was devilishly handsome, especially when he was still in the Mounted Police. I was little more than a girl when I met him, you know, and the sight of him in that dashing red uniform . . . well, I suppose it took my breath away."

"Scratch and I have met up with a few Mounties in our time. Good lawmen. We were along the border in Montana a few years ago, and there was a Mountie up there, just on the other side of the line, who was convinced we were running whiskey to the Blackfeet—"

"Were you?" Beatrice asked.

"Nope. Fact of the matter is, we were trying to help out this young fella who got mixed up with the whiskey runners because of a girl, and there was this other ornery little fella who called himself the Carcajou, who was really behind the whiskey running . . . Anyway, it's a long story, but we weren't really breaking the law even though that Mountie thought we were and tried to arrest us. I suspect your husband would've done the same thing."

"Not necessarily. He wasn't all *that* devoted to preserving law and order. In fact, he was quick to take off the uniform and resign from the Mounted Police when my father offered him a job with the steel company in Pittsburgh. We met while I was with my father in Toronto, while he worked on a business deal with a company up there."

"Your father owns a steel mill?" Bo was surprised by that. If Beatrice was an heiress, what was she doing traipsing off to marry somebody in an isolated little mining settlement in Alaska?

"Not at all," she replied. "He was one of the executives and was paid well enough, I suppose, but he was hardly a steel tycoon, if that's what you're thinking."

"Well, I wondered," Bo admitted.

"Still, he was able to offer Daniel a job, as an inducement to get us to move back to the States after we were married, and Daniel jumped at the chance." Slowly, Beatrice shook her head. "As it turned out, Daniel O'Rourke was not cut out to be an executive any more than he was a Mounted Policeman. He was too fond of drinking . . ." She took a breath. "And other women."

Bo frowned at her and said, "Now *that* I find mighty hard to believe, Miss Beatrice."

"Believe it," she said. "Daniel and I were still married at the time of his death, but we hadn't lived together in more than a year."

Bo had gotten caught up in her story, but suddenly he felt a little uncomfortable. "This is none of my business—" he began.

"No, it's all right," she told him as she moved her hand from the railing and laid it on his forearm instead. "You and Scratch have risked your lives for us, so I certainly don't see anything wrong with telling you more about me. If any of the other ladies wish to do so, that's up to them. Besides, talking is keeping my mind off the fact that I still don't feel absolutely steady."

Bo nodded and said, "Well, go on then, if that's what you want."

"Daniel is the one who left me. When he was in the Mounted Police, and even after he resigned, he'd heard rumors about gold being discovered along the Yukon. He promised he was going to win me back, and to do that he was going to strike it rich. Not that I cared about being rich, but Daniel never quite seemed to understand that."

"So he went to Alaska?"

Beatrice shook her head. "No, the Yukon runs fairly

deep into northwestern Canada, and gold has been found over there, too, I've heard. But Daniel didn't find any of it. I received a letter . . ." Her voice caught a little. "It took months to reach me. But it brought the news that he had died of a fever. His dreams were . . . unfulfilled."

Bo thought about that for a moment, then said, "So, are you trying to live those dreams for him, Miss Beatrice? Because I don't think that usually works out too well for folks."

She shook her head again. "No, that's not it. Daniel actually did talk about venturing on into Alaska in search of gold, but I'm not trying to do that for him. Honestly, I just wanted something different from my old life. We all did. And embarking on an adventure like this . . . well, it's going to be different, isn't it?"

"A whole heap different," Bo agreed. "And to be honest, ma'am, I'm not sure any of you ladies really understand what you're letting yourself in for. Alaska's a wilderness, and from what I've heard, the winters are mighty rough. So are the men who live up there."

"Such as the men we've agreed to marry?"

"Yes, ma'am, that's right."

"So what we're doing is a leap of faith, like everything else in life."

"You can look at it that way if you want."

"That's the way I choose to look at it, Bo." Her tone hardened, and Bo heard some of that steel, like her father helped manufacture back in Pittsburgh. "And it's your job, and Scratch's, to help us make that leap."

"Yes, ma'am, I suppose it is. And we'll carry out that responsibility to the best of our ability."

"I know you will, because that's the kind of men you

are. Now, if you'll excuse me, I believe I'll go back to the cabin . . ."

"Sure."

She started to turn away, then paused. "Don't think *too* badly of Daniel because of what I told you, Bo. He certainly had his flaws, but I have many fond memories of our time together. He swept me off my feet, and I was very happy for a time. I suppose . . . by going up into this far corner of the world . . . perhaps I hope to feel closer to those memories."

"Then I hope you find what you're looking for, Miss Beatrice," Bo said.

"I do, too, Bo. I really do hope that I find what I'm looking for."

Chapter 12

Just as Chart Kelly had predicted, Captain Saunders charged extra for the food that Bo, Scratch, and the ladies ate, and he insisted on being paid for it when the *John Starr* reached Juneau so the ship's cook could stock up on provisions. Bo thought that was fair, and since Saunders didn't seem to be gouging them on the amount he wanted, Bo paid up.

The ship was docked in Juneau for an afternoon while cargo bound for there was unloaded. None of the passengers went ashore, though. Bo and Scratch stood at the railing and looked at the numerous tree-covered islands to the west, through which various channels of water ran, and the ice-topped mountains just to the east of the settlement. The peaks and the water ringed Juneau, so according to Captain Saunders, no trails led into the settlement. The only way to come and go from there was by ship.

"I don't reckon I'd cotton to a place where you couldn't get on a horse and leave if you wanted to," Scratch commented.

"Neither would I," Bo agreed.

Later that day, the *John Starr* threaded its way back out

through the maze of waterways and reached the open sea again. Now began the big loop around the Aleutian Islands that would take another two weeks—a week out and a week back in to the mainland.

Captain Saunders proved to be a master at catching the wind and making good time. Because of the angle at which they were traveling, for several days the ship was completely out of sight of land, but then distant dark humps became visible on the horizon and slowly grew into mountain peaks.

One day after they had drawn even closer, Bo and Scratch were standing at the rail when Scratch suddenly said, "My eyes must be playin' tricks on me, Bo. I'd swear there's smoke comin' from the top of that mountain yonder."

Chart Kelly was passing along the deck behind them and overheard the silver-haired Texan's exclamation. He paused and said, "Aye, you're right, Mr. Creel. It is smoking. Many of the Aleutians are active volcanoes."

"Volcanoes?" Scratch repeated as his eyebrows climbed his forehead. "You mean they're liable to blow their tops? I've heard about such things but never seen one."

"Sure you have," Bo said. "There's that place down in New Mexico Territory, southeast of Raton Pass, that folks say used to be a volcano, thousands of years ago."

Scratch raked a thumbnail along his jawline as he frowned in thought. "Oh, yeah, I recollect now. We ran into that loco bunch of bandidos chasin' a pretty gal they figured on doin' some sort of sacrifice with, there on the rim of what used to be the volcano."

Kelly stared at Scratch and said, "Did that really happen, Mr. Morton?"

"Would I make up something like that?" Scratch asked with a disdainful snort.

"You two must have adventurous lives."

"We've gotten into a few ruckuses now and then," Bo said. "But you must, too, sailing all over the world."

Kelly grinned. "You mean like fightin' off Malay pirates and tobbo smugglers in the China Sea? Yeah, I've been in a few scrapes like that."

"And you want to give that up?" Scratch asked.

The young sailor's grin widened as he said, "For the love of the right woman, I'd be willing to settle down, I guess."

Scratch just shook his head.

The long archipelago stretched almost all the way to Russia, according to the captain. When the chain of rocky peaks turned to the northwest, the ship was nearly at the end of this part of the journey and would soon round the last of the islands and sail from the northern Pacific into the Bering Sea.

They were almost at that point a couple of days later when Bo noticed an even darker cloud than usual lying low on the northwestern horizon.

He pointed it out to Scratch, who gave a low whistle and said, "Dang, that reminds me of that big ol' blue norther that came roarin' in that time we were down in the Panhandle."

"When the blizzard covered up that town the outlaws had taken over?" Bo nodded. "Yeah, it'd be hard to forget about that."

"Can you tell if it's comin' this way?"

Bo shook his head. "No, but I think I'm going to ask the captain about it."

He headed toward the stern, where Jedediah Saunders stood on the raised deck next to the helmsman. As Bo went up the steps toward them, Saunders held up a stubby-fingered hand, palm out.

"Don't even ask," the captain said. "Aye, that's a storm, and aye, it's heading this way. Landlubbers always worry about such things, but I'm going to try to dodge the worst of it."

"Then it really is as threatening as it looks?"

"Hard to say just now. But I'm keeping my eye on it, I promise you that."

Saunders probably meant for that to be reassuring, but Bo didn't feel particularly comforted. When Bo looked again at the approaching cloud, the hairs on the back of his neck stood up. He trusted his instincts, and right now they were telling him loud and clear that trouble was on the way.

He rejoined Scratch. "The captain says he's going to try to dodge the worst of it."

"As big as that cloud is, I reckon he's gonna have trouble doin' that. I tell you, Bo, that thing gives me the fantods."

"Me too. Let's go warn the ladies they need to stick to their cabins the rest of the day."

"You gonna tell them we're in for a storm?"

"I think they've got a right to know," Bo said.

Beatrice, Martha, and Sally had just about recovered their color after their bouts with seasickness early in the voyage, but now they joined Caroline in turning pale as Bo told them about the approaching storm.

"Is there anything we can do?" Beatrice asked.

"Stay in your cabins and make sure everything is fastened down so it won't start flying around if the ship pitches too much," Bo said. "If you'd like to all stay together in one cabin, that would be all right, too."

"Reckon we just have to trust in the cap'n and ride it out," Scratch said. "Bo and I can do a heap of things, but steerin' a ship in a storm ain't one of 'em."

"You should stay in here, too," Caroline said. "We should all be together."

Bo nodded and said, "That sounds like a good idea. We'll fetch our rifles from the compartment where we've been sleeping."

"Your rifles?" Beatrice said. "You can't shoot a storm."

"No, ma'am," Scratch said, "but we're sort of in the habit of keepin' those Winchesters handy. Feels a mite strange if they're somewhere we can't get to 'em."

They hurried belowdecks to the storage compartment to get the rifles. When they came back up on deck, Bo noticed right away that the wind had picked up quite a bit, and the sea was rougher. The blue-black cloud seemed to be a freight train barreling down on the ship.

Crewmen shouted to one another and rushed around the deck as they brought in most of the sails before the wind got even worse. Two small triangles of canvas remained high on the masts, which Bo supposed gave the ship some steering capability.

Bo could tell that the *John Starr* was swinging to the south now in an attempt to skirt the worst of the bad weather. He glanced toward the quarterdeck and saw that the sailor who had been at the helm was no longer there. Captain Saunders stood alone behind the big wheel.

Scratch saw that, too, and said, "Lord have mercy, Bo,

the cap'n's got a rope around his waist, and the other end's tied to that pedestal the wheel's attached to. Why's he got himself tied to the wheel like that?"

"So the waves can't wash him away from it," Bo replied grimly.

"If the waves are gonna get big enough to do that, we're all doomed."

"Maybe not. These ships are made to sail through storms. Come on, let's get back to the ladies."

When they opened the cabin door, Bo saw right away that only three women were there.

"Where's Caroline?" he asked.

"She went next door to our cabin," Beatrice said. "We wanted a few things that are there."

"What sort of things?"

"Mementoes. Jewelry. A small Bible that belonged to Caroline's mother. Things that we wanted with us if . . . if we . . . sink." Beatrice wrung her hands anxiously. "Oh, I know it's silly! If we sink it won't matter whether we have those things with us. But Caroline thought it might make us feel better, and I didn't want to argue with her."

"It's all right," Bo told her.

"I reckon we're all scared," Scratch said. "I know I sure am."

"Did she leave right after we did?"

Beatrice nodded. "Yes, she did. I thought she'd be back by now . . ."

"Yeah, she should have been. I'll go take a look."

"I'll come with you," Scratch said.

Bo shook his head. "No, you stay here with the ladies. I won't be gone but a minute."

Scratch looked as if he wanted to argue, but he knew Bo was right. This errand didn't require both of them.

Besides, the ship was rising and falling, pitching and yawing, more with each passing second, and Scratch was starting to look a little green again.

"Don't take too long," he said.

Bo stepped out of the cabin and hurried along the companionway to the next door. It was closed, so he rapped on it and called over the sound of the rising wind, "Miss Caroline! Are you in there?"

There was no answer. Bo knocked again, and when there was still no response, he reached down and grasped the knob. It turned, and when he opened the door he saw the cabin was dim, as no lamp was lit and the light through the lone porthole had faded as the storm closed in. The daylight was almost gone. If this kept up, soon it would be dark as night outside.

At the moment, however, it was what was *inside* that concerned Bo, and what he saw made his heart slug his chest with alarm.

Caroline DeHerries wasn't here. Other than the bunks and the stowed baggage, the cabin was empty.

Chapter 13

Five minutes earlier, Caroline had been about to open the door of the cabin she shared with her aunt when hurried footsteps made her look toward the far end of the corridor. Steps there led up to the deck, and the hatch at the top of them was open at the moment.

One of the sailors had just rattled down the steps and stopped at a storage locker. As Caroline watched, he opened it, reached inside, took out a heavy coiled rope, and closed the door. The light here belowdecks was murky enough that at first she couldn't tell who he was, but as he turned back toward the steps, she recognized him as Chart Kelly.

Evidently he hadn't noticed her, because he went back up on deck without ever glancing in her direction.

He probably had to get that rope to lash something down, Caroline thought. She grasped the cabin door's knob again, but she still didn't turn it.

Instead, she took a deep breath and then hurried along the corridor toward the steps. They were steeper than regular stairs and climbing them wasn't easy. She had to put a hand on the wall to brace herself as she went up, and then she came out on the deck.

The wind immediately slapped at her, causing her to gasp at its ferocity. As she looked over the edge of the ship, she saw the jagged crests of the waves, and a shiver of fear shot through her. They looked like gigantic teeth, and she couldn't help but think that they were ready to gnaw the ship and everyone on it—and spit out what was left.

She forced her eyes away from the sea and looked around until she spotted Chart Kelly. He had just finished tying the rope around one of the masts. Caroline had no idea what he was tying down or why, but she assumed it was important or he wouldn't be doing it. He appeared to be finished with the task, though, so she called, "Mr. Kelly!"

He raised his head, glanced around, and then gave a little shake of his head as if he thought he had heard something but then dismissed the possibility. She didn't want him to turn and hurry off to do something else, so she raised her voice even higher and tried again to get his attention.

"Mr. Kelly!"

This time his head snapped toward her. He stared at her in surprise for a couple of seconds, then hurried over.

Behind him, the waves grew even higher and stronger. "Miss DeHerries!" he shouted as he came up to her. "What in the hell—I mean, what in the world are you doing out here?"

"I saw you, Mr. Kelly, and I wanted to be sure you were going to be all right!" Caroline had to raise her voice so much to be heard over the wind that it hurt her throat a little. "Shouldn't you go below?"

"The cap'n's not going below, and neither am I! Someone has to stand watch!" He grasped her arm, propriety forgotten. "You need to get out of here! Go to your cabin with the other ladies and stay there!"

"I'm going to, I just have to get a few things—"

"No time! A blow like this comes on you mighty quick! Please, Miss DeHerries—"

He stopped short as he looked down into her face. Rain had started to fall, just occasional drops but enough for Caroline to feel it on her cheeks. Her heart pounded even harder as Chart Kelly stared into her eyes, and then his lips moved as he muttered something. She couldn't make it all out, but she thought she heard him say, "time like this" and "be damned if I—"

Then he leaned down and kissed her, his lips hard and urgent against hers, and without thinking about what she was doing, her fingers clutched at his shirtfront and pulled her closer to him.

She wasn't sure how long the kiss lasted. It seemed a long time but probably was only seconds. But she knew how it ended: with a terrible roar like a locomotive. The sound made her jerk her head back. Both of them turned their heads to look toward the ship's bow and saw an awesome sight.

A giant wave, like a mountain range on the move, was bearing down on the *John Starr*. Caroline barely had time to open her mouth and scream before the watery juggernaut struck the ship with the power of a thousand explosions.

That was the way it seemed, at least. The deck tilted wildly under Caroline's feet, and she suddenly felt as if she was underwater. The stuff was in her mouth and nose, and she was drowning.

When she saw the massive wave about to strike, she had grabbed harder at Chart Kelly's shirt, but it was no use. The impact had knocked them apart, and she had no idea where the sailor was. She didn't know where *she* was, but she realized she was lying facedown and moving. Sliding . . .

Sliding along the steeply sloping deck toward those giant teeth she had seen earlier. Choking as she was, she couldn't even scream in terror at her impending death.

Then something clamped around her wrist and stopped her deadly plunge. The thing that gripped her felt as if it was made of steel cables, but as Caroline raised her drenched head and tried to blink the water out of her eyes enough to see, she realized that Chart Kelly had hold of her.

His left hand was wrapped around her right wrist. His right hand held a taut rope, the rope she had seen him tie a few minutes earlier. *He had been about to tie himself to the mast so he wouldn't be swept overboard*, she thought. And she had interrupted him.

She didn't know how he had managed to grab both her and the rope, but he had saved her life—for now. The storm still raged all around them. The ship pitched madly, rising so high that the masts must be poking holes in heaven, then plunging as if the entire world had dropped out from under it. Caroline and Chart went sliding the other way.

Chart was quick-witted enough, or perhaps experienced enough, to flip the rope in a loop around his wrist while he had some slack in it. That way he wasn't as likely to lose his grip on it. They slid past the mast as the ship tilted insanely in the other direction.

When they came to a sudden stop, the wrenching

pressure on Caroline's shoulder made it seem like the bone was going to pop right out of its socket. She cried out in pain. But Chart didn't let go of her, and she didn't go over the side into the hungry maw of the storm. The ship rose again, and as it did, Chart pulled her closer and shouted, "Grab on to me! Get your arms around my neck and hang on!"

He had to let go of her wrist in order for her to do that, and Caroline didn't want him to. She clutched at him with her other hand, and then when he released her wrist she threw that arm around his neck, too, even though it still hurt. His left arm went around her waist and closed like a metal band.

The ship dropped again.

This time, Chart twisted around and got his feet turned toward the mast so the soles of his boots slammed against the base of it, stopping them from sliding all the way to the other side of the deck. He wrapped more of the rope around his other arm, shortening the distance they could slide the next time the ship tried to turn on its side.

For what seemed like a coughing, choking, hellish eternity, Caroline and Chart slid back and forth as the waves tossed the *John Starr* this way and that. Gradually, though, Chart shortened the rope until they lay huddled against the mast and didn't move anymore.

Huge waves still broke over the ship's sides and completely inundated them, but Caroline learned how to keep her face pressed hard against Chart's broad chest so that she didn't swallow as much water. She felt his heart beating against her cheek and concentrated on that, willing everything else in the world to go away. That was the only thing in her universe—the strong, rapid thumping of Chart Kelly's heart.

It was a long time before she realized that the ship wasn't pitching around as much. The wind still howled, hard rain still lashed at her, and the ship rose and fell quite a bit, but the wild plunging had abated. She lifted her head and looked up into Chart's face.

"Are . . . are we dead?" she managed to ask.

"Dead? No, the storm's let up a bit. I reckon the cap'n's managed to get us past the worst of it. At least, the worst of the part we were in."

"What do you mean? It couldn't have been any worse!"

"Oh, aye, it was, off to the north. I could see it, and I was mighty glad we weren't in the really bad blow!"

That was the most insane thing she had ever heard. There had never been a worse storm than this one, not in any ocean, anywhere in the world, ever.

But if he wanted to think so, that was fine, as long as he continued to hold her.

It dawned on her that they were both soaked to the skin and entangled, arms and legs entwined in a way that would be completely improper and scandalous under other circumstances. Right now, however, Caroline couldn't bring herself to worry about that.

The rain dwindled from a downpour to a steady drizzle. The wind blew but was no longer a raging lunatic. The sea was rough but no choppier than it had been several times earlier in the voyage.

"Caroline! Caroline!"

As unbelievable as it seemed at the moment, that was her aunt's voice, Caroline realized. She lifted her head again and saw Beatrice coming toward them with Bo

Creel beside her, holding her arm. Beatrice's clothes and hair were wet, although she wasn't as soaked as Caroline and Chart.

"Caroline, are you all right?"

Chart's arm uncoiled from around her, and for a second, Caroline felt a pang of loss. But then Beatrice and Bo were there, lifting her to her feet. Beatrice embraced her tightly, sobbing, "I thought you were lost! I thought I'd never see you again!"

"No, I . . . Mr. Kelly . . . he saved me."

Bo extended a hand to Chart and helped him to his feet. "I'd say we're obliged to you, son," he said as he grasped Chart's hand and pumped it, "but that doesn't begin to cover it."

Beatrice moved back a little and rested her hands on Caroline's shoulders. She said, "What in the world were you *doing* out here when that terrible storm was about to hit?"

"I'm afraid that was my fault, Mrs. O'Rourke," Chart said. "I saw Miss DeHerries down below and called her up on deck to warn her about the storm. I didn't think it was going to hit as quickly as it did."

Bo frowned and said, "That doesn't make a lick of sense. Why would you get her up on deck at a time like that?"

"He didn't," Caroline said. "Mr. Kelly is just trying to protect me from having to admit that I did a very foolish thing. *I* followed *him* on deck so I could speak to him before the storm struck and wish him good luck. He tried to get me back down below in time but had no chance to do so. It was entirely my fault."

Beatrice shook her head and said, "Well, I don't care

about any of that. The important thing is that you're alive, the rest of us are alive, and the worst of the storm seems to be over. Oh, Caroline, I'm so sorry I got you into this!"

"Don't be, Aunt Beatrice. I knew perfectly well before we started out that there might be some risks. It's just part of the . . ." Caroline smiled weakly. "The adventure."

"Adventure! Oh, my heavens!" Beatrice put her arm around Caroline's shoulders. "Let's get you below and into some dry clothes. You look like you're half drowned!"

"More than half, I think," Caroline said as she allowed her aunt to lead her away.

Despite what Bo had said to her once before about looking back, she couldn't stop herself from doing it this time. She turned her head and looked over her shoulder at Chart Kelly, who stood there watching her go.

He had known that storm was bearing down on them, and he had taken the time to kiss her anyway. Because he thought it might be the only chance he would ever get?

Caroline didn't know. She was glad he had done it, had seized that moment, but his action—and her reaction—raised some questions she didn't want to think about right now.

She was too glad that the storm was breaking and she was still alive.

Chapter 14

The next day, the clouds actually broke for a change, and dazzling sunlight poured down over the sea and the islands visible from the *John Starr*. The light made the snow and ice glitter atop the peaks, and the plumes of grayish-white smoke rising from some of them stood out against the bright blue sky.

Nobody would ever guess from looking at their beautiful, peaceful surroundings that less than twenty-four hours earlier, the angry sea had almost swallowed the ship whole.

That day, the helmsman spun the wheel at Captain Saunders's command and the *John Starr* heeled over and rounded Attu Island, the westernmost of the Near Islands, which were called that despite being the farthest from the Alaskan mainland. Russians had given these islands that name, Saunders explained to Bo and Scratch, because they were the nearest to Russia.

"That bleak land is not far that way," Saunders explained as he pointed west.

"Sounds to me like we could be in Roosha quicker than we can get back to Alaska," Scratch commented.

"Oh, aye, that's true. A day's sailing and we'd be in

Russian waters, but it'll take us nigh a week to get back to the mouth of the Yukon, where we're headed."

Bo gazed off in the direction of Russia and shook his head. "Never figured I'd be in this part of the world," he said. "I wonder where else our travels will take us."

Scratch grinned and said, "Ain't no tellin'. That's the thing that makes life worth livin', ain't it?"

"A big part of it," Bo admitted with a smile and a nod.

"How's Miss DeHerries today?" Captain Saunders asked. "I haven't seen her out on deck."

"She's all right. Her arm and shoulder are a little sore from the strain put on them when Kelly was hanging on to her and keeping her from washing overboard, but that sure beats the alternative. Mostly she's just shaken up from almost being drowned like a rat. I'm sure she'll be fine in a day or two, though."

"I'm glad to hear it. And proud that we didn't lose a single soul durin' that big blow. 'Twasn't the worst I've been in, by any stretch o' the imagination, but bad enough, no doubt about that." The captain laughed. "I'll wager there was a lot of prayin' goin' on. I may have asked for the Good Lord's help a time or two myself, in between all the cussin' I was doin'."

Later that day, once the ship had made the big turn and was headed east again, Bo went looking for Chart Kelly and found the young sailor sending a man up the mainmast to the crow's nest. As third mate, Kelly was in charge of navigation and kept men aloft to maintain a watch on the sea around them.

"Afternoon, Mr. Creel," Kelly greeted Bo. "I was hoping to see you and ask how Miss DeHerries is."

"She's fine," Bo said without going into the same explanation he had given Saunders. "Thanks to you, son."

"No, I didn't really—" Kelly began, then stopped short. "I suppose there's no real point in false modesty, is there? If I hadn't grabbed her when I did, she would have been lost overboard as soon as the storm hit."

"That's true," Bo said, nodding slowly. "But from what I gather, she wouldn't have *been* on deck in the first place if she hadn't followed you there."

An uncomfortable look came over Kelly's face. "I didn't try to attract her attention and get her to come up there, Mr. Creel, I give you my word on that. I didn't even know she'd seen me down below when I went to fetch a rope to tie myself to the mast."

"Which doesn't change the fact that she's shown a considerable interest in you, son . . . or the fact that she's engaged to be married."

Kelly held up a hand and said, "I swear, as well, I didn't touch the young lady any more than I had to in order to save her life."

Bo had a hunch Kelly might not have been telling the complete truth there, but he didn't press the point. Instead he said, "I'm going to count on your sense of honor making sure you don't pursue her, Mr. Kelly. My job is to get her to Cushman and her intended bridegroom, and I intend to do it."

"Even if she doesn't want to go anymore?" Kelly's voice took on a challenging tone. "You'd force her?"

"If she comes to that decision on her own, she'll have to work it out with her aunt, who's sort of in charge of this little expedition. I never made any gal do anything she didn't want to do, so no, I'm not going to drag her up the

Yukon against her will. But I'd have to be convinced you didn't meddle in things, either."

For a moment, Kelly looked like he was going to continue to argue, but then he jerked his head in a curt nod and said, "I respect the young lady too much to force my attentions on her. You're asking me to steer clear of her?"

"I am," Bo said, although he wouldn't hesitate to *tell* Kelly to steer clear of Caroline if he had to. He was grateful to the young man for saving Caroline's life, but that gratitude only went so far.

Kelly sighed. "All right. I give you my word, Mr. Creel. I won't seek her out. But I can't do anything about it if she comes looking for me."

"Except remind her that she's already got somebody waiting for her."

"You drive a hard bargain, mister. But if you truly believe that it's best for Miss DeHerries . . ."

"I do."

"Then I'll go along with you."

"Thanks, Kelly."

From there, Bo went belowdecks, hoping to find Beatrice alone. He needed to have a talk with her, too. Unfortunately, the other ladies, including Caroline, were with her, so Bo had to wait until the next day before he caught Beatrice standing near the bow by herself.

"I reckon it'll still be a few days before we'll be able to see the mainland," he said. The Aleutians had fallen out of sight to the south as the ship sailed through the Bering Sea, so there was nothing around the *John Starr* at the moment except seemingly endless water.

Beatrice turned to him with a surprised smile. "I didn't hear you coming, Bo. You move very quietly."

"Habit," he said. "Comes from sneaking up on ornery fellas with mischief in mind."

She laughed. "I'm sure it does. And I'm sure you and Scratch have encountered plenty of those 'ornery fellows' in your lives."

"More than our share, I expect."

Beatrice turned her attention back to the water in front of them, and they stood in silence for a moment before she said, "Did you have something you wanted to talk to me about, Bo?"

"You're a pretty perceptive lady."

"Thank you. So you *do* have something on your mind?"

He didn't answer her directly. Instead he said, "Perceptive enough that you've probably noticed how Miss Caroline and that sailor, Chart Kelly, look at each other."

Beatrice's lips tightened slightly. "Yes, I've seen that. I also saw how he was holding her when we found them on deck after the storm. I realize he was just trying to protect her . . ."

"But that close together, with both of them soaked, and at their age . . . I don't reckon they could have helped but get some ideas, once they figured out they weren't fixing to die."

She still didn't look at him as she said, "It's not just young people who might get ideas when forced together in an intimate situation."

He wondered if she was thinking about that night in the Occidental Hotel when Rollin Kemp's men had snuck in to kidnap Caroline. He had wound up holding her while she wasn't wearing anything but a thin nightdress. He had certainly been aware of that, but he hadn't known until now that she had thought about it, too.

Well, that had been just circumstances and nothing was going to come of it, Bo told himself now. He went on, "I had a talk with Kelly and asked him to keep his distance. You might ought to do the same with Caroline."

"She's my niece, and I feel like I have to look out for her, but I'm not sure that gives me the right to interfere too much in her life." Beatrice paused, then continued, "On the other hand, we did make arrangements through Mr. Keegan's agency to marry those gentlemen in Cushman, and I consider those arrangements to be binding, unless there's a very good reason to set them aside. I'm not sure a brief infatuation on board a ship is enough of a reason."

Bo nodded and said, "That's what I was thinking. You'll talk to Caroline?"

"I will." She turned to him again and touched his arm. "And thank you for trying to look out for all of us."

"It's my job," he said gruffly.

"I know that. But I have a feeling you'd do it anyway, whether you were getting paid or not, simply because that's the sort of man you are. Mr. Morton, too. You're . . . knights errant, I suppose you could say. Wandering cavaliers looking for evil dragons to slay and beautiful maidens to rescue." She laughed. "I'd like to think that my friends and I qualify, even though Caroline is the only true maiden among us."

"That hombre Kemp could be considered an evil dragon, I reckon," Bo said. "And we might should have slayed him."

"He's all the way down in Seattle. Surely he's no threat to us now."

"I hope you're right, ma'am," Bo told her. At the same time, he knew he would feel better about things once they got to where they were going and the four ladies were safely married to their new husbands.

The Alaskan mainland was visible for a day before the ship got close enough for Bo and Scratch to make out any details. When they could, they saw that although plenty of mountains were visible in the distance, the coastline itself was low and heavily timbered, with large rocky bluffs jutting out into the water here and there. It looked like an approach from the sea would be tricky, so the Texans were glad that Captain Saunders had his experienced hands on the wheel.

The opening of a bay came into sight. Saunders headed for it. He waved Bo and Scratch onto the quarterdeck and told them, "That's Norton Sound ahead of us. We'll follow it a ways before one of the branches of the Yukon empties into it."

"One of the branches?" Scratch repeated. "I thought we were headed for the Yukon itself?"

"No, it's just not the main branch. But it's still the Yukon."

Bo said, "Like the Mississippi splits up into all that delta country down south of New Orleans?"

"That's right," Saunders said. "And St. Michael is where that branch empties in the sound. It's the only settlement for hundreds of miles up and down this coast, except for the Indian villages."

"There are Injuns up here?" Scratch asked sharply.

Saunders chuckled. "Yes, but they're all peaceful these days and have been for quite a while. They're fishermen, for the most part, although they'll hunt whales, too, or go inland after bear now and then. You don't have to worry about them scalping you, like the wild Indians where you come from."

"As long as they ain't Comanch' or Blackfoot or Apache, I'm fine with 'em," Scratch said.

By now, word had spread among the passengers that the ship was nearing its destination. They all came up on deck and lined the railing at the bow as the *John Starr* sailed into the harbor. The gold-hunters whooped and slapped each other on the back in excitement and anticipation. Some did little dances of glee that they were one step further on their quest for a fortune.

Beatrice and the other ladies were there as well, with Bo and Scratch standing beside them. They gripped the rail and leaned forward, displaying their own excitement— and considerable relief at the prospect of being back on solid land, Bo figured.

He saw Caroline glance over her shoulder, though, looking away from the shore for a moment. He wondered if she was searching for Chart Kelly. After a moment, she sighed and turned her gaze back to the land.

St. Michael consisted of a handful of streets lined with log buildings, tents, and even a few tar paper shacks. A couple of sturdy docks extended into the harbor, but no other ships were anchored there. A smaller wharf was located about a quarter-mile inland on the other edge of the settlement, and Bo spotted the tall smokestack of a steamboat tied up there. Beyond that wharf was the actual mouth of the river. It was several hundred yards wide, and according to the captain, this wasn't even the main branch of the Yukon.

Martha pointed to the steamboat and asked, "Is that how we'll get up the river?"

"I expect that's right," Bo said, "but we'll find out for sure when we get ashore."

Saunders himself was still at the wheel. He maneuvered the *John Starr* expertly alongside one of the docks extending into the harbor. Sailors were waiting to make the jump from the deck to the pier, taking ropes with them to tie up the ship to the dock's pilings. The ship rocked gently as Saunders called out orders for the crew to strike the sails and make all lines fast.

Still exuberant, the prospectors went ashore first, carrying carpetbags, canvas warbags, crates of supplies, picks, shovels, and axes. There were a couple of general stores in St. Michael where they could outfit themselves with any prospecting equipment they hadn't brought with them.

Once that was done, Chart Kelly appeared but kept his distance from Caroline as he led a group of sailors who unloaded the ladies' bags and stacked them on the dock. Bo supposed he and Scratch would need to rent a wagon to transport the bags to the riverboat.

With the ship safely docked, Captain Saunders ambled up to the Texans and said, "I've enjoyed havin' you fellows on board. You spun some good yarns whenever we got a chance to talk."

"You did, too, Cap'n," Scratch said. "I ain't sure which of us has gotten into the most scrapes."

"That just proves we're still vital and not ready for a rocking chair just yet." Saunders stuck out his hand and shook hands with both of them. "Good luck to you on the rest of your journey. And perhaps, when you're ready to return to Seattle, 'tis my ship you'll be doin' it on."

"That would be fine with us," Bo told him.

Saunders pointed at the riverboat and said, "That's the *Byron Mowery*, named after one of the first white men to go up the Yukon. The captain is Hal Cruickshank. I don't really know the man, but I haven't heard anything bad about him. He ought to be able to get you where you're goin'."

With a wave, he returned to the quarterdeck. Bo and Scratch turned to the four women, and Bo waved a hand toward the gangplank.

"Welcome to Alaska, ladies."

Chapter 15

Captain Hal Cruickshank of the *Byron Mowery* was a tall, scrawny scarecrow of a man with a tuft of gray beard that made him look a little like a billy goat, Scratch commented to Bo after they had gone on board the riverboat and introduced themselves.

Bo agreed about Cruickshank's looks, but he instinctively liked the captain and had confidence that he could get them upriver to Cushman.

"Sure, I don't mind carryin' female passengers," Cruickshank had said when Bo broached the question. "Some o' those seagoin' scalawags like Jedediah Saunders may be superstitious, but I never worried about such things. I figure I'm more levelheaded than that." Cruickshank snorted. "Shoot, the other riverboat that makes regular trips up and down the Yukon even has a lady captain!"

"Really?" Scratch had said. "I never heard of a lady boat captain."

"She inherited it from her pa," Cruickshank said by way of explanation. "And she's done a fine job runnin' it, from what I know. But she's somewhere upriver right now, and you need to get to Cushman, so your choices are waitin' a few weeks here in St. Michael for her to get back or bookin' passage on the ol' *Mowery* here."

"We're going upriver," Bo had said. "My friend and I, and four ladies."

"They aim to prospect, do they?"

Scratch had chuckled and said, "Only for husbands, and they won't have to do much prospectin' since they've already got fellas who've agreed to marry 'em just waitin' for them."

"You mean they're some o' them mail-order brides?" Cruickshank tugged at his billy goat beard. "Heard of such a thing, but I never seen any real evidence of it. Reckon I will now. Sure, bring 'em on board. Room on the forward deck for their bags. I got a few empty cabins left. There was kind of a rush once the *John Starr* docked, but I was expectin' that."

"When will you leave?" Bo had asked.

"First thing tomorrow mornin'. We're still takin' on wood for the firebox, and I don't like to head out this late in the day."

Bo had eyed the settlement, which consisted mostly of crude log buildings. A few structures were made of rough whipsawed lumber. Most of the roofs were tin and tar paper. "You're sure it's all right for the ladies to go ahead and come on board?" he'd asked. "Otherwise we'll need to find rooms for them in town."

"No, don't do that," Cruickshank said. "I've seen worse places in my life, but St. Michael can be hell with the hide off sometimes."

Scratch had said, "What about Cushman?"

"Oh, Cushman's a *real* boomtown. It's a hell of a lot

worse. Been plenty of killings and claim jumpin' up there, from what I hear."

That'd made the Texans exchange a worried glance. They'd started back along the muddy waterfront trail—it would be too generous to call it a street—toward the wharf where the *John Starr* was docked.

Then after Scratch made his comment about Captain Cruickshank reminding him of a billy goat, he said, "Are we doin' the right thing here, Bo, by takin' those ladies up the river like this?"

"It was their choice to agree to marry those men," Bo said, "and it's our job to get them there so they can do it."

"I know, but I'm startin' to worry that maybe they don't really understand what they're lettin' themselves in for. Sure, the weather ain't bad at this time of year, and the scenery's nice, but what about this winter when it stays dark all the time and the snow's ten feet deep and it gets down to fifty or sixty below at night? That ain't like nothin' they ever knew back where they come from. Not to mention, this here St. Michael looks like it's only one or two steps above a hellhole, and if Cushman's even worse . . ."

Bo sighed, then said, "You're not telling me anything I haven't thought for myself a dozen times over. And I sort of tried to say as much to Miss Beatrice. But she seems bound and determined to go through with it, and the others look to her to make up their minds for them. As things stand right now, I don't see any way out of it."

"All right," Scratch said with obvious reluctance. "I hope things work out."

"We'll have to see to it that they do," Bo said.

* * *

The ladies were waiting on the dock next to the pile of bags. Captain Saunders had promised to keep an eye on them from the quarterdeck while Bo and Scratch were off talking to Cruickshank, just in case anyone tried to bother them.

They weren't alone, however. Chart Kelly was there, too, although Beatrice was making a point of standing between him and Caroline.

"What are you doing here, Kelly?" Bo asked him. "Aren't you needed on board the ship?"

"I thought the ladies needed someone looking out for them," Kelly replied.

Scratch said, "Cap'n Saunders promised he'd do that while we were gone."

Kelly waved that away. "I'm sure he had good intentions, but the unloading of the cargo is going on, too, and he might have gotten distracted." The young sailor pointed. "As he's doing right now, in fact."

It was true that Saunders was leaning over the railing that ran along the front of the quarterdeck and yelling at some of the sailors scurrying around midships. He wasn't even looking toward the dock where the ladies waited.

"I admire the cap'n," Kelly went on. "You know that. But a man can only do so many things at the same time."

Bo's jaw tightened. He was annoyed with himself as much as he was with Kelly, maybe even more so. He should have thought of that, and he or Scratch should have stayed here while the other went to make sure they could arrange for the trip upriver on the *Byron Mowery*.

Beatrice must have seen and understood his reaction, because she said, "It's all right, Bo. There was no harm done. Now, tell us—are we going on that riverboat?"

"We are," he replied. "It's not leaving until tomorrow

morning, but the captain said it's all right to take your bags over there and load them, and you can spend the night in your cabins rather than having to try to find accommodations in the settlement."

Sally said, "That's good, because it doesn't really look like much of a settlement."

"There's a hotel," Kelly said, "but I wouldn't recommend it. It's right next door to a saloon." He laughed. "Of course, in St. Michael, almost everything is right next door to a saloon. There are more of those than anything else."

Bo figured it wouldn't hurt anything to be gracious, so he said, "Thanks for looking out for the ladies, Kelly."

"It was my pleasure, Mr. Creel. I know what a rough place this can be. The *John Starr* has docked here a number of times before."

"Did trouble break out on those occasions?" Caroline asked.

"Not *every* time. But enough to make me cautious." Kelly stiffened and stood up a little straighter. "As are those lads who are coming toward us right now."

Bo and Scratch turned and saw half a dozen men ambling toward the dock. They were all roughly dressed and heavily bearded, and the thick smell of unwashed flesh, tobacco, and liquor floated out ahead of them. *That's the way most of the prospectors who had been passengers on the* John Starr *would look and smell in a few months*, Bo thought. These men had been in Alaska for a while.

The Texans had run into plenty of hombres like this and knew right away that they were looking for trouble. Life in the goldfields was hard, no matter where, and these men probably hadn't had much luck. If they had, they would be up at their diggings, putting in the work to gouge the precious metal from the earth, rather than soaking up booze in some waterfront saloon in an attempt to dull their frustration and disappointment.

"Bo, what should we do?" Beatrice asked quietly.

"Just stay where you are," Bo told her as he and Scratch moved so that they stood between the ladies and the prospectors. Chart Kelly stepped up alongside them.

Under the circumstances, Bo wasn't going to ask the young sailor to get back on the ship. With Kelly, they were outnumbered two to one. Without him, the odds would be three to one. Bo didn't figure that was more than he and Scratch could handle, but it never hurt to have an extra friend anytime a ruckus broke out.

With any luck, though, it wouldn't come to that. Bo and Scratch were armed; Bo didn't see any weapons among the prospectors except for a few sheathed hunting knives. They probably wouldn't push their luck against a couple of gun-hung Texans.

The men stopped at the end of the dock, about fifty feet from where Bo, Scratch, and Kelly stood with the women. They milled around for a moment, talking among themselves in low, harsh voices, before one of them nodded to his companions and then stepped to the front. Clearly, they had picked him to be their spokesman.

He clearly had broad shoulders and powerful arms under the top half of his ragged, faded red pair of long underwear. He also wore canvas trousers with suspenders, mud-caked work boots, and a brown felt hat that looked as if its floppy brim had been chewed. The hair of his rust-colored beard and mustache jutted out awkwardly.

He hooked his thumbs under the suspenders as he called, "Howdy! Welcome to St. Michael, folks."

"Are you boys the official greeters?" Scratch asked.

"What? Naw, naw, we ain't official nothin'. We just seen this here ship come in, and we wanted to find out who was gonna be new to our little community, that's all." The man's tongue came out and licked over lips mostly hidden by his facial hair. "Sure never expected to see what we're a-layin' eyes on now, though."

Another man spoke up, saying, "Ain't no women in St. Michael 'cept for some Eskimo squaws, and a man's gotta have a powerful hankerin' for female company to put up with them fat, greasy cows."

"Reckon I'd rather cuddle up with a real cow," a third man said.

The rusty-bearded man leered over his shoulder and said, "I wouldn't be a bit surprised if you'd already done that, Haskell."

Bo snapped, "Watch what you're saying. In case you hadn't noticed, there are ladies present."

"Oh, we noticed, mister, we sure did," Rusty-beard said with a smirk. "We'd be obliged to you if you'd just move aside a mite so's we can get a better look at 'em."

"You boys best move on," Scratch said. "This is none of your business."

"Business, is it?" Rusty-beard said. He raked his fingers through the tangle of hair sticking out from his chin. "You come here on business, is that what you're sayin'? Does that mean you're gonna open up a house, and them gals is gonna work for you?" He turned his head and spat. "Three of 'em are a mite long in the tooth but not bad-lookin'. That young one, though I swear, I'd give a whole poke full o' gold dust for just one hour with her!"

A low growl came from Chart Kelly's throat. His hands

clenched into fists, and he leaned forward like a wild animal barely restrained at the end of a chain.

At the same time, Beatrice said in a voice that fairly shook with anger, "Mr. Creel, Mr. Morton, can you *please* do something?"

"Yes, ma'am," Bo said. He moved his hand to the butt of his Colt and called, "You men get out of here now."

They ignored the command and crowded forward onto the dock, led by Rusty-beard. He held out a filthy hand and said, "Hey there, little blondie, you come here to me. I'll pay you whatever you want. I can give you somethin' you ain't never had. You'll be beggin' me for more."

Caroline made a small choked sound of humiliation.

"Come on. Don't pay no attention to them two ol' whoremongers. I got a shack not far from here. We can go there and you can hike them fancy skirts and give me a look at—"

That was all Chart Kelly could stand. More than he could stand. With a bellow of rage, he charged the man, who had ambled forward and cut the distance between them to about twenty-five feet.

"Kelly, look out!" Bo shouted as he drew his Colt. Beside him, Scratch pulled the Remingtons. But neither man could fire with Kelly in the line of fire.

Then, a second later, before Kelly could reach the rusty-bearded prospector, the man yanked a broad-bladed knife from a sheath at his belt and slashed at the young sailor with a vicious stroke that threatened to spill his guts all over the dock.

Chapter 16

Caroline screamed as the blade flashed in the sun. Chart Kelly twisted aside at the last second so the knife's keen edge missed his belly by an inch, maybe two—but no more than that.

The missed stroke threw Rusty-beard off balance as Kelly's momentum carried him on into the man. His left shoulder rammed Rusty-beard's chest. The prospector yelled in alarm as he flew backward.

He would have fallen if his friends hadn't been crowding up right behind him. A couple of them caught him and kept him on his feet. Eager for a fight, they gripped his arms and thrust him back toward Kelly.

"Whip him, Dunston!" one of the men yelled.

"Cut him up good!" shouted the other.

Rusty-beard, or Dunston as they had called him, hadn't caught his balance yet. He tried to raise the knife, but he was still stumbling when Chart Kelly's right fist crashed into his jaw. It was a solid, well-aimed blow with plenty of power behind it. Dunston's head jerked far to the side under the impact, and his knees buckled.

Seeing Dunston going down, the other five men roared in outrage and charged Kelly.

Bo and Scratch still couldn't shoot with Kelly in the middle of the fracas like that. They jammed their guns back in the holsters and leaped into the melee themselves.

As Bo ducked a wild roundhouse punch that one of the prospectors swung at him, he heard Captain Saunders shouting on board the *John Starr*. The captain must have seen the fight break out on the dock; it would have been all but impossible to miss.

Bo hooked a hard left into his opponent's belly and then hit him under the chin with a right uppercut when the man bent forward. That snapped the prospector's head back and glazed his eyes for a second.

However, another man bored in from the side while Bo was doing that and caught him in the head with a fist. Bo's hat flew off, and he had to take a step to his left. The man who had just hit him hooked a foot behind Bo's right knee and yanked that leg out from under him.

Bo landed on his back with enough force to knock the wind out of him. The man he had stunned momentarily with the uppercut had recovered quickly and now crowded in with a foot raised, ready to stomp his muddy boot in Bo's face. Bo wasn't sure his muscles would work well enough to stop that brutal attack, but he tried to fling his hands up, anyway.

Bo caught the boot just before it landed, and he grunted with effort as he heaved. The man reeled away, windmilling his arms furiously in a futile attempt to keep his balance. His legs got tangled up and he fell.

The second man kicked Bo in the side, causing Bo to jerk away and groan. The man tried again, but before he could launch the kick, a figure in a dark blue dress appeared. Beatrice hovered over Bo, shoved the derringer in her hand at the prospector's face, and cried, "Get back or I'll shoot!"

The man recoiled and lifted his hands as if they would stop a bullet. At such close range, the derringer would be deadly.

An arm reached around Beatrice from behind. A dirty hand clamped around her wrist and jerked her arm up. "I got her, Clete!" shouted the man who had grabbed her. "I won't let her shoot you!" He dragged Beatrice back along the dock.

That distraction had given Bo time to recover a little, though. He pulled his leg up and launched a kick of his own. He drove his heel into the groin of the man who'd been kicking him. The prospector screamed and collapsed.

Bo rolled over and came up on one knee in time to see Sally Bechdolt pick up one of the carpetbags that had been unloaded from the ship and swing it two-handed. The bag slammed into the back of the head of the man grappling with Beatrice.

The unexpected attack made him let go. Beatrice twisted away from him and might have pointed the derringer at him, but before she could do that, Scratch was there planting a fist in the middle of the man's face.

The silver-haired Texan had lost his hat in the fight, too, and his clothes were rumpled. But he had a big grin on his face. Scratch loved a good tussle. He stepped back with his fists poised to strike again as the man he had just hit folded up on the dock.

All the prospectors were down, Bo saw as he pushed himself to his feet. Several of the crew members from the *John Starr* stood over them. Bo remembered hearing Captain Saunders shouting and knew the sailors had pitched in to help him, Scratch, and Kelly in the battle. More than likely, the prospectors had figured out pretty quickly that they'd bitten off a lot bigger hunk of trouble than they could chew.

It was all over now. Bo turned to Beatrice and asked, "Are you all right, Mrs. O'Rourke?"

"I'm fine," she said. "A bit mussed up, perhaps, but that's all. What about you, though? That terrible man kicked you really hard!"

Bo pressed a hand to his side and winced slightly. "Hurts, but doesn't feel like anything's broken. If he'd gotten me again, though, there's a good chance he would have busted a rib or two. I have you to thank for keeping that from happening."

"Well, you were risking injury or even death to protect us, so it was the least I could do."

Caroline stepped up to Chart Kelly after first casting a glance at Beatrice as if daring her aunt to stop her. She touched the sailor's arm and said, "Thank you, Mr. Kelly, for defending my honor."

"I couldn't let that scum get away with the things he was saying," Kelly replied.

"He might have killed you with that knife."

Kelly shrugged. "A risk I was more than willing to run, Miss DeHerries. Today or any day."

"Is there any law in St. Michael?" Beatrice asked. "Those men deserve to be locked up!"

Captain Saunders had come down the gangplank to join them. He said, "There might be a Mountie or two a few hundred miles away, across the border in Canada, but that'd be the closest law, ma'am. And they've no jurisdiction here."

"I'm familiar with the Mounted Police, Captain," Beatrice said. Bo recalled her telling him that her husband had been a Mountie for a while, but Saunders probably didn't know that.

"The closest American authorities are in Seattle," Chart Kelly said. "Up here in Alaska, things are much like they are at sea. Disputes are settled by the folks involved."

Beatrice looked at the sprawled, half-conscious prospectors. Some of them stirred a little and moaned softly, but the others appeared to be out cold.

"Was this dispute settled?" she asked. "Or will these men come looking for trouble again?"

Bo picked up his hat from the dock, grateful that it hadn't fallen off into the water, and slapped it against his thigh.

"If they come looking for trouble, they'll find it," he promised.

"In spades," Scratch added as he settled his own hat on his head.

There was one wagon in St. Michael for rent, along with a team of ancient-looking mules. The vehicle itself didn't appear to be in any better shape than the team pulling it, but maybe it would hold together long enough to make the trip from the dock to the *Byron Mowery*.

A little man with wispy white hair, a round pink face, and a high-pitched voice owned the wagon and drove the team as he hauled the ladies' bags to the riverboat. Bo worried that the wheels might get bogged down in the mud, but the man handled the reins perfectly and brought the bags to the *Byron Mowery* without any trouble.

"That'll be two dollars," the little man piped when the bags had been transferred to the riverboat's forward deck.

"A mite high on the price, ain't you?" asked Scratch as Bo dug out two silver dollars and handed them over.

"Everything costs more in Alaska, friend, and that's if you can even get it to start with. That's because we're so far from everywhere else. It's simple supply and demand."

"Well, we're glad you saved us from having to lug those bags over here through the muck, one or two at a time," Bo said.

The man slapped the wagon's side and said, "If you need to hire us again, you know where to find me."

"Same place we found you this time?" asked Scratch. "In Sudbury's Saloon?"

The little man cackled. "That's where I'll be, all right, in Sudsy's place."

He climbed onto the wagon, turned it around laboriously, and drove off with a rattle and clank.

Bo and Scratch stomped as much of the mud as they could off their boots as they went across the gangplank to the riverboat. The *Byron Mowery*'s main deck was lower than that of the sailing ship, so the gangplank didn't angle up as much.

The four ladies were waiting with Captain Cruickshank, who greeted the Texans with a friendly nod.

"I heard about that ruckus with Grady Dunston and his friends," Cruickshank said. "They're a mean bunch. You're lucky nobody was badly hurt."

"We had plenty of help," Bo said. "Chart Kelly and some of the other sailors pitched in. By the time it was over, we had those prospectors outnumbered."

"Bein' Texans, we had 'em outnumbered right from the start, just me and Bo," Scratch added, grinning.

Beatrice asked, "What are men like that doing here

in St. Michael? If they came up here to look for gold, shouldn't they be in Cushman or somewhere else upriver?"

"They were in Cushman for a while," Cruickshank replied with a nod that made his billy goat beard bob. "But they didn't have no luck findin' gold, and then they got in debt to Amos Lawson."

Bo saw Beatrice's interest quicken. Amos Lawson was the name of the man she was going to Cushman to marry, he recalled.

Cruickshank went on, "They couldn't pay up, of course, so they ducked out of town in a big hurry instead. Took off on foot, headin' back down the Yukon. They hailed me from the bank as the *Mowery* steamed past, a-wavin' and a-jumpin' around like mad to get my attention." The captain shook his head. "I thought about just leavin' 'em there, but I knew they'd starve if they was lucky or get et up by bears or wolves if they wasn't. So I put in to shore and let 'em come aboard. They didn't have no money to cover their passage, of course. They couldn't pay me any more than they could pay Lawson. But I worked 'em good and hard all the way back down the river. My crew didn't have to cut a stick of wood for the firebox the rest of that trip."

"So now they're just lingering around St. Michael?" Bo asked.

"Yep. They can't afford to buy passage on a ship back to Seattle, so they scrounge odd jobs from Sudbury and other businesses in town and claim they're savin' up for the tickets. I'll be surprised if they ever see the States again, though."

Scratch said, "As long as they don't come around and bother these ladies, I don't care what happens to the varmints. They can wander off and make a fine meal for bears or wolves, like you said."

"Mr. Morton!" Martha exclaimed. "What a terrible fate to wish on someone."

"I ain't wishin' it on 'em, necessarily," Scratch said. "But if that's how it was to work out, I wouldn't lose no sleep over it, neither."

Bo changed the subject by suggesting that the ladies go ahead and rest in their cabins for a while before supper. As on the *John Starr*, they were expected to provide their own rations. Once the mail-order brides were in their cabins, Bo and Scratch could walk into the settlement and gather supplies for the trip upriver at one of the general stores.

Beatrice and the others were agreeable to that. The day had been stressful, and the chance to rest and freshen up obviously appealed to them.

Caroline looked rather sad and upset, though, and Bo wondered if that was because the knowledge she would probably never see Chart Kelly again was sinking in on her.

Bo told Scratch to go ahead and start walking over to the settlement, adding that he would catch up in a few minutes. Scratch looked puzzled by that request, but he said, "Sure, I reckon I can do that." He headed for the store, leaving Bo standing on the riverboat's deck with Cruickshank.

"Can I ask you a question, Captain?"

Cruickshank nodded and said, "I thought you looked like you had somethin' on your mind, mister. What is it?"

"Earlier you said Dunston and those other prospectors ducked out of Cushman in a hurry because they owed money to Amos Lawson and couldn't pay him. Why didn't they just stay and do something to work off their debt?"

Cruickshank's mouth tightened. "I reckon Lawson didn't give 'em that option."

"And they were so afraid of him that they rushed off like that, even though it was dangerous? What sort of man *is* Amos Lawson, anyway?"

"The sort of man I do business with, carryin' goods up the river for him to sell in his store, so it ain't my place to say," snapped Cruickshank. "What affair is it of yours?"

"I told you those ladies are on their way to Cushman to marry some men there. Mrs. O'Rourke is betrothed to Amos Lawson."

Cruickshank pursed his lips and frowned in thought for a moment before saying, "I can see why you might be concerned, so I'll say this much. Alaska's a hard land, Mr. Creel. And I reckon you know what sort of men it takes to survive in a hard land."

Bo nodded and said, "Men who are just as hard as the land."

"Well, Amos Lawson ain't just survived. He's thrived up here. And that oughta tell you somethin' about him. But that don't mean he ain't a good man, and neither does the fact that he would've been hard on Dunston and the rest of that no-account bunch if he'd caught up with 'em. I generally don't claim to know things I ain't seen with my own eyes or heard with my own ears. Good, bad, or indifferent, I can't tell you about Amos Lawson. All I can tell you for sure is that he's always handled his business with me fair and square. That's all I ever asked of him."

"Fair enough," Bo said. He left the riverboat and headed along the trail toward the settlement's business buildings. He could see Scratch up ahead, taking his time and looking back over his shoulder to see if Bo was following him yet.

When Scratch spotted his old friend, he paused and waited for Bo to catch up. Then he said, "You find out what you wanted to know from Cap'n Billy Goat?"

"Why do you think there was something I wanted to ask him?"

Scratch snorted. "After all these years, you figure I can't tell when you've got wheels spinnin' around up there in your head? You wanted to know why Dunston and his pards were so scared of Amos Lawson that they went on the run when they couldn't settle up with him."

"The thought crossed my mind," Bo admitted. "And you're right, I should've known better than to think you didn't notice the same thing about that story I did."

"So what did the cap'n say?"

"Not much, really," Bo replied with a shake of his head. "He said that Lawson is a hard man but that it takes a man like that to survive in Alaska."

"That sounds about right. You're still worried, though, ain't you, about Miss Beatrice marryin' up with him?"

"I don't want her getting into something she's going to regret." Bo blew out a frustrated breath, but he didn't know if he was more frustrated with himself or with the situation. "However, she's a grown woman, and I'm not some busybody of a maiden aunt. Our job is to keep the varmints away from those ladies, not to sort out their love lives for them."

"That's right," Scratch said. Then he added, "Varmints are a lot easier to deal with. Them, you can just shoot."

Chapter 17

After buying what they hoped were enough supplies for the trip upriver, Bo and Scratch returned to the riverboat with the bags and crates and stored them in the ladies' cabins, splitting them up between the two compartments.

The Texans would have a cabin of their own on this leg of the journey, although they would have been willing to spread their bedrolls on the deck if they needed to.

All six of them ate supper in the cabin shared by Beatrice and Caroline, then Bo and Scratch went back out on deck so the ladies could turn in if they wanted to.

At this time of year, the sun barely dipped below the horizon at night, so it never really got dark. Bo had read about that phenomenon, but he hadn't figured he would ever see it for himself. They had gotten a taste of it on the *John Starr*, but now that they were on land again, it was more obvious. The strangeness of it was both impressive and a little unsettling.

"I ain't sure I'd ever get used to it bein' light for six months, then dark for six months," Scratch commented. "That just don't seem natural."

"No, it doesn't," Bo agreed. "But one thing you can say,

being light all the time must make it more difficult for enemies to sneak up on you."

"Yeah, durin' half the year. The other half, they've got a free shot at you."

Bo chuckled, then grew serious as he went on, "I was thinking it might be a good idea to stand watch tonight."

"Because of Dunston, Clete, and that bunch? You figurin' they might try somethin' else?"

"They didn't strike me as the sort to accept defeat gracefully."

"That's for sure." Scratch nodded toward the riverboat's upper deck rising to the pilot house behind them. "I imagine Cap'n Billy Goat has crew members standin' watch at night."

"Maybe, but they're probably not as used to dealing with trouble as we are."

"Probably not," Scratch agreed. "I'll go along with the idea. Split the night in half?"

"Yeah," Bo said. "Would you rather have the first half or the second half?"

"I'll take the first half. I never did like gettin' up early." Scratch looked around at the light still spilling over the timbered landscape and shook his head. "Although how you'd ever know early from late in this loco part of the world, I ain't sure."

Bo was already awake when Scratch came into the cabin to wake him for his turn on guard duty. Over the adventurous decades, both Texans had picked up the ability to sleep whenever they had a chance and wake up when they needed to.

"Any problems?" Bo asked.

"Nope. I could hear some racket from the saloons in the settlement, but they closed down after a while and after that everything was quiet."

Bo nodded, buckled on his gunbelt, and shrugged into his long dark coat. He put on his hat and stepped out onto the deck. He closed the door behind him, knowing that Scratch would be snoring within moments.

At this hour of the "night," the sun was below the horizon, but not by much, so it was like dusk outside. The sky wasn't dark enough for any stars to be showing, but it *had* faded to a deep cobalt blue in places. The air was still, with just a hint of coolness in it. Bo heard a strange whooping cry somewhere far in the distance that puzzled him, but after a few moments he realized it was a bird.

The settlement was quiet, as Scratch had said. Bo didn't see anyone moving around. He supposed people actually *did* get accustomed to the strange pattern of light and dark to be found in these far northern latitudes. Either that or they left and went back down to the States.

Footsteps on the deck at the other end of the boat made him turn in that direction. One of the *Byron Mowery*'s crew members was ambling in his direction. Bo supposed the man was standing this watch. From what he had seen, the crew numbered only half a dozen men or so, smaller than the complement of sailors on the *John Starr*. It didn't take as many men to operate a steam-powered riverboat without all those complicated sails and rigging.

This man had a black stiff-billed cap like Captain Cruickshank's, pulled low over his forehead and eyes, and his head was down as he shuffled along. He yawned as if he was having trouble staying awake. Bo didn't know when watches changed on board the boat. The man might be near the end of his shift, trying to stay alert until he was relieved.

"Morning," Bo said quietly as the man came up to him. "At least, I suppose it is. Hard to tell with the sun like that, but it's bound to be after midnight by now."

The man grunted, said, "Yeah, it is," and started to step past to continue his circuit of the boat.

As he did, Bo glanced down and saw fresh mud on the man's boots. If he had been on board the *Byron Mowery* all night, he couldn't have gotten into fresh mud. But if he'd just recently come from the settlement . . .

Bo acted on instinct. If he was wrong, he could apologize. His left hand shot out, hooked under the bill of the man's cap, and flipped it back off his head.

The angry face of the former prospector called Clete snarled at him. Clete whipped his right arm around toward Bo's head. Bo caught a glimpse of a short wooden club in the man's hand and flung his arm up to block the vicious strike.

He only partially succeeded. The club caught him on the head with a glancing blow, but it was powerful enough to knock Bo's hat off and make him lurch backward. He grabbed for his gun and had just closed his hand around the Colt's butt when, with a sharp snap of the wrist, Clete hit him again.

This impact was enough to make explosions go off behind Bo's eyes. His knees buckled. Clete struck for the third time, and this blow made Bo pitch forward. He landed with his face pressed against the rough boards of the deck, and even though he tried to push himself back up, he couldn't do it. His brain was too stunned to force his muscles to work.

Bo lay there, not quite unconscious but barely clinging to awareness. He felt the riverboat shift slightly under him. After thinking about that for what seemed like an hour but probably was only a second or two, he realized that several men had just come aboard.

Dunston and the rest of that bunch, he thought. They had returned to avenge the beatings they had suffered, and quite possibly to try to grab the four ladies as well. It wasn't likely they would ever get away with kidnapping and assaulting respectable women—such things were seldom tolerated on the frontier, and Alaska was certainly a frontier—but if they were filled with hate and lust, they might not be thinking ahead that far.

Bo bit back the groan that tried to well up his throat. Clete probably believed he was out cold. That was the only reason the man had left him where he fell and not done anything else. If he knew Bo was conscious, he might strike again with that club—and another such blow could stove-in Bo's skull!

So even though it was difficult, since he didn't know what else was happening on the riverboat, he lay there silent and motionless, gathering his wits and letting strength seep back into his muscles and nerves.

Then the sharp reek of coal oil stung his nose.

There was only one reason he'd be smelling that now: the varmints were going to set fire to the riverboat! If such a blaze caught hold, the *Byron Mowery* probably would burn to the waterline, incinerating everybody on board.

Bo couldn't wait any longer to act. He drew a quick

breath and pushed himself up, hoping that this time his muscles would cooperate.

They did. He came up on his knees. The sun had dipped under the horizon a little more, causing the dusk-like atmosphere to thicken, but Bo could still see well enough to spot a couple of men on this side of the deck— one fairly close to him and the other near the big paddle wheel at the back of the boat.

Both of them were sloshing cans of coal oil across the deck and on the outside walls of the cabins. Bo figured there might be more men on the other side of the cabins, carrying out the same sort of sabotage.

He reached for his gun, only to have his hand slap empty leather. The Colt must have fallen out after Clete walloped him with that club. A quick glance didn't reveal the weapon lying anywhere near him, and he didn't have time to hunt for it.

Instead he surged to his feet and lunged toward the man closest to him.

The man heard the soles of Bo's boots slapping against the deck and whirled toward him. When he did, some of the coal oil in his can flew out and splattered on Bo's clothes, but that didn't slow down the Texan. He slammed into the man and drove him back against the cabin wall with a heavy thud that was undoubtedly heard by whoever was inside—probably one of the gold-seekers bound for Cushman. Sure enough, a man shouted in sleepy alarm on the other side of the wall.

The man dropped the can, letting the rest of it splash out. The reek from the stuff on the deck and on his clothes choked Bo and made him want to gag.

He fought down the impulse and concentrated on the

battle instead. He hooked a right into the man's belly with enough force that his fist sunk more than halfway to the wrist. The punch made the man lean forward and gasp, but he had plenty of fight left in him. He swung a wild left that clipped Bo on the head and made him take a step back. When he did, his foot slipped on the oily deck and he went down again.

As he was falling, Bo grabbed his opponent's shirt and pulled the man down with him. They rolled across the deck, wrestling and slugging each other.

The man who had been spreading coal oil at the other end of the boat had heard the ruckus and now ran toward them, pulling a gun from behind his belt as he did so. Bo wouldn't have risked a shot if Scratch was in the middle of a hand-to-hand battle, but this hombre might not be that careful about his friend's safety.

The second man skidded to a stop and raised his gun, but before he could fire, Scratch threw open the door of the Texans' cabin and stepped out with a Remington revolver in each hand. His silver hair was tousled from sleep, and he wore only a set of long red underwear and a pair of gray socks, but he was wide awake and alert, possessing the same ability Bo did to throw off sleep in a hurry.

Scratch needed only a split-second to take in the scene and understand the situation. His right-hand Remington came up and spouted fire. The .44 caliber slug drilled through the man's shoulder and twisted him around as he cried out in pain. The gun in his hand went off as he jerked the trigger out of reflex action. The bullet went through the wall and into the cabin beyond.

The gun's muzzle was close to the wall when the weapon went off, and unfortunately sparks flying from the barrel struck the coal oil that had been splashed around. With a *whoosh!* it caught fire.

Bo had just struggled to his feet and thrown a punch at the man he'd been battling. His fist crashed into the man's jaw and sent him reeling backward. The man stumbled against the flames, and his clothes, which had soaked up coal oil while he and Bo were rolling around on the deck, instantly burst into flame.

The man screeched and lunged away from the burning wall, but it was too late. The blazing clothes engulfed him. He rushed back and forth on the deck and screamed, evidently in too much pain to think straight and realize that the water was close by.

Bo, who was covered in coal oil himself, had to back away swiftly to avoid the same grisly fate.

The burning man finally came close to the edge of the deck, tripped, and accidentally fell into the river, extinguishing the flames.

At the same time, the man Scratch had shot was trying to get back up after having fallen. Scratch stepped closer and lashed out with one of the Remingtons. The blow landed with a solid thud, and the man went down and stayed down.

The man who had gone into the river had vanished underwater and hadn't come back up. Bo called to Scratch, "Get around to the other side of the boat! They're probably trying to set it on fire, too!"

Scratch ran toward the bow, since that was the closest way to reach the other side of the deck.

Bo hurried to the cargo stacked at the front of the deck, where he had seen a pile of blankets that could be draped over the crates to protect them. He grabbed one and leaned over the edge to soak it in the water, then whirled toward the section of wall and deck that was on fire and started slapping at it with the sodden blanket.

With coal oil smeared all over him, he didn't dare get too close, or else he would turn into a human torch, too, like the man who had fallen in the river.

The other passengers were pouring out of their cabins now, alarmed by the shooting, screaming, and smell of smoke. Bo shouted at them, "Grab blankets and get them wet! We have to put this fire out!"

They scrambled to do that, and as more men pitched in, Bo backed away from the flames.

"Watch out for the coal oil on the deck!" he warned them.

More shouts made him look toward St. Michael. The uproar had reached the settlement, and men had emerged from the buildings and were running along the trail toward the riverboat landing.

The blaze had spread quickly because of the coal oil and had come within a whisker of catching hold well enough that no one would have been able to save the *Byron Mowery*. Under the circumstances, though, Bo thought the men had a pretty good chance of getting it under control.

Shots suddenly roared around on the other side of the boat.

"Scratch," Bo breathed, then he was running around the stacks of cargo to reach the part of the riverboat where his old friend had gone.

He spotted Scratch kneeling at the corner of the cabins. The silver-haired Texan fired toward the paddle wheel at the other end of the boat. Colt flame blossomed in the shadows as someone down there returned the fire.

Bo heard a slug whine past his head, not too far from

his ear. Even though the gunman was shooting at Scratch, Bo was in the line of fire, too. He crouched behind one of the crates and wished he had his Colt.

The boat wasn't burning over here on the port side. The would-be arsonist must not have had a chance to set it on fire before Scratch interrupted him.

All it would take, though, was one lucifer flicked in the right direction to create a new catastrophe.

"Scratch," Bo called softly, "is there just one of them?"

"As far as I can tell," Scratch replied over his shoulder, just before snapping another shot toward the other end of the boat.

"Keep him pinned down."

Scratch's head jerked toward Bo for a second. "What in blazes are you gonna—"

It was too late to finish that question. Bo had already dashed back to the other side of the *Byron Mowery* so the man near the paddle wheel couldn't see what he was doing. He peeled off his coat, yanked his boots from his feet, and slipped over the side into the chilly water of the Yukon River.

Chapter 18

Bo pulled himself along the boat until he reached the bow. Then he drew in a couple of deep breaths before going under.

Because of the stern-wheeler's shallow draft, the river didn't have to be very deep for the *Byron Mowery* to navigate it. Bo felt the muddy bottom brushing against his fingers when he reached down. He stroked with his arms, swimming underwater toward the stern. The water muffled the booming gunfire above him as Scratch continued trading shots with one of the varmints who'd come to burn the riverboat.

There was enough light for Bo to see when he'd reached the stern. He was glad, because his lungs were starting to feel a little tight. He wasn't capable of holding his breath as long as he'd been able to when he was younger.

He pushed his head up carefully so as not to cause a splash that might attract the gunman's attention. His fingers hooked over the edge of the deck.

He pulled himself high enough to see the man using the rear corner of the superstructure for cover as he tossed shots in Scratch's direction. The man looked vaguely familiar. He was one of the former prospectors who had been with Grady Dunston the day before. Bo had halfway expected it to be Dunston himself.

The man wasn't paying attention to what was going on behind him. Bo raised his right leg, hooked it on the deck, and used it to lever himself up and over the edge, onto the boat. He rolled on the planks and came up already unleashing a punch.

The gunman had heard the splash when Bo came out of the water and was turning in that direction when Bo's fist smashed into his jaw. The man dropped his gun and fell back toward the wall behind him. He bounced off and collapsed on the deck, clearly stunned.

At the same time, a couple of struggling figures appeared at the superstructure's other corner. Grady Dunston was one of them. He had his left arm wrapped around Caroline DeHerries's waist while his right hand was clamped over her mouth to keep her from crying out. Her bare feet were off the deck and kicking frenziedly as she tried to get loose from Dunston's grip. She wore only a filmy nightdress.

Bo knew instantly what had happened. Dunston had used the commotion on board the riverboat as a distraction, allowing him to slip into the cabin Caroline and Beatrice shared and grab the beautiful young blonde. Bo felt a second's worry about Beatrice and hoped that Dunston hadn't hurt her.

At the moment, however, he had to concentrate on the threat to Caroline. He bent and scooped up the gun the other man had just dropped. If he was lucky, there were still some bullets in it.

"Dunston!" he called as he leveled the weapon. "Let her go!"

Dunston twisted toward Bo, bringing Caroline around in front of him so she served as a shield. The former prospector's rust-colored beard jutted forward as he barked, "Creel!" He took his hand away from Caroline's mouth to fumble for a gun stuck behind his belt.

She screamed, a piercing sound that attracted plenty of attention from the men rushing onto the *Byron Mowery* to help fight the fire. Several of them shouted angry curses at the sight of Caroline being handled roughly.

Dunston jerked his head in their direction, then back toward Bo. He had to be aware that in a matter of seconds, he would be swarmed—and the citizens of St. Michael wouldn't take kindly to him treating a woman like that.

"You want her?" he snarled at Bo. "Take her!"

With that, he gave Caroline a hard shove that sent her stumbling toward Bo, putting her directly in the line of fire.

At the same time, Dunston finally yanked out his pistol and cocked it as he brought it up. Bo didn't know if the man intended to shoot Caroline in the back or wanted to fire past her at him.

Either way, it wasn't good, so as he crouched, he shouted, "Caroline, get down!"

She used her momentum to her advantage then, diving forward onto the deck just as Dunston's gun belched flame and noise. The bullet sizzled through the air next to Bo's ear. The gun he had picked up from the deck still had at least one round in it, because it roared and bucked against his palm when he squeezed the trigger.

Dunston grunted in pain and twisted halfway around as the slug smashed into his torso. He dropped his gun and stumbled to the side as he wrapped both arms around himself. He pitched face-first into the river and disappeared under the surface.

Bo kept the gun pointed at the spot where Dunston had gone underwater as he knelt beside Caroline. He was glad he had a reason to focus his attention somewhere else other than all the creamy female flesh partially visible through the nightdress. He wasn't sure why he kept winding up in awkward situations such as this.

"Are you all right, Miss Caroline?" he asked.

She lifted her head. Her hair was tangled and tousled from sleep, not to mention the tussle with Dunston. She said breathlessly, "I . . . I think so. He didn't really hurt me."

"What about your aunt?"

"Oh!" Caroline gasped. "He struck her and knocked her down when she tried to protect me from him! I don't know how badly she's hurt."

Bo wanted to go check on Beatrice, but he had no way of knowing how badly he had wounded Grady Dunston. He didn't want the man climbing back onto the riverboat and causing more trouble.

"You run back to your cabin and see about her," he told Caroline as he straightened to his feet. He took hold of her arm and helped her up. "I need to make sure the boat's safe."

"Dunston and his friends tried to set it on fire! We smelled the smoke." Caroline made a face. "And you have coal oil all over your clothes."

"Yeah, I know. They were even worse before that little dunk in the river I took."

Caroline nodded and turned to go back to the cabin she shared with her aunt. She had barely started in that direction before Scratch came up and used a boot toe to prod the man Bo had punched.

"Looks like you knocked him cold, pardner," he commented when the man groaned slightly but didn't stir otherwise.

"Yeah, I know, and my hand's probably going to be sore, too," Bo said. "What about those fellas around on the other side of the cabins?"

"Some of the crew have 'em rounded up. If they try anything else funny, they'll wind up gettin' stomped into the deck."

"Is the fire out?"

"Yeah. It did some damage, but nothin' too serious. The cap'n said it shouldn't take more than a day to put it right."

"But we'll be delayed a day on our trip to Cushman," Bo said.

Scratch shrugged. "I reckon those bridegrooms have been waitin' long enough that another day won't matter."

"Yeah, you're probably right about that."

"Was that Dunston I saw back here a minute ago?"

"Yeah," Bo said, "he was trying to get away with Miss Caroline. I stopped him."

"Permanent-like?"

"I don't know. I shot him, and he fell into the water there." Bo pointed. "As far as I could tell, he never came up."

"Good riddance," Scratch said.

Bo couldn't argue with that sentiment.

Captain Cruickshank stalked up to them, looking a little like a scarecrow in a nightshirt but with his captain's cap perched on his head. He had the stem of an unlit pipe clenched between his teeth.

"Creel, you look a mite like a wet rat." Cruickshank

sniffed and made a face. "And smell worse'n one. I hope you got some other duds. You might not ever get the stink of coal oil outta those."

"You're probably right about that," Bo said.

"But there's a Chinee woman in the settlement who runs a laundry. You might see what she can do with 'em. Meantime, are those ladies you're in charge of all right? Some of the fellas said they heard screamin' a few minutes ago."

"Dunston tried to kidnap one of them," Bo explained. "I stopped him."

"Did he get away?"

"I shot him and he went in the river. Never saw him come up."

"If he's dead he will, once he bloats up some. Might not be here, though. He might float out into deeper water. And if he ain't dead—"

"He's either dead or hurt bad," Bo said. "I hit him solid. I don't think he'll give us any more problems, either way."

"Hope you're right about that." Cruickshank looked around and added, "Here come some of the bunch from the *John Starr*."

He was right. Half a dozen sailors, led by Chart Kelly, hurried along the trail toward the riverboat landing. Spotting the Texans back near the paddle wheel, Kelly headed straight for them once he was aboard.

"We heard shots and all kinds of commotion," the young sailor said. "What happened?" He paused for a second, then added what was obviously uppermost on his mind. "Is Caroline all right?"

"Yeah, she is," Bo said, and the relief was visible on

Kelly's rugged face. "Maybe shaken up a little, but no real harm done."

As if to confirm that, Caroline called from farther up the deck, where she had just emerged from her cabin, "Mr. Kelly!"

He turned sharply toward her and began, "Ca—" but then stopped short and went on in a more formal tone. "Miss DeHerries, I'm glad to see that you're unharmed."

She had put on a quilted dressing gown, and while her hair was still a little disarrayed, Bo could tell that she had run a brush through it, anyway.

He didn't pay too much attention to Caroline, though, because he was looking past her at Beatrice O'Rourke, who followed Caroline with Martha Rousseau and Sally Bechdolt behind her. All the women wore dressing gowns over their nightclothes.

Bo was glad to see that Beatrice appeared to be all right, but then he noticed the bruise forming on her jaw, in front of her right ear. He moved to meet her and said, "Caroline told me that Dunston hit you. Are you hurt?"

Beatrice put a finger on her jaw and said, "It's going to be sore where he struck me, I can tell that already, but I believe I'll be fine, Bo. Especially since you saved Caroline from being carried off by that . . . that . . ." She took a breath. "I'm afraid I can't come up with a word to describe Mr. Dunston that's not completely unladylike."

"Well, I ain't a lady," said Scratch, who had come up to join Bo in greeting the mail-order brides, "so I don't mind sayin' that he was a rotten, low-down son of a—"

"Never mind about that," Bo said. "The important thing is that he's gone."

Beatrice turned to Cruickshank and asked, "Captain,

how much of a setback will this be? Will you still be able to take us upriver to Cushman, or will we have to wait for the other riverboat to return?"

"No, ma'am, we'll have things set a-right in no time," Cruickshank promised. "I'm hopin' we'll be able to leave the day after tomorrow."

"That would be wonderful."

"Until then," Bo said, "we'll be doing a better job of standing guard. Scratch and I are sorry we let you down."

"Plumb sorry," Scratch added.

Beatrice shook her head and said, "There's no need to apologize. Without you two gentlemen, not only would this boat have been destroyed and a number of us probably killed, but that brute Dunston would have carried off Caroline as well. I'd say we owe you our thanks instead of you owing us an apology."

"That's the truth," Sally said. Martha nodded in agreement.

"It's nice of you to say so," Bo told them, "but that doesn't stop us from feeling like we let you down."

"It won't happen again," Scratch vowed.

"I'll help see to that," Cruickshank put in. "I'll double the watch until we've put St. Michael behind us." He frowned and tugged at his beard. "Now I got another question for you: What'll we do with those varmints who got caught tryin' to set the boat on fire? I'm thinkin' that hangin's too good for 'em!"

Chapter 19

Unfortunately, since there was no real law in St. Michael, stringing up the would-be arsonists seemed to be the only option as far as punishment went. Since they had failed to do anything other than damage the riverboat, Bo and Scratch figured stretching their necks was a mite too harsh.

Bo didn't trust the prisoners enough to just let them go, however, despite believing it was unlikely they would try anything else without Grady Dunston prodding them on.

"Why not see if the folks in the settlement will agree to lock them up somewhere and keep them there until we're safely on our way upriver to Cushman?" he suggested to Cruickshank. "Maybe they ought to fork over any money they have, too, to help pay for the damage they did."

Cruickshank frowned in thought and then slowly nodded. "That ain't a bad idea," he said. "There's a good solid smokehouse in the settlement, and if those varmints are locked up in it, at least we'll know they won't be gettin' up to any more mischief." He let out a disgusted snort. "As for your other idea, Creel, more than likely they don't have two coins to rub together between 'em, but we'll give it a try, at least, and make 'em empty their pockets before we lock 'em up."

That was the way it worked out. Cruickshank's prediction turned out to be a little pessimistic; the three former prospectors who had been taken prisoner had almost five dollars once they pooled their money. They argued that that ought to be enough to buy their way out of being locked up, but Cruickshank was adamant and the settlers in St. Michael went along with him. Travel up and down the Yukon River would be very difficult without the paddle wheelers, and without that traffic the settlement wouldn't be anything more than an Indian fishing village.

Bo and Scratch were surprised to see that the *John Starr* didn't set sail the next day, while Cruickshank's crew, along with some of the men from the settlement, were repairing the *Byron Mowery*. Captain Jedediah Saunders strolled over to the riverboat landing to visit and explained that he had his crew working, too, taking care of damage done to the ship in the big storm they had come through.

"We'll be finished and sailin' in a few days," Saunders said. "I hate to lose the time, but I'd rather the ship be in top shape before we make that long trip around the Aleutians again." He sighed. "Although it's hard to put up with Kelly moping around, him knowin' that girl is so close but still on her way to marry another man."

"They'll get over each other," Bo said, although a little feeling of unease stirred inside him. It bothered him that, in a way, his job was to keep Caroline and Chart Kelly apart even though they obviously had feelings for each other.

Of course, the whole mail-order bride business was just that: a business. Romance didn't always enter into it.

In fact, the folks who found their mates that way were usually lucky if such feelings played even a small part in the arrangements they made.

"Don't worry about him comin' over here and pesterin' you," Saunders went on. "I've given him strict orders to stay on board the *John Starr*. Still and all, it probably would have been easier if you'd been able to leave this morning like you planned."

"It sure wasn't our idea to cause all that trouble and delay our departure," Bo said. "Cap'n Cruickshank assures me we'll be leaving as soon as we can."

"He's a good man, Cruickshank is," Saunders said, nodding. "For a riverman."

Bo chuckled. He knew that if Cruickshank had overheard that, there would have been an argument about the relative merits of navigating the Yukon River as opposed to the Bering Sea and the northern Pacific, and that was a quarrel that no one could really win.

Cruickshank proved to be better at predicting how long it would take to repair the damage to the riverboat. The next morning, he declared that the *Byron Mowery* was ready to depart from the landing at St. Michael. He warned Bo and Scratch that if they or the ladies had any last-minute business in the settlement, they needed to take care of it right away.

"There's nothing else we need to do, Captain," Bo assured him. "We're ready to reach our destination."

"We'd best get started, then," Cruickshank said. He shouted orders to the crew to cast off the lines, then climbed to the pilot house and pulled on the cord that sounded a long, piercing blast on the boat's whistle.

The engine already had steam up, and its rumble grew louder as the captain applied the throttle. The big paddle wheel at the stern began to revolve, slowly at first, then faster and faster, turning backward so that it pushed the boat away from the dock and the shore.

Knowing that they were about to leave, the ladies hurried out on deck in response to the engine's louder growl. They shaded their eyes from the sun with their hands and looked toward the settlement as the *Byron Mowery* backed away from the landing.

"We're really going," Martha said.

"One step closer," Sally added.

"Any regrets?" Beatrice asked them.

"None at all," Martha replied. "I think it's going to be a grand adventure."

Sally nodded in agreement.

Bo and Scratch stood beside the ladies. Bo could tell that Caroline wasn't really looking at the rough buildings of St. Michael. Her attention was centered on the tall masts of the sailing ship still docked there.

Suddenly a figure appeared at the *John Starr*'s railing. An arm waved over the man's head. Caroline exclaimed in a small voice, "Oh!"

Even though at this distance it was impossible to be sure the man waving at them was Chart Kelly, Caroline seemed convinced that it was. She lifted her arm and returned the wave.

Bo figured that was Kelly at the railing, too. So did Beatrice, who moved closer to her niece and rested a hand on Caroline's arm.

"I'm sorry," she said. "You know I'd never force you to do something that makes you unhappy."

"No, I made a promise," Caroline said without taking her eyes off the distant ship and the figure at the railing.

"I wouldn't hold you to it."

"I intend to honor it anyway, Aunt Beatrice." Caroline lowered her arm and summoned up a smile. "Besides, as Martha just said, it's going to be a grand adventure, isn't it?"

"I certainly hope so," Beatrice said.

Up in the pilot house, Captain Cruickshank shouted orders into the speaking tube that connected him with the engine room. The paddle wheel slowed to a stop as the Yukon's current made the *Byron Mowery* drift around in a turn. The wheel came to a complete stop, then gradually began revolving in the other direction, churning the water and powering the boat forward against the river's current. They moved into the broad estuary and drove ahead, following the Yukon inland. St. Michael—and the *John Starr*—fell out of sight behind them.

All of them—the Texans, the mail-order brides, and the other prospectors bound for Cushman—turned to look ahead now, facing in the direction where their destiny lay.

A man stood in some trees not far from the riverboat landing and watched as the *Byron Mowery* backed away and then turned into the estuary and vanished upriver.

When the paddle wheeler was out of sight, he walked away from the water and along a narrower, even muddier path until he came to a ramshackle log building that was part shed, part cabin. The crude structure looked as if it might collapse if a hard wind came along.

The man pulled the latch string on the door and went inside. There were no windows, but the gaps between the logs let in enough light to reveal the inside of the cabin. A man lay on a crude bunk with a filthy blanket pulled up to his waist. Above that, dirty, bloodstained rags were tied together and wrapped around his torso to serve as crude bandages.

"The boat's gone," the newcomer told the man on the bunk, who had been alone in the cabin until now. "I reckon that means maybe they'll be lettin' Clete and the other two fellas out of that smokehouse sometime soon."

Grady Dunston's breath rasped in his throat every time he inhaled. His face was pale and haggard above the jutting beard. His arms lay at his side, but his fingers dug into the thin mattress on the bunk as his lips drew back from his teeth in a snarl.

"Those two Texans . . . they were on the boat? They went with the women?" Dunston's voice was thin and strained from the pain of his wound.

"Yeah, sure. After comin' all this way, where else would they go?"

"I just wanted to make sure . . . I know where to find them . . . once this bullet hole heals up. They'll be . . . upriver in Cushman."

"You might ought to leave those Texans alone," the other man said as he pointed a grimy finger at Dunston. "Sure, I wanted to get even with 'em for what they done, and I wouldn't have minded spendin' a little time with that blonde. She wouldn't be so prissy when I got through teachin' her how to be a real woman. But hell, Grady, you nearly got yourself killed. Probably should've died, gettin' shot and goin' in the river like that. If I'm bein' honest . . . you might die yet."

"No," Dunston whispered. "Not gonna die. Not until I . . . settle the score . . . with that fella who shot me. You tell the boys . . . when they turn 'em loose . . . that I'll be ready to travel soon . . . and we'll go get . . . what's comin' to us." Rage burned in his eyes like fires, and the emotion inside him gave him the strength to prop himself up on an elbow. "No matter where we have to go . . . or how long it takes . . . I'm gonna track that Texan down . . . and kill him!"

Chapter 20

After everything that had happened so far on this journey, Bo and Scratch wouldn't have been a bit surprised if all hell broke loose more than once on the trip up the Yukon River.

Instead, the trip went about as smoothly as anyone could have hoped. The weather was good: a little drizzle now and then, but mostly sunny, with spectacularly blue skies dotted here and there by brilliant white clouds. The scenery was gorgeous, with thickly forested hills, breathtaking canyons, and towering mountains where the snow and ice came down fairly low on the slopes and glittered in the sun. In the middle of the night, when the sun was at its lowest point, those ice and snow fields turned red and it appeared that the slopes were covered with carpets of fire.

"Will we be able to see the northern lights?" Caroline asked one day when they were all on deck. "I've heard about them but never seen them."

"I have, when I was living in Canada with Daniel," Beatrice said. "They're not visible at this time of year, but later in the summer and on through the fall and winter, they'll put on quite a show, I promise you."

"I'm looking forward to it," Caroline said.

A wistful expression still came over her face now and then, which made Bo believe she was thinking about Chart Kelly and the doomed attraction between them. Most of the time, however, she was smiling and happy and seemed to be looking forward to reaching Cushman.

According to Captain Cruickshank, it would take the *Byron Mowery* ten days to reach Finbar Creek. At that point, half a day's journey on up the smaller stream would bring them to Cushman. Since Cruickshank had made the trip up there on numerous occasions, Bo and Scratch sat down with him when they got the chance and asked him about the settlement.

"When the place started, it was just a few tents scattered in the mouth of a gulch where an even smaller stream with no name runs into Finbar Creek," the captain said. He had the *Byron Mowery*'s wheel at the moment, watching through the pilot house's front window as the paddle wheel drove the boat steadily upriver. "A handful of stubborn prospectors tramped up and down that gulch, lookin' for color and hardly ever findin' any. But they came across just enough to keep hope alive. They were too mule-headed to give up."

"That seems to be true of prospectors the world over," Bo commented as they stood in the pilot house, high above the water, with Cruickshank. "They always believe they're right on the verge of striking it rich."

"Sure. If they didn't think that, they wouldn't be able to stand the conditions they live in most of the time," Scratch put in. "We've done some prospectin', too. Remember Cutthroat Canyon down yonder in Mexico, Bo?"

"It would be hard to forget it, what with all the trouble we had there."

Cruickshank went on, "Most of the time, those poor deluded fools wind up freezin' or starvin' to death, but enough of 'em find their fortune to keep more comin' in all the time, like those boys sittin' on the cargo down there, headed for Cushman. Ever' one of 'em is convinced that by this time next year, he'll be rich." The captain shook his head. "Anyway, who am I to be sayin' they ain't right? Quite a few fellas have done mighty well for theirselves, up there on that creek. Fella name of Lew Cushman made the first real strike and named the camp after himself, and it stuck. After that, more and more gold-hunters flocked in around his claim and found plenty of color, too. And once word got around about that, the men who follow the strikes moved in."

"The businessmen, you mean?" Bo said. "The ones who built Cushman up into a boomtown?"

"That's right. There are half a dozen stores there now . . . and two dozen saloons and whorehouses. That's about all a minin' camp really needs. Places for prospectors to outfit theirselves and pick up supplies, and places to spend whatever gold they come back with. Cushman's got both those things handled. Or maybe I should say . . . Amos Lawson's got that handled."

"Lawson again," Bo said.

"He's the big skookum he-wolf in those parts, sure enough," Cruickshank said with a nod. "Owns half the businesses in the settlement and has his eye on the rest."

"Sounds like a pretty hard-nosed character," Scratch commented.

"You didn't hear me say that, and I sure don't want it gettin' back to Lawson that I said so."

"You're afraid of him?" Bo asked sharply. Maybe he was being too much of a meddler, but Amos Lawson was the man Beatrice intended to marry, and Bo didn't want her getting hitched to a man who was trouble.

"Like I said before, Lawson and me do business, and I don't intend to go around tellin' tales about folks like that. You'll see what he's like when you get there."

Bo and Scratch exchanged a quick glance. The captain's words and attitude certainly didn't make them confident that Lawson was going to prove a suitable husband for Beatrice.

"Anyway," Cruickshank continued, "Cushman's a good-sized settlement now, three or four times bigger than St. Michael. There are still some tents, but with so many trees around, there are plenty of logs for buildin'. I wouldn't be a bit surprised if sooner or later I'm bringin' bricks up there for even more substantial structures. It'll be a real town." The captain shrugged his skinny shoulders. "Or else all the gold'll peter out, everybody'll leave, and in ten years it'll all be gone and nobody'll be able to tell anything was ever there."

That sounded like a pretty gloomy prediction to Bo, but he knew Cruickshank was right. He and Scratch had seen enough ghost towns in their wanderings to be aware of just how fleeting so-called civilization could be.

"You told us there have been plenty of killings and claim jumpin's up there," Scratch said. "I'm guessin' there's no law in Cushman, just like there's not any in St. Michael."

"There's *one* law," Cruickshank said. "You boys are packin' it on your hips."

"And that's what we're taking those four ladies into," Bo said with a bleak edge in his voice.

"They're full-growed, as far as I can tell, and got a right to make up their own minds."

"Problem is," Scratch said, "I ain't sure they really understand just what they're gettin' into."

"I know quite well what sort of place Cushman is," Beatrice O'Rourke said tartly. "You don't think I would have agreed to come up here—and more importantly, persuaded my niece and my friends to come along—without investigating the situation thoroughly, do you?"

After their conversation with Captain Cruickshank, Bo and Scratch had talked it over between themselves and agreed that they couldn't, in all good conscience, continue this trip without at least discussing their concerns with Beatrice and the other ladies.

Since Beatrice was the unofficial leader of the group, they had approached her first and were talking to her now while the three of them were on deck. The other ladies were resting in their cabins.

"You know the sort of man that Amos Lawson is?" Bo asked.

"I know he's a successful businessman and one of the leading citizens in the settlement. I also know that in order to be successful in difficult environments, a man has to be very practical and pragmatic."

Scratch said, "Ruthless is what you mean."

"Call it what you will," Beatrice said. "I've exchanged numerous letters with Mr. Lawson, and he's never made any secret of his dealings, or sugar-coated them, either. I believe such an individual will be a good match for me, since I take a fairly pragmatic view of life myself. Remember, I was raised around the steel industry, and that's a rather uncompromising business." She smiled faintly. "Ruthless, if you will, Mr. Morton."

"All right," Bo said, "but what about the other ladies? How much do you know about the men they're supposed to marry? How much do *they* know?"

"Well, I haven't pried and asked them about what was written in the letters they exchanged, if that's what you mean."

"How about their names?" Scratch asked. "Do you know those?"

"Of course," Beatrice replied rather indignantly. "Caroline is marrying a young man named Eli Byrne. Martha is betrothed to Franklin Nebel, and Sally's intended is Walter Heuman." She paused. "All of them work for Mr. Lawson. Mr. Nebel is his bookkeeper, and Mr. Heuman runs one of his saloons."

"What about Eli Byrne?" Bo asked when Beatrice didn't elaborate about him.

"I'm not sure. I believe he's some sort of general assistant to Mr. Lawson."

Scratch said, "Don't it strike you as a mite funny that all of those gents work for Lawson?"

"Not at all. As I mentioned, Mr. Lawson is the most successful businessman in Cushman. It stands to reason that he would employ the most men. So the law of averages says there's a good chance any men seeking wives would work for him."

"I suppose that makes sense," Bo said with a nod, not sounding completely convinced.

Beatrice looked keenly at the Texans and said, "I believe you gentlemen are charged with escorting us to our destination and seeing to it that we arrive safely. Once we're in Cushman, though, your responsibility is at an end. There was nothing in our arrangement with Mr. Keegan stipulating that the two of you had to approve of our fiancés before we could marry them."

"No, ma'am, you're absolutely right. All Scratch and I are supposed to do is get you there. Once we've done that, our job is finished."

"I reckon we'll be headed back downriver with Cap'n Cruickshank as soon as he leaves," Scratch added.

"Please," Beatrice said quickly, "don't take offense at what I just said. If I made it sound as if we don't appreciate what you've done for us, that's certainly not true. We appreciate you a great deal. All of us feel that way." She smiled. "We never would have made it this far without you."

As if giving in to an impulse, she put a hand on Bo's arm, leaned in, and came up on her toes to brush a kiss across his cheek. She turned and did the same to Scratch. Both Texans looked vaguely embarrassed.

"I feel like you're two of my favorite uncles," Beatrice went on. "But even so, this is something we have to do, and I won't let you talk us out of it."

"We won't try," Bo said. "That's not our place, I reckon. You've made that clear."

He hoped he could keep that promise.

Beatrice patted them both on the shoulder and then strolled toward the bow. Scratch's eyes narrowed as he watched her go.

"That there is one determined little lady," he said.

"She sure is," Bo agreed. "Stubborn, even. And I hope that stubbornness doesn't get her into more trouble than she's expecting once we reach Cushman."

Chapter 21

Nothing happened to slow down the journey up the Yukon. Late in the afternoon of the tenth day after the *Byron Mowery* left St. Michael, the riverboat came to the mouth of Finbar Creek, which flowed into the larger stream from the north. Captain Cruickshank steered the boat into the creek. The river was a hundred feet wide here, the creek about half that. Cruickshank turned the boat toward the western shore and slowed the engine and the paddle wheel to a stop as crewmen waded ashore with ropes to tie the boat to trees along the bank. They had been tying up every night since Cruickshank considered the Yukon too treacherous to keep traveling after dark, so this was nothing new.

"We'll get an early start in the mornin' and be at Cushman by midday," the captain told Bo, Scratch, and the other passengers as they gathered on the deck.

"How long will you stay there before heading back downriver?" Bo asked.

"Depends on how many passengers want to head in that direction and how much cargo I got to haul. We won't leave before mornin' after next, at the earliest. That'll give us time to fill up the woodbox." Cruickshank squinted at Bo and Scratch. "Will you gents be headin' right back down to St. Michael?"

"That's the plan, I suppose," Bo said as he glanced at Beatrice. Her face was impassive, giving nothing away.

Scratch said, "You won't be back up here for close to three weeks, ain't that right?"

"Around that," Cruickshank said. "The timing ain't exact on these things."

Bo said, "So if we don't take the boat, we're stuck there in Cushman until you get back?"

"Maybe, maybe not. We didn't meet the *Yukon Queen* on the way upriver, so Cap'n Ridgway must've gone on farther east toward Canada. Could be she'll be comin' back down sometime while I'm gone, so you might be able to catch a ride with her. But there ain't no guarantees of that."

Beatrice said, "There won't be any reason for you and Scratch to stay, Bo. You can go back with Captain Cruickshank. We'll be fine."

"But we'll miss you," Caroline added.

"We certainly will," Sally said, and Martha nodded in agreement.

That evening, after the ladies had retired for the night, Bo and Scratch stood on the deck and watched the sun creep lower and lower, retreating slowly below the horizon.

"Voyageurs of the midnight sun," Bo mused. "That's what I heard somebody call the fur trappers who were the first white men to venture up here into this part of the world."

"Frenchmen, weren't they?" Scratch asked.

"That's right. Part of Canada belonged to France then."

"Rooshans on one side, Frenchies on the other. I ain't sure why that fella Seward was so anxious to buy Alaska."

Bo chuckled and said, "That's why some folks called it Seward's Folly, I reckon. But just look around you. Any country this pretty has to be worthwhile."

"We've seen country just as pretty down in the States. Plenty of gold to be found there, too."

Bo couldn't argue with that. He was still impressed with Alaska, anyway.

After a moment, Scratch went on, "Are we really gonna turn right around and leave once we deliver those gals to the fellas waitin' for 'em?"

"That's the job," Bo said heavily.

"And you know as well as I do that after comin' this far with 'em, you feel just as much responsibility as I do. We didn't run off from Silverhill, down there in New Mexico Territory, just because we got the gals there safe and sound. There was a whole lot more to it than that."

"No, we didn't," Bo agreed. "That doesn't mean it'll be the same in Cushman."

"Maybe not, but I reckon we ought to take a good long look at the situation before we get back on this boat and head downriver."

Bo had to agree with *that*, too. That was exactly what they would do.

Whether Beatrice O'Rourke liked it or not.

Finbar Creek twisted and turned among the foothills of the mountains, snaking its way north so that it was difficult to estimate how many miles they had actually come from the Yukon River. Captain Cruickshank was right about how long it would take them to reach Cushman. It was midday when the riverboat rounded a bend in the creek and the settlement appeared on the right-hand bank.

Bo, Scratch, and the four mail-order brides were standing at the bow along with the would-be prospectors. The gold-seekers let out a ragged cheer at the sight of the buildings. As Cruickshank had said, most of them were made of logs, although Bo saw maybe a dozen tents still scattered among them. A number of tents sat back a short distance from Cushman's single street, too, no doubt serving as residences.

That street was wide and muddy. Unlike the cattle towns where the Texans had been, no wagons were parked in front of the buildings, and there were very few saddle horses, all of them tied to posts supporting awnings in front of building entrances since there were no hitchracks. Most of the folks in Cushman had come in by boat, either the *Byron Mowery* or the *Yukon Queen*, and there wasn't really anywhere to go that couldn't be reached on foot.

Because of that, some prospectors used crudely made handcarts to haul supplies, and Bo saw several of them sitting in front of businesses.

The street stretched for about a quarter of a mile, and at the far end of it loomed a tall bluff with a lot of timber growing on top. A gulch maybe a hundred yards wide formed a slash through that bluff, and where the gulch opened, the street ended. Bo recalled Captain Cruickshank saying that a smaller creek ran through that gulch, but from here he couldn't see it. A sturdy dock extended into the creek to form the riverboat landing. Cruickshank aimed the *Byron Mowery* toward it. As the boat approached, people began to emerge from the buildings and head toward the landing. A boat's arrival, bringing goods and newcomers, would be an attention-worthy event in a frontier settlement like this, where all too often life would be grueling and monotonous.

Cruickshank blew the steam whistle, which brought out even more people. A crowd of at least a hundred had assembled on the shore near the dock by the time the captain maneuvered the riverboat expertly alongside it. Some of them cheered, too, as crewmen jumped onto the dock to tie the boat to it.

The paddle wheel came to a stop with water pouring from it. The rumble of the engine died. Cruickshank blew the whistle again to let off some of the steam.

The prospectors had already grabbed their gear. They didn't wait for the gangplank to be put in place but jumped from the deck to the landing and hurried ashore excitedly.

Bo noticed that the first ones to meet the prospectors were women wearing plain dresses open an immodest amount at the throat. Smiling and laughing, they linked arms with the newcomers and led them up the street while some of the male citizens of Cushman hooted and slapped the prospectors on the back. It was a pretty brazen display.

Other men had noticed Beatrice, Caroline, Martha, and Sally and were eyeing them with open lust. Beatrice leaned toward Bo and said quietly, "Those men take us for, ah, soiled doves, don't they?"

"I suppose they figure no woman would come to a place like this for any other reason," Bo said.

"I'm surprised Mr. Lawson and the others didn't make it clear to everyone that they were expecting us today."

One roughly dressed, unshaven man crowded forward

and called, "Hey, you gals, come on ashore. We'll get together a big welcome party for you. Won't we, boys?"

That prompted laughter and whoops of agreement from some of the other men.

"Oh, no," Caroline said. "It's going to be like what happened in St. Michael all over again."

Bo and Scratch thought so, too, but a moment later that changed. A deep voice roared, "Out of the way, you timber rats! And mind your tongue when you're speaking to respectable ladies!"

The crowd parted abruptly as men scrambled aside to form a path. A burly, impressive figure with a thatch of iron-gray hair and matching side whiskers strode forward. He wore a gray tweed suit and carried a thick gnarled walking stick, although he wasn't using it to help him walk. He seemed to be doing fine with that on his own.

Three men followed him closely. One of them was young, lean, and wiry, with light brown hair under a thumbed-back black hat. A holstered Colt rode on his right hip. Judging by his clothes, he could have been a cowboy, but he was a long way from any cattle range to ride.

The next man also wore a suit, although it didn't appear to be as expensive as the one worn by the man with the walking stick. This gent had curly dark hair and a mustache, and a pair of pince-nez spectacles perched on his nose. Despite the suit and the spectacles, he had a rough-hewn look about him, as if he could handle himself in a fight.

The fourth man had bushy eyebrows, but that appeared to be the only hair on his bullet-shaped head. He wore black trousers and a faded blue shirt with the sleeves rolled up over heavily muscled forearms.

Bo and Scratch glanced at each other. Scratch said, "That's a tough-lookin' bunch. That young one strikes me as a fella who fancies himself fast on the draw."

"Yeah, I thought the same thing," Bo said. He and Scratch had encountered scores of gun-wolves over the years, and both of them were able to recognize the breed.

"The way he was bellowin' orders, that big fella with the side whiskers is Lawson, I'm bettin'," Scratch muttered. "And the other three are his friends who are supposed to marry up with the ladies."

Bo nodded. What he was seeing didn't make him feel any better about the situation.

As the four men reached the dock, Bo turned to Beatrice and asked, "Is that Amos Lawson? The one in the lead?"

"It is," Beatrice replied. "He sent me his tintype. They all provided pictures so we'd know them when we got here. The young man is Eli Byrne, the man with the mustache is Franklin Nebel, and the, ah, bald man is Walter Heuman." She looked up at Bo. "See, they're all very respectable."

Bo wasn't sure about that. The next instant gave him even more doubts, because one of the men who had been calling out to the ladies before Lawson and the others showed up suddenly said loudly and angrily, "You got no right to keep them pretty gals all to yourselves. We're all citizens of this here settlement, and it oughta be share and share alike!"

The young man called Eli Byrne stopped short and pivoted sharply toward the complainer. As he did, the gun on his hip came out of its holster slick and fast. He pointed it at the man who had spoken and eared back the hammer.

"What'd you say, Mitchell?" he demanded, tight-lipped.

On board the *Byron Mowery*, Caroline gasped and Martha said softly, "Oh, dear."

Mitchell's eyes had gone wide with fear as he found himself staring down the barrel of Byrne's gun. He licked his lips and said, "T-take it easy, Eli. I didn't mean nothin' by it. I just thought . . . well, since there's so few women here in Cushman . . . that it'd be fair if . . . if . . ."

"Are you sure you want to keep sayin' what you're sayin'?" Byrne asked.

"N-no, I'm gonna shut up now—"

"Good idea."

Amos Lawson had paused at the foot of the dock. He looked back over his shoulder and said, "Eli! Ignore that trash and come on." He turned toward the boat again, grasped the lapels of his suit coat, and tugged them down a little. "We have to meet our brides."

He strode forward, trailed by the other three men, and everyone on shore had gone quiet as they watched the momentous meeting about to take place.

Chapter 22

By now, a couple of the *Byron Mowery*'s crewmen had put the gangplank in place. Beatrice and the other three ladies moved toward it, but Bo and Scratch got there before them.

"Let us go ashore first and meet those men," Bo said.

"We've got to make sure they're the right fellas," Scratch added.

Beatrice said, "But I told you they sent us pictures . . ." She shook her head. "All right, I'm not going to argue about it. Go ahead, if that's what you want to do."

The Texans nodded to each other and went down the gangplank side by side.

"Amos Lawson?" Bo said to the man with the side whiskers when they reached the dock.

"That's right." Impatiently, Lawson thumped the walking stick he carried against the planks. "Who are you?" Without waiting for an answer, he went on, "Step aside, you two. You're in my way."

Scratch held out a hand and said, "Hold on there. My

name's Morton. My friend's Creel. We're responsible for those ladies' safety—"

Eli Byrne stepped in front of Lawson and said, "Maybe you didn't hear my boss, you old coot. He told you to get out of his way." His hand hovered near the butt of his gun, and his voice was a little breathless with anticipation as he went on, "You better do what he said, or else . . ."

He didn't complete the threat, but everyone there knew what he meant. The crowd remained quiet as they waited to see what was going to happen.

"I reckon you don't want to do that, son." Scratch's words were calm and steady.

Byrne sneered. "Why? Do you really think you can outdraw me?"

"I don't know about that. But I'm pretty sure you can't outdraw *both* of us, and whoever you go for, the other one is gonna kill you dead as can be a split-second later."

Bo and Scratch stood there, ready to draw. Bo hoped the ladies had gotten out of the line of fire, but he couldn't take his eyes off Eli Byrne in order to check. After all the long, perilous years, the Texans knew every sign that a man was about to make his move.

Lawson clamped his free hand on Byrne's shoulder and pulled the young gunman roughly aside. "There's not going to be any shooting," he snapped. "Eli, step back—*now*."

"But Mr. Lawson, these old codgers disrespected you—"

"If it's their job to escort those ladies who have come here to honor us by accepting our proposals of marriage, then we have to let them carry out that task." Lawson looked at Bo and Scratch and continued, "We've gotten

off on the wrong foot here, gents. As I said, I'm Amos
Lawson, and these other gentlemen are my associates,
Mr. Byrne, Mr. Nebel, and Mr. Heuman. I believe the ladies
can identify us. We've never met in person, but we've
corresponded and they have tintypes of each of us."

Bo and Scratch knew that was true. They had known it
all along, Bo thought, and maybe he and Scratch had
butted in more than was actually warranted.

He didn't like the looks of these four, though, and
Lawson's obvious arrogance rubbed him the wrong way.
He knew Scratch had experienced the same reaction. They
weren't going to just stand aside and turn the ladies over
to these men without making sure they were aware that
Beatrice and the others had somebody standing up for
their best interests.

Lawson was trying to smooth things over now, though,
and the Texans could only stand in his way for so long.
Bo and Scratch exchanged a glance and nodded in agreement. They moved aside. Lawson eagerly put a foot on
the gangplank to go onto the riverboat, where the ladies
were waiting.

Instead, Beatrice said coolly, "Stop right there, Mr.
Lawson."

Frowning in surprise, Bo looked over his shoulder.
Beatrice stood near the gangplank with the other three
women behind her. She wore a serious, determined expression, and so did Caroline, Martha, and Sally. In fact,
Bo had never seen the four of them look more resolute.

"Mrs. O'Rourke?" Lawson asked. "That *is* you, isn't
it? I must say, you look even lovelier in person—"

"There's no need for compliments," Beatrice interrupted him.

"Well, now," Lawson said, putting an oily, insincere smile on his face, "if a fella can't compliment the beautiful woman he intends to marry—"

"That's just it," Beatrice broke in on him again. "I'm not going to marry you."

She must have decided she didn't like the looks of Lawson, or of this situation, thought Bo. He couldn't blame her for feeling that way. He instinctively disliked Lawson, too.

The smile disappeared abruptly from Lawson's face. "We had an arrangement."

"I'm aware of that," Beatrice replied coolly.

"Wait just a damned minute here," Eli Byrne burst out. He pointed at Caroline. "You're Miss DeHerries, ain't you? You and me are still gettin' hitched, ain't we?"

Caroline shifted her feet nervously and looked at Beatrice, clearly waiting for her aunt to respond to Byrne's question.

"My niece will not be marrying you," Beatrice said. "I have to inform you that *none* of us will be getting married."

Burly, bald-headed Walter Heuman rumbled, "That's crazy. We're supposed to be gettin' wives, blast it. You there! Sally Bechdolt! You're Sally, aren't you? You said you'd marry me!"

"I'm sorry, Mr. Heuman," Sally replied. "Like Beatrice said, there aren't going to be any weddings."

Franklin Nebel pushed his spectacles up his nose, cleared his throat, and said, "Is this true, Mrs. Rousseau?"

"I'm afraid it is, Mr. Nebel," Martha told him.

"Well, then, did you *ever* intend for us to wed?"

Martha shook her head and said, "I'm sorry, but . . . not really."

Scratch looked over at Bo and asked quietly, "What in blazes is goin' on here?"

Bo shook his head and said, "I'm just as surprised as you are, partner. It seems like nobody ever bothered to tell us the whole story."

"So nobody's getting married?" Amos Lawson's voice was louder now, and as angry and demanding as it had been before.

"That's right," Beatrice said.

"Even though we had a deal? Even though I paid that man Keegan good money to send the four of you up here?"

"Hold on," Bo said. "You paid the expenses and fees for all four ladies?"

"That's right." Lawson sneered at him. "What business is it of yours, cowboy?"

"It's not the usual arrangement—"

"These men work for me, and Keegan took the money. A deal's a deal!"

Eli Byrne said, "That's right! Those women are *ours!*" He stepped around Lawson and started up the gangplank. "And I'm gonna get mine!"

Caroline let out a little cry of alarm and shrank back.

Scratch lunged up the gangplank after Byrne. His hand shot out, closed on the collar of Byrne's shirt, and jerked the young man to the side. Byrne yelled in surprise and anger as he suddenly found empty air under his boots. He toppled from the dock and went into the waters of Finbar Creek with a big splash.

Lawson growled a curse and lifted the walking stick, which would be a formidable weapon. As Lawson took a step toward Scratch, Bo drew his gun and leveled the Colt at him.

"I wouldn't do that, Mr. Lawson," he said.

Lawson froze and glared murderously at Bo, but he slowly lowered the stick.

With an angry rumble, Walter Heuman started forward as well, with his hands clenched into mallet-like fists. Bo's gaze flicked toward the saloonkeeper. He said, "Better call him off, Lawson, or you'll need somebody else to run your saloon."

"Stay back, Walter," Lawson ordered. "You, too, Franklin. We'll get to the bottom of this."

Nebel nodded, even though he hadn't made any move to force his way onto the boat.

Eli Byrne was thrashing around in the water. Scratch drew both Remingtons, pointed one toward the dock and the other toward Byrne, and asked, "Can that young varmint swim?"

"I don't know," Lawson snapped, "and it doesn't matter anyway. Eli! Stand up, you fool. That creek's not deep enough to drown in."

Lawson's sharp words got through to Byrne. The young gunman stopped flailing his arms and kicking his feet and splashing water high in the air. He let his legs sink to the bottom and stood up.

His clothes were soaked, and his hair was plastered to his head. His hat floated a few feet away. He looked embarrassed and furious at the same time.

Byrne's gun was still in its holster. When he reached for it, Scratch waggled the barrel of the left-hand Remington and said, "Don't try it, boy. You ain't near fast enough to get that gun out before I can ventilate you. Anyway, it might not work right after that dunkin'."

Curses spilled from Byrne's mouth. Scratch pulled

back the Remington's hammer, and the metallic ratcheting was ominous enough to make Byrne shut up, at least for the moment.

"Watch your language," Scratch told him. "There are ladies present."

"I'm not sure about that," Lawson said. "I don't know what I'd call women who make promises they don't intend to keep, but I don't think 'ladies' is the right word."

Bo said, "That's enough of that kind of talk."

Lawson scowled at him. "Don't you think we deserve an explanation?" He looked at Beatrice. "How about it, Mrs. O'Rourke? Shouldn't you at least tell us *why* you lied to us?"

Beatrice's mouth was a thin line, but she nodded and said, "I suppose you're right. If you'll stay there on the dock, I'll tell you why we're really here."

Bo wouldn't mind hearing that explanation himself.

Chapter 23

Lawson made a curt motion toward Byrne, who was still standing in the creek, and told Heuman, "Get him out of there."

Heuman went over to the edge of the dock, leaned down, and extended his hand to Byrne, who grasped it. With seemingly little effort, Heuman hauled the young gun-wolf out of the water.

Byrne had grabbed his floating hat. He stood there on the dock with a disgusted look on his face and water streaming from his clothes as he wrung out the hat.

"All right," Lawson said to Beatrice. "Let's hear what you've got to say."

He had stepped back onto the dock from the bottom of the gangplank. Scratch came back down, too, and moved to the other side of the little group from Bo so that they could cover Lawson and his men from both directions.

Beatrice held out a hand toward her companions and told them quietly, "Stay here." Then she moved down the gangplank until she stood on the dock, too, facing Amos Lawson.

He was a lot bigger than her and gave off a definite air

of intimidation, but Beatrice looked cool and collected and not the least bit frightened. In fact, her chin lifted defiantly as she faced him.

"First of all," she said, "I suppose I should apologize to you, Mr. Lawson, for dealing with you under false pretenses."

"Damned right you should," Lawson snapped.

Bo wouldn't have phrased it so bluntly, but Beatrice and the other ladies had dealt with him and Scratch under false pretenses, too, not to mention Cyrus Keegan. He felt as if the so-called mail-order brides had taken advantage of all of them.

He hoped they had a good reason for what they had done.

"I'm sorry we led you to believe that we would marry you," Beatrice went on.

"You didn't 'lead us to believe' that. You out-and-out said it."

Beatrice inclined her head slightly in acknowledgment of Lawson's point. She said, "I assure you, there was no intent to harm you and your associates. It was a necessary subterfuge in order to get us up here." She shrugged. "We couldn't have afforded to travel to Cushman otherwise."

Scratch couldn't restrain himself. He said, "Why in the world would you want to come 'way off up here in the first place?"

Beatrice pointed at the spot where the gulch opened up in the bluff and said, "Because a mile or so up that gulch is the gold claim that I inherited from my late husband, Daniel."

"Gold claim!" Bo exclaimed. "You told me he never got over here but did all his prospecting in Alaska."

She turned to him, smiled sadly, and said, "I'm sorry, Bo. I lied to you. There's no other way to put it."

Lawson stared at her. "You're Dan O'Rourke's widow? You never told me—"

Beatrice didn't let him finish. She said, "I most certainly did. You knew good and well that Daniel was my husband *and* that he had established a claim up the gulch. You're just trying to save face now by claiming that you didn't."

Franklin Nebel said, "But the O'Rourke holdings are worthless. There's no gold there."

"We'll see about that," Beatrice told him.

Bo squinted at her and asked, with a feeling of foreboding going through him, "What do you mean by that?"

"We're going to work the claim."

For a moment, all Bo and Scratch could do was stare at her. Everyone else on the dock who had heard Beatrice's bold statement looked equally amazed and dumbfounded. Somewhat surprisingly, it was Walter Heuman who found his voice first.

"You mean you and the other ladies are gonna be prospectors?" The saloon man let out a bray of harsh laughter. "The four of you who look like you never done a day's real work in your whole lives?"

Coldly, Beatrice said, "I assure you, sir, that is exactly what I mean."

Bo couldn't believe it any more than Heuman could. Delicate Caroline, elegant Martha, refined Beatrice . . . Sally was the only one of the ladies who seemed sturdy enough to work a mining claim, and even that idea was far-fetched enough to be unbelievable.

"That's not a good idea, Mrs. O'Rourke," he said. "I

don't think you realize how hard it is to work a mining claim."

"Strong men break their backs at it," Scratch added. "I don't reckon you ladies would last a week."

"You don't, do you?" Beatrice said. Bo winced at the stubbornness he heard in her tone. That was just about the worst thing Scratch could have said to her. With some women, telling them they couldn't do something was like waving a red flag at a bull. They would stampede full-speed ahead with whatever it was, just to prove that they could.

"I think what Scratch means—" Bo began.

"I know precisely what Mr. Morton means," Beatrice interrupted him. "I assume you feel the same way, Bo."

Lawson said, "Everybody in this camp feels the same way, Mrs. O'Rourke. What you're proposing is insane. A bunch of women can't work a mining claim!"

"It belongs to me. My friends agreed to come up here and work it with me."

"By cheating me out of the money to pay for this crazy jaunt!" Lawson waved the walking stick in the air as he let out the angry words.

For the first time, Beatrice looked truly regretful.

"I'm sorry about that," she said. "I told you I owe you an apology for deceiving you, even though it was necessary. Once the claim begins to be profitable, I'll pay you back every cent you spent bringing us up here. I give you my word on that, Mr. Lawson."

"I don't want your blasted money."

Beatrice's chin jutted out stubbornly again. "Nevertheless, I insist on repaying you."

"You can insist on whatever you want. I can tell you're

one of those women who are used to always getting your own way. But you're in Alaska now, lady, and I think you'll find that things don't work here the way they do in the rest of the world!"

Beatrice crossed her arms and said calmly, "We'll see."

"Boss," Eli Byrne whined, "you're not gonna let these gals get away with this, are you? We had a deal. You paid for them to come up here, and they were gonna marry us. That pretty blond one, she was gonna be my wife!"

Lawson turned on him and roared, "I know that, you numbskull! You think I like it? What do you suggest we do, drag them back to the saloon by their hair?"

Bo said, "I don't reckon you'd get very far if you tried that."

Lawson sneered at him. "You don't think these men are the only ones I've got, do you, cowboy? I do what I want around here!"

A few mutters came from the crowd. Some of the men frowned in disapproval of Lawson's bold words. Lawson might be the most influential man in these parts, since he owned most of the businesses in Cushman, but that didn't mean he was all-powerful. Many of the men who had come up here to seek their fortunes were Westerners, and they wouldn't tolerate women being mistreated or even disrespected.

Bo knew that, and he suspected that Lawson did, too, because after a tense few seconds, the man made a disgusted sound deep in his throat and turned away.

"Do whatever you want, Mrs. O'Rourke," he flung over his shoulder, "but I'll lay even money you'll come to regret it."

He jerked his head for his men to follow him as he

stalked off. Eli Byrne was still whining and complaining, but Lawson ignored him. Walter Heuman glared at the Texans but turned away. Franklin Nebel just gave them a speculative look and rubbed his chin for a second before trailing the others.

The crowd parted for Lawson again. He and his men walked through the gap, which closed behind them as the bystanders remained near the landing, watching curiously.

Beatrice's back was still stiff and inflexible until Lawson was out of sight. Then Bo saw a tiny shudder go through her as she allowed herself to relax a little. She sighed and said, "That was unpleasant. But really, I never expected it to be otherwise."

"And it's not over yet," Bo said as he slid his Colt back into its holster. "Now I reckon you owe Scratch and me an explanation for why you lied to us."

Chapter 24

"Once we'd gotten to know you, that was actually the worst of it," Beatrice said a short time later. "Deceiving you, I mean. Even though it was for a good cause."

The Texans and the four mail-order brides were in Captain Cruickshank's cabin aboard the *Byron Mowery*. The captain had seen and heard the confrontation a few minutes earlier and was as flabbergasted by the revelations as Bo and Scratch were. He had offered to let them use his cabin to hash things out.

The ladies were seated at a table that had a map of Alaska Territory spread out on it. Scratch had taken a ladderback chair, reversed it, and straddled it. Bo was the only one still on his feet, so mad that he had to suppress an impulse to pace back and forth. The cabin wasn't really big enough for that.

Scratch thumbed his hat back and said, "Deceivin' is a pretty word. I'd call what you did out-and-out lyin', ma'am."

"Was anything you told me on the *John Starr* true, Mrs. O'Rourke?" Bo asked.

"Nearly all of it was," Beatrice said. "And I don't appreciate being called a liar."

"Then maybe you should try telling the truth."

Caroline said, "Aunt Beatrice didn't have any choice. She thought that if you knew why we were coming up here, you wouldn't bring us."

"Darn right we wouldn't have brought four ladies to work a gold claim in the middle of Alaska," Scratch said. "That's the most loco notion I've ever heard."

Beatrice leaned forward in her chair and looked at Bo as she said, "Listen to me, please. My husband . . . my late husband . . . actually was a member of the Mounted Police at one time. He arrested a man who had crossed over from Canada into Alaska and did some prospecting in that gulch. That was before anyone had found gold in this area. Cushman didn't even exist then. But this man told Daniel he was convinced there was gold here, and that gave Daniel the idea of coming to look for it someday.

"Then my father got him the job at the steel mill and lured us back to Pittsburgh. But Daniel never forgot about trying to find that gulch the man had told him about. When he . . . left me . . . he came up here . . . and he found it."

She shrugged and went on. "Of course, by that time, other men had discovered gold in this region, too, and it wasn't wide open anymore. Even so, he made what he believed was a good claim, and he got a letter out to tell me about it. He . . . he said that if anything happened to him, he wanted me to have it. He put in the legal paperwork he got from the clerk here in town when he filed the claim."

"Did he actually die of a fever?" asked Bo.

Beatrice shook her head. "No, he was killed in an avalanche. At least, that's what Mr. Nebel told me."

"Nebel?" Scratch repeated. "The bookkeeper fella?"

"Yes. He wrote and informed me of Daniel's death.

He offered to dispose of Daniel's belongings and send the money to me. I accepted that offer, and that's how I came to know Mr. Lawson, as well. He proposed to buy the claim from me."

Bo frowned. "Lawson did?"

"Yes. He didn't offer much money, you understand. He said the claim was basically worthless, but he wanted to see me get *something* out of it, since I was a widow and all. I'm sure he believed I would jump at the offer and send the claim document back to him."

Bo and Scratch looked at each other, both clearly thinking the same thing. Bo said, "There's a good chance Lawson had your husband killed to try to get his hands on that claim, Miss Beatrice."

"I know that," she said, her voice level. Her hand trembled slightly where it lay on the table, and Caroline reached over to clasp it. Martha rested a hand on Beatrice's other shoulder.

After a moment, Beatrice swallowed and continued, "I thought it was very unlikely I could ever prove such a thing, and as you've pointed out more than once, Bo, there's no real law up here, anyway. But my suspicions made me more determined than ever to find the gold on Daniel's claim . . . and *not* to let Amos Lawson have it. So I decided to come up here, and while I was trying to figure out how to go about that, Caroline mentioned seeing an ad for Mr. Keegan's matrimonial agency in a magazine. I wrote to Mr. Keegan immediately and engaged his services."

"And decided to get Lawson to pay for you comin' up and ruinin' his plans," Scratch said.

Beatrice smiled. "We were already corresponding, and

it was easy to play up to him and sell him on the idea of bringing me and three of my friends up here. And you have to admit, it does seem like poetic justice, doesn't it?"

"It seems like a foolish stunt that could get you all killed," Bo said. "In fact, it nearly has, already, more than once."

"But we're here," Sally said, "and we're going to help Beatrice teach that Lawson scoundrel a lesson."

"By working that claim? That's backbreaking, man-killing work. No offense, ladies, but no matter how determined you are, I don't think you can handle it."

"We're stronger than we look," Caroline said.

Scratch tried to hold back a laugh but couldn't do it. He said, "Let me see your hands, Miss Caroline."

She frowned in puzzlement but held out her hands, which were soft and smooth and pale.

"Have you ever used a shovel or swung a pickax?" Scratch asked her.

"Well . . . no. But I'm certain I can learn. I've always been good at picking up new skills."

"Knowing how to do something and being able to, especially for ten or twelve hours a day, are two different things," Bo said. "Before the first day's over, those hands will be just giant bleeding blisters. Your feet will get the rot from tramping around in an icy creek. Any skin that's uncovered will burn. You'll be too tired and hurt too bad to move a muscle."

"You won't frighten us," Beatrice said, but judging by the uneasy expressions on the faces of Caroline, Martha, and Sally, Bo had scared them already—which was exactly what he was trying to do.

Martha said, "Perhaps we can hire some men to work the claim for us."

"With what?" asked Scratch. "You couldn't afford to come up here on your own, remember?"

Beatrice said, "We can promise to pay them from the profits once we've found the gold and the claim is producing."

"Most fellas aren't going to take a deal like that," Bo said. "Anyway, you're forgetting Lawson."

"He doesn't scare me, either," Beatrice insisted.

"Maybe not, but I'll bet he scares plenty of other folks around here. He owns the saloons, so he can cut men off from having a place to drink."

"And the whorehouses," Scratch put in, "so he can tell 'em they can't—"

Bo lifted a hand to stop his old friend from continuing. He said, "It's the same thing with the stores. The men need to buy supplies. Lawson controls the supplies. All he's got to do is put the word around that he doesn't want anybody hiring on to work for you, and you'll be out of luck."

"But that's not fair!" Caroline burst out.

Bo shook his head. "On the frontier, fair doesn't have much to do with it."

"Then what do you suggest we do?" asked Beatrice, her voice a little chilly now. "Turn around and go back down the river with Captain Cruickshank? Sell Daniel's claim . . . *my* claim . . . to Lawson, who may well have had him killed? Or perhaps we should just go through with the marriages! I'll marry my husband's murderer. Why not?"

"Blast it, that's not what we're saying," Bo responded with frustration in his voice now.

"Then what *are* you telling us to do, Mr. Creel?"

They looked at each other in silence, their eyes dueling across the table, for a long moment until Caroline said tentatively, "What about . . . what about the two of you?"

"Us?" Scratch said.

"That's right. You said you'd had some experience as prospectors, and you obviously would know what you were doing. And you wouldn't have to do *all* the work. The four of us could at least help."

"Now hold on a minute," Bo said.

Sally leaned forward and said, "That's a good idea. You two are tough enough that nobody would bother you, and you're not afraid of Lawson and his men, anybody can see that."

"Maybe not," said Scratch, "but we didn't sign on to—"

"That's a ridiculous idea," Beatrice snapped. "These two men are done with us. Their job is finished. We're here in Cushman, and they can go on to whatever assignment Mr. Keegan has for them next."

"Well, that ain't exactly true," Scratch said. "Our job is to deliver you to your prospective bridegrooms, and since there *ain't* any bridegrooms, as it turns out . . . well, hell! I don't know if we finished our job or not." He looked at his old friend. "I'd say we didn't, Bo. We've got to see it through until these ladies are hitched, or unless until they're betrothed for real."

Bo shook his head. "You're letting them talk you into something."

"Nobody's trying to talk you into anything," Beatrice insisted. She came to her feet. "I told you, go on back downriver with Captain Cruickshank. We'll be all right."

"No, you won't be—"

Martha broke in, saying, "Didn't the captain say it would be about three weeks before he's back here? We could all give it a try for three weeks, couldn't we? I mean, if Bo and Scratch agreed to stay and help us? That way, we could see how hard it really is, and we might decide not to continue."

"I'm not giving up," Beatrice said.

"Just a trial period," Martha continued as if she hadn't heard. She looked around the table. "That's reasonable, isn't it?"

"I'd say so," Sally replied.

Caroline smiled and said, "That would be long enough for me to learn how to use a pickax."

Scratch groaned and shook his head. "I reckon there ain't enough time in the world for that, Miss Caroline," he said. "But it would give you a taste of what you came up here for."

"Adventure," Sally said with a smile.

"And one hell of a lot of trouble," Bo said, trying not to grumble about it but not really succeeding.

On the other hand, he had suspected that something like this might be coming even before Caroline suggested it, and he had seen the fires of excitement light up in Scratch's eyes when she did. There was nothing the silver-haired Texan liked better than a good fight—and with Amos Lawson angry because he'd been duped, and having his eye on the O'Rourke claim in the first place, he wouldn't accept defeat gracefully. Bo knew that.

Lawson would come after these women, striking hard and fast, and even as he sighed, Bo accepted that there was no way he and Scratch could abandon them to that fate.

"Three weeks, or until Cruickshank gets back," he said.

Caroline clapped her hands in delight. Martha and Sally both smiled, and after a couple of seconds, Beatrice nodded and said, "All right. I suppose three weeks won't hurt anything."

"You could be mighty wrong about that," Bo told her.

But in three weeks, he thought, *they could change their minds . . .*

Or they might all be dead.

Chapter 25

Amos Lawson slammed the walking stick down on the desk in his office, making the papers, spread out there, jump. He spewed curses.

"I agree with you, Amos," Franklin Nebel said, breaking off the flood of profanity, "but getting angry really isn't going to solve anything."

The bookkeeper had followed Lawson into the office. Walter Heuman remained out in the saloon's main room, behind the bar, and Eli Byrne was leaning on the hardwood, more than likely throwing back his second or third whiskey by now as he tried to drown his humiliation.

The office was located in the back of the Avalanche Saloon, the biggest and best of the drinking establishments Lawson owned. For an office in a settlement that had been a mining camp full of crude tents only a year earlier, it was comfortably—even luxuriously—furnished, with a thick rug on the floor, an impressively solid desk, and several well-upholstered leather chairs. Heavy curtains that would help keep out gusts of winter wind hung at the single window, although they were open at the moment to let sunlight spill through the glass. A cast-iron wood-burning stove sat in the middle of the room with a vent pipe leading up through the ceiling and roof.

Lawson sank into the red leather chair behind the desk and reached for a jug of brandy sitting beside the papers. He poured some of the liquor in a cup for himself but didn't offer any to Nebel. He drank the fiery stuff down and said, as he replaced the cup on the desk, "I should have known better. I should have known I wouldn't be lucky enough to have that claim fall right into my lap like that—along with a beautiful woman."

"The woman might be worth more than the claim," Nebel said dryly.

Lawson shook his head. "I'm convinced there's gold to be found on that claim. You know that O'Rourke had a good-sized nugget he dug out, somewhere up there."

"I know O'Rourke *said* he had a nugget like that," Nebel replied. "But none of us ever actually saw it, did we, Amos? Wouldn't it have turned up somewhere? Wouldn't he have hidden it in his cabin, or spent it here in the settlement?"

Lawson scowled. "Maybe he had it on him when that avalanche buried him."

"Maybe. And maybe there was no reason to make sure an avalanche *did* bury him."

"I'm going to forget you said that, Franklin," Lawson responded as his eyes narrowed and glittered angrily.

"Please do." Nebel waved a hand that was well mani-cured, considering the surroundings. "It was an intemper-ate thing to say, and pure speculation on my part."

"Damn right it was," Lawson growled. He sat back in the chair and went on. "What do we do now?"

Nebel pulled up one of the other chairs in front of the

desk and sat down without waiting for an invitation. Both
men knew which of them was the boss, but Nebel enjoyed
a little more leeway in his words and actions than Heuman
or Byrne did. Heuman was a brute and Byrne a callow
gunman, but Lawson relied on Nebel's keen brain for
advice.

"It's almost impossible that those ladies will be able to
work O'Rourke's claim," he said. "Since they had to trick
you in order to get up here in the first place, it's unlikely
they have any money to hire men. Not that anybody would
sign on with them anyway, if you made it plain you didn't
want that."

"Make it plain," Lawson ordered. "Make sure the word
gets around. Nobody works for those so-called ladies."

Nebel leaned back in his chair and nodded, then pursed
his lips in thought.

"The only real wild card I see in this deal is those men
who came up here with them. They sounded like Texans to
me . . . which means they may be crazy and unpredictable."

Lawson snorted. "You're talking about two men, and
they looked to me like they're past their prime. Texans or
not, I don't think we have to worry too much about them."

"But they might decide to stay on and help the women
with the claim. We don't have any guarantee they'll leave
with Cruickshank. They might prove to be an annoyance,
if nothing else."

Lawson's eyes narrowed. He said, "Maybe we need to
make sure they realize it'd be in their best interests to get
out of Cushman. You think you can make that happen,
Franklin?"

"I think so," Nebel answered without hesitation. "Of

course, sometimes men get caught up in the moment and these things spiral out of control . . ."

"And I'm not going to give a damn if that happens," Lawson snapped. "Without those two old codgers to help them, the women won't stand a chance of holding on to that claim."

"Which might still prove to be worthless," Nebel reminded him.

Lawson grabbed the walking stick and banged it down on the desk again.

"I don't care if there's not an ounce of gold in that ground," he said. "I'll be damned if I'm going to let *that woman* think she can get away with putting one over on Amos Lawson!"

There was a hotel in Cushman, but Bo and Scratch thought it would be better if the ladies spent one more night on the *Byron Mowery*, and Captain Cruickshank agreed. The next day, they would take a ride up the gulch and see the situation at Daniel O'Rourke's claim.

"That's assumin' you can find anybody willin' to rent you some horses," Cruickshank commented as they had supper with the captain that evening. "Lawson's probably put the word out already that nobody's supposed to deal with you."

"Can he get away with that?" Caroline asked.

Cruickshank shrugged. "He's got the idea that Cushman's his town to do with as he wants, and he's pretty much right."

"Not this time he won't be," Beatrice declared.

"There's another problem," Scratch said. "You need supplies and equipment to work a minin' claim, and you won't be able to get any. Bo pointed out that Lawson controls the supplies around here when he said you wouldn't be able to hire anybody to work for you. It's still true."

"There might still be some equipment at the claim," Bo said. "If it hasn't all been stolen by now."

"Do you think there's a chance of that?" Beatrice asked.

"Hard to say. Most miners will respect another man's goods, because they know that if they get caught stealing, there's a good chance they'll wind up decorating a tree branch."

Martha said, "I'm not sure what that means . . ."

"Strung up," Scratch said. "Lynched. There may not be any law in these minin' camps, but there *is* justice, sometimes."

"Oh," Martha said faintly.

Beatrice said, "We may not have to worry about supplies and equipment right away. When I knew for certain we were coming up here, I took steps to address that problem."

Bo looked at her with keen interest and asked, "What have you done now?"

Instead of answering him directly, Beatrice turned to Cruickshank and asked, "Does the name Wilbur Peacock mean anything to you, Captain?"

"Nope, I can't say that it—" Cruickshank stopped short and frowned. "Wait a minute, that name is sorta familiar. Let me think . . . It's on some of those crates of cargo the boys are gonna be unloadin' in the morning!"

"That's right, and Wilbur Peacock will be there to take delivery, because *I* am Wilbur Peacock."

"You shipped the goods to yourself," Bo said as understanding dawned.

"Hold on," Scratch said. "How'd you know you'd be arrivin' in Cushman on the same boat?"

"Now, when it comes to that, I didn't know," Beatrice admitted. "That was just a stroke of good luck. I tried to arrange the shipment so that we would reach here at approximately the same time, but there was a chance the crates would get to Cushman first and would be held until we arrived, or else we'd beat them here and have to wait for them. But they were on the *John Starr*, and then they were transferred to this boat, so things worked out perfectly."

Caroline said, "I'd take that as a good omen."

"What's in the crates?" Bo asked.

"Picks, shovels, axes, saws, hammers, nails, pans, and anything else I could think of that might be used for mining. Along with flour, sugar, coffee, beans, dried, salted meat, canned tomatoes and peaches, and other food items that won't go bad. My hope was that once we got here, we might be able to hunt for fresh meat and perhaps even grow a few vegetables. I tried to purchase and ship enough that we wouldn't starve while we were discovering if the claim is indeed worth pursuing."

"How'd you plan on doin' that huntin'?" Scratch asked with a frown.

"There are rifles and shotguns, along with ammunition, among the supplies as well."

Bo thought Beatrice looked and sounded pretty pleased with herself. He said, "I thought you were broke and couldn't afford your passage up here. That's why you had to rook Lawson into the whole mail-order bride scheme."

"You make it sound awfully sordid," she said. Then she shrugged and went on. "Buying all those things and arranging to have them shipped up here took nearly all of my available funds. I had just enough left for our living expenses on the way west."

That made sense, Bo supposed, and it was more evidence that Beatrice O'Rourke was a pretty canny woman. She had to be to come up with such an audacious plan.

Cruickshank chuckled and said, "Seems like you've thought of just about everything, ma'am. But there's still the problem of gettin' up the gulch yonder."

"We'll walk if we have to," Beatrice said. "And if we need to, we'll build one of those handcarts like I saw in the settlement to carry the supplies."

Bo knew it would wind up being him and Scratch who did most of the work hauling those supplies, if not all of it. But they had given their word that they would stay and help the women at least until the *Byron Mowery* returned to Cushman in a few weeks. They weren't going to go back on that promise.

"You see," Beatrice said, "this wasn't some lark, some wild whim. I put a lot of planning into this. And I know it's going to work out."

"I hope so," Bo said.

But he knew that all the planning in the world couldn't always account for what angry, ruthless men might do.

Later, after the ladies had turned in, Bo and Scratch stood on the riverboat's deck with Cruickshank. Coils of smoke from the captain's briar pipe wreathed his head. He puffed on the pipe for a moment, then said, "The ladies are safe here tonight. Not even Lawson would dare bother 'em out in the open like this. I can't say the same about you lads, though. Somebody might come after you."

"The same thought occurred to us," Bo said.

"That young fella Byrne's bound to be carryin' a pretty good grudge against me," Scratch added. "I threw him in the creek, after all."

"Yeah, and Eli Byrne ain't the sort who'll forget that," Cruickshank agreed. "He's a man-killer, too."

Bo said, "He's actually good with that gun? It's not just bravado?"

"He's good. He's killed four men that I know of, in fair fights. And I wouldn't be surprised if there were others."

"But not in fair fights," Scratch said. "So he's a bush-whacker."

"Men that Amos Lawson has trouble with have a habit of turnin' up dead, or sometimes they just disappear. Lawson ain't the kind to handle such things himself, but he'd sure pay to have it done, I'm thinkin'."

"I thought you didn't want to get on his bad side," Bo said.

"I don't. I sure as *blazes* don't." Cruickshank puffed on the pipe again, then said, "But I like you fellas. You seem like good sorts. I'm just sayin' for you to keep your eyes open."

"We're in the habit of that," Scratch said.

Cruickshank pointed with the stem of his pipe and said, "If it ever comes down to it, don't underestimate Lawson himself, either. One night I saw a fella go after him in the Avalanche. That's the saloon Lawson uses as his headquarters. He took that stick he always has with him and beat that poor fella plumb to death. When Lawson got through with him . . . well, his head didn't look like nothin' human, I can say that."

"We'll be careful," Bo promised.

"I'm glad to hear it. Good night."

Cruickshank ambled back to his cabin. The Texans lingered on the deck. It was late enough now that the sun was below the horizon, and the thick twilight that was the closest thing to night at this time of year had settled over the rugged landscape and the boomtown alongside the creek. Faint strains of music could be heard coming from the saloons.

"We've gotten ourselves into some loco dustups over the years," Scratch said, "but this may be one of the locoest."

"And one thing's for sure," Bo said, smiling, "we came farther than we ever have before to do it, too."

"Yeah." Scratch waved a hand toward the stacks of cargo still waiting to be unloaded. "Reckon we'd better go check and make sure ol' Wilbur Peacock's goods are still there?"

"They didn't get up and walk off by themselves, but it wouldn't hurt to look."

As they walked along the shadowy deck, Scratch said, "Wonder where Miss Beatrice came up with a name like that, anyway?"

"She just made it up, according to what she told me when we were talking about it after supper. She thought it sounded like the sort of man who would go to Alaska to look for gold."

"Bo . . . if there really is gold on that claim, and

Miss Beatrice cuts us in for a share . . . we could wind up bein' rich men. You ever thought about what we'd do if we wound up rich?"

Bo shook his head. "Honestly, I can't say as I ever have. We've always been able to come up with enough money to get us on down the trail and over the next hill, so to tell you the truth, I figured we were rich all along."

"Yeah," Scratch mused, "that ain't a bad way to look at it—"

Bo couldn't have said what warned him—a flicker of movement in the gloom, a rustle in the brush that grew up close to the creek just south of the landing, maybe a faint sound that could have been a gun hammer being drawn back—but at that moment he grabbed Scratch's arm and dived to the deck, pulling his friend down with him.

And as soon as Bo moved, guns roared and tongues of flame lashed out from the bushes as hidden killers went to work.

Chapter 26

Bo and Scratch hit the deck planks hard as slugs whipped through the air above them and slammed into the boat's superstructure. Most of the cabins were empty now, the prospectors who had taken the *Byron Mowery* up here to Cushman having gone into town, so Bo hoped the bullets wouldn't hit anyone after punching through the walls.

Beatrice and the other ladies were farther toward the stern, so there was a good chance they were safe.

"I'll cover you," he told Scratch. "Head for those crates of cargo and fort up there."

"Got it," the silver-haired Texan replied.

Bo drew his Colt, rolled over, and fired toward the brush where the gunmen were hidden. The gun roared and bucked in his hand as he emptied it in a long, rolling peal of gun thunder. The muzzle flashes flickered like an explosive burst of lightning.

While he was doing that, Scratch surged up, took a couple of fast steps, and launched himself in a dive that carried him among the crates and burlap sacks stacked on the forward deck. He scrambled to a good position and pushed himself up on one knee as he unleathered both Remingtons and thrust them toward the bushwhackers.

Bo probably hadn't hit any of the hidden gunmen, but his swift volley had forced them to duck and stop shooting for a moment. They recovered quickly, however, and opened up on him again as his Colt fell silent. Bullets chewed splinters from the planks around him and whined dangerously close to his ears. The splinters stung his cheeks.

Then Scratch joined in the ball as footlong flames spurted from the muzzles of his Remingtons. He set the bushes on the shore to shaking with the storm of lead that lashed through them.

Bo took advantage of that onslaught to leap to his feet and dash among the crates. He threw himself down a few feet from where Scratch was crouched. When the hammers of Scratch's guns clicked on empty chambers, he ducked below the top of the stack and started reloading.

Bo was already thumbing fresh cartridges into his Colt's cylinder. "Reckon we've hit any of them?" he called to Scratch as he snapped the loading gate closed.

"Don't see how all those shots could've missed," Scratch replied.

"I don't know. They've thrown a heap of lead at us, but none of it tagged me yet. How about you?"

"Fine as frog hair," Scratch said. "A mite too old for all this runnin' and jumpin' and landin' hard, though."

"Yeah, we'll be sore in the morning. It'll hurt to climb out of our bunks." Bo chuckled grimly. "But then, how will that be different from any other morning?"

"As long as we wake up, I reckon we're ahead of the game. You ready?"

"Let's give 'em hell," Bo said.

"Texas style!" Scratch called as he raised up and opened fire again.

Bo did likewise. He emptied the Colt, and this time it had held a full wheel instead of the usual five rounds. The shots smashed out rapidly.

Since Scratch had twelve rounds total in his Remingtons, it took him a heartbeat longer to finish triggering his barrage of lead. As the Texans' guns quieted, no return fire erupted this time. Instead a choking moan filled the sudden silence, then more crackling in the brush followed by running footsteps slapping the ground.

"There they go!" Scratch exclaimed as he used one of the empty revolvers to point. "The rascals are headed for the tall and uncut!"

Bo saw the shadowy shapes darting through the gloom, too. He reloaded as quickly as he could, but by the time he had the Colt ready again, the fleeing bushwhackers had vanished.

A rifle suddenly cracked sharply from somewhere else on the boat. Whoever had the rifle fired twice in the direction of the would-be killers, then hurried along the side of the boat toward the forward deck.

"Creel!" the familiar voice of Captain Hal Cruickshank called. "Morton! You boys up there?"

"We're here, Cap'n," Scratch replied. "Was that you with that Winchester just now?"

"Yeah," Cruickshank replied. "I heard the shootin', saw what was goin' on, and figured I'd better take a hand.

I'm damn sick and tired of people shootin' holes in my boat and tryin' to burn it!"

"At least they didn't set any fires this time," Bo said. "Better stay back, Captain. I think they all lit a shuck, but I'm not sure about that."

"We'd best go check," Scratch suggested as he finished reloading again. "I know we hit at least one of the varmints. I heard him carryin' on."

"Yeah." Bo stood up. "Keep your rifle pointed at that brush, Captain, and if it moves around, cut loose your wolf. We'll see what we can find."

He wanted to make sure Beatrice and the other ladies were all right, but first they needed to be certain the threat was over. He and Scratch trained their guns on the brush as they went down the gangplank and then along the shore.

Nothing happened. They reached the little thicket, pushed into it, and found it deserted. Scratch spotted something dark on the ground, though, and holstered his left-hand gun so he could use that hand to flick a lucifer to life with his thumbnail.

The flare of light revealed a bright splash of blood. "We hit one of 'em, all right," he said. "Pretty solid, too, from the looks of that gore."

"But either he was still able to run or the others carried him," Bo said. "I guess they didn't want to leave anybody behind."

"Because if they had, that would've pointed right back to Lawson. I'd bet a hat on that."

They went back to the gangplank and crossed it to the deck. Captain Cruickshank was waiting for them.

"I'm gonna go see to my men," he said. "Make sure all of 'em are all right."

"That's a good idea, Captain. We'll check on the ladies."

Beatrice stepped forward from the shadows along the superstructure and said, "There's no need for that, Bo. We're all fine. None of the bullets penetrated our cabins."

Bo nodded in relief. "That's probably because Lawson warned his men that you weren't to be hurt. They were just after Scratch and me."

"There's no proof Lawson was behind it," Cruickshank pointed out. "You never got a good look at the varmints, did you?"

Scratch scoffed. "Who else in these parts would want us dead?"

"Oh, I ain't sayin' you're wrong, just that you can't prove it." With that, Cruickshank went to check on his crew, leaving Bo and Scratch standing there with Beatrice.

"You've traded letters with Lawson," Scratch said to her. "You know him better than any of us. Do you reckon he's the one to blame for this?"

"I don't doubt it for one second," she said.

Bo pouched his iron and nodded toward the settlement.

"Now that the shooting's over, folks are coming to see what happened."

A good-sized crowd was headed down the street toward the riverboat landing. A couple of men carried lanterns. When they reached the foot of the dock, Bo saw that one of the men with a lantern was Franklin Nebel.

"What happened here?" the bookkeeper called. "We heard a great deal of shooting."

"Sounded like a war, in fact," commented another man.

"Close to it," Scratch said. "Somebody bushwhacked us, tried to kill Bo and me."

"Good Lord," Nebel said. "That's terrible. Were you harmed?"

"Nope," Bo replied. "Can't say the same for the bunch that ambushed us, though. At least one of them got drilled pretty good, judging by the blood he left behind."

"Well, perhaps that will help us determine who's responsible," Nebel said. "I'll ask around about a wounded man."

"You do that," Scratch said dryly. "See what you can find out."

"Of course." Nebel lifted the lantern a little higher. "The, ah, ladies weren't harmed, were they?"

"Not a bit," Bo said.

"We can be thankful for that. Is there anything I can do to help you, gentlemen?"

"No, we can take care of ourselves . . . *and* the ladies," Scratch told him.

"Very well. I hope you don't have any more trouble tonight."

Nebel shepherded the rest of the curious crowd away, back toward the settlement. As the group drifted off into the twilight, Scratch asked quietly, "That hombre sounded like he wanted to be helpful, but do you trust him, Bo?"

"Not as far as I could throw him," Bo replied.

Chapter 27

Amos Lawson was pacing back and forth in his office when Franklin Nebel came in. Lawson swung around sharply and demanded, "Well? Are Creel and Morton going to trouble us anymore?"

Nebel sighed. "They're both still alive and well, if that's what you mean."

"Blast it, Franklin! You were supposed to have Eli and some of the other men scare them off."

"Scare them off" meant kill them, of course, and both men knew it. Nebel didn't mind keeping up the facade, though. He said, "Evidently, they don't scare easily."

Lawson snorted disgustedly. "With that much shooting going on, the blasted riverboat ought to be full of holes and sunk! How did Creel and Morton survive?"

"According to Eli, they're a lot faster than you'd expect men that age to be. Somehow, Creel realized they were about to be ambushed and got himself and Morton out of the way of the first volley. Then they fought back, and did an exceptional job of it." Nebel cleared his throat and added, "Good enough, in fact, that Ben McDowell is dead."

Lawson stared at him for a long moment, then repeated, "Dead?"

"Don't worry, Amos, they didn't leave him there, and he didn't actually die until they were back at the warehouse. There's no proof you had anything to do with what happened."

Lawson looked relieved, then said, "Still, McDowell was a good man. I don't like losing him. That's one more mark against those blasted Texans."

"We'll get a chance to settle the score. Walter just told me that a couple of members of Cruickshank's crew were in here earlier, and he overheard them talking about how Creel and Morton are going to help the ladies work O'Rourke's claim, just as we thought they might."

"It'll be harder to get at them when they're off up the gulch somewhere," Lawson said, scowling.

"Maybe, maybe not. There are a lot fewer witnesses around once you're out of the settlement."

Lawson's eyes narrowed in thought. "Are you saying we ought to let them go up to the claim with those women without trying to stop them?"

"It might simplify matters considerably."

Lawson rubbed his chin and said, "They'll need horses, a wagon. I was going to make sure they weren't able to get those things."

"Why not back off a little instead? Get them where we want them, and then we can deal with them efficiently."

After thinking about it for a few more seconds, Lawson nodded abruptly. "All right, that's what we'll do. Eli's not going to like it, though."

"He certainly won't. He wanted to get some dynamite and blow that riverboat out of the water tonight."

"Tell him to get himself under control," Lawson snapped. "We'll act when I say it's time to act, and not before. If he can't take orders, I won't have him working for me, no matter how good he is with that gun."

"He'll do as he's told," Nebel said with a sharp, icy edge to his voice. "I'll make sure of that."

The next morning, Bo and Scratch walked from the landing up the street toward a barn that Captain Cruickshank told them was Cushman's only livery stable. The captain stood on the dock with his Winchester carbine tucked under his arm, the same weapon he had used to shoot at the bushwhackers the previous night. He was supervising the crewmen as they unloaded the cargo from the riverboat, and he'd promised not to let anybody bother "Wilbur Peacock's" goods.

As the Texans approached the livery barn, they heard a lot of loud barking going on. Scratch said, "That don't sound like any stable I've ever been around."

"Some places keep a dog or two because the horses get to be friends with them."

"All that barkin' sounds more like twenty or thirty."

Bo had to admit there was a lot of barking and yapping going on, and it got even louder when they entered the barn. They looked all the way through the building along a center aisle to a large pen behind it. A high wooden fence, with the poles closer together than a typical corral, surrounded the pen. A swinging gate stood between it and the inside of the barn. The barking became a real ruckus as several dozen large dogs swarmed on the other side of the gate and raucously greeted Bo and Scratch.

The right side of the barn had regular horse stalls, half a dozen of them. Four of the stalls held big, heavy draft horses, while the other two were occupied by smaller animals that looked like saddle mounts.

Several of the handcarts Bo and Scratch had seen on Cushman's single street sat to the left, along with a buckboard and half a dozen sleds. When Bo saw the sleds, he nodded in understanding. During the winters up here, folks got around using sleds drawn by dog teams, more than anything else. This was a livery stable, all right, but one set up to meet the needs of Alaska's hardy pioneers.

A man was repairing some of the lashings on one of those sleds when Bo and Scratch came in. He straightened from where he was kneeling and came toward them, saying, "Howdy, gents. What can I do for you?"

He was short, a little on the scrawny side, and had thinning, grayish-brown hair. His face was tanned and weathered until it looked like old saddle leather. His right eye was a brilliant blue, but where the left one should have been was only an empty, puckered socket. He wore a flannel shirt, canvas trousers with suspenders, and lace-up work boots.

"This is your place?" Bo asked him.

"It sure is. Name's Ed Lerch." He stuck out a strong, work-gnarled hand.

The Texans shook hands and introduced themselves, then Bo nodded toward the gate leading into the dog pen and said, "Looks like you've got yourself some fine animals back there."

Lerch grinned and gestured for them to follow him. "Come on and take a look at 'em. Nothin' they like better than havin' company."

The three men walked over to the gate, where the dogs jumped on it and stuck their noses through the gaps to get them scratched. Bo saw malamutes, St. Bernards, and plenty of mutts that were a mixture of two or three breeds. Maybe a little wolf strain here and there, too. The dogs were all big and strong and had thick coats.

One stood off a ways and regarded them coolly instead of coming up to the gate and begging for affection. He was a magnificent black, white, and gray specimen, mostly husky but with some malamute thrown in, Bo thought. He nodded toward the dog and asked Lerch, "Who's that?"

"The big fella? That's Nemo. The boss of this bunch, let me tell you."

Scratch said, "He doesn't look too friendly."

"That's because he don't know you yet. Once he gets used to you, he warms up some. But he still don't put up with no nonsense from man nor beast, either."

"You own all these dogs?" Bo asked.

"Yep. I rent out teams and sleds durin' the winter. Sometimes sell 'em, if a man's willin' to pay the price for top dogs, 'cause that's the only kind I have, the best you'll find in the whole territory."

"What about the horses and wagons?"

"They're for rent, too. Don't get as much call for them, but sometimes a fella needs more than a sled. What are you boys in the market for?"

"Those two saddle mounts," Bo said. "Maybe the buckboard and a couple of draft horses later on."

Lerch regarded them shrewdly. "I know who you are, don't think for a second I don't. You're the men who came in on the riverboat with those ladies Amos Lawson and his men figured on marryin'."

"No sense in denying it, is there?"

"Not a bit. And you want the horses so you can ride up the gulch and locate Dan O'Rourke's claim." Lerch grinned. "I keep up with the news in Cushman, such as there is of it."

Scratch asked, "Did you know O'Rourke when he was in these parts?"

"I did." Lerch nodded. "And even though you didn't ask me, I'll tell you I wasn't overfond of the man. Seemed a mite full of himself. Still, he always dealt fair and honest with folks, as far as I know. I never had no trouble with him."

"I'm a little surprised that Amos Lawson doesn't own this outfit," Bo said.

Lerch grimaced. "He made me an offer, or I should say, he had his flunky Nebel make one, but I didn't take him up on it and he never tried to force my hand." The man shrugged. "Could be he just ain't got back around to it yet. I'd say Amos Lawson has got his mind set on ownin' everything in Cushman, and all the way up Ten Mile Gulch, too."

"That's what they call it, Ten Mile Gulch?"

"Yeah, on account of it's ten miles to the other end, up in the mountains."

"Are there gold claims all along it?"

"Pretty much. Nobody's struck it rich yet, but there's color, both in the creek and in the slopes. Just depends on whether a fella wants to pan for it or dig for it, or both."

"Which did O'Rourke do?" Scratch asked.

"Couldn't tell you," Lerch replied with a shake of his head. "I never went up there. No reason to. My business is right here."

"And it looks like a good one," Bo said. "How about it, Mr. Lerch? You'll rent us those horses?"

"Sure. Saddles and gear, too."

Lerch named a price, and they quickly came to an agreement. Bo and Scratch saddled the two mounts, a buckskin and a roan, and led them out of the stalls.

"You know where you're goin?" asked Lerch.

"We've got directions to the claim," Bo said.

"From O'Rourke's widow, I reckon. Well, good luck, boys. Don't get yourselves killed. Or if you do, be sure to turn them horses loose first. They'll come back here all right, I reckon."

Chapter 28

The two saddle horses were good mounts, a little less spirited than what Bo and Scratch were used to, maybe, but each had a nice, easy gait and plenty of strength and stamina.

Ten Mile Gulch wasn't hard to follow; once they were inside its walls there was nowhere else to go. Those walls weren't sheer, but they were very steep. A man could have climbed them, but a horse would have no chance. Both rimrocks were topped with pine, fir, and spruce trees. A few hardy bushes clung to the rocky walls.

The creek was only five feet wide and anywhere from six inches to a foot deep, flowing fast enough over a rocky bed to create bubbling music. When it left the gulch, it made a sharp turn to the south and meandered for a couple of hundred yards before turning again and emptying into Finbar Creek. That bend was why it wasn't visible from the riverboat landing.

The gulch itself varied in width from a hundred yards to less than twenty. In some places, there were grassy banks along the stream; in others, only trails of hard-packed dirt and rock wide enough for a pair of horsemen

or one of the handcarts, no more. The walls rose high
enough that the bottom of the gulch was mostly in shadow.
Despite that, it wasn't gloomy as long as the sun was
shining, although Bo imagined it would be during the long
winter.

According to the directions Beatrice had given them,
her late husband's claim was some four miles up the
gulch.

"You'll know it because there are two ridges that jut
out from the right-hand wall," she had explained. "They
extend about fifty yards and then curve in toward each
other, like a pair of hands wrapping around the outside of
a cup. That's what Daniel said he was going to call his
mine . . . the Golden Cup. The opening formed by the
ridges is fairly small, but then the claim opens back up
inside them and forms a rough circle. At the rear of the
area is a cliff. That's where Daniel did most of his
prospecting, along the base of that cliff. He told me in one
of his letters that he had managed to start several tunnels
back there."

"Hackin' out tunnels from hard rock like that is mighty
hard work," Scratch had told her. "Sometimes you have
to use dynamite to get very far."

"You and Bo have experience with that, though, don't
you?"

"We do. But you'll still need dynamite."

"There's a case of it among the supplies. I thought it
might be necessary."

Scratch had looked at Bo and muttered, "Lord have
mercy."

Now as they rode east along the gulch, they heard
distant, muffled booms and knew that other prospectors

were using dynamite or blasting powder to gouge holes in the earth in the hope of uncovering a vein of gold ore. They passed several men panning for gold dust in the creek, and on a couple of claims, men had built sluices and were washing dirt and gravel down them, attempting to sift out tiny grains of the precious metal. Sometimes it seemed that there were as many different ways to hunt for gold as there were men doing it, because everybody took a slightly different approach.

The sound of shovels crunching and picks ringing on stone also filled the air. Sometimes the prospectors they passed stopped whatever they were doing to stare at the two men on horseback.

"Hey, Tex!" a bearded gold-hunter called as he leaned on a shovel. "What are you doin' out here?"

His partner said, "Maybe they're gonna start a cattle ranch so we can have fresh steaks to eat!"

Scratch grinned and ticked a finger against his hat brim in salute as he replied, "You know, that ain't a bad idea. You boys may be onto somethin' there!"

They all laughed as Bo and Scratch rode on.

"We should be getting pretty close to O'Rourke's claim," Bo said a short time later.

Scratch squinted up at the rimrock on both sides of the gulch and said, "I halfway expected Lawson's boys to try to ambush us again before now."

"I don't know if he'd make a move in broad daylight like this. Skunks like that usually skulk around in the dark."

"Yeah, but it don't ever get full dark around here at this time of year."

Bo chuckled and said, "I reckon you have to consider

that, too. But I've been keeping my eyes open, and I haven't seen anything unusual yet."

"That don't mean they ain't up there somewhere, watchin' us. You can't ever tell when Comanch' or Apache are doggin' your trail."

"No, usually you can't," Bo agreed. Like Scratch, he kept his head on a swivel, and from time to time he glanced over his shoulder at their back trail and the rimrock behind them, too.

Half a mile west along the gulch, riding a narrow trail along the rim, a gunman who had only ever given his name as Ketchell said to Eli Byrne, "If we keep hangin' back like this, they're gonna get away from us."

"You think so? Where the hell are they gonna go, Ketchell? Once a man's down in that gulch, he either keeps going or turns around and rides back out. I've been all the way to the end and back more than once. There are no side canyons where they can veer off." Byrne blew out his breath disgustedly. "Anyway, we know where they're goin'. They're headed for the O'Rourke claim. Once they get there and stop, we'll catch up to them without any trouble."

Ketchell shrugged and said, "Fine with me. I'm just along for the twenty bucks. That's not much for killing a man . . . but, come to think of it, I've killed folks for less than that."

"If things go as planned, you'll get paid that double eagle for doin' nothing," Byrne said. "I want to kill both of those troublemaking Texans, especially the one in that cream-colored hat." The young gunman took off his own hat and looked at it disgustedly. "Mine's all stained up from that dunk in the creek. Fella's got to pay for that."

"Even though Lawson didn't give the order?" The smirk on Ketchell's lantern-jawed face made him even uglier than usual.

"I may work for Lawson, but that don't mean he gets to tell me everything I can or can't do," snapped Byrne. "I've got a score to settle for what they done to me and for poor Ben McDowell, too."

Along with Byrne and McDowell, Ketchell had been among the half-dozen men who had opened fire on Creel and Morton from the brush near the riverboat landing the previous night. He had dodged the slugs the Texans threw at them and had helped carrying McDowell's bloody, writhing body away from the ambush site. McDowell had been shot twice through the body and hadn't stood a chance. He had died less than five minutes after they got him back to Lawson's warehouse.

At the mention of that, Ketchell's smirk disappeared and a bleak expression settled over his face.

"Yeah, Ben was a good fella," he agreed. "Those two deserve to die for what they done to him. You can have first shot, Eli, but I want in on the killing."

"Fine," Byrne said. He slowed his horse. "We're gettin' pretty close to O'Rourke's claim. We'd better go ahead on foot. We don't want them to hear these horses up on the rim and get nervous about bein' followed."

The two men reined in, swung down from their saddles, and tied the horses to tree trunks. Then they pulled Winchesters from saddle sheaths and cat-footed ahead, following the rimrock trail to a point overlooking the claim that had belonged to Daniel O'Rourke.

* * *

Bo and Scratch rested crossed hands on the saddle horns and leaned forward to ease their bones and muscles as they looked at the entrance to what Daniel O'Rourke had referred to as the Golden Cup.

The bluffs jutting out from the gulch's southern wall curved around just as Beatrice had described them, making the location impossible to miss. The creek bubbled past a few yards from the entrance.

"You reckon O'Rourke's claim goes all the way to the middle of the creek?" asked Scratch. "That's usually the way these things work."

"Yeah, I'd say so," Bo replied. "But according to Miss Beatrice, he was digging for gold, not panning for it."

"Might be a good idea to give it a try once the ladies get up here. I'll bet I could teach Miss Sally how to use a pan. Some of the others might be able to get the hang of it, too. It ain't an easy job, but it ain't as hard as swingin' a pick all day, either."

"I suspect that's what you and I will be doing," Bo said dryly.

"Yeah." Scratch nudged the roan into motion. "Let's take a look at the place."

They rode through the gap into the "cup," which was a rough circle approximately seventy-five yards in diameter. At the back, the wall of the gulch rose eighty feet and was too sheer for any creature other than a mountain goat to climb. From the entrance, the Texans could see the dark mouths of four tunnels begun by Daniel O'Rourke.

"Why do you reckon he didn't stick with any of them?" Scratch said. "None of 'em appear to be very deep. What did he do, dig a few feet, then give up and try somewhere else?"

"That's what it looks like," Bo said. "You've got to remember, from what we know of O'Rourke he never stuck with anything for too long. He was a Mountie, then he worked for Miss Beatrice's father in the steel business, and then he took off to become a prospector."

"And he left Miss Beatrice, too, after not bein' too faithful to her." Scratch shook his head. "I never met the fella, of course, but I get the feelin' I wouldn't have cottoned to him if I had."

"He probably wasn't all bad, or Beatrice never would've married him in the first place. Some hombres just can't ever settle down with one woman . . . or with one thing they want out of life."

"And some are so dad-blasted set on one particular thing, they let it ruin everything else." Scratch chuckled and added, "It's a good thing you and me are so sensible and levelheaded, not like most folks."

Bo laughed and said, "Yeah, that's a good description of us, all right."

It didn't take long for them to ride all over the claim. Some of the ground was covered with brush, and there were a few scrubby trees. Enough grass grew to provide graze for horses, but it wasn't what anybody would call lush.

Along the back wall, between two of the rudimentary tunnel mouths, O'Rourke had built a shelter of sorts out of logs and brush. It was a shed-like affair with a roof, two sides, and an open front.

"We'll have to close that up and make it nicer for the

ladies," Scratch said as he nodded toward the shelter. "Make it closer to bein' a real cabin."

"In the meantime, there are tents in those supplies Miss Beatrice had shipped up here. They'll have to stay in those starting out."

"As long as the weather holds, I don't mind spreadin' my bedroll outside." Scratch looked around the claim. "We've stayed in worse places. Good water handy."

"Yeah, that part of it ought to be fine. Let's take a closer look at those tunnels."

They dismounted and tied the reins to one of the posts holding up the shelter's roof. They walked over and stood in front of the nearest tunnel mouth.

"How deep would you say it is?" asked Scratch. "Ten or twelve feet?"

"About that," Bo said. He fished a lucifer from his shirt pocket. "I want to see what the rock face looks like back there."

He didn't need the match to see where he was going; enough light penetrated into the short tunnel to reveal the rocky, irregular floor and the rough walls. The tunnel was barely tall enough for Bo to stand up straight, and he had to take his hat off to do that. The ceiling brushed against his hair as he stepped inside. Scratch took off his hat as well and followed him.

Daniel O'Rourke hadn't extended the tunnel far enough to require shoring it up, but it was deep enough that Bo felt a little closed in. He ignored that discomfort, snapped the lucifer to life, and held the flame close to the rock wall at tunnel's end. He moved the match back and forth as he studied the rock.

"No quartz," he announced. "No sign of color at all that I can see."

"Reckon that's why he gave up and tried somewhere else. Seems to me that prospectin' is one of the most frustratin' things a fella can do. There could be a big vein of pure gold six inches farther on, or six inches to one side or the other. Or nothin'. You just never know. You can break your back and your heart and never do a lick of good . . . but every time you quit and move on, there's a little voice in the back of your head whisperin' *Just a little more. Just a little farther on.*"

"That's why we never spent a lot of time looking for gold or silver," Bo said. "A man's got to be mighty single-minded to make that his life's work."

Scratch grinned. "Yeah, and our life's work has always been wanderin'."

"It suits us," Bo said as he shook out the match, which had burned down almost to his fingers. "Let's see if we can turn around and get out of here."

They stepped back out of the tunnel. Scratch said, "Once we pick one and start extendin' it, we'll want to shore up the roof. I didn't like thinkin' about all those tons of dirt and rock right over our heads with nothin' much to hold 'em up."

"Neither did I," Bo agreed. He put his hat on, and so did Scratch.

But the silver-haired Texan had barely settled his Stetson on his head when it leaped off again and the sharp crack of a rifle shot split the air.

Chapter 29

Bo grabbed Scratch's arm and lunged back into the tunnel, pulling his old friend with him. The ceiling knocked Bo's hat off when they went through the opening.

"Blast it!" Scratch exclaimed as he and Bo stumbled to a stop after the hasty retreat, about halfway to the end of the tunnel. "If whoever that varmint is put a hole in my hat and ruined it—"

"He nearly put a hole in your *head* and ruined it," Bo interrupted. "Are you all right?"

"Yeah, yeah, that bullet didn't come close enough to even part my hair. But now what are we gonna do? We're kinda stuck here in this tunnel."

"I know, but this was the closest cover. It sounded to me like that bushwhacker was up on the rim. If we tried to make a run for the horses or some of those trees, he could've picked us off without much trouble, if he's any kind of shot at all."

"You reckon there's a chance he was aimin' for my hat? You know, firin' a warning shot?"

"Do you think anybody up here we've run into so far

would go to that much trouble instead of just trying to kill us?"

Scratch chuckled, but there was no real humor in the sound. "No, you're right about that," he said. "Lawson and his bunch want us dead. They ain't made no secret about that. And I can't think of anybody else who'd come after us."

"That's one of Lawson's men up there, all right. Maybe more than one."

"Knowin' that doesn't get us outta this fix, though. We're still pinned down. And there's no back door in this tunnel."

No more shots had sounded since the one that had knocked Scratch's hat off his head, but Bo knew it was only a matter of time. Whether there was only one bush-whacker or several, whoever wanted them dead could work around and get an angle to fire into the tunnel. Emptying a rifle into the tunnel mouth would create enough ricochets that anyone taking cover in here wouldn't have a chance of surviving. If he and Scratch waited, they'd be cut to pieces.

"There's only one way out of this," Bo said. "One of us has to die."

Eli Byrne cursed bitterly as he knelt near the rimrock's edge and kept his rifle trained on the tunnel mouth where the two Texans had disappeared.

"Don't take on so, Eli," Ketchell said. "We've got 'em trapped. If they so much as stick their noses out of that hole, we'll blow 'em to hell."

"Damn sights must be off on this rifle," Byrne muttered. "I never miss a shot like that."

"I'm not so sure you did."

"What do you mean? You saw that hat go sailing off."

"Yeah, but for all you know, you hit him in the head, too. The bullet could've gone through his hat and drilled him through the brain."

Byrne shook his head. "I don't think so. I didn't see any blood fly."

"It all happened pretty quick, though," Ketchell pointed out. "That other old codger grabbed him and jerked him back in the tunnel before I could get a good look at what happened. He's got mighty fast reflexes for somebody that long in the tooth."

Byrne didn't want to hear excuses. He was too filled with anger for that. He just wanted the Texans dead.

Ketchell might be right, though, he told himself. He couldn't be sure he'd missed Morton. Maybe Morton was lying down there in the tunnel, already dead or dying. . . .

"I'll work my way along the rim until I'm in a good position to keep them covered," Ketchell went on. "Then I'll watch the tunnel while you join me, and then we'll both pour enough lead in there to make sure they're both dead. That sound like it'll work?"

"Yeah, I suppose," Byrne said grudgingly. "We need to get this over and done with, though. Some of the other men who have claims nearby might get curious about that shot and come to see what's going on. I'd just as soon not be spotted up here. They could cause trouble. The boss doesn't run *everything* in these parts yet."

"Just a matter of time," Ketchell said with a grin. Holding his rifle, he stood up from where he'd been kneeling. "I'll move on around—"

An anguished cry from the tunnel broke in on what he was saying.

"Scratch! Scratch, damn it! Don't die! *Scratch!*"

"Why do I have to be the one who dies?" Scratch had asked a few minutes earlier.

"Because you were the one who got his hat knocked off, and there was only one shot," Bo had explained. "Unless you figure they'll believe that slug bounced off your cast-iron skull and got me on the ricochet. Come to think of it, that's not completely far-fetched—"

"Yeah, yeah, I get it. I reckon what you're sayin' makes sense. And I *am* a better shot than you, so if your plan stands any chance of workin', it's better that I do the shootin'."

"We can argue about that some other time. Give me one of your Remingtons."

Scratch handed over the ivory-handled revolver from his left-hand holster.

"You need to stay on the move," he told Bo. "Don't let 'em draw too good a bead on you."

"I don't intend to. Are you ready?"

Scratch drew the other Remington and held it up next to his head with the barrel pointed at the tunnel ceiling. "Ready as I'm gonna be, I reckon," he said.

Bo nodded and drew in a deep breath. He let it out in a loud cry full of anger and grief.

"Scratch! Scratch, damn it! Don't die! *Scratch!*" He moved closer to the tunnel mouth and went on. "He's dead! You killed him, you—"

He added some of the most obscene epithets he could

think of, then bellowed inarticulately and charged out of the tunnel, zigzagging and firing both guns wildly toward the rim where he thought the shot had come from, while continuing to yell at the top of his lungs.

"There's the other one!" Ketchell exclaimed as he stopped where he was on the rimrock and flung his rifle to his shoulder. "He's gone loco! I'll get him!"

The Winchester belched flame. Dust flew in the air as the slug hit the ground near Creel's feet, but it was still a clean miss.

A few yards from Ketchell, Eli Byrne aimed and fired, too, but the way Creel was darting around, it was hard to settle the sights on him. Byrne could tell he missed, and as Ketchell fired a second time, that slug didn't stop Creel's mad dashing around, either.

Understanding suddenly burst in Byrne's brain. He yelled, "Ketchell, get back! It's a trick!"

As gun thunder filled the air and the echoes bounced back and forth in the gulch to create a great racket, Scratch stepped out of the tunnel mouth and lifted his other Remington. A part of him wanted to watch Bo and make sure his old friend didn't get hit, but he knew he couldn't afford to do that.

Instead he raised his eyes to the rim and spotted the man standing up there firing a rifle toward Bo. Scratch brought the Remington up and lined the sights in one swift, smooth movement. The range was a mite long for a handgun, and shooting up at a sharp angle like that was tricky, too, but Scratch knew he could make the shot.

The Remington boomed and bucked against his palm.

The man on the rim dropped his rifle and jackknifed, bending almost double as he came up on his toes. That made him lean forward, and he was too close to the rim to catch himself, even if Scratch's .44 slug hadn't punched deep into his guts. He toppled into empty space, too far gone even to scream as he made a complete revolution in midair before crashing to the ground on his back.

Scratch heard another rifle crack and felt the wind-rip of a bullet past his ear. He swung the Remington to the left. Another bushwhacker was up there, kneeling a few yards away from the man the silver-haired Texan had just drilled. Scratch triggered again just as he saw the muzzle flash of a second shot erupting from the rifle.

The would-be killer had hurried this shot. It plowed into the ground a good ten feet to Scratch's left. Scratch's shot struck a rock right in front of the bushwhacker and blasted it into gravel, making the man flinch.

Bo had stopped running around like a chicken with its head cut off, and he opened fire again with his Colt and the Remington he had borrowed from Scratch. His shots lashed at the rimrock. Scratch kept up the barrage, too. He saw the bushwhacker's hat fly in the air as the man threw himself backward, out of the line of fire.

"Come on, Bo!" he called. "Head for the trees!"

They ran hard for a clump of scrubby pines with trunks thick enough to offer some protection. They put the trees between them and the rim where the ambushers had been and pressed their backs to the trunks.

"Here you go," Bo said as he tossed the Remington to Scratch, who caught it deftly. "Thanks for the loan."

"You could've kept it until we got out of here."

"No, I'm a one-gun man. Toting two throws my balance off a mite."

"Well, I never understood how you could carry just one. Don't it make you walk slanchwise?"

"No, I've packed an iron on my hip for so long I figure I couldn't walk a straight line if I *didn't* have one weighing me down."

They were reloading during this banter, but as they finished and snapped their guns' cylinders closed, a new sound came to their ears.

Hoofbeats. Heading away from the rim in a hurry.

"Sounds like the one we didn't ventilate is getting out of here while the getting's good," Bo said. "Did you see any more than just the two of them?"

"Nope, I think that was all. Judgin' by those hoofbeats, he's takin' his pard's horse with him, too."

"No reason to leave it behind."

"Reckon we should go take a look at the fella lyin' over there?"

"Let's give it a few minutes," Bo said. "Just in case that other hombre is trying to play it tricky."

Only a minute or so had gone by, though, when several men ventured cautiously through the gap between the two bluffs at the entrance to the claim. A couple carried rifles, and the others brandished pickaxes. One of them hailed the Texans.

"Hey, are you fellas all right?"

Bo waved a hand and replied, "We're fine. Just a little problem with bushwhackers."

The newcomers strode on in. Bo and Scratch stepped out to meet them, figuring that even if the remaining ambusher was still lurking up there, the man wouldn't try anything with this many witnesses on hand.

"We were workin' our claims when we heard all the shootin'," said the spokesman for the group. Bo realized now he was the bearded prospector who had called out to them earlier as they rode up the gulch, the one who had called them "Tex." He went on. "We try to be neighborly around here and figured we'd better see if you needed some help."

"Claim-jumpers, eh?" said another man, this one stocky and round-faced.

"I'm not sure about that," Bo said, "but there's one of them, lying over there where he fell off the rim after my partner ventilated him."

They all walked over to the dead man. If Scratch's bullet hadn't killed him, the fall would have. His head had struck a rock when he landed and busted open in gruesome fashion.

The man's face was still relatively unmarked, though. The bearded prospector looked at him and said, "That's Ketchell. Never heard a front handle for him."

"Does he have a claim around here?" Scratch asked.

"Him?" The prospector made a face and shook his head. "Huntin' gold would be too much work for the likes of him. Only prospectin' he does is for whiskey and whores, and maybe a poker game now and then. He hangs around the Avalanche, mostly, or one of the other saloons."

"One of Amos Lawson's men, eh?" Bo said.

"I didn't say that. Don't recall ever seein' this fella with

Lawson. 'Course, that don't really mean anything one way or the other."

The stocky prospector said, "This used to be Dan O'Rourke's claim. Are the rumors I've heard true? O'Rourke's widow and some other women have come up here to take it over?"

Scratch said, "That's the plan. And we're workin' for them. Gonna help them work the claim and make sure they stay safe."

The stocky hombre shook his head. "Well, all I can say is that you boys are gonna have a mighty big job cut out for you." He looked down at the dead bushwhacker. "From what I can see, though, you just might be up to it."

Chapter 30

"We'll go ahead and rent that buckboard from Ed Lerch," Bo explained to Beatrice and the others when he and Scratch got back from the claim and gathered with them on the *Byron Mowery*. "That way we can take the supplies up to the claim first and then come back for you ladies."

"Won't that be taking a chance on someone stealing the supplies?" asked Beatrice.

"We thought of that," Scratch said. "I'll be stayin' up there to keep an eye on 'em while Bo fetches y'all."

Martha said, "But if you're there by yourself, couldn't that tempt some of those awful . . . bushwhackers . . . to attack you again?"

Scratch grinned. "I won't be by myself. We sort of made friends with a couple of fellas named Clarke and Emery who have claims close by. They volunteered to come and keep me company while I'm waitin' for you and Bo to get back. We'll spend the time gettin' tents set up and makin' the place as livable as we can."

"What a generous thing to do, giving up that time when

they could be working on their own claims. We'll have to do something to repay them," Beatrice said. "Perhaps have them over for dinner once we get settled in."

Bo had to smile to himself. Beatrice's comment about having the prospectors over for dinner indicated that she didn't quite understand just what a hardscrabble existence mining for gold could be. It wasn't the sort of life that included dinner parties.

But she would come to realize that once she was at the claim.

"Gold-hunters are like anybody else, I reckon," he said. "You'll find some nice ones—"

"And plenty of downright skunks," concluded Scratch with a grin.

They got busy making the arrangements with Ed Lerch, accompanied by another loud chorus of barking from the sled dogs. After hitching four draft horses to the buckboard, Bo and Scratch took it back to the riverboat landing and loaded the supplies on it, with some help from Cruickshank's crew.

The captain was anxious to be headed back downriver, but he had agreed to remain until the Texans could take the ladies up the gulch to the O'Rourke claim. He hoped it was that afternoon, in time for him to depart and put a few miles behind the *Byron Mowery* on its return trip.

On their way to deliver the supplies to the camp, Bo handled the team while Scratch rode beside him with a Winchester across his lap, eyes constantly scanning the rimrocks on both sides of the gulch for any sign of an ambush. They felt that it was unlikely the man who'd survived the earlier bushwhack attempt would come back and try again so soon, but the chance of that couldn't be ignored.

Nothing happened, however, and when they reached the claim, they found Clarke and Emery using shovels to tamp down the dirt of a grave on the other side of the creek, well away from the stream.

"Didn't figure you'd want that fella planted where he'd foul the creek," Clarke explained. He was the tall, bearded member of the pair.

"Hope we didn't cause a problem by planting him," added the short, stocky Emery. "Didn't see that taking him back to the settlement would serve any purpose, though, unless maybe you wanted to dump him at Amos Lawson's feet. Sorry we didn't think about that until after we had him in the ground."

"No, that's all right," Bo assured them. "It's not like there's any big mystery behind who our enemies are up here. Lawson's made it plain enough already. No need to shock a confession out of him."

The two prospectors pitched in and helped unload the supplies and equipment. Bo left Scratch there with them and headed back to Cushman. This time he had to both drive and watch out for trouble, but he didn't encounter any problems on the way to the settlement.

Eli Byrne leaned on the bar and nursed the whiskey Walter Heuman had poured for him a short time earlier. He hadn't gone back to Amos Lawson's office to report what had happened, and he was deep in a debate with himself whether he was even going to say anything to his boss about the failed ambush. Lawson hadn't sent him up the gulch to kill those two Texans, after all, and he could get proddy about his men acting without orders.

Eventually, someone would notice that the gunman called Ketchell wasn't around anymore. Whether anybody would care was another question entirely. Most people would just assume that he had drifted on to some other mining camp farther up the Yukon, or maybe even across the border in Canada.

Byrne straightened instinctively as someone stepped up beside him. His hand drifted toward the gun on his hip.

Then he relaxed as he realized the newcomer was just one of the soiled doves who worked in the saloon. She was a short, chubby girl with auburn hair, and after a moment he recalled that she went by the name Dolly, which was almost certainly not her real name.

She leaned toward him, giving him a good look at her freckled bosom as it tried to spill out of her low-cut dress, and said, "Hello, Eli. Buy me a drink?"

"I don't have to buy you a drink," he snapped, still on edge. The whiskey hadn't dulled his frustration. "You know that."

It was true. As one of Amos Lawson's inner circle, he had the right to claim any of the girls who worked in the Avalanche, any time he wanted, without it costing him anything. He had been with Dolly a few times in the past; she was all right, nothing special.

But maybe right now, spending an hour or so with her was just what he needed to make him forget his failure to kill Creel and Morton—as well as the sound Ketchell's head had made when it hit the ground. He kept hearing that grisly thud in the back of his mind.

Dolly looked a little hurt that he had spoken to her so sharply, so he said, "Sorry. Sure, I'll buy you a drink." He signaled to Heuman, who got a glass and a bottle from under the bar. The bottle held colored water, Byrne knew. Lawson wasn't going to waste actual booze on whores.

Heuman poured the drink and said, "On your tab, kid?"

"Sure." It wasn't like that tab would ever be collected, at least not as long as he worked for Lawson. Like spending time with Dolly or one of the other doves if he wanted to, it was one of the benefits of the job.

"Maybe we could go back to my room later," Dolly suggested with a coy smile.

"Maybe . . ." Byrne said.

His voice trailed off as a transformation seemed to take place right before his eyes. Instead of Dolly standing there beside him, Byrne suddenly saw the taller, more slender, blond, and definitely more elegant Caroline DeHerries. His heart slugged in his chest at the vision.

Eli Byrne knew good and well that Amos Lawson didn't care if any of his men got wives out of the deal he'd made. He just wanted to get his hands on the O'Rourke claim, and marrying O'Rourke's widow was the easiest, simplest way to do that. Paying for the other three mail-order brides was just part of the scheme.

But Byrne had enjoyed reading the letters he'd gotten from Caroline DeHerries. He wasn't much of a hand for writing, but he had tried and she'd seemed to respond.

Now, of course, he knew that Caroline was part of an underhanded deal, too. She hadn't ever intended to marry him. She'd probably just been pretending that she cared anything at all about him. He knew he ought to hate her for her treachery. Despite all that, however, she was beautiful. As lovely a young woman as Byrne had ever laid eyes on. And now, as he imagined her standing there beside him instead of Dolly, he knew two things.

He wanted her—and he was going to have her.

No matter who or how many he had to kill to get her.

"Eli?" Dolly said in a frightened little voice. "Are you all right?"

He snapped out of his reverie. "What?" he rasped. "What did you say?"

She looked even more scared now. "I just asked if you were all right. You looked like you were a long, long way off just then."

"I'm fine," he said in a flat, hard tone.

"We can go back to my room any time you—"

"Forget it," he told her. "Find somebody else."

"Eli," she said plaintively as he turned away from the bar and stalked toward the saloon's entrance. "Eli, whatever I did, I'm sorry!"

Byrne ignored her. A whore was no substitute for Caroline DeHerries. He strode down the street toward the riverboat landing.

Bo parked the buckboard at the foot of the dock. Beatrice, Caroline, Martha, and Sally were waiting for him on the deck of the *Byron Mowery*. Captain Cruickshank stood with them.

They all crossed the gangplank to the dock. Each of the women carried a small bag, the last of the possessions they had brought with them. The rest had been taken up to the claim on the previous trip.

Bo extended his hand to Cruickshank. "Captain, I can't tell you how much I appreciate you staying here and keeping an eye on the ladies until we had things ready for them."

Cruickshank clasped Bo's hand and said, "I reckon I've gotten a mite fond of them, although I'll admit, havin' them along on this trip made for more excitement than usual!"

Beatrice laughed and said, "We're sorry about that, Captain. Trust me, none of the trouble was our idea!"

That wasn't strictly true, Bo mused. It had been Beatrice's idea to come to Alaska in the first place, and ultimately that was what had led to the various ruckuses.

Each of the women hugged Cruickshank in turn. He patted them on the back awkwardly and wished them luck.

Caroline, Martha, and Sally climbed onto the buckboard and sat with their feet dangling off the back. Bo helped them get up there, then gave Beatrice a hand onto the driver's seat, where she perched beside him as he swung up and took the reins.

"We're really close to our goal now, aren't we?" Beatrice asked, sounding a little nervous.

"Another hour and you'll be at the claim," Bo told her. "That's not really the goal, though, is it? That's actually just the beginning of getting what you're after."

"That's true. But I'm going to feel a sense of accomplishment in making it that far."

"And you should. It hasn't been an easy trip."

Bo flapped the reins and got the team moving. The buckboard rolled away from the landing and up the street toward the mouth of the gulch at the other end.

They had barely gotten started when Bo spotted Eli Byrne up ahead, walking toward them with an arrogant swagger, his thumbs hooked in his gunbelt. For a second, Bo thought Byrne wasn't going to get out of the way, but then the young gunman stepped aside and stood there, glaring.

Bo felt the hate coming from Byrne like a physical

thing, almost like a slap in the face. Looking at him, Bo suddenly had a hunch that Byrne was the bushwhacker who had gotten away that morning. Whether Amos Lawson had ordered that attempt on their lives, he didn't know. Byrne looked as if he would have killed both Texans just for the pleasure of it.

Then as the buckboard passed him, Byrne turned his gaze toward Caroline, who was sitting on the side closest to him. His gaze was so intent that Caroline must have felt it, just as Bo had. He didn't slow the team, didn't look back, but he had to admit, he wasn't 100 percent sure Byrne wouldn't whip out his gun and try to plug him, even though it was broad daylight in the middle of the settlement.

Nothing happened, though, as they left him behind. Beatrice turned slightly on the seat to peer over her shoulder and said, "Heavens, Caroline, you're white as a sheet!"

"I know, Aunt Beatrice," Caroline replied. Sally was sitting beside her, and she slipped an arm around the girl's shoulders. "Mr. Byrne looked at me like he . . . like he was a hungry animal and I was a piece of meat!"

"That's a good way to put it, Miss Caroline," Bo told her. "Fellas like that are half wolf. But Scratch and I are going to be around to make sure he doesn't bother you."

"Thank you, Bo. That makes me feel a lot better."

Bo didn't know whether she really meant that. He just hoped he and Scratch would be able to keep that promise.

The buckboard rolled on, left Cushman behind, splashed across the hard and rocky bed of the shallow creek, and moved into Ten Mile Gulch, bound for the Golden Cup.

Chapter 31

Scratch poked a fingertip through the hole in the crown of his hat and said, "Yep, that's how close I came to gettin' this old noggin of mine ventilated. A few inches lower and that would have stung a mite."

"But you don't know who shot at you?" Beatrice asked.

"We have a few ideas," Bo replied, but he didn't go into details. Nor did he explain that one of the bushwhackers now lay on the other side of the creek in a shallow grave. He didn't want to cast too much of a pall on this occasion.

Scratch, Clarke, and Emery had pitched two good-sized tents where the ladies would sleep for now. Scratch had also cleaned out the dead brush and the pine needles that had collected in the shed, as well as gathering rocks to build a fire ring and stacking up a nice pile of firewood. He'd had a blaze going and a pot of coffee boiling by the time Bo and the ladies arrived.

"All the comforts of home," he'd announced proudly with a sweep of his hand.

Clarke and Emery had gone back to their claim already. Bo had paused the buckboard there and introduced the ladies to them. The two rough prospectors had been shy and awkward in the presence of such beauty and elegance, shuffling their feet as Beatrice thanked them for their help.

Now they sat around the fire and sipped coffee, using crates of supplies as chairs. Scratch had some salt pork frying in a pan, resulting in a delicious smell. The sun was low on the horizon, giving the evening a tranquil feeling, and a breeze heavily laden with the tang of pine trees drifted through the gulch.

"It's beautiful here," Caroline said. "Much nicer than I imagined."

"It's nice now," Bo agreed. "In a few months, when winter sets in, it won't be the same story."

"It can't be too bad, though," Beatrice said. "I mean, people live here year 'round, don't they?"

"The Indians do," Scratch said. "But that's all they've ever known. It really hasn't been that long since white men moved into this part of the world. You may not want to stay out here once the snow starts. I reckon that gulch might get impassable durin' the worst months."

"Where would we go?" asked Martha. "Into Cushman?"

"Or back down to Seattle," Bo suggested.

"No," Beatrice said flatly. "That would be an invitation for someone else to take over this claim. I won't stand for that. Daniel wanted me to have it, and I intend to hang on to it." She looked around. "Me and my friends. Share and share alike."

The other three women nodded in agreement.

"We're getting ahead of ourselves," Bo said. "First there's a matter of seeing if we can even find any gold here, as well as turning that shed into an actual cabin. There's going to be plenty of work to keep us all busy."

"I'll drink to that," Scratch said as he lifted his coffee cup. "Hard work's a good thing. Keeps a fella outta mischief." He grinned. "Most of the time."

There were no opportunities for mischief over the next two weeks, but there *was* plenty of hard work.

Bo and Scratch felled trees and built a front wall for the shed, turning it into an actual cabin. They added bunks, and Martha and Sally used canvas from the supplies to make mattresses filled with pine needles. All the supplies were moved into the cabin to get them out of the weather.

While doing that, they didn't neglect the search for gold, devoting more than half the time to chipping out the tunnel that Bo and Scratch decided looked the most promising. The Texans wielded the picks while the ladies hauled out the rocks and gravel created by their efforts. Bo and Scratch cut down more trees to fashion beams that shored up the tunnel's ceiling. Their progress was slow, only a few inches a day, but they continued finding small streaks of quartz in the rock, an indication that gold might be present.

Scratch also taught the ladies how to pan for gold in the creek. As he'd predicted, Sally took to it, and Beatrice proved to be fairly adept, too. Caroline and Martha struggled and never could quite master the art of swirling a mix of water, gravel, and dirt from the stream bed in a pan until the lighter stuff floated out and the heavier flecks of gold were left.

That was the idea, anyway. None of those flecks showed up, even though Sally and Beatrice were doing it right.

Dave Clarke and Milt Emery visited from time to time

and were always quick to offer to help with anything that needed to be done. It didn't take long for Bo to figure out what was going on. During those visits, Clarke always seemed to be somewhere around Martha Rousseau, and Emery was never far from Sally Bechdolt. Neither of the women appeared to be bothered by the attention, either.

The traveling outfits they had worn on the way up had been replaced by garments more suitable for work: long-sleeved flannel shirts and long canvas or corduroy skirts. Their hair was pulled back and tied out of the way. Faces burned and then tanned. Soft hands roughened.

Even so, Clarke and Emery obviously believed Martha and Sally were the most gorgeous creatures they had ever laid eyes on. Bo and Scratch discussed that among themselves and agreed that the prospectors seemed like decent hombres, so they didn't discourage Clarke and Emery from visiting.

There had been no sign of Amos Lawson or any of his men.

The Texans also debated whether to continue deepening the tunnel they had been working on or give up on it and switch to another one.

As they stood leaning on their picks in front of the rock face, studying it in the light of the lantern that burned on the tunnel floor behind them, Bo suddenly reached out and rested his hand against the rough stone.

"Blast it, Scratch," he said, "it's like I can hear that ore in there, just taunting me."

"What's it sayin'? *Dig a little deeper*?"

"That's exactly what it's saying. But what if it's not there?"

Scratch shrugged. "Then it ain't. Some fellas claim to

know a whole heap about rocks and such and can point to a place and declare that there's gold here or there, but in the end it always comes down to the same thing. It's just a roll of the dice, Bo, and it always has been."

Bo nodded slowly, patted the rock face, and said, "You're right. But it's mighty frustrating, anyway."

"Well, maybe you were right when you said blast it."

"No, I was just—" Bo stopped short and looked at his friend. Scratch was grinning. "You think?"

"Could be time for that," Scratch said.

Bo peered at the rock and nodded again. "Could be. If nothing else, it would shut up that little voice for a while, wouldn't it?"

"Let's go warn the gals."

Beatrice and the other three flocked around, eager and excited as Bo explained that they were going to use dynamite on the tunnel.

"The rock's gotten so hard we're not making much progress anymore," he said. "We're hoping that if we blow some of it out of there, it'll tell us whether it's worth our time to continue with this tunnel or if we ought to try another."

"What can we do to help?" asked Beatrice.

"Just stay back a good long ways," Scratch replied. "All the way out by the creek, maybe, and 'round on the other side of one of them bluffs."

"But you'll be running all the risks," she objected.

"That's what we're here for," Bo said. "But don't worry. After that blast goes off, there should be plenty of rubble to clear out of there."

They hadn't put *all* the supplies inside the cabin. In

fact, Scratch had carried the case of dynamite as far away from the structure as he could, placing it inside the tunnel the farthest distance from the cabin. Daniel O'Rourke had hacked it out only a few feet deep, but that would make a good place to store the explosives, anyway. Scratch had covered the crate with a piece of oilcloth to protect it from the elements. Without a blockhouse in which to keep the dynamite, that was the safest method of storage.

Scratch went over there now and brought back a single cylinder wrapped in red paper, as well as a piece of fuse and a blasting cap.

"I hope this fuse burns at the same rate as the other stuff we've used over the years," he commented. "We haven't checked it yet."

"I'd be generous with it, if I was you," Bo said.

"That's the plan. One of us needs to chip out a hole for it."

Bo hefted the pick he had brought out with him. "I'll take care of that."

He worked for a while, preparing the rock face for the blast. Scratch stood back watching him. When Bo had the hole ready, he stepped aside and motioned for Scratch to place the dynamite. While Scratch was doing that, Bo retreated to the tunnel mouth to check on the ladies.

They were standing about twenty yards away. Bo waved them back and called, "Go on out yonder by the entrance."

With an obvious mixture of nervousness and reluctance, they moved farther away.

"I used what ought to be about three minutes worth of fuse, just for good measure," Scratch said, his voice echoing in the tunnel. "Ready out there?"

"Ready," Bo said. He planned to move to one side, well away from the tunnel mouth, as soon as Scratch emerged.

He heard a match scrape to life, saw the brief flare of light from inside the tunnel. A couple of heartbeats went by, then Scratch burst out of the entrance, running.

"Go, go!" Scratch yelled as he waved at Bo. "It's burnin' faster'n I thought it—"

The loud boom chopped off his words midsentence. Rock flew out of the tunnel mouth, followed by a huge cloud of dust. The ground shook from the explosion.

Scratch had veered away from the tunnel as soon as he was outside, so the full force of the blast missed him. But it was still strong enough to knock him off his feet and send him rolling on the ground.

Bo yelled, "Scratch!" and hurried toward him as dust continued to billow out of the opening and echoes swarmed along the gulch. They would have been louder if the curving bluffs hadn't blocked the sound to a certain extent.

Coughing and shaking his head, Scratch sat up before Bo could get there. He grinned up at his old friend and said, "We should've played around with that fuse a mite beforehand."

"You loco old pelican!" Bo exclaimed. "Are you all right?"

"I think so." Scratch took the hand Bo held out to him, climbed to his feet, rolled his shoulders, and waved his arms around. "Everything seems to be workin'."

The ladies rushed across the claim to join them. "Scratch, are you hurt?" Beatrice asked as she clutched his arms.

"No, I'm fine," he assured her. He grinned as he added, "That dynamite blowed up real good, didn't it?"

"Why is there still smoke coming out of the tunnel?" asked Caroline.

"That's not smoke, it's dust," Bo explained. "It ought to thin out in a few minutes, and then maybe we can get a look in there. We'll need to be mighty careful, though. That blast might have weakened the ceiling. We don't want a cave-in."

"We certainly don't," Beatrice agreed. "Maybe we should wait even longer. Until tomorrow, maybe."

Scratch shook his head and said, "Nope. I want to see what happened in there."

Bo's prediction proved to be correct. Within ten minutes, the dust had settled. He and Scratch approached the opening cautiously. The support beams they had placed a couple of feet inside the tunnel mouth were still there; they could see those, and they appeared solid and intact. Squinting, Bo moved just inside the opening and peered along the tunnel, lifting the lantern he took with him so its yellow glow extended deeper.

"The next set of beams is all right, too," he reported. "I'll go a little farther."

"Bo, be careful," Beatrice urged.

"It looks fine. I'll just—Holy cow!"

"What is it?" Scratch asked sharply as Caroline and Martha both let out frightened little cries.

Instead of answering directly, Bo said, "Everybody, stand clear of the opening. Scratch, take a look at this."

A moment later, a fist-sized chunk of rock sailed out of the tunnel mouth and bounced a couple of times on the ground. Scratch picked it up, cradled it in his hands, and frowned as he studied it intently.

Bo appeared in the opening and asked, "What do you think?"

"The quartz has gotten streaky, all right, no doubt about that. Is that . . . ?" Scratch picked at the rock with a fingernail, then said, "By grab! This might still be fool's gold, but I believe it's the real thing!"

The ladies crowded around him. "Gold?" Beatrice said, wide-eyed.

"Real gold?" Caroline added.

In the hand that wasn't holding the lantern, Bo gripped another rock. He held it out and said, "Have a look at this one, ladies. Unless I miss my guess, there's a good-sized vein of this stuff in there that was uncovered by the explosion." He grinned at Scratch. "I told you it kept talking to me."

"And you weren't hearin' things," Scratch agreed. He had picked away more of the quartz and dirt, revealing an inch or so of dully gleaming rock. "I remember seein' an assay office in Cushman. We need to get this ore in there and have the fella take a look at it, find out how much it's gonna assay out per ton."

Beatrice licked her lips and said, "Is it good? Is this a strike? A bonanza?"

"It might be," Bo told her. "It's hard to say for sure just yet. But right now, we need to move all that rubble out of the tunnel so we can get a better look at the rock face the way it is now. Also, we'll need to bust up the smaller rocks and pick out the gold ore. It's possible we'll find enough for a pretty good payoff just doing that."

"We're going to be rich," Martha breathed. She looked over at Sally. "We're going to be rich!"

"There's plenty of hard work to do yet," Bo said, "but honestly, I'd say you've just taken a big step toward getting there."

Chapter 32

They spent the rest of that day and all of the next cleaning out the tunnel and searching for bits of gold among the rubble. Clarke and Emery showed up, having heard the blast, and immediately volunteered to help with the hard work, steadfastly refusing any offers of pay for doing so. Bo felt a little like they were taking advantage of the two prospectors being smitten with Martha and Sally, but at the same time, he was glad to have the help.

Beatrice, Caroline, and Martha used small hammers to chip away at the chunks of rock until they split apart and revealed their secrets. By the time the tunnel was cleared out, they had a small leather bag more than half full of pebble-sized pieces of ore.

The men had added more timbers to support the roof, and Bo felt like it was safe enough in the tunnel now to bring the women in there and show them how things looked.

By lantern light, he pointed out the quartz seam running in a zigzag line up the rock face that the blast had uncovered.

"That's where the gold is coming from," he explained. "It's embedded in that softer rock."

"It doesn't seem very soft when you're trying to break it up," Caroline said.

"Well, no, but compared to what's around it, it is. What we'll do is just dig out this part as far as we can without extending the tunnel. Then if we need to, we'll take it deeper and expose more of the vein."

"How deep do you think it goes?" asked Beatrice.

"There's no tellin'," Scratch replied. "It might peter out in six inches, or it might run hundreds of feet up in there."

"If it does, we'll be really rich," Sally said with a note of breathless excitement in her voice.

Bo said, "Chances are it'll wind up being somewhere between those two extremes. But for right now, we need to take the gold we've gotten out so far into the settlement to have it assayed. That'll tell us how much it's worth."

"It wouldn't hurt to pick up a few more supplies while we're there," Martha said.

"If any of the stores will sell to us," added Sally. "Mr. Lawson may have ordered them not to do business with us."

Beatrice snapped, "Amos Lawson doesn't own everything in Cushman. We just need to find someone willing to stand up to him. There have to be plenty of people in town who don't like the way he's tried to take over."

"More than likely," Bo said, nodding. "But when Lawson gets wind of the fact that you've found color, he's liable to be even madder than he was before."

"That's too bad. Perhaps what we'll do, if this claim pays off as well as it looks like it might, is start our own store."

That's actually not a bad idea, thought Bo. The ladies could hire men to work the claim while they stayed in the settlement. It would still be a rougher life than what any of them had come from, but not as rough as staying out here in the gulch.

But Amos Lawson would regard such a move as a direct challenge to his ambitions, and Bo had a hunch that could have only one outcome.

Lawson would declare war.

Sally drove the buckboard when they headed into Cushman the next morning, with Beatrice on the seat beside her and Caroline and Martha in the back while Bo and Scratch rode the saddle horses they had rented from Ed Lerch.

When they passed the claim belonging to Dave Clarke and Milt Emery, the two prospectors stopped working on the tunnel they were digging into the side of the gulch and came out to wave at them. The ladies returned the waves, and Clarke called, "Good luck on the assay!"

As Sally drove on, Beatrice said, "We don't need to worry about those two going up to our claim and stealing any ore, do we?"

"Dave and Milt?" Sally said. "They'd never do that."

"You only say that because Mr. Emery is smitten with you."

"You trust my judgment, don't you? Otherwise you wouldn't have asked me to come along on this expedition."

"Of course I trust you," Beatrice said.

"Well, then, believe me when I say those two men are honest," Sally said. "Not only will they not steal from us, I think there's a good chance they'll keep an eye on the claim while we're gone."

"For what it's worth," Bo said, "I reckon I agree with that."

"So do I," added Scratch.

Beatrice said, "Well, I'm certainly not going to argue with all of you." She smiled. "I'm glad Mr. Clarke and Mr. Emery have befriended us, to tell you the truth. We can use some allies up here. At times I've felt like we were surrounded by enemies."

"That's because you were," Scratch told her. "Luckily, we've been able to deal with 'em so far."

The little procession reached the settlement late in the morning. As they emerged from the gulch, crossed the stream, and started along the street, Bo saw people looking at them with interest. It had been a couple of weeks since the ladies were in Cushman, and now that they had returned, folks had to be wondering why—and what was going to happen next.

The assay office was next to one of the general stores, about halfway along the street on the right-hand side. As the Texans led the way toward it on horseback, a man stepped out from the open door of one of the other buildings and strode toward them, lifting a hand in a request for them to stop.

Bo and Scratch reined in as Sally brought the buckboard to a halt behind them. The man who had stopped them didn't look particularly threatening, but Bo and Scratch kept their right hands close to their guns anyway.

The man was tall and slender, clean-shaven, with a rumpled thatch of graying dark hair. He wore a canvas apron over a white shirt, black vest, and black trousers. He didn't have a tie around his neck. Ink stained the long fingers of the hand he lifted, which made it impossible not to recognize his profession.

"Hello!" He greeted them with enthusiasm. He smiled at Beatrice and went on. "Do I have the honor of addressing Mrs. O'Rourke?"

"You do, sir," she replied coolly. "But you have the advantage of me."

"I beg your pardon, ma'am. My name is George Sullivan." He gestured toward the log building from which he had emerged. A neatly painted sign attached to the wall next to the door read CUSHMAN CHRONICLE. "I've started a newspaper here in town."

"I didn't know there was a newspaper here."

"That's because I just published my first edition last week. I was already in Cushman when you arrived a few weeks ago, but I didn't have my press set up yet, so I didn't introduce myself. But now I can, because in the first issue of the *Chronicle*, you four ladies were the leading story! I still have some copies and will be happy to give one to each of you."

Beatrice frowned. "I don't know that we're worthy of so much attention from the press."

"Are you joking, ma'am?" asked George Sullivan. "Because I can assure you, four beautiful young women coming to Alaska to work a gold claim is definitely newsworthy!"

The newspaperman seems an excitable sort, as so many of them are, thought Bo. He said, "If you'll excuse us, Mr. Sullivan—"

"Oh, I know, I know, you must be in town on business, otherwise you'd be up the gulch at the claim. I just want to ask you, Mrs. O'Rourke . . . would you and your companions consent to an interview?"

"For the newspaper, you mean?"

"Exactly. You ladies are news, and the citizens of Cushman want to read about you."

Beatrice said, "I'd be willing to wager that not everyone feels that way, Mr. Sullivan. In fact, I think it's likely some of the people in this town wish we'd never even shown up."

The grin dropped off Sullivan's face as he said, "You mean Mr. Lawson." It wasn't a question. Nor did Sullivan look or sound pleased that the subject of Amos Lawson had come up.

"Lawson and the people he has influence over . . . which seems to be most of the population of Cushman."

"Actually, there may be fewer than you believe, ma'am," Sullivan said.

Bo wondered what he meant by that. Had the newspaperman already clashed with Lawson? That was sort of the way Sullivan's comment sounded. Some journalists fancied themselves crusaders, and their targets tended to be those in power.

There was no question that Amos Lawson wielded more power here in Cushman than anyone else.

"Be that as it may, Mr. Sullivan," Beatrice said in response to the man's statement, "I don't believe we'd be interested in being interviewed. I'm sorry."

"I'd like the opportunity to change your mind. Over dinner at the café, perhaps?"

That was another tendency of fellas who worked for newspapers, thought Bo. They were usually stubborn, if not downright pushy.

"No, thank you," Beatrice said. She lifted the reins and flicked them against the backs of the team. As the horses started forward, Sullivan had no choice but to step aside.

"I'll check with you later and see if you've changed your mind," he called to her as she drove past.

"Don't bother!"

Bo moved his mount alongside the buckboard's seat and said quietly to Beatrice, "I'm glad you didn't mention the ore we found. Probably best to keep that as quiet as we can for now."

"But the news will get out eventually, won't it?" asked Caroline. "I mean, we can't go into the assay office without being seen, and what other reason would we have for visiting the place?"

Scratch said, "You've got a good point, Miss Caroline, but Bo's still right. Let's play our cards close to the vest as long as we can."

Beatrice brought the buckboard to a halt in front of the assay office, which was housed in another log building. A sign on a post in front of it read BURTON PECK, ASSAYER AND CLERK.

Bo dismounted and helped Beatrice down from the seat. Scratch remained on his horse and said to the others, "Why don't we wait out here, ladies? The place is a mite small, and we'd likely feel crowded in there."

"I have a better idea, Mr. Morton," Caroline said. "We could go ahead and walk down to that store." She pointed along the street. "It's only a couple of doors away."

Scratch looked at Bo, who nodded.

"Keep an eye out for trouble, and don't hesitate to yell if you need help," Bo said.

Sally drove the buckboard on down the street toward the store with Scratch riding alongside. Bo cupped his left hand under Beatrice's right elbow as they stepped up onto the rough walk in front of the assayer's office. She had the canvas bag containing the chunks of ore in her hand.

They went inside and found a short, heavy-set man with curly dark hair sitting behind a table with several pieces of paper spread out before him. A couple of leather-bound ledgers lay on the desk as well. His fingers were stained, but by the chemicals he used in his job rather than ink, like George Sullivan's.

He glanced up at them, smiled, and began, "What can I do for—" before stopping short and looking at the visitors with greater interest. He stood up hastily and went on. "I beg your pardon, ma'am. I'm not accustomed to having ladies come in here. Or females of any sort, to be honest."

"That's all right, Mr. Peck," Beatrice assured him. "I assume you *are* Burton Peck, as the sign outside says?"

"At your service, ma'am. You'd be Mrs. O'Rourke?"

"That's right."

"I read about you and your friends in the first edition of our new newspaper. Cushman's a real town, I reckon, now that it's got a newspaper. How can I help you?"

Beatrice set the bag on the table. "I have some ore here I'd like to have assayed."

"Well, you've come to the right place."

Peck picked up the bag, opened the drawstring, and reached inside with stubby fingers to take out a couple of the small chunks of rock. He let them lie on his palm as he studied them. His eyes slowly widened.

"There appears to be gold laced through this quartz," he said. "And of fairly high quality."

Bo said, "Could be fool's gold, though."

"That's possible, but I don't believe it is. I've had con-siderable experience in assaying, in both California and

Nevada, before I came up here. We can certainly find out for sure in a matter of minutes."

He left the bag sitting on the desk but took the two samples over to another table on which sat glass jars and beakers. Bo had seen assays conducted before, so he knew what to expect as the man placed one of the samples in a beaker and poured a couple of different chemicals in it. He swirled them around, lifted the beaker, and intently watched the chemical reaction taking place inside it.

Beatrice watched, too, with an anxious expression. *She has a lot riding on this*, thought Bo. If the ore proved not to be gold, or was of such poor quality that it wouldn't be worth mining, she might have to reconsider her whole plan.

Of course, there were other tunnels on the claim. One of them might prove worthwhile even if the first one didn't. But Bo knew that Beatrice would find failure very discouraging.

After several long moments, Burton Peck set the beaker down on the table and turned to Bo and Beatrice.

"It's gold," he announced.

"Oh, thank heavens," Beatrice said as she let out the breath she had been holding in a relieved sigh.

"I can't say yet how much it will assay out per ton," Peck went on, "but my educated guess is that it's pretty high quality. Some of the best I've seen up here so far, in fact."

"That's wonderful news."

Peck held up a hand. "I don't want to be too encouraging just yet, Mrs. O'Rourke. I'll need to run some more tests before I can give you anything like a definitive answer. That will take a while. Why don't you leave this other sample and maybe one or two more with me, and I'll get busy on the job?"

"How long will it take?" asked Bo.

"Half an hour, perhaps an hour."

Bo nodded. "We'll be at the general store a couple of doors along the street. You can find us there if we don't check back with you first."

"Volney's Emporium. That's fine," Peck said. He smiled at Beatrice. "Congratulations, Mrs. O'Rourke. I feel confident in saying that much, although I'm not sure yet just how hearty those congratulations are going to be."

Chapter 33

Eli Byrne knocked on the door of Amos Lawson's office, and when Lawson answered with a curt, "What is it?" the young gun-wolf opened the door and looked in.

"Fella out here wants to see you, Mr. Lawson," Byrne said.

"I don't have time for some damn prospector who wants to mooch a grubstake off me," Lawson said without looking up from the glass of whiskey into which he had been staring.

"And *I* don't need to mooch a damn grubstake," the visitor said angrily as he shouldered Byrne aside.

Byrne stumbled, caught his balance, and started to reach for his gun. He stopped short as revolvers appeared as if by magic in the hands of the three men who had come into the Avalanche with the swarthy mustachioed gent who had just bumped Byrne out of the way.

All of them wore town suits and bowler hats, as did the man who seemed to be their leader. Byrne felt an instinctive hatred for them because they had gotten their guns out too quickly for him to make a draw.

But that is only because they took me by surprise, he told himself. In a straight-up fight, when he was ready to slap leather, he'd be faster than all of them, he didn't doubt that for a second.

Lawson pushed himself to his feet, rested his fists on the desk, and glared at the mustachioed man.

"Who the hell are you?" he demanded.

Instead of answering, the visitor growled a question of his own. "You're Amos Lawson?" Then, in a slightly less challenging tone, he added, "I'm told you're the man who runs things in this town."

That comment appeared to mollify Lawson a little. He drew in a deep breath that made his nostrils flare. He straightened from his aggressive stance and hooked his thumbs in his vest pockets.

"That's true," he said. "I'm Lawson, and if you're looking for the biggest man in town, you've found him."

"Rollin Kemp," the visitor introduced himself. "From Seattle."

Lawson's bushy brows drew down as his eyes narrowed.

"Kemp," he repeated. "I've spent some time in Seattle. I recall hearing the name. You run a saloon there, don't you?"

"Among other things." Kemp took a cigar from his pocket and clamped his teeth on it. Around it, he said, "I reckon I occupy the same position in Seattle that you do here. And Seattle is a hell of a lot bigger."

Lawson's face darkened at that veiled insult.

"What do you want, Kemp?" he asked. "I don't have a lot of time to waste on some puffed-up popinjay who comes swaggering in here."

For a few long seconds, the two men's gazes dueled. Then Kemp shrugged and said, "All right. This is your town. Maybe I came on a little too strong. But I'm a man who's accustomed to getting what he wants, when he wants it. Actually, that's why I'm here."

"There's something in Cushman you want?"

"Someone." Kemp's teeth clenched harder on the cigar. "A young woman named Caroline DeHerries."

Anger welled up inside Eli Byrne when he heard Caroline's name. The three toughs Kemp had brought with him had lowered their guns but still held the weapons at their sides. When Byrne sidled into the office through the still-open door, they didn't try to stop him, but he knew that if he made any sort of suspicious move, they would start shooting. They watched him closely as they followed him in.

Despite that, he couldn't stop himself from blurting, "What do you have to do with Miss DeHerries, mister?"

Kemp glanced back at him, then said to Lawson, "Tell this young whelp to stop yapping at me like a stray cur."

Gunmen or no gunmen, Byrne could only take so much. As his eyes widened in fury and his hand started toward his gun, Lawson said, "Eli! Stop it right now, you fool. What are you doing in here? I didn't ask you to join us. Get out!"

"But, boss, this fella's talkin' about Miss Caroline—"

"Whatever business brings Mr. Kemp to Cushman is with me, not you." Lawson nodded toward the door. "Go tell Walter to give you a drink." He added, "And take those three with you."

"Kind of free in ordering around my men, aren't you?" said Kemp.

"I get the feeling you and I are a lot alike, Kemp. I think we can deal with each other straight on, man to man, without a lot of flunkeys crowding us."

Kemp thought about it for a moment, then shrugged and nodded. He turned to his men and said, "Get yourselves a drink, boys."

"Are you sure about that, boss?" one of them asked.

"You're not in the habit of questioning my decisions, Dex," Kemp snapped. "Don't start now."

"Sure, sure," the man called Dex murmured. He replaced the Colt in the cross-draw holster at his waist.

Kemp added, "Oh, and take one of those men we picked up in St. Michael with you to get some tobacco and ammunition. That fellow Dunston claims to know his way around up here. That's why we brought him with us. He might as well be useful."

Dex nodded, then crooked a finger at Byrne. "You too, cowboy. We'll leave our bosses alone to talk."

With a sullen glare on his face, Byrne followed the three men out of the office. At Lawson's barked order, he closed the door behind him.

A large sign that read VOLNEY'S GENERAL STORE AND EMPORIUM was nailed on the wall above the entrance to the building down the street from the assay office. Scratch looped his horse's reins around a hitchrack made of peeled pine poles and stepped up onto the walk just as Caroline, Martha, and Sally got there. He would have helped them down from the buckboard, but they had already disembarked from the vehicle on their own.

The general store was a dim, sprawling, low-ceilinged place that reminded Scratch a little of a bear's cave. Barrels, crates, and crude shelves crammed with goods crowded in from all sides. Work boots, canvas overalls, and flannel shirts shared space with frying pans, Dutch ovens, and tin cups. Shovels and pickaxes rested on nails that served as pegs in the log walls. A long counter in the rear ran the width of the building. The store smelled of sawdust, grease, coffee, tobacco, spices, whiskey, coal oil, and unwashed human flesh. Half a dozen roughly dressed men stood at the counter. They all turned to stare in unconcealed amazement at the women who had just come in.

Scratch was confident that even dressed in their work clothes, the ladies were the most attractive visitors the store had ever welcomed. The rapt gazes of the customers were more proof of that hunch, not that he needed it.

A man behind the counter hurried around the end of it. He wore a canvas apron over a big gut and had a pleasantly ugly face. A few strands of dark hair were plastered over a mostly bald head. In a deep, raspy voice, he said, "Howdy, ladies. Welcome to Volney's. I'm Ham Volney. I own the place."

"Hello, Mr. Volney." Martha returned the greeting, then looked around. "My, you have a . . . a nice store."

That compliment was obviously a little forced, but it drew a chuckle from Volney. "Nice ain't exactly the word for it, ma'am, but my customers don't really care about fancy. They just want a place to buy supplies and prospectin' equipment and clothes to replace the ones that get wore out workin' all day. And what can I do for you?"

Before any of the ladies could answer, Volney frowned slightly, cocked his head to the side, and added, "Say, I thought there was supposed to be four of you. That's what it said in the paper."

"There are four of 'em," Scratch said. "The other lady is handlin' some business up the street."

Ham Volney's bushy eyebrows climbed his forehead. "At the assay office?" he guessed. He leaned forward, almost quivering with excitement. "You found color up there on the O'Rourke claim?"

The customers instantly crowded behind him, keen interest on their bearded, grimy faces.

"We just came to pick up some supplies," Scratch said, a little sharper than his usual mild-mannered fashion, "not to gossip. That all right with you?"

Volney waved a hand with sausage-like fingers and said, "Sure, sure. Can't blame a fella for askin' questions. I mean, gold is the whole reason for this settlement's existence. Cushman wouldn't be here without it." The storekeeper paused, then went on. "Say, you're one of those Texans who came up here with the ladies, ain't you?"

"That's right."

"Some of the boys who came up on the *Byron Mowery* with you claim that you fellas are ring-tailed roarers when it comes to a fight."

"We don't ever go lookin' for trouble," said Scratch. "But we don't shy away from it when it finds us, neither."

The store's front door opened again. Volney glanced past Scratch and the ladies, then looked again. He frowned and said, "That's good, I reckon, because it may be about to find you, sure enough."

Scratch didn't like the sound of that. He turned to see who had just entered the store, easing around as he did so that he was between the ladies and the newcomers.

Two men had just stepped through the entrance. They came to an abrupt halt as they spotted Scratch and the three women standing in front of the counter.

Scratch was just as surprised to see them as they were

to see Scratch. The tall, lean, rusty-bearded hombre was Grady Dunston, who had fallen in the Yukon River after Bo shot him back in St. Michael, when Dunston and his friends tried to burn the riverboat. All too obviously, he hadn't died after all.

The man with Dunston was an even bigger surprise. The last time Scratch had seen him was back on Seattle's Skid Road, standing behind the bar at the Timber Treasure Saloon. It took a second for Scratch to come up with his name—Dex.

He was Rollin Kemp's right-hand man, and as Scratch's jaw tightened, he wondered if Dex's presence meant that Kemp was here in Cushman, too.

Dex smiled and started forward again. He'd had his arm in a sling back in Seattle, which had led Bo to suspect Dex was the would-be robber he had winged when the gang of outlaws tried to hold up the train. Dex must have recovered enough by now that he didn't need the sling anymore.

Dunston had been wounded, too, and the way he moved gingerly along the aisle next to Dex told Scratch that the injury might not have healed completely. Dunston was spry enough to be dangerous, though, and judging by the murderous scowl on his face, he might be in the mood for that.

Dex put an insincere smile on his lean face and said, "Morton, isn't it? Didn't expect to see you here. We figured you and Creel would have gone back downriver after you delivered the ladies to their bridegrooms. That was the deal, wasn't it?"

"Plans change," Scratch said curtly. "What do you want, Dex? And since when did you start travelin' in the company of skunks?"

Dunston's mouth twisted in a snarl under the rusty beard. He took another step and said, "Why, you old son of a—"

Dex put a hand on his arm and stopped him. "We didn't come in here hunting for trouble, remember? We're after cartridges and tobacco."

Ham Volney said hurriedly, "I can sure fix you up with those two things, gents." He motioned for the men to follow him. "Come on back here to the counter, and I'll fix you right up."

Scratch and the ladies moved aside to let Dex and Dunston step up to the counter. Caroline said in a low voice, "I think we should come back later."

That'll look like we're running away, Scratch mused, and that idea stuck in his craw. But he had more to worry about here than his own pride. The ladies' safety came first.

"Yeah, that's probably a good idea," he said.

He ushered the ladies toward the front of the store, but as he was about to follow them, his curiosity got the better of him. He paused and said to Dex, "Is Kemp here in Cushman, too?"

"I reckon you'll find out soon enough," Dex replied with a smile.

Scratch didn't like the sound of that. Didn't like it at all.

Chapter 34

Inside Amos Lawson's office, Lawson walked over to a sideboard, where several bottles of whiskey sat along with some glasses, and asked his visitor, "Care for a drink?"

"You have anything there worth drinking?" asked Rollin Kemp.

Lawson let the arrogance of that question go by. It would be easy to fight with Kemp, but he wanted to find out what the man wanted—and if there was any way he could make use of him.

Chances were, Lawson thought wryly, Kemp was thinking the same thing right now. . . .

Without answering Kemp's question, Lawson picked up one of the bottles, pulled the cork, and splashed amber liquid into a couple of glasses. He carried them over to Kemp and handed one to the man.

"Try that," he said. "And you can light that cigar if you want to. I don't object."

"I like to chew on 'em. Helps me think."

"Suit yourself." Lawson sipped the whiskey in his glass.

As if he'd been waiting for Lawson to do that, as proof

that the liquor wasn't doped, Kemp took the cigar out of his mouth, lifted the glass, and downed a healthy swallow of whiskey. He stood there in reflection for a moment, then inclined his head as if acknowledging a point Lawson had made.

"It's not bad," he said. "Not as good as my private stock at the Timber Treasure, of course, but not bad."

"We're a long way from anywhere up here," Lawson said. "We have to make do with what we can get."

"Except when it comes to women. At least in one particular case. You have one woman here who would be the finest in any settlement, big or small."

Lawson cocked an eyebrow and said, "You're talking about Caroline DeHerries."

"I am, indeed," Kemp admitted.

Well, that's interesting, mused Lawson. Despite his gruff, hard-boiled facade, Rollin Kemp sounded a little like a man who was lovesick. Was that possible? Could a woman—the *right* woman—sneak up on even a man such as Kemp and pierce his defenses?

"I've met Miss DeHerries," Lawson said. "She's quite beautiful. So are the other ladies who journeyed to Cushman with her."

Kemp waved the hand that held the cigar. "I suppose so, but Caroline's the one who interests me. They came up here to marry some men who sent for them as mail-order brides." His voice sharpened. "Has that happened already? Does she have a husband now?"

Lawson looked at him in silence for a moment, then couldn't hold back a laugh.

Kemp's face flushed again. "I don't see how that question is amusing," he snapped.

"You don't know, do you?" said Lawson. "You really don't know."

"Know what?"

Lawson threw back the rest of the whiskey in his glass and thumped the empty glass down on the desk.

"Those women never intended to get married," he told Kemp, not bothering to keep the disgust and anger out of his tone. "It was all a lie."

Kemp leaned back a little, as if someone had just slapped him across the face.

"The hell you say! How do you know that, Lawson?"

"Because I'm the one who paid for them to come up here. Mrs. O'Rourke was supposed to marry *me*, and the other women were intended to be brides for three of my men." Lawson laughed coldly. "That young gunman who let you in here, Eli Byrne, was Caroline DeHerries's betrothed."

Kemp struggled to get the surprise off his face. He grimaced, drank the rest of his drink, and set the empty glass next to Lawson's. After rubbing his jaw for a moment, he said, "What in blazes happened?"

"When they arrived, that O'Rourke witch told us to go to hell. She and her friends didn't come up here to get married. They came to work a gold claim she inherited from her husband, damn his Canadian soul."

Kemp shook his head and said, "This is one hell of a note. And one hell of an audacious scheme by the O'Rourke woman. Thinking back to the run-ins I had with her in Seattle, though, I reckon I'm not really that surprised. I knew then she was stubborn and smart." He chuckled. "So she tricked you into footing the bill for their trip up here."

"It was fraud, that's what she did, promising they'd marry us when they had no intention of doing so."

Lawson didn't say anything about his own intentions, which had been to get his hands on Daniel O'Rourke's claim by marrying the man's widow. Nor did he mention his own involvement in *making* Beatrice O'Rourke a widow . . .

"All right, when you get down to it," Kemp said, "what's important to me is that Caroline DeHerries isn't married. That means I can take her back to Seattle with me and make her my wife."

"You came all this way just for that? For a woman?"

Kemp's lips tightened to a thin line under the mustache. "Like I said, I'm a man who's accustomed to getting what he wants."

"So am I." Lawson stroked his chin as the wheels of his brain turned rapidly. "Maybe the two of us could do each other some good."

"The same thought occurred to me," said Kemp. He paused for a second, then went on. "This gold claim you mentioned . . . is it valuable?"

"I don't know. I have a hunch it is. I know I'd like to find out."

"If those lying, troublesome women were gone . . . if someone took them back to Seattle, let's say . . . you'd likely have a free hand at it, wouldn't you?"

Lawson cocked his head to the side and shrugged.

"Normally, I'd say that men don't work *with* me," Kemp went on. "They work *for* me. This might be one of those rare occasions when a partnership of sorts would benefit us both."

"Cushman is my town," Lawson snapped. He didn't

want to admit it, but he knew a significant percentage of the citizens resented his dominance and would defy him if they thought they could get away with it. "I don't need any help running things from a bunch of Seattle sharpers."

"I brought half a dozen good men with me," Kemp continued, as if he hadn't heard Lawson. "Make sure I have a free hand with those women, and I think I can solve both of our problems."

"Do you intend to cause any trouble here in town?"

Kemp shook his head.

"Then I can't very well object to anything you do anywhere else, can I?" Lawson summoned up a smile. "Alaska's a big place. I can't be expected to know and control everything that's going on."

Kemp put the cigar back in his mouth and said, "You certainly can't." He thought for a second. "You said that fellow Byrne was betrothed to Caroline DeHerries. He struck me as a hothead—and a man who doesn't want to give her up."

"You let me worry about Eli Byrne. He won't cause you any trouble. I give you my word on that."

Byrne's a good man, thought Lawson. But if it came down to a choice between him and that gold claim . . . well, that wasn't much of a choice.

"I'd say we have a deal," Kemp declared as he stuck out his hand.

Lawson clasped that hand and said, "We do."

He didn't hesitate to agree, because he knew that if he needed to later on, he could always double-cross Rollin Kemp and kill him.

Of course, Kemp was probably thinking the same thing about *him* right now. . . .

* * *

Normally, Beatrice was the calm, unflappable type, although she had moments when her emotions got the better of her, such as the night she had wound up clinging to Bo in the Occidental Hotel, despite wearing only her nightdress at the time.

But excitement definitely gripped her today as she walked along Cushman's single street with Bo, heading from the assay office to the general store where they were supposed to meet Scratch and the other ladies.

"I knew it," she was saying. "I just knew there was gold on that claim."

Bo chuckled and told her, "I might have put a little less stock in that hunch of yours if I hadn't heard the blasted stuff calling out to me, too, while Scratch and I were working in that tunnel. You can ask him. I put my hand on the rock and *heard* it."

"I don't doubt it. All the Irish are touched by the spirits. Daniel, you, me . . . My maiden name was Monaghan, you know."

"No, I don't reckon I ever heard your maiden name until now. But maybe we'd better not talk too much about spirits and things like that. We wouldn't want folks to start thinking we're touched in the head."

Beatrice laughed. "If you believe I give two figs what people think about me, Bo Creel, it just shows that you don't know me very well after all."

"Well, that could be. Here's the store."

Bo had already seen the buckboard and Scratch's horse

in front of the building. He opened the door and held it for Beatrice to go inside ahead of him.

When she stopped short just past the threshold, he almost bumped into her, hauling himself to a halt at the last second. She stood there stiff-backed as two men ambled toward them from the rear of the store.

Bo looked over Beatrice's shoulder and recognized both men instantly. He remembered Grady Dunston's name right away, and after a couple of seconds he recalled that the other man was known as Dex. It had been more than a month since Bo had seen him back in Seattle, behind the bar of the Timber Treasure Saloon.

Did Dex's presence mean that Rollin Kemp was in Cushman, too? And what in blazes was he doing with Dunston?

For that matter, thought Bo, why wasn't Dunston dead? He knew good and well he had shot Dunston back downriver in St. Michael, during the battle on the *Byron Mowery.*

He had worried a little when nobody fished Dunston's body out of the Yukon River. It looked like maybe he had been right to be concerned.

A mocking smile spread across Dex's face. He said, "Hello, Creel. I don't reckon you expected to see me again so soon."

"It would have been all right with me if I never saw you again," Bo said.

Dunston's lips pulled back in a snarl as his hand crept toward the lapel of his jacket.

"You keep reaching like that, and my friend's going to

put a bullet in the back of your head, Dunston," Bo warned him.

Dunston froze at the sound of Scratch cocking the Remington he held. Dex cocked an eyebrow and said, "You'd shoot a man from behind, Creel?"

"Bo won't have to shoot anybody," drawled Scratch. "I'll take care of that. And I never lost a minute's sleep over shootin' some skunk, no matter what direction it was from."

"Take it easy, both of you." Dex had a paper-wrapped bundle under his left arm. He nodded toward it and went on. "We just came in to pick up a few things. No need to get proddy."

"Tell that to your friend," Bo said. "He was the one about to reach for a gun."

"Come on, Dunston." Dex smiled and touched the fingers of his right hand to his hat brim. "If you'll excuse us, ma'am . . ."

Bo and Beatrice moved aside so the two men could go past them and out the door. He kept a close eye on them the whole time as they turned and headed up the street. Dunston threw one last murderous glare over his shoulder.

"What in the world were those awful men doing here?" asked Beatrice.

"It's even worse than that," said Scratch as he came toward them, pouching the iron he had pulled when the two men confronted Bo and Beatrice. "They ain't alone."

"Kemp is here?" Bo asked.

"Yeah. Evidently another riverboat has started makin' runs up the Yukon, and Kemp, Dex, and some other fellas were on it, along with Dunston and a couple of *his* friends from the bunch that gave us trouble in St. Michael."

"They're working together now?"

Caroline walked up to them and said, "That man Dex was very smug about it, but from what they said, I gather Dunston found out somehow while Mr. Kemp was in St. Michael that he was looking for us, and he insinuated himself and the others into Mr. Kemp's group."

"That means they've got eight or ten fellas on their side," Scratch said. "We're outnumbered, Bo."

"Not by that much," Beatrice said. "There are six of us."

Bo shook his head and said, "No offense, Miss Beatrice, but none of you ladies are exactly the gunslinging type."

"I'll bet we could learn," Sally said. "We have rifles and pistols. Maybe we should start practicing."

"That ain't a bad idea," Scratch said.

Beatrice looked back and forth between the Texans and said, "It's not your responsibility to protect us, you know. That officially ended when you delivered us here to Cushman."

"Maybe as far as Cyrus Keegan's agency is concerned, it did," Bo said. "But we've thrown in with you now, so you're stuck with us."

"I can't say that I'm unhappy about that," Beatrice responded quietly as she touched Bo's arm for a second.

Scratch said, "We'd best pick up some extra ammunition while we're here if we're givin' you ladies shootin' lessons." He turned to address the storekeeper. "Mr. Volney, you have plenty of .45 rounds in this emporium of yours?"

"Yes, sir, I do," said Volney. "And I'd be plumb happy to sell some of them to you."

"There are fellas in these parts who might not be happy about that."

"If you're talkin' about Amos Lawson and his cronies, I can't say as I care whether they're happy or not," Volney replied in his rumbling voice.

Bo said, "You ladies go ahead and look around, pick up whatever you need."

"Oh!" Caroline exclaimed. "I just remembered. You didn't tell us how it went at the assay office."

Beatrice smiled and said, "We should be able to afford whatever supplies we need."

The women smiled. Caroline clapped her hands together in excitement.

"It's good news?" she asked.

"Good news," Beatrice said. "Possibly very good news."

The ladies clustered together, talking animatedly, while Bo and Scratch stood back and watched. Quietly, Scratch said, "I reckon that ore must've had good color in it."

"It did. The assayer said it was some of the best he'd seen around here."

"I ain't a bit surprised. I could tell it was high grade just by lookin' at it." Scratch raked a thumbnail along his jawline. "When word of the strike gets around—and it won't take long—that'll draw some attention."

"That it will," Bo agreed.

"Which means things are about to get more compli-cated . . . and dangerous."

"More than likely."

"There's something else that occurred to me . . ."

When Scratch hesitated, Bo told him, "Just spit it out. You've never had any problem talking plain."

"Now that Kemp and some of his bully boys are here

in Cushman, what's to stop them from throwin' in with Lawson? I mean, Lawson's got a grudge against us, too. Seems like a natural partnership."

"Yeah, I thought of that," Bo admitted. "And I don't like the idea one bit."

"We're liable to need that extra ammunition for more than target practice."

"Could be," Bo said.

Chapter 35

Dave Clarke and Milt Emery were waiting for them when they came back up the gulch late that afternoon.

Sally pulled back on the reins and brought the buckboard team to a halt as the two prospectors approached them. Clarke lifted a knobby-knuckled hand in greeting and said, "Have any luck in town?"

On the way up here, Bo and Scratch had discussed with the ladies what they ought to say in response to the inevitable questions. They knew that news of what they had found was going to get around Cushman, anyway; that was inevitable. Clarke and Emery had been friendly and helpful so far and seemed trustworthy, so keeping the discovery a secret from them didn't strike the Texans as being necessary.

Sally spoke up. "We found gold," she replied with excitement in her voice. "The man at the assay office says it's good ore!"

"Say, that's mighty fine news!" Emery exclaimed. "I'm happy for you, Sally."

"So am I," Clarke said as he stepped up to the side of

the buckboard where Martha sat. He almost sounded disappointed as he added, "I reckon now that you're rich, you'll be heading back home, Miss Martha."

"Oh, we're far from rich," she told him. "It was just a little handful of rocks."

"If it assays out to be high-grade ore, though, you'll have plenty of money before you know it."

"Not necessarily," Beatrice said. "Bo and Scratch just uncovered the vein with that explosion. We have no idea how far it's going to run."

Emery said, "We'll hope it's nice and deep. Although we'll miss havin' you ladies for neighbors, that's for sure."

"Actually," Bo said, "we were wondering if you fellas might be interested in working the claim with us. Scratch and I could use the help."

That had been Sally's idea, and Bo knew it was prompted partially by her growing friendship with Milt Emery. But if the vein ran very deep, there actually would be plenty of work for four men at the Golden Cup, so he and Scratch had been fine with the suggestion. Beatrice didn't mind, either.

Clarke and Emery hesitated in answering. Beatrice said, "We wouldn't expect you to work for wages, gentlemen. Would a five percent share in whatever we take out of there be a suitable arrangement?"

"Five percent to split between us?" asked Clarke.

"Each." Beatrice smiled.

Scratch said, "Unless you boys are makin' a heap more than that from this claim."

Emery waved a hand and said, "From this worthless piece of ground? We're barely makin' enough to eat!"

"Some weeks we don't make that much," Clarke added solemnly.

"Then come and work with us," Martha urged.

The men looked as if they were about to accept the offer, but before they could commit to that, Bo said, "You need to remember one thing, though: Amos Lawson's not happy about the ladies working this claim."

Emery let out a contemptuous snort. "We don't give a da—I mean, a darn what Amos Lawson thinks. He may believe he's the boss of everybody in these parts, but that ain't true."

"Not by a long shot," added Clarke.

"I'm glad to hear you fellas say that," Scratch said with a nod. "Lawson may not be the only one you'd have to worry about, though."

"What Scratch means," Beatrice said, "is that another old enemy of ours has shown up in Cushman. There's a chance he may join forces with Mr. Lawson, but together or separately, they're threats either way."

Emery chuckled and said, "Too late, ma'am. You're not gonna scare us off now. We're gonna accept your generous offer, aren't we, Dave?"

"We sure are," Clarke said. He smiled at Martha, who flashed him a smile in return and then looked down shyly like a girl half her age.

"You might as well bring your tent over and pitch it at the Golden Cup," Bo told the prospectors.

"And have supper with us tonight," Sally added. "I'll have a nice pot of stew and some biscuits cooking by the time you get there."

"That sounds mighty fine to me." Emery took his hat off, and so did Clarke. They stood there rather awkwardly as Emery went on, "We're much obliged to you ladies for your kindness. We'll do our best to earn it."

"I reckon there's a good chance you will," Bo said.

He just hoped they wouldn't earn it by getting shot at . . . but with what he knew about Rollin Kemp and Amos Lawson, the odds of that were slim.

A lot of hard work went on for the next few days, and all eight people at the Golden Cup turned in at night weary but satisfied with the knowledge that they had done a good job that day. With Bo, Scratch, Clarke, and Emery doing the digging and the ladies hauling out the ore and going through it, they made significant progress in uncovering more of the gold vein.

It varied in width from two to four inches, and so far was six inches deep. It might run for hundreds of feet into the side of the gulch, in which case this would be a real bonanza. But it might peter out at any time, and the men were experienced enough to know that.

The women were all giddy with optimism, even the normally reserved Beatrice and Martha. Bo had to admit that, so far, he hadn't seen any reason for them *not* to be optimistic.

They didn't work all the time. As Sally had suggested, the ladies practiced shooting, burning enough powder that the echoes of the shots rolled up and down Ten Mile Gulch.

Even if they never got very good at it, Bo considered the practice time well spent. Every prospector for miles around knew now that those ladies were working on their gun-handling skills, and that might make any would-be thieves or claim-jumpers think twice before skulking around.

"You're good teachers," Beatrice complimented the Texans one day after an hour's practice with the extra rifles.

"On the job before this one, down in New Mexico Territory, we taught those ladies how to shoot," Scratch explained. "Or tried to, anyway. Some of 'em never did pick it up very well. But a couple of 'em got pretty good at it."

"How are we doing?" Caroline asked.

Bo said, "You're doing fine. You're getting familiar with the guns, and you have decent aim. The thing is, you can get good at shooting one rock off another rock, but that's not the same as having to defend yourself in case of trouble."

"Shooting at other people, you mean," Beatrice said.

"That's what it comes down to," Bo said. "And unfortunately, you'll never know for sure what you'll do in that situation unless you're faced with it." He shrugged. "With any luck, you never will be."

"You forget," Beatrice said coolly, "I wounded that man in the hotel, back in Seattle."

"That's true." *She had done more than wound him*, thought Bo. She had killed him. But she didn't know that. "You kept a cool head that night and did just fine. I expect all you ladies will, if it ever comes to that." He changed the subject by adding, "Right now, I reckon Scratch and I had better get back to work."

In the evenings, they sat around the campfire and enjoyed the meals that Sally and Martha cooked. Not surprisingly, Clarke and Emery praised the grub every night. They helped the ladies clean up afterward, too.

Just because they hadn't run into any trouble up here so

far didn't mean that would remain the case. Bo and Scratch were in the habit of taking turns standing guard, and after a couple of nights, the two prospectors came to them and volunteered to take shifts, too. That would make things easier, and Bo's instincts told him it would be safe to trust them.

"I don't know what sorts of trouble you fellas may have been mixed up in before you came up here," Bo told them, "but Kemp's men are hard cases, and Dunston and his friends are vicious. Plus that young hombre Eli Byrne is a gunfighter, or at least fancies himself one."

"He's fast, all right," Clarke said. "He's killed at least a couple of men who tried to draw on him."

Bo nodded. "All right. You know what we may be up against."

"What Bo's sayin'," Scratch put in, "is that if you have to pull the trigger . . . shoot to kill."

"You can count on us," Emery said. He glanced toward the campfire, where the four women were still sitting after supper. "We won't let anything happen to those ladies."

"Try not to get any holes shot in your own hides while you're at it," Scratch said. "Bo and me don't want to have to finish diggin' that gold by ourselves."

The next night, well after midnight, four men approached the claim on foot. The liveryman back in Cushman had insisted that he didn't have any horses to rent to them, so they'd had to make the long walk up Ten Mile Gulch. Grady Dunston wasn't sure he believed the liveryman, but he could settle that one-eyed old pelican's hash later, after they were finished with the job that had brought them up here.

Dark gray clouds had moved in during the late afternoon, with the promise of possible rain later on, so the gloom was thicker than usual. There had been no midnight sun tonight. It was still brighter than a normal night in more southern latitudes, but it was as good for sneaking around as Alaska got this time of year.

"How much farther is it?" asked Jethro Anderson, one of the men Kemp had brought with him from Seattle. Anderson's chest heaved as breath rasped in his throat. He was a saloon tough, unaccustomed to tramping through the wilderness in the dark.

"We're almost there," Dunston whispered. "The boys and I prospected in this gulch when we were up here before, so we know our way around."

To tell the truth, they hadn't really spent all that much time prospecting. Swinging a pick all day was damned hard work. When fortune hadn't fallen into their laps right away with a minimum of effort, they had given up pretty quickly. Even so, Dunston and his friends knew this gulch a lot better than any city boy did.

"They'll probably have a sentry posted," Dunston went on. "Lije, you go on ahead and cut the varmint's throat."

Lije, a lean, dark-faced Cajun from the swamps of Louisiana—far, far from Alaska—nodded.

"Once the way is clear, yell like a loon. That'll be the signal for the rest of us to charge in there and start shootin'. But remember, nobody shoots toward that cabin, because that's where the women are. We'll pour bullets into those tents, though, and that ought to take care of the three men who'll be in there."

For the past couple of days, Lije had been spying on the Golden Cup, and he had brought back the information about the sleeping arrangements. Dunston had asked—practically begged—Rollin Kemp for the chance to avenge himself on Creel and Morton. Kemp had agreed, but he'd insisted on sending Anderson along so he'd have a man on hand to take part in the killing. Kemp puredee hated those Texans.

But not as much as Grady Dunston did.

Dunston drew the gun from behind his belt and gripped it tightly as he said to Lije, "Go ahead. We'll be waitin' for your signal."

The Cajun drifted off silently into the shadows. Dunston licked his lips as he stood there waiting with the other two men. He was ready for the killing to start.

And after that . . . well, the blond beauty he'd had his eye on was promised to Kemp, and Dunston couldn't very well go against the man. Kemp had too much money and too many men backing him up, including the fellas working for Amos Lawson, who had thrown in with him.

But there were three other women, and they were all mighty easy on the eyes, too.

Dunston supposed he'd just have to make do with one of them.

Chapter 36

Bo leaned his shoulder against the trunk of one of the scrubby pines growing near the gap between the two bluffs that formed the entrance to the Golden Cup.

He was standing the second guard shift tonight. Milt Emery had started off the watch, Dave Clarke would have the next turn, and then Scratch would finish up—and poke the fire back to life and get the coffee on to brew.

Bo rolled his shoulders to ease the weariness in them. Although he'd slept for a couple of hours, he was still tired. At his age, it took a lot of rest for him to recover fully from a day of hard work. Mostly he just stayed tired and achy. By now that seemed like his normal state. It never stopped him from doing what needed to be done.

The thick overcast made it almost feel like night, although some gray light lingered in the sky. Bo's gaze roved constantly over the opening between the bluffs, as well as the rugged outcroppings themselves. It was always possible that somebody might try to bushwhack them from one of the rims again, although the bad light would make accuracy difficult right now.

Somebody might try climbing down one of those rough

walls, too, but they would have to be young and spry to do that. Of course, that description fit Eli Byrne and no telling how many other men who worked for Amos Lawson.

Bo heard footsteps approaching and turned his head to see a dim shape coming toward him from the direction of the tents. That would be Dave Clarke relieving him on guard duty. Bo still leaned against the tree, but he began to straighten as Clarke approached.

Clarke was about twenty feet away. Bo could make him out fairly well now. The prospector lifted a hand in greeting, but as he did, something moved behind him. Another shape leaped forward, and Clarke was jerked to an abrupt stop as somebody grabbed him from behind, looping an arm around his neck.

The attacker's other arm lifted high above his head. Bo caught a glimpse of a knife clutched in the man's hand. In a swift move, he brought his Winchester to his shoulder. Shooting in this bad light was tricky, all right, but Bo had no choice—and not much of a target at which to aim, either.

He squeezed the trigger. The rifle's crack split the night air.

The attacker's arm jerked wildly as the bullet struck it. He cried out in pain. The knife flew out of his hand as he lost his grip on it.

Getting shot made the man lose his grip on Clarke, too. The prospector tore loose and whirled around. He slammed a fist into the jaw of the man who'd jumped him. The intruder went down hard.

Bo ran a few steps toward them, then stopped short. Thoughts raced through his brain like bolts of lightning.

The way he had been standing under the tree and leaning against the trunk, it was possible that the man who had attacked Clarke hadn't ever seen him until it was too late. The man might have believed he was disposing of the only guard when he tried to knife Clarke.

Bo didn't think a lone man would try to attack a camp with four armed men in it by himself. That meant the hombre he'd just wounded probably had others with him, and there was a good chance that shot would goad them into action . . .

All that flashed through his mind in a split second. He acted instantly, whirling back toward the gap—just in time to see a flurry of muzzle flashes and feel the hot breath of a slug as it whipped past his cheek.

A moment earlier, crouched just outside the gap, Grady Dunston had heard the shot and knew something had gone wrong. If Lije had disposed of the guard, he would have done it silently.

So they wouldn't take Creel, Morton, and those other two by surprise after all. They could still strike hard and fast enough to slaughter the men and grab the women.

"Come on!" Dunston called to his companions as his hands tightened on the rifle he held. "And go in shootin'!"

Bo dropped to one knee with the Winchester against his shoulder and fired three times as fast as he could work the repeater's lever. He tracked the barrel from left to right as he shot, spraying lead across the gap.

More tongues of orange flame licked out in the gloom

as the raiders charged. Another rifle cracked behind Bo and to his right. Dave Clarke was getting in on the fight. They met the assault with stiff resistance.

Between booming echoes, Bo heard a man cry out. A gun fired toward the sky. That told Bo the man who had pulled the trigger had done so while he was falling backward, probably driven off his feet by a bullet.

"Damn it!" a harsh voice yelled. "Let's get out of here!"

Bo caught a glimpse of a couple of darting shapes as they raced back through the gap. He threw a couple of slugs after them to hurry them on their way.

Clarke ran up beside him and asked, "Should we go after them?"

"They probably have horses tied up somewhere close by," Bo said. "Even if they don't, they can hunker down out there and pick us off if we take a step outside the claim."

"So we just let them go?" Clarke didn't sound happy about that.

"We downed two out of the four. Maybe they'll tell us who was behind this."

Clarke snorted disgustedly and said, "I reckon we know that already. Has to be Amos Lawson or that fella Kemp."

"Having proof of that might allow us to raise enough support to run them out of these parts."

"Or enough men backing our play to wipe them out."

"That sounds like something Scratch would suggest," said Bo. "And it may come to that. Right now, though, why don't you go back to the tents and the cabin and make sure nobody was hurt by all that lead flying around. I can keep an eye on the gap, just in case those two varmints try to double back."

"What about the fella you shot and I knocked out?"

Before Bo could answer that question, he heard footsteps hurrying toward them and Scratch called, "Bo! Bo, are you all right?"

"Over here by the trees," Bo replied. "Yeah, we're fine."

Scratch and Milt Emery ran up to them, having hastily crammed their feet in boots when they rolled out of their blankets. Emery had a rifle in his hands, and Scratch toted both Remingtons.

"Dead man back yonder," Scratch reported.

Bo jerked his head around. "Dead? I winged him in the arm."

"Maybe so, but there was a big pool of blood around him. I reckon your bullet must've glanced off a bone, gone up his arm, and nicked a vein so all the red stuff leaked out of him."

"Blast it!" Clarke said. "If I hadn't knocked him out, he might not have bled to death."

"Don't lose any sleep over it," Bo told him. "He was about to plant a knife in you. That's why I shot him." In a few words, he explained to Scratch and Emery what had happened, then continued, "Dave, Milt, go check on the ladies. Scratch and I will check out the other fella who got hit."

Bo could see the body sprawled about thirty yards away. The man hadn't moved since Bo's shot knocked him off his feet.

Clarke and Emery headed back to the cabin while the Texans advanced cautiously on the motionless shape. Bo held his rifle at the ready. Scratch kept one Remington pointed at the fallen man and the other aimed toward the gap. He said, "You take a good look at the varmint, Bo. I'll keep an eye out in case any more show up."

By the time they reached the man, Bo had a hunch he was dead. It didn't take much to confirm that. The front of the man's shirt was black with the blood that had flooded from a bullet-ripped throat.

Bo knelt, snapped a lucifer to life, and studied the man's face in its glare. The coarse, beard-stubbled features were vaguely familiar.

"I think this is one of the men who was with Dunston at St. Michael. A couple of them survived that shoot-out, as I recall."

"You know, I thought that other one looked familiar, too," Scratch said. "Could be that's where I was rememberin' him from. Neither one of 'em was Dunston, though."

"No," Bo agreed. "If he was here tonight, he got away."

"Which means he's liable to keep on givin' us trouble."

"Unfortunately, yes."

For the time being, they left both corpses where they were and went back to the cabin. Dave Clarke and Milt Emery were waiting for them just outside the door.

"The ladies are all fine," Emery reported before they could ask him. "A couple of the bullets hit the cabin but didn't go through the wall. Those logs are too thick for that."

"That's why we built it that way," Scratch said.

The door opened and Beatrice stepped out in a quilted robe. Lantern light inside the cabin revealed the other three women looking out anxiously.

"Are you and Scratch all right, Bo?" asked Beatrice.

"We're both fine," he assured her. "Milt told us that you ladies are, too."

"Who was that? Lawson's men? Kemp's?"

"The two who got left behind were friends of Grady Dunston's, part of the bunch that gave us trouble at St. Michael."

"Left behind?" Beatrice repeated with a frown. "Where? Do you mean . . . ?"

"Yes'm," said Scratch. "They've both crossed the divide."

"I would have liked to have asked them a few questions," Bo added, "but when bullets start flying around, they don't always do exactly what you want."

"But neither of them was Dunston himself?"

Bo shook his head. "No, he's still out there somewhere."

"Which means we're not done with him."

"More than likely," Bo said.

Since it was the middle of the night—well past the middle of the night, really—Dunston didn't know if he and Anderson ought to wake up Rollin Kemp when they finally trudged back into Cushman.

"Trust me, the boss will want to know what happened," Anderson said. "He's probably waiting up to hear. And he won't be happy about it, either."

"I never knew Lije to mess up a job like that before," Dunston said. He heard the whine in his own voice and despised it, but there was nothing he could do about it.

Anderson heard it, too, judging by the contempt in the snort he let out.

They went to Kemp's room in the Lawson Hotel, named after the man who owned it, of course. The promptness with which Kemp answered Anderson's knock told Dunston that Anderson had been right about the man waiting up to hear their report.

And waiting to take possession of Caroline DeHerries, as well, since they'd been ordered to bring the women back with them.

Kemp glared darkly at them as they stepped into the room—without the four mail-order brides.

He was sitting at a table, fully dressed, with a bottle of whiskey and a glass in front of him. The glass had about an inch of amber liquid in it. He shook his head, lifted the drink and threw it back, then said, "You failed, didn't you?"

"They were ready for us, somehow," Anderson said. "Or else they reacted mighty quickly. I know from what happened back in Seattle that those two old Texans will surprise you." He looked over disdainfully at Dunston. "We should have taken more men with us, our own men, instead of trusting those woods rats."

Dunston stiffened. "You can't talk about me and my friends like that!"

"Shut up," Kemp snapped. "You wanted a chance to get revenge on those two Texans. I gave it to you, and you failed. I won't be trusting you again, Dunston. Get out."

"But that's not fair. It was a good plan. We just had some bad luck, that's all."

Kemp ignored him and said to Anderson, "We'll get together with Lawson later today and figure out our next move. I'm not going to wait around for some incompetent who's consumed by the need for revenge."

Dunston's face burned hotly at that insult. He said, "If you give me another chance, Mr. Kemp, I won't let you down again."

"Are you still here?" Kemp asked coldly. "Get out."

"But—"

Anderson gripped Dunston's arm and turned him toward the door. "You heard the boss," he said. He used his other hand to open the door, then shoved Dunston through it into the hall. Dunston stumbled and came up hard against the wall on the other side of the corridor. Pain bit into his side from the bullet wound, which had never healed up completely.

Anderson closed the door.

Dunston pushed himself upright. His lips curled into a snarl as he looked at the door of Kemp's room. He had come to Cushman with a powerful hate for those Texans, Creel and Morton. But there was plenty of hate in him to go around, and he could spare some for Kemp and Anderson. They would be sorry for treating him this way over something that wasn't his fault. He didn't know how just yet, but sooner or later he would even the score with them.

He turned and left the hotel, grimacing at the nagging discomfort in his side. Even though it was very late, the lamps were still lit at the Avalanche Saloon. Dunston licked his lips and headed in that direction, thoughts of bloody revenge whirling around in his head.

Chapter 37

The gold vein petered out the next day, turning into plain, hard rock.

Scratch made that discovery while he was working in the tunnel with Dave Clarke. He left Clarke staring at the rock wall in dismay and went out to find Bo.

As soon as Bo saw the doleful look on his old friend's face, he knew what had happened. He and Emery were breaking up some of the larger chunks of rock that had been dug out. Bo rested his pick on the ground and said, "The color ran out, didn't it?"

"It sure appears so," replied Scratch.

Caroline was close enough to overhear. She said, "No! That can't be. We were going to be rich."

"Mining is like almost everything else," Bo told her. "Never count on something happening until it actually does."

The other three ladies saw them talking and must have sensed that something was wrong. They hurried over. Beatrice asked, "What is it?"

"We lost the vein," Bo said.

Beatrice stared at him. "You mean . . . it's still there, but you can't find it? Or . . . it's gone?"

"We won't know until we dig some more," Scratch said. "Or blast." He turned to Bo. "We uncovered that gold with dynamite. Might find it again the same way."

Bo considered the suggestion and nodded. "We can give it a try. Let's get everything cleaned out of the tunnel."

They worked for several hours preparing the diggings for the blast. They hauled out all the ore they had already chipped off the rock face and added some timbers to shore up the roof even more than it already was. Then Bo drilled a hole for the cylinder of dynamite, set the blasting cap, and strung the fuse. Based on their experience the first time, he unrolled considerably more fuse than Scratch had. It extended several feet from the tunnel mouth.

Everyone else backed off to the gap between the bluffs. Bo looked at them, nodded to himself, once satisfied that they were far enough away, and took a match from his pocket. He snapped the lucifer to life, bent over and touched the flame to the fuse, and turned to run as the cord sparked behind him. Those sparks raced along the fuse and into the tunnel.

Bo reached the others and turned toward the tunnel just as the explosion made a heavy thump and caused the ground to shake under his boots. As before, a huge cloud of dust billowed out of the opening.

Milt Emery whooped in excitement. "That blowed up real good," he said.

"Now if it just uncovered more gold," Dave Clarke added.

"As soon as the dust clears, we'll see if we can find out," Bo told them.

Emery started forward, his enthusiasm obviously getting

the better of him. "I'm gonna take a look now," he said over his shoulder.

Bo was about to call out for him to wait a minute when Emery suddenly yelped and twisted around. At the same time, a rifle shot sounded.

"Milt!" Sally cried as the stocky prospector collapsed. She ran toward him.

"Get behind the bluff!" Scratch shouted at the others. He waved his arm. "Move!"

More shots rang out. Clarke grabbed Martha's arm and hustled her toward the curving bluff, which would provide good cover against the gunfire as it came from the far side of the gulch.

Bo realized that was where the shots originated from, too, and had hold of Beatrice and Caroline, gripping their arms and running for shelter with them.

That left Scratch to deal with Sally and Emery. He saw blood staining the right leg of Emery's canvas trousers as he ran toward them.

"Go with the others!" he ordered Sally. "I'll get Milt!"

"I'm all right," Emery insisted, even though clearly he wasn't. He clutched his wounded leg with both hands and grimaced as blood seeped between his fingers.

Bullets kicked up dirt only a few feet away as Scratch stooped, got his hands under Emery's arms, and hauled him to his feet. Emery was no lightweight. Scratch had to grunt with the effort it took to lift him.

He got Emery upright, though, then slung an arm around the man's waist and pulled Emery's arm around his shoulders.

"Let's go!"

Sally said, "I'll get on his other side and help!"

"No!" Emery said. "Get out of here, Sally!"

She ignored him and put an arm around his waist from the other side. She and Scratch practically carried him toward cover. He had to hop a little only every few feet.

The bullets were going over their heads now, Scratch noticed as he stayed cool even under fire. That meant the bushwhackers didn't want to risk hitting Sally. The other five had already retreated behind the curving bluff, so they had a lot of rock and dirt between them and the men shooting at the claim.

They reached safety a moment later without getting hit. Scratch and Sally lowered Emery to the ground. Sally knelt beside him and asked anxiously, "How bad is it, Milt?"

"I dunno," he said, his face and voice revealing the strain he was under from the pain. "I don't think the slug busted the bone, just tore through the muscles pretty good."

Bo knelt on the other side and used his knife to cut away part of Emery's trouser leg. That revealed the blood-welling holes in the front and back of his leg.

"Straight through, from the looks of it," Bo said. "That's good. We'll tie it up nice and tight for now, until we get a chance to clean and bandage the wounds properly."

"What about those varmints shootin' at us?" asked Scratch. "You reckon they've given up?"

The rifle fire had stopped. Bo thought for a second, then said dryly, "I don't think I'm going to step out there and find out just yet."

Scratch let out a grim chuckle. "No, I don't rightly think I will, either. I wish we could get to our Winchesters, though, so we could make things hot for those sons of . . . Well, you know what I mean."

"You can say it as far as I'm concerned," Beatrice told him. "I was thinking the same thing."

Sally tore some strips off her underskirt and used them to bind up Emery's leg. Clarke knelt, squeezed his friend's shoulder, and said, "You're gonna be all right, Milt."

"You're blasted right I am," Emery replied. "This won't hardly slow me down."

With Sally and Clarke hovering over the wounded man, Bo straightened and joined Scratch, Beatrice, Caroline, and Martha near the end of the bluff.

"It seemed to me that after they wounded Milt with that first shot, they were firing either high or wide most of the time," he said.

"That's the way I saw it, too," Scratch said.

"Why would they do that?" asked Beatrice.

"Because they didn't want to hit any of you ladies," Bo said. "They didn't even want to risk ventilating you by accident."

"So it's right back to Kemp being behind this," Beatrice said grimly. "Or Amos Lawson. They want us alive."

"Kemp does, that's for sure. He wants Caroline, and I suspect he'd just as soon the rest of you weren't hurt, either. On the frontier, a man who hurts a respectable woman, or allows her to be hurt, can't expect any kind treatment, even from men who are pretty bad in every other way."

Scratch asked, "You reckon Lawson still wants the ladies as brides for himself and his men?"

Beatrice shook her head and said, "Goodness, I can't believe he'd think that would ever happen."

Bo frowned in thought. "Lawson's the sort of man who likes to maintain the appearance of being law-abiding. He wanted to get his hands on this claim by marrying you. Since that's not going to happen, he'd rather buy it from you—at his own price—rather than kill you and take it."

"That's what this is, isn't it?" Beatrice waved a hand to take in the scene around them, including the wounded Emery. "This ambush, I mean. Lawson wants to frighten me into selling to him."

"That could well be."

"Well, I won't do it!" Beatrice clenched her hands into fists, and for a second Bo thought she was going to stamp her foot in anger and frustration. "I won't let that man force me into doing anything."

Scratch said, "Sooner or later, there's a good chance he'll lose his patience and try to grab this claim any way he can. He may be gettin' pretty close to that point now."

"We'll fight him!" Sally declared hotly from where she still knelt beside the wounded Milt Emery. "He's not going to get away with this."

"Now, hold on, Sally," Emery said. "Don't get yourself all worked up over me gettin' winged like this. I told you, it's not really that bad—"

"That's easy for you to say. You . . . you don't know how I felt when I saw you lying there on the ground with all that blood on your leg!"

She bent over him then and kissed him, putting a hand on the back of his head to steady him as she pressed her lips to his. After a second, Emery lifted a hand to her shoulder as he returned the kiss.

The others looked away for a moment, not wanting to embarrass the two of them. Then Scratch said, "Since there hasn't been any shootin' for a while, I'm gonna make a run for the tents and grab a couple of rifles."

"I'll cover you with my Colt, just in case they're still there," Bo said. He had a hunch the bushwhackers were up on the opposite rim of the gulch. That was long range for a handgun, but at least if they opened fire on Scratch, he could give them something to think about.

He moved to the end of the bluff, drew his Colt, and nodded to his old friend. The silver-haired Texan sprinted toward the tents, zigzagging as he ran to make himself a more difficult target.

No shots sounded.

Scratch reached the spot where the rifles had been left leaning against some trees. He grabbed a couple of the Winchesters and ducked behind the trunks. A tense silence still hung over the claim.

After a few seconds, he called to Bo, "Looks like they lit out."

"Maybe. Let's give it a little more time."

Nothing happened. Eventually, Bo's instincts were satisfied that the ambushers were gone. He holstered his gun and said to the others, "All right, let's get Milt back to the cabin so we can do a better job of patching up that leg. Dave, you and Sally help him. You other ladies go ahead in front, but stay close to the bluff and follow the curve around so anybody who's still lurking won't have as good an angle on you if they decide to start shooting again."

"They're not going to shoot," Beatrice said. "They've already done what they came here to do. They just want to scare us into abandoning the claim. And that's not going to happen."

Bo admired her stubbornness. He wasn't in the habit of letting himself get spooked, either, and he didn't intend to start now.

During the next half hour, they got Milt Emery onto one of the bunks in the cabin and Bo used a flask of whiskey to clean the bullet wounds, then bandaged them with strips of clean cloth. Emery drank a slug of the whiskey, too, which helped with the pain.

"I'm much obliged to all of you, but I reckon I'm ready to get back to work," he said. "We need to check that tunnel and see if the blast uncovered anything."

Sally put a hand on his shoulder and pressed him back down on the mattress. "You're not going anywhere," she told him. "That's my bunk, and you're staying there. I mean—" Her face started to turn red. "I mean, you should rest for a while. You lost a good amount of blood."

Emery lay back and nodded. "All right," he agreed. "For a while."

Bo said, "Scratch and Dave and I will go check out the tunnel. You ladies stay in here with Milt. It's safer that way."

"We'll have to go back outside and help with the claim sometime," Beatrice said.

"Yeah, but not right now. Not until we're sure those gunmen are gone."

Bo could tell that Beatrice didn't like it, but she didn't argue. He and Scratch and Clarke left them there and headed for the tunnel, taking rifles this time.

Dealing with the ambush had given the dust time to settle. Bo lit a lantern and headed into the tunnel, stepping over the large chunks of rocks scattered around. He held the light up so it would shine on the rock face where the blast had gone off, hoping to see glints of gold there.

Nothing. Just dull stone.

Scratch and Clarke could tell by his face when he came out what he had found. Scratch sighed and said, "I reckon that one little vein was all that was there."

"We can't know for sure, but that's my hunch, too," Bo said. "We'll have to decide now whether we want to keep digging or try one of the other tunnels." Bo paused. "Or start a brand-new one. I reckon we could do that, too."

Clarke said, "The ladies should have some say in that. It's their claim."

"Yes, it is," Bo agreed. "And I'm sure Miss Beatrice will have an opinion on it, too."

When Bo posed the question of what they should do next, Beatrice's answer surprised him.

"I'll leave the matter of which tunnel to you and Scratch," she said. "You know more about that than I do. But what *I* intend to do is go into Cushman."

"Why in the world would you do that?" Bo asked with a frown.

"I want to talk to George Sullivan."

Bo had to think for a second before he recalled who that was.

"The fella who runs the newspaper. The *Chronicle*. Isn't that what it's called?"

"I believe so," Beatrice said. "He wanted to interview me, but I turned him down. Now I intend to let him have that interview after all."

"What do you figure on saying to him?" Bo asked warily.

"I want to let him know that my friends and I intend to continue working the Golden Cup and that we won't be scared off or run out, no matter who's trying to do that."

Bo nodded slowly. "So you're going to throw this right back in the faces of Lawson and Kemp and dare them to do even worse next time?"

"Are you saying that's a bad idea?"

"Nope. Letting folks know what's going on is liable to

get more of them on your side. But it's an approach that has some danger to it as well."

"Earlier today they were shooting at us. Poor Milt is lying there in the cabin with two bullet holes in his leg, and this isn't the first time we've been attacked. I'd say we're well past the point of worrying about whether something is dangerous. Just being here is dangerous."

Bo laughed and said, "Well, I can't argue with that. When did you want to go to town?"

"The sooner the better. Tomorrow, I think."

"I'll come with you. Scratch and Dave can keep an eye on things here and maybe check out those other tunnels."

"This feels like we're taking the fight to the enemy at last." Beatrice smiled. "I think I like the feeling."

If Bo was being honest, so did he.

Chapter 38

After a quiet night, Bo hitched the pair of draft horses to the buckboard the next morning and then put his saddle on one of the other horses.

Beatrice came out of the cabin pulling on the gloves she used for driving.

"Ready to go?" Bo asked her.

"I certainly am." She wore a long skirt and a corduroy jacket over her soft flannel work shirt. A flat-crowned black hat rested on her dark hair, with its strap taut under her chin.

She had one of the carbines in her left hand.

Bo nodded to the weapon and said, "You're going armed?"

She placed the carbine on the floorboard in front of the driver's seat and asked, "Do you think that's a bad idea?"

"Actually, no, I reckon it's not. You've done pretty well practicing with that repeater. You don't want to use it unless you have to, though."

She smiled and said, "I'll try to withstand the temptation to blaze away if we encounter Lawson or Kemp . . . although it won't be easy."

Bo chuckled. "I know what you mean."

Scratch and Dave Clarke were already working in one of the other tunnels, the digging that the Texans had decided was the most likely to hold any color. Of course, that was just a hunch. An educated guess, at best.

Milt Emery was still resting in Sally's bunk, despite his insistence that he was in good enough shape to go back to work. The ladies had strung up a blanket to separate that bunk from the rest of the cabin and give them some privacy.

Caroline was in the cabin keeping an eye on Emery and tending to any needs he might have. She was the least physically suited to the hard labor of prospecting, so she was the easiest to spare. Sally and Martha were at the tunnel helping Scratch and Clarke.

They saw Bo and Beatrice getting ready to leave and hurried over to say their good-byes.

"Be careful, Beatrice," Martha cautioned. "We have a lot of enemies in that settlement."

"But we have some friends, too, and I'm hoping to make more by letting Mr. Sullivan interview me."

Beatrice hugged her friends, then climbed onto the buckboard's seat. Bo had swung up into the saddle already. He lifted a hand in farewell as he turned the horse and nudged it into motion.

His still-keen eyes scanned the rimrock on both sides of the gulch as he and Beatrice left the claim and headed for Cushman. He didn't see any movement or spot sunlight reflecting off rifle barrels—but that didn't mean the coast was clear.

He felt bad about leaving the claim with one less gun

to defend it, but he had complete confidence in Scratch. His old friend had never let him down.

As she drove, Beatrice said, "You know, I hope that you and Scratch staying up here with us won't cause trouble for you with Mr. Keegan when you finally go back."

"Don't worry about that," Bo told her. "Scratch and I have enjoyed working for Cyrus, but if he were to decide not to give us any more jobs, we wouldn't lose a minute of sleep over it." He grinned. "Shoot, we've already worked at this job longer than we do at most of them."

"Don't you ever have the urge to settle down?"

He didn't tell her that once, many years ago, he *had* settled down, with a ranch, a wife and kids, everything a man needed to be happy. Then tragedy had torn it all away from him and set him on the path to all those wandering decades with Scratch. Even now the memory hurt, which was why he tried to keep it behind him most of the time.

Instead he said, "Thought about it now and then, I reckon. A while back, Scratch and I visited the part of Texas where we were raised, and for a time it looked like we might stay. We have family and friends there . . . even a couple of ladies who would have been pleased for us to hang around . . . but the urge to drift got to be too much." He shook his head and added, "I reckon we're just too shiftless to ever amount to much."

"I wouldn't say that," Beatrice replied. "I think you both amount to quite a bit, in your own way."

"Kind of you to say. After all this time, it's pretty clear we're going to just keep wandering as long as we can."

"You don't want to become Alaskan mining tycoons?"

Bo threw back his head and laughed. "No offense, ma'am, but that just sounds like too much work!"

They chatted about other things during the trip into town. Finally, the mouth of Ten Mile Gulch came into view, and they emerged from it and followed the trail that became Cushman's only real street.

The women who had come to take over the Golden Cup claim were celebrities in the settlement and had been ever since the first confrontation with Amos Lawson, so Beatrice's presence drew a lot of immediate interest. The men on the street and the rough boardwalks would have stared at her anyway because she was so attractive, but they were even more fascinated by the trouble she and her friends had stirred up. Some of them began trotting alongside the buckboard, tipping their battered hats and trying to get Beatrice to talk to them.

They backed off when Bo gave them a hard look. The Texans had reputations as being bad men to cross.

Beatrice drove straight to the newspaper office. George Sullivan must have heard the commotion when she and Bo entered the settlement, because he stepped out the door as Beatrice was pulling the buckboard to a stop.

"Mrs. O'Rourke!" He greeted her with a smile. "It's good to see you again."

"I'm glad you think so, Mr. Sullivan," she said as she wrapped the reins around the vehicle's brake lever, "because I want to talk to you."

His smile vanished and he looked a little surprised. "To me, ma'am? Are you upset about something?"

"Not at all." Still perched on the buckboard seat, Beatrice frowned slightly. "Why on earth would I be upset with you?"

Sullivan rubbed the back of his neck and smiled sheepishly. "It's just that, ah, whenever anybody comes looking for a newspaperman, they're usually angry about something he printed, or something he *didn't* print."

"Oh. Well, I'm not the least bit angry . . . with you."

"Now that sounds intriguing. You don't mind if I ask who you *are* angry with?"

"You can ask me anything you like. I'm here to give you that interview you wanted."

"Oh! Well . . . well, that's wonderful. Let me help you down, and we can go on in the office . . . I apologize in advance, it's not very fancy. Nothing like what you're accustomed to, wherever you come from, I'm sure."

He took her hand to steady her as she climbed down from the buckboard. Bo was still mounted, leaning forward with both hands resting on the saddle horn. He said, "I'd better come with you, Miss Beatrice—"

"I don't think that's necessary," Beatrice said. "I'm sure Mr. Sullivan will be happy to look after me, and at our age, we hardly need a chaperone."

"No one will bother you, Mrs. O'Rourke," Sullivan said. He looked around and added, "I assure you, you have more friends in Cushman than you may be aware of."

"That's one of the things I want to discuss," she told him as she allowed him to link arms with her and lead her toward the newspaper office's open door.

"All right," Bo said, although not without a certain amount of reluctance. He didn't believe either Lawson or Kemp would try anything too blatant right here in the middle of the settlement, in broad daylight, but a part of him still worried about leaving Beatrice in George Sullivan's care.

They had come to Cushman to let their enemies know

that they weren't going to cut and run, though, and Bo knew another very good way of doing that.

He kneed his mount into a walk and headed for the Avalanche Saloon.

That got some attention, too. Bo had a small crowd of men following him by the time he reined up in front of the saloon. None of them looked hostile, just curious and eager to see what was going to happen. He swung down from the saddle and looped the reins around one of the posts holding up the awning.

The Avalanche had batwing doors at the entrance, but they were fastened back. Bo opened one of the double doors and stepped inside. It was a fairly warm day for Alaska, but it was hot and stuffy inside the saloon because a fire was burning in the potbellied stove in the corner. Bo left the door open, and some of the bystanders trailed in behind him.

His gaze darted around the room. He spotted Eli Byrne sitting at a table, idly playing with a deck of cards. Walter Heuman was behind the bar, along with another apron-clad bartender. Bo didn't see Amos Lawson or Franklin Nebel. They were probably back in Lawson's office.

There was also no sign of Rollin Kemp or his men. Bo didn't know where they were, but he figured he'd be wasting his time by hoping they might have left Cushman and headed back to Seattle.

Byrne dropped the cards on the table's green felt top and sat up sharply when he saw Bo come in. Heuman leaned both hands on the bar and frowned. Neither man made a move to start trouble, though.

Bo hooked his thumbs in his gunbelt and walked to the

bar. He gave Heuman a curt nod and said, "I'll have a mug of beer, please."

"Can you pay for it?" asked Heuman with a sneer on his blocky face.

Bo used his left hand to take out a half dollar and drop it on the bar. "As a matter of fact, I can."

Heuman grunted disdainfully, but he reached for a mug to draw the beer.

From the corner of his eye, Bo saw Eli Byrne get to his feet and come toward the bar. Some of the men who were close by started easing away, as if they figured it would be a good idea to get out of the line of fire.

"You've got some nerve comin' in here, Creel," Byrne said as he stopped a few feet away. His hands hung loose at his sides, but the tenseness that gripped his body overall showed that he was ready to draw.

"Oh?" Bo said. "Why's that?"

"You and that other old coot probably talked those women into not keepin' their promise and marryin' us."

"If you'll think back, what Mrs. O'Rourke said that day came as just as much of a surprise to Scratch and me as it did to you and your friends."

Several of the men in the saloon muttered and nodded in agreement with what Bo had just said. They had been on hand when the Texans and the mail-order brides arrived on the *Byron Mowery*.

"Nah, it was all just a trick. You worked it out ahead of time, I'll bet. You're a liar, Creel. Nothin' but a no-good liar."

Byrne was trying to goad him into drawing. Bo knew that. He had come up against countless young firebrands who thought they were the fastest guns to ever come along. Most of them were dead now, and Bo was still alive.

It wouldn't do any good to explain that to Eli Byrne, though. Bo knew that, too.

Heuman finished drawing the beer and set it in front of Bo roughly enough that some of the froth sloshed out. "Drink up," Heuman said with a grin. He pushed Bo's coin back across the bar. "It's on the house. Least I can do, considerin' it'll be your last beer, Creel."

"Well, then, I reckon I'm obliged to you." Bo reached for the mug with his left hand.

Heuman noticed that and the sudden realization that Bo was about to do something flashed across his face, but he didn't react in time. Bo took hold of the mug and snapped it up from the bar, flinging the beer in Heuman's face. The burly man reeled back, pawing at his eyes.

In a swift continuation of the same move, Bo whirled and threw the mug at Byrne, who had started clawing his gun from its holster. The heavy glass mug struck Byrne in the center of the face with enough force to make him jerk his head back.

Bo's Colt was in his hand as he leaped at the young gunman. He struck hard and fast, slamming the gun against the side of Byrne's head. Byrne went down with a crash on the sawdust-littered floor.

An alarmed yell made Bo look around. The crowd in the saloon stampeded, with men scrambling and diving to get out of the way as a figure rushed through the open front door, thrusting a double-barreled shotgun in front of him.

"Die, Creel!" howled Grady Dunston as his fingers tightened on the Greener's triggers.

Chapter 39

B o knew he couldn't turn and fire before Dunston loosed that double load of buckshot at him. At this range, it might kill Eli Byrne, too, but Dunston was too consumed with hate and the need for revenge to care about that.

Before Dunston could pull the triggers, though, a big fast-moving shape loomed up behind him and tackled him, driving him forward and down. Both barrels of the shotgun went off with a deafening double boom, but the buckshot tore into the puncheon floor rather than human flesh.

The man who had grabbed Dunston and saved Bo's life lifted a fist and hammered it into the back of Dunston's head. The blow smashed Dunston's face against the floor. He went limp, out cold just like Eli Byrne.

The heroic man grinned at Bo, who stared at him in surprise.

"Looks like I got here just in time, doesn't it, Mr. Creel?" Chart Kelly asked.

After a moment, Bo got over his shock at seeing the brawny young sailor again and said, "Where in blazes did you come from, Kelly?"

"Up the Yukon," Kelly replied as he got to his feet. "In a canoe."

It seemed amazing that anyone could accomplish such a feat, but if anybody could, it would be this young Hercules, Bo supposed. And he could make a pretty good guess as to Kelly's motivation for undertaking such an arduous journey, a guess that was confirmed as Kelly went on. "Where's Miss Caroline?"

Before Bo could answer, Walter Heuman stormed out from behind the bar with beer still dripping from his face and a bung starter in his hand as he bellowed at Bo, "I'll stove your head in, you damn Texas troublemaker!"

Chart Kelly stepped forward with his hands clenched into fists, obviously ready to intervene on Bo's behalf again. Bo still had his Colt in his hand, too. He figured looking down its barrel might make Heuman settle down a mite.

Neither of those things were necessary, because at that moment Amos Lawson stepped out of his office and snapped, "Walter! That's enough."

Franklin Nebel emerged from the office behind Lawson. Both men held pistols. They must have heard the shotgun go off and hadn't known what was going on, so they had come prepared for more gunplay.

"Damn it, Amos," Heuman said as he came to an abrupt halt. He trembled with the anger that wanted to propel him toward Bo again. "This blasted Texan threw beer in my face and buffaloed Eli."

"They had me whipsawed," drawled Bo. "I didn't cotton to the idea of just standing there and letting them kill me."

"Did you think you'd be welcomed here with open arms?" Lawson asked.

"I didn't much care one way or the other. After riding into town, I was thirsty."

"Not all that thirsty," said Nebel, "if you wasted a mug of beer by throwing it in Walter's face."

"Seemed like the thing to do at the time," Bo said with a shrug.

Lawson jerked his head at the burly Heuman and ordered, "Walter, go see about Eli. Make sure he's all right."

Heuman snarled one more time at Bo, then tossed the bung starter onto the bar and went over to Byrne, kneeling beside him and lightly slapping his face. Byrne began to shift around a little and groaned.

"He's alive," Heuman reported. His blunt fingers probed Byrne's skull. "He'll have a goose egg on his head, but other than that I reckon he'll be all right."

"What about that one?" Lawson asked, nodding toward Dunston. "He's one of Kemp's men, isn't he?"

Bo said, "He latched on to Kemp in St. Michael. Kemp didn't bring him all the way from Seattle."

Heuman cast an unfriendly glance toward Chart Kelly, who had stepped back; then Heuman hooked a foot under Dunston's shoulder and rolled him onto his back. Blood smeared Dunston's face. The brutal collision with the floor had broken his nose. Black circles were already starting to show around his eyes. Air rasped and bubbled in his flattened nostrils.

Lawson slipped his gun back into the shoulder holster he wore under his coat. He regarded Kelly coolly and said, "I don't recall seeing you in Cushman before. Who are you, and what are you doing here?"

"I'm a friend of Mr. Creel's," Kelly said boldly, with a defiant jut of his chin. "And a friend of the ladies with him, as well. I sailed on the *John Starr,* the ship that brought them to Alaska."

Nebel frowned and asked the same question Bo had. "How did you get here? There hasn't been a riverboat come this way for a while, and the *Mowery* isn't scheduled to arrive again for a few days yet."

"I paddled up the river in a canoe."

"That's a lie!" Heuman burst out. "Nobody would paddle this far up the Yukon."

Bo said, "The old fur trappers used to paddle thousands of miles, almost from one side of the continent to the other. Some of them, like the one they call Preacher, are still alive and probably could do it even now. So I believe this young fella."

"It doesn't matter how he got here," Lawson said. "If he's your friend, he's not welcome in the Avalanche any more than you are. Get out, both of you."

Kelly looked over at Bo and said, "Not very hospitable, is he? What's his problem?"

"It's a long story," Bo said. "Maybe we'd better go somewhere else, and I'll tell you all about it."

Kelly looked like he didn't care for the idea of being run out of the saloon, but he had to be curious about Caroline, too, and probably was eager to ask Bo about her. So he nodded and said, "All right, Mr. Creel. We'll go." He looked coolly from Heuman to Lawson and Nebel. "But that's not to say I won't be back."

Bo put his left hand on the young sailor's arm and turned him toward the entrance. He kept his Colt in his other hand as he backed away, not wanting to turn his back on their enemies.

They were almost at the door when Eli Byrne suddenly

regained his senses enough to bolt up from the floor. Byrne staggered and almost fell again, but Heuman was there to catch hold of his arm and steady him.

Byrne lifted his other arm and pointed at Bo. "You're a dead man, you old coot!" he yelled. "Nobody wallops me like that and lives! You understand?"

"I understand you've got a mouth on you, kid," Bo said. "I don't reckon you can back it up, though."

"Let go of me!" Byrne raged at Heuman. "I'll kill him!"

"Eli!" Lawson's voice lashed out like a whip. "I don't want this place shot up." He looked at Bo. "There'll be other chances."

Bo just nodded at him and backed the rest of the way out of the saloon. He didn't pouch his iron until they had walked halfway along the block toward the newspaper office.

"Where are we going?" asked Chart Kelly. "And where's Caroline? She's all right, isn't she, Mr. Creel?"

Instead of answering Kelly's questions, Bo looked over at him and asked, "What did you do, jump ship in St. Michael?"

"That's right," Kelly replied without hesitation. "I hated to do that to Cap'n Saunders, but I realized I couldn't live without Caroline." His broad shoulders rose and fell in a shrug. "The riverboat had already left, so I didn't have any choice but to buy a canoe from a fella, pick up some supplies, and set off after you. It took a lot longer with just me and a single paddle, though, instead of that paddle wheel on the *Byron Mowery*."

Bo shook his head. "I know the old mountain men did it, like I said in there, but coming this far upriver like that is quite a feat, son. You must really want to see that girl again."

Kelly stopped and gripped Bo's arm, bringing him to a halt as well. With an earnest expression on his face, he said, "Tell me the truth, Mr. Creel, and don't spare my feelings. Did Caroline take a husband the way she was supposed to?"

The youngster looked so solemn that Bo had to chuckle. "She's not married," he said.

Kelly's eyes went up to heaven as if in thanksgiving, and he let out a long sigh of relief.

"In fact, that hotheaded young gunman back there who threatened me was the one she was betrothed to," Bo went on.

Kelly stared at him in disbelief. "That scoundrel? Really?"

"Like I told you, it's a long story. Let's go to the newspaper office and you can hear all about it. Miss Beatrice is there, talking to the fella who publishes the paper. I've got a hunch he's going to think you're a pretty good story, too."

Bo's hunch was right. Once George Sullivan found out that Kelly had paddled this far up the Yukon River in search of a girl, instead of gold, he grabbed another pad of paper from his desk and started making notes for a story in the paper. He already had a couple of pages full of scribbled notations from his interview with Beatrice.

"I'm going to have plenty of material for the next issue of the *Chronicle*, that's for sure," Sullivan said with a grin.

"I still don't understand," Kelly said to Beatrice. "You didn't marry those fellas you came up here to marry?"

"We never really intended to marry them," she explained

to him, her voice gentle. "I'm sorry that we had to lie to you, to all of you, the men on the ship . . . and to Bo and Scratch, as well. But there was a good reason. *Gold.*"

She spent the next few minutes telling Chart Kelly about her late husband's claim and the plan for her and her niece and friends to come up here and work that claim.

"And it's paid off," Beatrice concluded excitedly. "We've found gold. High-grade ore, according to Mr. Peck, the assayer. The Golden Cup is going to be one of the best mines in the entire territory."

Bo frowned slightly in puzzlement. The way Beatrice was making it sound, the vein hadn't played out and they were still taking valuable color out of the mine. That wasn't the case at all. He wondered why she was lying to George Sullivan and Chart Kelly.

"Of course, we still have to deal with some problems, as I've been explaining to Mr. Sullivan here," she went on. "Amos Lawson and his men have a definite grudge against us, and I'm certain he wants that claim for himself."

"Lawson's the fella who came out of the office and was giving orders at the saloon," Bo said for Kelly's benefit.

"And that man Kemp, who tried to persuade Caroline to marry him back in Seattle, by force if necessary, has shown up here, too, with some of his ruffians in tow. So you see, Mr. Kelly, we're surrounded by enemies."

"Well, you've got another friend now," said Kelly. "I'll stand with you, Mrs. O'Rourke, and do anything I can to help you and the other ladies."

Sullivan looked at Bo and said, "I heard some gunfire a little while ago. Sounded like a shotgun going off. Do you know anything about that?"

"As a matter of fact, I do," Bo said. "Grady Dunston tried to plant a double load of buckshot in my hide."

Beatrice's eyes widened in alarm. "You're not hurt, are you?"

"No, thanks to Chart here. He showed up just in time to jump Dunston and stop him from ventilating me."

Sullivan was writing furiously. "Keep going. I want the whole story."

Eventually the newspaperman was satisfied that he had enough facts to fill up a couple of pages, which would account for half of the paper's next issue. Bo and Beatrice had told him about the ambush and how Milt Emery had been wounded the previous night.

"I can't come right out and accuse anyone of being responsible for that except Dunston," Sullivan said. "Even though I'm sure either Lawson or Kemp—or both—were actually behind it. But I promise, when the citizens of Cushman get through reading my stories, they'll know exactly who's to blame." His forehead creased with worry. "You know, of course, Mrs. O'Rourke, that that's liable to stir up even more trouble."

With a fierce look glinting in her eyes, Beatrice said, "Mr. Sullivan, that's exactly what I want. To force those cockroaches out into the open . . . so they can be squashed!"

Chapter 40

Chart Kelly made arrangements with Ed Lerch, the liveryman and sled dog breeder, to leave his canoe at Lerch's barn. Then he climbed onto the buckboard's seat next to Beatrice for the ride out to the Golden Cup.

The vehicle was still sitting in front of the newspaper office, and as Beatrice lifted the reins, George Sullivan came out of the building to say good-bye.

"Thank you for the interview, Mrs. O'Rourke," he told Beatrice. "And I'm not saying that just as a journalist." He cleared his throat, squared his shoulders, and continued in a visible display of bravery. "To tell you the truth, I find you rather . . . ah . . . enchanting, madam."

"Why, Mr. Sullivan, that's a very sweet thing to say," Beatrice replied with a smile. "Although it *is* a bit bold."

"Faint heart ne'er won fair lady, as the poets say. Next time you come to town, you will stop and see me, won't you?"

"Of course," Beatrice replied. "I'll probably have another news story for you."

With that, she flicked the reins and got the team

moving. The buckboard rolled up the street toward the gulch.

"So long," Bo said to Sullivan as he turned his horse to start after the buckboard.

"Good-bye, Mr. Creel. Be careful out there."

Bo could have said the same thing to Sullivan. If Sullivan wrote those stories the way he'd said he was going to, Lawson and Kemp were liable to be pretty upset when the next *Chronicle* was published. Bo hoped they wouldn't try to retaliate against Sullivan. Attacking the newspaperman might turn even more of the citizens of Cushman against Lawson, but if he was mad enough, he might not care.

As Bo pulled up alongside the buckboard, Kelly was saying to Beatrice, "Do you think Caroline will be glad to see me?"

"She'll be surprised, I know that. I certainly was." She smiled at him. "But I think she'll be happy, too. You were very kind and attentive to her on the ship. And, of course, you saved her life during that storm."

"I don't want her just feeling grateful, though," Kelly said. "I think what we have is more than that."

"If that's what Caroline wants, then I wish you well. Both of you."

Bo said, "I reckon you're going to have a suitor, too, Miss Beatrice. Mr. Sullivan made that pretty clear."

"Oh, he's just a newspaperman," Beatrice responded. "They'll say anything to get a story."

"You'd already given him the story, though," Bo pointed out.

"I suppose that's true," she admitted, still smiling.

With Chart Kelly's arrival, George Sullivan's interest

in Beatrice, and the already developing romances going on at the camp, it seemed that all four ladies now had legitimate suitors, Bo mused. Although there was no way of knowing when—or if—any marriages would result from that, it was looking as if the job that had brought him and Scratch to Alaska really was near its end.

Despite that, there was no way the Texans would be going anywhere as long as trouble loomed over those ladies. They had never run away from a ruckus, at least not since the Texas revolution, when they were kids and their families had fled from Santa Anna's army with all the other Texican settlers—only to turn and make a stand at San Jacinto and kick that fancy-pants dictator back to Mexico where he belonged.

They weren't going to run away from the likes of Amos Lawson and Rollin Kemp, either.

Chart Kelly looked around wide-eyed at the rugged, timber-covered landscape. "I've seen plenty of Alaska, but only from the shore. This is downright magnificent."

"If you've seen it only from the shore, you've barely touched the place," Bo told him. "It's huge. I don't think we're even halfway to the Canadian border yet. Looking at it on a map, Alaska seems almost half as big as the United States. I reckon a fella could wander around up here for a long time and not even come close to seeing all of it."

"The way you and Scratch have wandered around the frontier all these years?" asked Beatrice.

"Yes, ma'am. Since this territory is part of America now, I suppose you could call it the last frontier."

"That has a nice ring to it."

"It does," Bo agreed.

"Is there any chance you'll stay up here?"

Bo considered for a moment and then shook his head.

"Not likely," he said. "When winter starts coming on, Scratch and I usually head south, like the wild geese. Too much snow and ice is bad for our old bones."

As they drove up the gulch toward the Golden Cup, most of the men they passed who were working other claims stopped what they were doing to come out and talk briefly or wave or just stare at them with great interest.

Kelly watched those reactions for a while, then said, "I suspect those lads have never seen anyone like you and the other ladies before, Mrs. O'Rourke."

"Maybe not, but they ought to be getting used to us by now," Beatrice said. "We've been around these parts for a while, and we don't intend to leave until we've established a successful mine."

"I hope you'll allow me to help you." Kelly grinned. "One thing I have is a strong back. I'd be happy to help with anything you need done around that claim."

Beatrice gave him a shrewd glance. "For a share in the profits, I suppose."

Kelly's eyes widened. He looked shocked as he shook his head.

"That's not what I was thinking at all, ma'am," he said. "I just want to help. I'll be happy to do it for the sheer pleasure of being around Miss DeHerries."

"We'll see, Mr. Kelly. If you throw in with us, as Bo and Scratch would put it, you can be sure that you'll be treated fairly."

"Yes, ma'am, I appreciate that. But I don't want you or

any of the other ladies feeling beholden to me. Like I said, I'm just glad to help."

Smiling, Bo told him, "Quit while you're ahead, youngster. Anyway, we're almost there."

It was true. In another few minutes, they reached the bluffs that curved out from the wall of Ten Mile Gulch to form the Golden Cup. Beatrice drove through the opening toward the camp.

Scratch, Dave Clarke, Martha, and Sally stopped working in the tunnel and came to greet them. Caroline stepped out of the cabin where she'd been looking after Milt Emery and shaded her eyes with a hand as she gazed toward the buckboard.

Then she lowered that hand and broke into a run toward the vehicle.

"Chart!" she called. "Oh, Chart, is that really you?"

The young sailor dropped to the ground before Beatrice even brought the buckboard to a stop. Caroline rushed into his arms. He wrapped them around her and lifted her off the ground as he hugged her. She wrapped her arms around his neck and clung to him.

After a moment, Kelly lowered her so her feet were on the ground again. He bent down and kissed her, and her arms tightened around his neck. When he lifted his mouth from hers, she said, "Chart, I didn't think I'd ever see you again."

"Neither did I," he told her. "That's why I decided I couldn't just sail away from St. Michael. I jumped ship and came after you."

Her eyes widened. "Won't you get in trouble for that?"

"In trouble with who? There's no law up here. Anyway, I'm pretty sure Cap'n Saunders knew what I was doing and was willing to go along with it. He knew I wouldn't be any good to him as a sailor while I was pining away for you!"

"Well, you're here now, and that's all that matters." Caroline suddenly looked worried. "You *are* going to stay, aren't you?"

Kelly nodded. "I've already told your aunt I want to help with the mine any way I can." He grinned. "I reckon you're all stuck with me."

Scratch clapped a hand on his shoulder and said, "Glad to hear it, son. You might've torn off a bigger chunk than you figure, though. We've got a heap of enemies to deal with up here."

"I know," Kelly said. "Mrs. O'Rourke and Mr. Creel told me all about it."

Bo said, "Chart saw it for himself, too. He showed up just as Grady Dunston was about to let daylight through me with a shotgun."

That brought surprised gasps from Caroline, Sally, and Martha. Bo told them about the ruckus in the Avalanche Saloon, then concluded by saying, "I don't know if Kemp or Lawson actually sent Dunston after me. He's got a big enough grudge against us that he could've been acting on his own. But I'm pretty sure Eli Byrne and that fella Heuman were trying to seize their chance to kill me while they had me between them. That's why I made my move first."

"And it's a good thing you did," said Clarke. "Byrne's pretty fast on the draw, and Heuman's as strong as a bear."

"Lawson's got to be getting tired of having us around," Bo said. "And he's going to be even angrier when he sees the next issue of the newspaper."

"I made it clear to Mr. Sullivan, the editor, that Lawson and Kemp are to blame for our troubles," Beatrice said, "as well as telling him how successful the mine is."

Scratch frowned and said, "But we're still lookin' for more color. Haven't found a speck of gold since that other vein petered out."

"Lawson and Kemp don't need to know that."

Understanding dawned on Scratch's rugged face. He nodded and said, "You're tryin' to prod those varmints into comin' out in the open."

"That's the general idea, yes."

Caroline said, "But isn't that just asking for more trouble?"

"The trouble's not going to go away," Bo said. "The only way to placate men like that is to give them everything they want. That would mean turning this claim over to Lawson—and turning *you* over to Kemp, Miss Caroline."

Kelly put his arm around Caroline's shoulders and declared, "That's never going to happen."

"I should say it's not," Beatrice added emphatically. "Whenever they try to cause trouble again—and I'm sure they will—we'll be ready for it . . . and we'll fight." She looked around at the others. "Am I right?"

Caroline still looked worried, but after a second her chin came up and determined fires kindled to life in her eyes.

"You're right, Aunt Beatrice," she said. "We'll fight, and we'll win."

"That's the spirit," Scratch told her.

The Texans exchanged a wary glance without the others noticing, though. Out of all the people here, they were the only ones who had a real idea of what men like Amos Lawson and Rollin Kemp were capable of, because they had clashed with hard cases like that in the past.

Given the number of gun-wolves those two could muster, quite a battle was looming in the near future.

Chapter 41

In the meantime, there was work to do at the claim. Chart Kelly proved to be a valuable addition to the group. He was a tireless worker, capable of swinging a pick or wielding a shovel for hours on end with seemingly little effort.

He often took his shirt off while working in the tunnel, and when he came outside his skin was very white in the sun, standing out in sharp contrast to his deeply tanned face, hands, and forearms. Caroline always had some excuse for being around any time Chart was shirtless, and to be honest, the other ladies seemed to appreciate the sight as well.

A week passed without any luck in the search for more gold. The men moved on to one of the other tunnels, then another, but there was no sign of ore in either place, and the Texans' instincts told them they were wasting their time.

The two remaining tunnels hadn't been extended, and the dynamite was stored in one of them. Scratch suggested blasting to start with on the next tunnel, but Bo vetoed the idea.

"We don't want to blow too many holes in the wall of

this gulch. Besides, if we use up the dynamite, we don't know how long it would be before we could get more."

"And we've got Chart to help with the digging now," said Milt Emery, who was getting around on a crutch he had fashioned from a pine branch. The jovial Emery had formed a friendship with the young sailor already. "He's like having two or three extra fellas when it comes to working."

"So let's get back at it," Kelly suggested. He grinned and added, "I'm starting to understand the lure of gold. You know in your gut that it's somewhere in there, buried in that rock. You just have to find it."

Amos Lawson was in his office with Franklin Nebel when the two men heard voices raised in anger in the saloon's main room.

"Step aside, you young pup! I'm going in there to talk to Lawson."

"Not unless I ask him about it first." That was Eli Byrne, who had appointed himself the guardian of Lawson's sanctum. "You just step back and don't crowd me, mister."

Lawson jerked his head at Nebel and said, "Get out there and put a stop to that before the young jackass shoots one of Kemp's men and the others fill him full of lead."

Lawson had recognized Rollin Kemp's voice as the man from Seattle demanded entry.

Nebel stood up, went quickly to the door, and opened it. "It's all right, Eli," he said. "Mr. Lawson will see Mr. Kemp."

Byrne stood there just outside the door, curled in a tense crouch with his hand hovering near the butt of his gun. He glanced over his shoulder at Nebel, then straightened reluctantly.

"Folks shouldn't think they can just barge in here and bother the boss any time they want to," he muttered.

"Don't worry about it," Nebel told him. "Amos knows how loyal you are." He stepped back and held out a hand to usher Kemp into the office. Two of Kemp's toughs were with him, but he motioned curtly for them to wait for him and went into Lawson's office alone. Nebel closed the door, cutting off his view of Byrne's surly expression.

Kemp clutched a folded-up newspaper. He strode over to Lawson's desk, slapped the paper down in front of him, and asked, "Have you seen that?"

Lawson was leaning back in his leather chair, holding the same issue of the *Chronicle*. He rattled the paper meaningfully, then folded it to toss it down on top of the copy Kemp had brought.

"As a matter of fact," he said dryly, "I was just catching up on the news here in Cushman."

"The news that we're trying to have those Texans and their friends murdered so you can steal a gold claim and I can kidnap a young woman?"

Lawson regarded his visitor coolly and said, "I'm not going to steal any gold claim. I intend to buy it from Mrs. O'Rourke once she's realized it's more trouble than it's worth."

"You mean when her protectors are dead?"

Lawson ignored that and went on. "As far as Miss DeHerries goes, I assume you intend to court her and convince her that you're a good match for her. How forcefully you conduct your pursuit is no business of mine."

Kemp grimaced. "Damn it, Lawson, I don't like all this

pussyfooting. You care too much about trying to look respectable." He balled a fist and thumped it on the desk. "When a man wants something, there comes a time when he needs to just take it!"

Lawson regarded him intently for a long moment, then said, "You may be right, Kemp." He reached out and tapped a finger against the newspaper. "The . . . drivel . . . that fool published makes us look bad. Worse than that, it makes us look *weak.*"

Kemp drew in a deep breath and nodded. "Now you're starting to understand. I'll have my men go down to that newspaper office and teach Sullivan a lesson. He can't print any more papers if somebody takes a sledgehammer to his press, can he? He can't even write anything else if he has a broken arm!"

Lawson blew out a disgusted breath. "It's broad daylight out there. If you wreck his press and have him beaten when people can see you do it, you're just proving all those insinuations for him, aren't you?"

"Why do you give a damn about that?"

Lawson finally came to his feet, surging up from his chair. "Because I still have to live and do business here once you've gone back to Seattle with that little blonde! I've invested a lot of time and effort and money in this town, Kemp. I'm not going to throw it away just because you're mooning over some girl who's half your age, no matter how pretty she is!"

They stood there, angry gazes dueling over the desk, as tense seconds ticked by. Until Franklin Nebel said, "Excuse me, gentlemen, but you're both right."

The two men turned their heads to look at him.

"If you wait until everyone has gone to bed for the

night to make your move against Mr. Sullivan and the *Chronicle*, no one will be able to prove that the two of you are responsible. Most people will *suspect* that's true, of course, but if you don't rub the truth in people's faces, they'll ignore it if that's the most convenient thing for them to do." Nebel spread his hands. "By the same token, if you go out to the O'Rourke claim in force tonight, once the work here in town is done, you can do what's necessary without a lot of witnesses. But I would recommend overwhelming force, because Creel and Morton have proven to be amazingly resourceful when it comes to dealing with threats."

"Take enough men to wipe them out, you mean," growled Kemp.

"Your words, sir, not mine."

Lawson said, "Nebel's got a point." He grunted. "And you're showing a surprisingly ruthless side, Franklin."

"Enough is enough," said Nebel. "Those Texans have defied you, and now that defiance has spread to George Sullivan. It's time to put a stop to it, sir, by whatever means necessary, before it infects the entire settlement and the surrounding area."

"I like the sound of that," Kemp said. "We'll put an end to this and get what we want. Tonight."

The lamp on George Sullivan's desk was turned low. The thick overcast made it almost seem like night outside. Sullivan leaned back in his chair, sipped from the cup of coffee in his hand, and sighed in satisfaction. He had run off the latest edition of the *Chronicle* the day before, then spent today distributing it. It felt like a job well done.

Footsteps on the boardwalk outside made Sullivan look up. He set the cup on the desk and pulled open the drawer to his right. Sitting in that drawer was a loaded Colt .45 revolver.

The door swung back, and Eli Byrne swaggered into the newspaper office with his thumbs hooked in his gunbelt. Bulking up behind him was Walter Heuman from the Avalanche Saloon. Three more men, all burly and dressed in town suits and bowler hats, followed Byrne and Heuman. Sullivan recognized them as toughs who worked for Rollin Kemp.

"Good evening, gentlemen," Sullivan said coolly. "It's getting a little crowded in here, wouldn't you say?"

Heuman raised a sledgehammer with both hands. "It'll be less crowded once we finish busting that press of yours to pieces, you damn lying inkslinger."

"I won't deny the inkslinger part, but what have I lied about?"

"You made all kinds of insinuations against our boss, and theirs," said one of the bowler-hatted toughs. "You can't just print whatever you want."

"I can if it's true," Sullivan said. "That's the way the newspaper business works."

Byrne said, "You can't print anything without a press. And without a press, there won't be any reason for you to hang around these parts. You can skedaddle on back wherever you came from." He sauntered closer and smirked. "Unless you want to get busted up the way that press is about to."

The printing press itself was in the building's other room, with the door behind Sullivan's desk. That door opened abruptly, and Ed Lerch stepped through and moved to Sullivan's right, holding a shotgun in both hands.

"I'd say this scattergun trumps that sledgehammer of yours, Heuman," the one-eyed liveryman said.

Ham Volney followed Lerch out of the press room, also armed with a shotgun. The storekeeper spread out to Sullivan's left. Burton Peck, the assayer, stepped out next and took a position at Sullivan's left shoulder. He held a rifle with the barrel pointed in the general direction of Byrne, Heuman, and the other men.

Sullivan lifted the Colt from the drawer and rested his hand on the desk with the weapon pointed at the intruders.

"We thought today's paper might provoke a reaction such as this," he said. "So the honest citizens of Cushman got together and decided to arrange this little committee."

Byrne's face flushed dark red with anger. "You won't get away with this," he blustered. "You act like you've got some say in how things are run around here. But you're wrong. This is Amos Lawson's town. Always has been, and always will be."

"We'll see about that. None of us object to Mr. Lawson remaining in business in Cushman, as long as he conducts his affairs in an honest manner. That doesn't include hiring gunmen and bullies and running roughshod over anyone who doesn't agree with him."

"You're full of talk," said Heuman with a menacing scowl. "But we'll see how talkative you are when you don't have any guns backing you up." He jerked his head at the other men. "Come on."

"But I can—" Byrne began.

"I don't care how fast on the draw you think you are,"

Heuman interrupted him. "Those Greeners are cocked and ready."

"And we'll pull the triggers, too," Lerch put in.

"Nobody can beat a setup like that," Heuman went on. "But there'll be another time."

"Not if your boss—and that bookkeeper of his—are as smart as they think they are." Sullivan got to his feet but kept the Colt trained on the men in front of him. "People around here are fed up, Heuman. They'll give Lawson another chance, I expect . . . but that generosity is coming to an end."

He gestured with the gun barrel. "Go on and get out of here."

Despite the odds being stacked against them, Byrne looked as if he wanted to reach for his gun, anyway. One of Rollin Kemp's men grasped his right arm and said, "Come on, kid, let's get out of here."

Reluctantly, Byrne allowed himself to be steered out of the newspaper office. The door slammed behind the delegation Lawson and Kemp had sent.

The men in the office lowered their weapons. Ham Volney said, "Heuman was right, you know. This ain't over yet."

"No, I don't imagine it—" Sullivan began.

That was as far as he got before gunshots slammed through the air outside and the office's front window shattered from the volley of lead that crashed into it. The four men dived to the floor as bullets whipped through the air. Volney bellowed a curse.

The savage onslaught lasted only about ten seconds—long enough for the attackers to empty their guns and then light out. As an echoing silence settled over the office, Sullivan raised his head and asked, "Is anybody hurt?"

"One of those flying pieces of glass cut my cheek," Burton Peck answered, "but it's not serious."

Lerch and Volney chimed in, declaring that they weren't hit.

"I guess Byrne couldn't stand not getting the last word," Sullivan said. "But the damage can be repaired, and none of those bullets would have hurt the printing press."

Hoofbeats swept past outside as a large group of riders left Cushman in a hurry. Sullivan ignored the warnings from the others and leaped to his feet, hurrying out onto the boardwalk. "They're headed up the gulch," he said as he peered through the gloom in that direction. "I couldn't really see them, but it sounded like a dozen or more."

"Where do you reckon they're goin'?" asked Lerch.

"There's only one place they *could* be going," Sullivan answered grimly. "I think Lawson and Kemp have sent all the gunmen they can muster to wipe out those Texans and the other fellows at the Golden Cup."

Chapter 42

Eli Byrne was still seething with fury as he rode at the head of the group charging up Ten Mile Gulch. He had a lot of things to be mad about, but first and foremost on his mind was the way people kept running down his talent with a gun.

He could have drawn his Colt and killed all four of those men in the newspaper office before they ever got off a shot. He was sure of that.

Of course, if he'd been wrong, that would have meant multiple loads of buckshot, along with rifle and pistol bullets, might have blown him and his companions to hell. But that was the risk you ran when you set out to impose your will on other men, and Walter Heuman and the others should have realized that.

You had to take some chances to get what you wanted out of life.

And Eli Byrne wanted Caroline DeHerries.

Lawson's orders had been simple. Destroy the printing press at the newspaper office, give Sullivan a beating he would never forget, then ride up to the O'Rourke claim and kill those meddlesome Texans and anybody else who got in their way.

Once that was done, they would bring the women back to town, and Lawson would tell them how it was going to be. The O'Rourke woman would sell him the Golden Cup. Caroline would go back to Seattle with Rollin Kemp, and the other women could stay in Cushman or do whatever else they wanted to, as long as they didn't make any more trouble.

That was where Byrne planned to change things up a mite.

Once they had the women, he was going to take Caroline and head for the high lonesome with her. He had done some exploring around these parts, when he wasn't working at any chores for Lawson, and he knew the area better than anybody realized. If anyone tried to stop him, even Heuman, Byrne would feed him a bullet.

Once he got up in the mountains with Caroline, nobody would ever find them. They would live off the land, and she would come to love him as much as he loved her. The fact that they hadn't really said a dozen words to each other didn't matter. Some things were just destined to be.

Somebody nudged his horse up next to Byrne. He looked over and, in the shadowy half light, recognized Grady Dunston. The bruises under the man's eyes had faded, but his nose was grotesquely crooked from being broken by Chart Kelly.

"Eli, I been thinkin'," Dunston said in his wheedling voice. "I know how we can get those damn Texans."

"We're gonna ride in there and shoot them," Byrne said. He inclined his head toward the dozen men behind them. "We've got plenty of guns."

"Yeah, but that's liable to put those women in danger, too. And you don't know what it's like tryin' to finish off Creel and Morton. They've got the luck of the devil ridin' with them."

"So what's your idea?" asked Byrne, as much to placate Dunston and maybe shut him up as anything.

"They've got a crate of dynamite, and I know where they keep it. I saw Creel fetch a stick of the stuff a while back."

Byrne looked at Dunston with more interest. "While you were spying on the claim?"

"Yeah. It's in one of the tunnels. If I was to sneak in there and get a stick of it, then set it off, that would draw those Texans and the other fellas out in the open where you could pick 'em off without any trouble."

Byrne frowned in thought and slowly nodded. "That might actually work."

"Well, why wouldn't it? You don't think I'm dumb, do you?"

Byrne didn't answer that. Instead he said, "You might hang on to a few more sticks of that dynamite, in case we need it to blow those Texans to hell."

An ugly laugh came from Dunston. "I like the sound of that."

"You really think you can sneak in there without them catchin' you?"

"Sure I can. Like I said, I've been watchin' the place. I know my way around."

Byrne knew he ought to talk it over with Heuman and make sure the big saloonman was in agreement, but he was tired of taking orders. He was more suited to giving them.

"All right, Grady," he said. "When we get there, that's

what we'll do. There'll be a lot riding on you, though, so don't let us down."

"I won't. You can count on me. I'll do whatever it takes to see those damn Texans dead."

That day's work hadn't produced any better results than all the previous days recently. Still no color.

It had been easier not to let weariness grind them down when they had been taking high-grade ore out of the first tunnel. Now everybody was stretching and yawning and ready to crawl into their blankets almost before supper was over.

Someone still had to stand guard, though, and Bo had the first shift tonight. As everyone else was turning in, he walked out into the shadows under the trees, his usual spot.

No trouble had cropped up since his and Beatrice's visit to Cushman a week earlier. Bo didn't know exactly when George Sullivan was going to publish the next issue of the newspaper. Surely it had come out by now, though, he mused as he stood there with his Winchester cradled in his left arm.

There were bound to be fireworks when Lawson and Kemp read what Sullivan had to say. Men with that much pride, who relied on fear to maintain their dominance, couldn't afford to let anybody get away with defying them.

Knowing that, Bo was especially alert tonight. For some reason, his gut was telling him that all hell might be about to break loose.

Maybe his senses were heightened because of that. Whatever the reason, he heard a faint noise from the other side of the claim and stiffened in response to it.

With his Winchester held ready at a slant across his chest, Bo cat-footed toward the wall of the gulch. It was impossible to be sure about such a small thing, but he believed the noise he'd heard had come from the vicinity of the last tunnel.

That was the tunnel where the case of dynamite was stored. He felt a cold ball of fear form in his stomach at that thought. There were enough explosives cached in there to cause a heap of trouble if the wrong person got their hands on them.

Bo paused as he neared the tunnel mouth and listened intently. Somebody was in there, all right. Bo heard a man muttering to himself, then steps shuffled toward him.

Bo lifted the rifle to his shoulder, and when a shadowy figure stepped out of the tunnel, he called softly, "Hold it right there, mister."

The man stopped short and exclaimed, "Creel! Blast it, no! You can't be *that* lucky."

"Luck's got nothing to do with it, hombre," Bo told him. "You just weren't as stealthy as you thought you were." He was pretty sure he'd recognized the man's voice. "Come on out of there, Dunston, and drop your gun."

Instead, Grady Dunston dropped whatever was in his hands and clawed for the gun on his hip instead. That coldness inside Bo suddenly grew even larger. He knew Dunston must have been trying to steal some of the dynamite, no doubt to use against him and Scratch. He hated to risk a shot, but he couldn't just stand there and let Dunston gun him down.

He squeezed the Winchester's trigger as Dunston cleared leather.

The rifle cracked. Dunston didn't get a shot off as the

bullet ripped into him and spun him halfway around. He dropped his gun as the impact made him fall to one knee.

Pressing his left hand to the wound in his belly, Dunston reached out with his right and grabbed one of the sticks of dynamite he had dropped. He surged to his feet and threw himself into the tunnel mouth.

"Damn you, Creel!" he cried. "You've killed me!"

Bo stepped quickly to the side, out of the line of fire in case Dunston had another gun on him.

Dunston had something else in mind, though. Bo heard a rasping sound, and the sudden flare of light inside the tunnel told him that the crazed former prospector had just lit a match.

Bo lunged toward the tunnel mouth and shouted, "Dunston, get out of there!"

"Go to hell!" Dunston screeched back at him. The tunnel was about ten feet deep, and in the light cast by the sparks flying from the fuse attached to the stick of dynamite in Dunston's hand, Bo saw that the man had collapsed next to the open crate of explosives. Dunston's shirt front was sodden with blood. He was mortally wounded, all right, but the bullet wasn't going to get the chance to kill him.

The blast that was about to go off would.

Bo's brain worked with lightning speed. The fuse was short and burning fast. He didn't have time to dash in there and get the dynamite away from Dunston so he could snuff it out.

All he could do was run.

As he did so, dashing along the wall of the gulch perpendicular to the opening, Dunston's maniacal laughter echoed from the tunnel. It blended with the swift rataplan of hoofbeats as a large group of riders charged through the gap and into the Golden Cup. Gun thunder welled up, and muzzle flashes split the twilight gloom as the attackers opened fire.

Bo barely noticed that as he kept his head down and ran, forcing as much speed out of his aging body as he could. In the back of his mind, he knew the horsemen had to be the rest of the bunch that had come to attack the claim. The gunshot had warned them that Dunston's sneak attack had failed, so now they were launching an all-out frontal assault.

Scratch, Chart Kelly, Dave Clarke, and Milt Emery spilled out of the tents and returned the raiders' fire. They didn't know what was about to happen.

"Get down!" Bo shouted as he ran toward them. "Hit the dirt!"

He didn't know if Scratch or any of the others heard him. His time was just about up. That fuse was going to reach the blasting cap any time now. . . .

The roar was almost too much for the human mind to comprehend, like being in the middle of the world's biggest thunderstorm and having it all crash at once. Bo was already diving to the ground, obeying his instincts, or else the blast wave would have struck him even harder and slapped him right off his feet. As it was, he felt as if a giant fist had crashed into him and sent him rolling.

He came to a stop on his belly, cocooned in silence because the blast had bludgeoned his ears beyond the point of working. He didn't know if his hearing would come back, but his brain, even though stunned, functioned well enough to remind him that he had other things to worry about right now. He raised his head and looked around for the attackers.

Some of them were down, and so were their horses, kicking and screaming. The explosion had flung chunks of rock across the claim with so much speed and power that they had become deadly missiles.

Other men were still mounted, though. The shooting had stopped for a moment in the aftermath of the explosion, but now it started again, ragged but no less deadly. Bo couldn't hear the shots, but he saw the muzzle flashes and pushed himself back to his knees as he aimed at them.

He triggered shot after shot as he worked the Winchester's lever. More attackers fell.

From the corner of his eye, he saw Scratch meeting the charge with a long-barreled Remington revolver in each hand. Walter Heuman tried to draw a bead on the silver-haired Texan, but Scratch fired first and the twin .44 rounds smashed into the saloonman's chest, driving him from the saddle.

Bo spotted Eli Byrne and snapped a shot at him, but the young gunman's horse reared at just the wrong instant and took the bullet meant for Byrne. The horse whinnied and went over backward. Byrne leaped clear just in time.

Bo squeezed the Winchester's trigger again as Byrne rolled over and came up with a Colt in his hand. The rifle's hammer clicked. Bo had emptied it.

"You and me, Creel!" howled Byrne as he charged forward on foot, firing as he came.

Bo stood up and calmly palmed out his own revolver. He felt the wind-rip of a bullet past his ear as he triggered his gun. Byrne rocked back, then stumbled forward another step. His gun hand sagged.

"I . . . I'm faster than you," he gasped as he made a monumental effort and raised the Colt again.

Bo's gun roared and bucked against his palm. Byrne went back and down, losing his gun and landing in a huddled heap that quivered a couple of times before going still.

"And deader, too," Bo told the gunman, then realized he'd heard what Byrne said, muffled but understandable. His hearing was coming back, and he was glad of that.

As he lowered his Colt, he realized that the shooting had stopped. He heard more hoofbeats and looked around to see another group of riders entering the claim.

These were friends, though. He saw George Sullivan in the front, along with Ed Lerch and Ham Volney and Burton Peck. From the looks of things, the honest citizens of Cushman had banded together and come to give them a hand, only to arrive just as the fight was finished.

Scratch hurried over and asked his old friend, "Are you all right, Bo?"

"Yeah, I reckon so. My brains are a mite scrambled up from being so close to that blast, but no real harm done. Are all those varmints done for?"

"I expect so. Chart and Dave are checkin' on 'em right now. The ones who didn't get cut down by the blast, we took care of." Scratch shook his head. "I don't reckon they expected that much hell to break loose. I know I didn't. What happened?"

"That loco weasel Dunston tried to steal some dynamite. He figured on using it on us, I imagine. But he wound up setting it all off instead."

A thick cloud of dust hung over the claim, but it was starting to settle, and as Scratch looked toward the wall of the gulch, he said, "He blew a mighty big hole in the ground, too."

"Bo! Scratch!"

The female voice made them look around. Beatrice led

the other three women toward the Texans. They hurried up in their nightclothes. Beatrice clutched at Bo's arm.

"Are you all right?"

"Sure," he said. "It'll take more than a little explosion to hurt a tough old bird like me."

"That was no little explosion!" Martha exclaimed. "It sounded like the world was coming to an end."

George Sullivan rode up with the other men from the settlement. "Mrs. O'Rourke, is everyone all right?" he asked.

"We all appear to be. What are you doing here, Mr. Sullivan?"

The newspaperman looked a little uncomfortable on horseback. He dismounted awkwardly and said, "Byrne and Heuman and some of the other men who work for Lawson and Kemp came to the newspaper office to destroy my printing press, but we were ready for them." He nodded toward the other men who had come with him. "When the same bunch went charging out of town a short time later, we figured they were on their way up here to attack you."

"So we lit out after 'em," Ed Lerch put in. "Had to scrounge up every horse we could find to do it, too, includin' some extra mounts that belong to Lawson." He laughed. "I reckon that makes us hoss thieves, but I don't think anybody's gonna be callin' in the law."

"They'd have to go a long way to do that," said Bo.

Sullivan said, "As it turned out, our assistance wasn't really needed, but I'm glad we came, anyway. We can take these bodies back to town." He looked around at the scattered corpses and shook his head. "This appears to be just about all of Lawson's and Kemp's men. I don't know what they'll do now."

Before any of them could speculate on that, a startled cry made them all look around. Milt Emery was hobbling toward them on his makeshift crutch, moving fast despite his healing injury. He thrust out a hand and said, "Look at that!"

Chart Kelly and Dave Clarke came along behind him, Kelly holding up a lantern he had gotten from the cabin. Its light shone on the large ragged piece of rock in Emery's hand.

Shone . . . and glittered.

"Is that . . . ?" Sullivan began.

"Looks like it," Bo said.

Burton Peck stepped forward and said, "Let me take a look at that." He bent over the rock Emery held for several long seconds, then raised his head and looked around at the group. "I'll have to run some tests, of course, but I feel confident in saying that's some incredibly rich ore."

"But . . . where did it come from?" Beatrice asked.

"From that last tunnel," Bo said, nodding toward the gaping hole the explosion had blown in the wall of the gulch. "It was there all along. Dunston just helped us find it sooner." He paused. "I have to admit, I never would have risked a blast that big."

"Then something good came out of this after all." Beatrice took the chunk of rock from Emery when he held it out to her. "This time we really are going to be rich, aren't we?"

"We'll have a better idea once we've cleaned up all this mess."

"And we still have one more mess to clean up," said Scratch. "Lawson and Kemp aren't here. That means they're waitin' in Cushman to find out what happened."

"I reckon we'll just have to ride in and tell them," Bo said.

Chapter 43

The Avalanche Saloon was closed, but four men were still there drinking at what would have been a predawn hour in most places in the world. Here in Alaska at this time of year, the sun was already climbing above the trees.

Amos Lawson refilled his glass, along with Franklin Nebel's. He slid the bookkeeper's drink over to him. They sat at one table with a bottle; Rollin Kemp and the man called Dex sat at another. The air in the room was thick with tension.

Finally, Lawson growled, "Damn it, they should have been back before now."

"That explosion we heard a couple of hours ago must have done quite a bit of damage," said Nebel.

Kemp said, "It better not have hurt Miss DeHerries. My men had strict instructions that she wasn't to be harmed, Lawson."

"And *my* men knew that all four of those women were to be protected, if possible," Lawson snapped. "We're not fools, Kemp, no matter what you may think of us." His mouth tightened into a thin line. "A man who runs a Skid Road saloon shouldn't be acting so damned superior."

Dex leaned forward angrily, but Kemp held out a hand to forestall the reaction.

"We need to remember that we're on the same side," he said. "It's those troublesome Texans and their friends who are the enemy."

Franklin Nebel stood up and went to the saloon's front window, taking his glass of whiskey with him. He sipped from it as he looked out at the new day.

Then he stiffened, let out an uncharacteristic curse, and said, "Amos, you need to see this."

Lawson wasn't the only one who got to his feet and hurried over to the window. As all four men peered through the glass, Kemp cursed, too.

Bo Creel and Scratch Morton were riding slowly down Cushman's lone street. A larger group of riders followed them, a couple of hundred yards behind. The buckboard carrying all four women rolled along beside those horsemen.

Dex pulled a gun from under his coat and started toward the door. Nebel stopped him by saying, "I think they want to parley, otherwise they wouldn't have ridden into town ahead of the others like that."

"Parley about what?" asked Lawson.

Nebel shrugged. "I don't know, but it might be a good idea to hear them out. I don't see Eli or Walter or any of Mr. Kemp's men among that group following them. It looks like just Sullivan and his friends." The bookkeeper sighed. "Clearly, the men we sent up the gulch last night failed."

"I say we go out there shooting," Dex declared.

Kemp shook his head. "Nebel's right. We'll see what the Texans want. Maybe we can salvage *something* from this mess." He looked at his second-in-command. "Dex, stay in here, out of sight. Be ready if there's any trouble, though. That way you can take them by surprise."

"You, too, Franklin," Lawson said to Nebel, who looked as if he wanted to argue, then shrugged in reluctant agreement.

Kemp took a pistol from under his coat and said, "I'm not going out there without a gun in my hand."

"That's a good idea," Lawson said, drawing his own weapon from its shoulder holster. The two men moved to the doors, where Lawson opened one of them and stepped out onto the boardwalk in front of the saloon. Kemp was right behind him.

Creel and Morton had just reined in. The four men faced each other from a distance of about twenty feet.

Bo saw right away that Lawson and Kemp had guns ready at their sides. He and Scratch left their own guns holstered for the moment. They had turned their horses so they were facing the Avalanche.

Bo glanced at the far end of the street, where the others had all come to a halt. The ladies had complained about being left out of this confrontation, and so had Chart Kelly, Dave Clarke, Milt Emery, George Sullivan, and the other men from Cushman. Bo and Scratch had insisted on having this showdown with Lawson and Kemp—just the two of them. Ending this with no further bloodshed was unlikely, Bo knew, but it might still be possible.

Lawson spoke up first, rasping, "Whatever you've come to say, spit it out."

"All right," Bo said. "You're done here, Lawson. Done in Cushman. All your men are dead. It would be better if you just packed up and left."

Lawson stared at the Texans for a moment, then said, "You can't run me out of town. I'm an honest businessman—"

Scratch's laughter cut his declaration short and made his face flush in anger.

"I reckon everybody here knows you're as crooked as a dog's hind leg, Lawson. You hid behind Byrne and those other gunmen and hard cases you hired, but the whole blamed town knows who was callin' the shots. And most of 'em are tired enough of it to do something about it, too."

"As for you, Kemp," Bo said, "you came up here to take Miss Caroline back to Seattle with you, but that won't be happening. She's engaged to be married."

"She already said she wasn't going to marry Byrne—" Kemp began.

"She's betrothed to Mr. Charles Kelly."

As of earlier this morning, that was true.

"So if you're willing to go back where you came from," Bo went on, "you can leave peacefully, just like Lawson. Captain Cruickshank and the *Byron Mowery* will be here in a few days, and I'm sure he'll take you both back downriver to St. Michael. From there you can go anywhere you want."

Lawson lifted his left hand and rubbed it wearily over his face. His expression when he looked up at Bo and Scratch was bleak.

"You're asking me to give up everything I worked so hard to get," he said.

"I'm asking you to accept the generosity of people you've wronged and leave with your life," Bo responded.

Scratch smiled, leaned forward in his saddle, and said, "Reckon there's one more thing you ought to know before you go, though, Lawson. That claim of Mrs. O'Rourke's that you wanted so bad . . . After one of your men set off a big explosion out there, this is what we found."

He reached into one of his saddlebags, took out a chunk of rock, and tossed it so that it landed at the feet of Lawson and Kemp.

"That's gold ore," drawled Scratch. "And mighty high-grade gold ore, at that. The vein's wide and deep, and that claim's fixin' to bring those ladies a fortune."

Both men stared down at the rock for a moment. Then Lawson's head snapped up. Hate twisted his face as he yelled, "Damn you!" and jerked the gun in his hand up to point at Scratch.

The silver-haired Texan was already drawing his Remingtons, though, and they came level a fraction of a second before Lawson's gun. Flame geysered from both muzzles. The slugs hammered into Amos Lawson's chest and threw him backward against the saloon's big front window. It shattered under the impact. Pieces of broken glass flew as Lawson fell over the sill and landed with his legs still hanging out limply.

At the same instant, Kemp tried to bring his gun into play, but Bo was ready and beat Kemp to the shot, even though Kemp was already holding his gun and Bo had to draw and fire. The boom of Bo's shot blended with the roar from Scratch's Remingtons. Kemp doubled over as the bullet punched deep in his midsection. His finger jerked the trigger, but his gun arm had sagged and the slug chewed splinters from the boardwalk at his feet. He dropped the gun, folded up in a heap, and didn't move again.

Howling curses, Dex burst out of the saloon and fired a shot that whistled between Bo and Scratch, who were having to work to control their suddenly skittish mounts. These horses weren't as accustomed to gunplay as the animals that the Texans had left in Seattle.

Before Dex could trigger a second shot, a gun blasted from the saloon's open door. The bullet struck Dex and threw him forward. He stumbled off the edge of the board-walk and pitched into the street, landing on his face. A dark bloodstain began to spread on the back of his coat.

Bo and Scratch swung their guns to cover the man who stood in the doorway. Powdersmoke curled from the muzzle of the pistol in Franklin Nebel's hand. He set it quickly on the planks at his feet when he saw the Texans covering him.

"Don't shoot," Nebel said. "I'm on your side."

"Since when?" Bo demanded.

Nebel looked at the sprawled bodies on the boardwalk and in the street and said, "Since about three seconds ago, I'd estimate."

Several days later, Bo and Scratch stood at the riverboat landing and watched as Franklin Nebel crossed the gang-plank, carpetbag in hand, and boarded the *Byron Mowery*. Nebel glanced at them, then looked away.

Scratch said, "I still don't like lettin' that varmint just

leave like this. He was up to his neck in all the deviltry that Lawson was behind."

"Yeah, I reckon he was," Bo agreed, "but he also took our side during that gunfight."

"By shootin' Dex in the back! Anyway, we would've killed Dex our own selves in another half a second or so."

Bo nodded. "Sure. Nebel's just one of those fellas who always finds a way to survive, even if it means double-crossing his partners. He knew we wouldn't gun him down in cold blood or let any of the other folks in town lynch him if he promised to leave and never come back."

"Yeah. I hate it when no-good skunks like that take advantage of our better nature."

Nebel disappeared into one of the cabins as Captain Hal Cruickshank came along the deck and across the gang-plank to join the Texans.

"Are you sure you boys don't want to head downriver with us?" Cruickshank asked.

"We'll wait until the next trip," Bo told him. "By then the Golden Cup Mine ought to be operating well."

"And there ought to be another engagement or two in the works," added Scratch. "Maybe three, the way George Sullivan is courtin' Miss Beatrice. He's bound and deter-mined to win her over."

"I think he's got a good chance of succeeding," Bo said.

Cruickshank tugged at his little billy goat beard and frowned. "Didn't I hear that you boys are partners in that mine?"

"We have shares in it," Bo said. "Beatrice has promised to send along any profits that are coming to us. For a long time, we've kept a bank account in Denver—"

"Durned near empty most of the time, but still there," Scratch put in.

"So we'll have that to draw on if we need it."

"From what I've heard about that ore, if the vein holds out, you two are gonna be rich men," the captain said.

"It seems to me we've been rich all along. We've lived our lives the way we wanted to."

"And we haven't had to sit around in rockin' chairs, whittlin' and gettin' bored."

Cruickshank shook his head and said, "No, you just get shot at and have varmints tryin' to kill you half the time."

"It keeps us out of trouble," Bo said dryly.

"Are you still gonna be in the mail-order bride business?"

"I don't suppose we'll know that until we make it back to the States and get in touch with Cyrus Keegan. If he has something else for us to do, we'll probably take on the job."

"Providin' that it sounds excitin' enough," Scratch said.

"Well, I wish you good luck." Cruickshank shook hands with both of them. "I'll see you in three weeks or so."

"We'll be here," Bo promised.

They watched the riverboat's crew cast off, then the big paddle wheel began to revolve and pull the boat back out into the Yukon. From the pilot house, Cruickshank lifted a hand in a wave of farewell.

The Texans returned the wave, then walked up the street toward Volney's Emporium, where the ladies were doing some shopping, accompanied by Chart Kelly. Dave Clarke and Milt Emery were up at the claim, along with several other men Beatrice had hired to help with the work.

"Rich men," Scratch mused. "I never figured anybody would ever describe us that way."

"Don't go counting your fortune yet," Bo advised. "That vein of ore could still play out any time."

"You really think it will?"

Bo considered, then said, "No. No, I don't feel like it will."

"So we actually *could* stop driftin' if we wanted to."

"I suppose. Have you seen the other side of all the hills you want to see?"

Scratch let out a snort. "Hell, no."

"Me neither," Bo said. He smiled. "I reckon we can keep on being fiddle-footed for a while longer."

Scratch chuckled, and the Texans moved on.

Keep reading for a special preview!

National-Bestselling Authors
William W. Johnstone
and J. A. Johnstone

THE
INTRUDERS

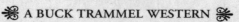 A BUCK TRAMMEL WESTERN

Pinkerton. Sheriff. Lawman. Buck Trammel has spent his life fighting for justice. Now, he must defend a town against corrupt businessmen and scurrilous outlaws from turning it into a bloody battleground.

Blackstone, Wyoming, belongs to "King" Charles Hagen. The rancher bought land, built businesses, and employed most of the townsfolk. Unfortunately, Sheriff Buck Trammel is not on His Majesty's payroll. The lawdog won't be tamed or trained to accept the king's position as master of the territory, but neither will he threaten his empire.

Adam Hagen, the king's oldest son, is vying to take control of his father's violent empire in Blackstone. Sidling up with the notorious criminal Lucien Clay, Adam is adding professional gunmen to his gang of murderous hired guns who perform his dirty deeds without question. But moving against his father means crossing paths with his former friend Buck—the man who once saved Adam's life.

A civil war is coming to Blackstone. And when the gunsmoke clears, Buck Trammel is determined to be the last man standing . . .

Look for THE INTRUDERS, on sale now!

Chapter 1

"Clean up Blackstone! Clean up Blackstone!"

So yelled the thirty or so marchers from the Citizens' Committee of Blackstone. Their number was enough to fill the width of Main Street in front of the Pot of Gold Saloon.

Sheriff Steven "Buck" Trammel stood guard in front of the saloon to prevent the crowd from storming the place. He might only have been one man, at several inches over six feet tall and two-hundred-and-thirty solid pounds, he loomed large over the crowd. He looked larger still from the boardwalk.

The piano player from the Pot of Gold mocked the marchers by banging out "The Battle Hymn of the Republic." The patrons joined in, slurring the words loudly.

"Blasphemy!" Mike Albertson exclaimed. Trammel had heard the man with the crooked back was a retired freight driver who had given up the life of a long hauler to do the work of the Lord. He was the leader of the marchers and raised his voice louder than his followers as he said, "How dare they mention the Lord in a den of such iniquity! Let us go amongst them and defend His holy name from the mockery of drunken rabble."

The marchers, who were mostly older men and women, took several steps toward the boardwalk.

Trammel took a single step forward and said, "That's enough. You've had your say. Now go home. All of you."

The crowd's chants of "Clean Up Blackstone" died down and their banners sagged. Some of the marchers at the back of the crowd took a couple of steps backward.

Because everyone knew Buck Trammel did not say much, so when he spoke, it was best to listen.

But Albertson held his ground. Instead, he limped forward and pointed his finger up at Trammel. "Last time I checked, Marshal, this here territory was still part of the United States of America, and that means we can march anywhere whenever we're of a mind to do so. Says it right in the Constitution." He glared up at Trammel. "Or are you one of those types who never got around to learning to read?"

Trammel stepped down from the boardwalk without using the steps. He still towered over all of the marchers. Most of them moved back a couple of steps as the big lawman approached.

Only Albertson held his ground. "You don't scare me, big fella. I've gone through tougher and bigger than you."

"No, you haven't." Trammel pointed at the star pinned to his vest. "Says 'Sheriff,' not 'Marshal.' Or are you one of those types who never got around to learning how to read?"

Albertson did not look at the star. He stood with a stoop, probably from all his years spent hauling freight all around the territory and beyond. "I don't care what you call yourself, Trammel. You've got no right to order us to leave."

His followers cheered as Albertson pointed past Trammel toward the Pot of Gold Saloon. "But you do have every right to tell them to leave. To tell them to obey the law. Them and their kind. It's getting so it ain't safe to walk around town, be it morning, noon, or night. Drunken cowhands from the Blackstone Ranch and miners roaming the streets in a laudanum stupor."

Albertson pointed to a shrunken old woman clutching a bag. "Why, Mrs. Higgins here found one of them passed out on her porch the other morning. Gave this poor, God-fearing woman the fright of her life."

"I know all about it." Trammel looked at Mrs. Higgins and said, "I came right over and got him out of there, didn't I, Helen?"

The old lady's scowl turned into something of a smile. "Yes, you did, Sheriff. You came in and dragged him away in no time flat."

Trammel looked back at Albertson. "I kept that drunk in a cell until he sobered up. Then I fined him and threw him out of town. I know you're new around here, Albertson, but this town is used to drunks and knows how to handle them."

The old freighter pointed to the new buildings that had more than doubled the length of Main Street. The locals had taken to calling that section of town New Main Street. "And just how do you expect to handle all of them new places once they're open, Trammel? How many of them are going to be saloons? Your friend Hagen sure ain't telling us."

Trammel said, "Adam Hagen's not my friend, but he

does own those properties. Why don't you ask him what he has planned? Or ask Mayor Welch."

But Albertson and his followers had come to Main Street to shout and argue, not for answers. "Asking either of them is pointless," Albertson said. "Hagen is crafty enough to keep his true plans hidden, and Welch is gullible enough to believe him. And King Charles Hagen is content to look down on us from his ranch house and watch this town crumble without so much as lifting a finger."

The crowd offered a full-throated cheer, and Albertson raised his voice so he could be heard over them. "We will not be deterred by lies and placation. We will not be fooled into thinking Hagen's plans are for the benefit of anyone but himself."

The old freighter's eyes narrowed in defiance as he glared up at Trammel. "And we will not allow a Judas goat with a star on his chest to tell us to be calm and go home."

Trammel snatched Albertson by the collar and pulled him toward himself before he realized he had done it. He easily lifted the man just enough so that Albertson was standing on his toes.

The marchers gasped and now took several steps back.

"You listen to me, Albertson, and listen well," Trammel said. "I'm nobody's Judas goat, got it? I don't belong to either of the Hagens. I don't belong to Montague down at the bank. I don't belong to anyone or anything but the law and the town of Blackstone. If you ever doubt it, come see me at the jail and I'll be more than happy to convince you."

He released Albertson with a shove that sent him stumbling back toward the marchers he led. Several of them rushed to keep him from falling down. He knew he would regret manhandling the rabble-rouser later on, but now was not the time.

He faced the crowd. "You've all made your point. You've had your march. You've spoken your mind and you've been heard. Now it's over. If I see any of you clustered together within the next five minutes, I'll lock you up for disorderly conduct."

Trammel did not have to ask if he had made himself clear. Judging by the looks on their faces, they knew.

And from how they had just seen him take on Albertson, none of them wanted to risk the same treatment.

Trammel stood his ground alone as he watched the marchers reluctantly fold their banners and head back to their homes.

As the crowd thinned out, only one man was left in the middle of Main Street. A thin man in his late twenties, his black hair and spectacles gave him a studious look. This man was not Albertson, but Richard Rhoades of the town's newspaper, *Blackstone Bugle*.

Trammel shut his eyes and hung his head. He had not seen the reporter during the march. If he had, he would have tried to keep a better handle on his temper. Grabbing Albertson would be the bright bow his story needed for the paper's next edition. And he couldn't blame Rhoades for printing it. He could only blame himself for giving the newsman something to print.

"How long have you been there?" Trammel called out to him over the heads of departing marchers.

"From the beginning." The reporter finished jotting something down in his notebook as he walked toward Trammel. "I was with them when they began gathering at Bainbridge Avenue and followed them the whole way here. They had about thirty marchers by the time you broke it up. An impressive number for a town this size if you ask me."

Throughout his career as a policeman in Manhattan, and then as a Pinkerton, Trammel always had a healthy distrust of newspapermen. They tended to distort the truth to fit whatever message they were trying to convey. But Rhoades was a different sort. Since he had come to town a year before, Trammel found his reporting honest and had even grown to like the man.

"Guess you're happy I grabbed Albertson like I did. That ought to make a nice addition to your story."

"Maybe," Rhoades agreed, "but I'm not going to use it."

Trammel hadn't been expecting that. "Why not? Your readers will love it."

The reporter shook his head. "Albertson said he wouldn't be manipulated by anyone, and neither will I. He goaded you into grabbing him because he knew I was there. When he gathered everyone together, he told me to keep an eye on him because he was going to give me 'one hell of a story' for my article. I won't give him the satisfaction of printing it."

Trammel's mood improved some. "I'll make it a point of keeping a better handle on my temper when he's around. He won't rile me so easily next time."

Rhoades leaned in closer so no one could hear him say, "Personally, I think you should've slugged him for stirring up all this trouble."

Trammel had thought about that a lot since Albertson had first come to town six weeks before. The crippled freighter had started grousing about conditions in the town almost from the start. People were always looking for a reason to complain, and men like Albertson had a knack for getting the worst out of them. "What do you think his aim is? About starting up all this trouble, I mean. I've known a lot of freighters in my day, and every one of them would prefer whiskey and women over marches and such. It doesn't make any sense to me."

"Me neither," Rhoades agreed. "He claims he was a freighter, but if he was, he's the most eloquent mule skinner I've ever heard."

The small question that had been rattling around in Trammel's mind now loomed large. "That's been bothering me, too. You think he's a phony?"

"He seems sincere in his complaints," Rhoades said. "There's no denying that. Now, as for his motivation, I'm still trying to figure that out." Trammel watched an idea dawn on the reporter's face. "He says he's worked freighter outfits in Texas and Missouri and Kansas. I have colleagues in those areas. I'm going to write them to see if they've heard of him. I doubt we'll learn much, but I'll feel better having tried it."

Trammel watched Albertson walk back toward Bainbridge with two old ladies on his arms. He was gesturing wildly, probably carrying on with the same rhetoric he had used in front of the saloon.

"Think you could wire your friends instead?" Trammel asked. "The town will pay for it."

"In that case, of course." Rhoades looked curious. "But why the urgency?"

"Because I think Albertson is working up to something big," Trammel said. "Today's march proves it. His attempt to barge into the saloon tells me he's looking to escalate things. The sooner we know who and what he is, the quicker we'll know what he's really up to. Might be able to stop him before he does it."

"Let's hope so." Rhoades pushed his hat further back and scratched his forehead. "I've got to tell you, Sheriff, for a small town, Blackstone's sure got a lot of intrigue going on."

Trammel could not argue with him there. "Too much for my taste. When do you think you could get down to Laramie and send out those telegrams?"

He pulled his watch from his waistcoat and frowned. "It'll be well on dark if I leave now and I have tomorrow's edition to get out. I'll do it first thing in the morning. That soon enough for you?"

It wasn't, but it sounded like it would have to be. "I appreciate it, Rich. And I appreciate you leaving my grabbing of Albertson out of your article."

"Don't give it a second thought." Rhoades grinned. "Besides, no one wants to read anything that casts 'the Hero of Stone Gate' in a bad light."

"Knock it off." Trammel had hated that moniker since the day Rhoades had hung it on him after he kept a group of Pinkertons from taking over King Charles Hagen's Blackstone Ranch the previous year. "I told you not to call me that."

"That's the problem with you, Buck. You're too modest. I spelled your name right and gave you a legend. You should be pleased. The people of this territory have put you on a pedestal."

Trammel knew he was right. And he also knew what people did with things on pedestals.

They pulled them down after they were sick of looking at them.

Chapter 2

Adam Hagen had watched the entire spectacle unfold from the second-floor balcony of the Clifford Hotel. His hotel.

From there, he could watch the whole town. He could see the carpenters working on the structures he had ordered to be built on lots he had purchased along Main Street. He could see the new houses he was building on the new Buffalo Street, too, in anticipation of the people who would flock to Blackstone when his plans took shape. He had even seen the marchers assemble on Bainbridge, then head toward his Pot of Gold on Main Street. He had watched them pick up more followers along the way until they reached his saloon and hurled insults and prayers at the place.

He almost felt sorry for the poor fools. They were so ardent in their righteousness. Strident in their belief that they could change the future of Blackstone.

But Adam Hagen knew there was only one man who could do that, and it was not King Charles Hagen. Soon, it would be King Adam Hagen.

He had ordered the porch to be added to his room to aid

in his convalescence after having been shot in the right arm by renegade Pinkerton men several months before.

He squeezed the small bag of sand in his right hand again for the countless time that day. He ignored the sharp pain that webbed through his body following each squeeze. His convalescence had taken a toll on him, particularly his looks. His fair hair had begun to turn white in places, though he was just past thirty. His smooth skin, which the ladies loved, now had lines brought about by pain that had not been there before.

A doctor down in Laramie had told him the exercise was his best chance of regaining some use of his right arm. The doctor had been cautious enough to tell him that he was unlikely to ever have full use of the arm again, but with diligent exercise, he might be able to hold a fork again. Perhaps even write his name without much difficulty.

But as for gambling and gunfighting, those activities were out. The doctor advised him to learn how to make do with his left hand for now.

But Adam Hagen had no intention of making do with anything. He had made do long enough as the banished son of King Charles Hagen. And now that he knew the man he had called "Father" all those years was actually his uncle, he planned on going far beyond making do.

He intended on making revenge.

Hagen had almost cheered when Trammel snatched Albertson by the neck. The old man had been baiting him and almost got what he deserved. But Buck was a smart man, quick to anger and even quicker to calm down and listen to reason.

It was why the people of Blackstone loved him. It was the quality Hagen had admired most in his former friend.

And it also happened to be the only weakness in his considerable armor. A weakness he intended to exploit when the time came.

He knew Trammel would rebel at first. After all, Hagen hadn't nicknamed him Buck without a reason. But eventually he would see that his old friend was right and had given him an embarrassment of riches. Hagen hoped Trammel would be prudent enough to focus on the message and not the messenger. Hagen still owed him for saving his life by getting him out of Wichita the year before.

If he did not, Hagen just might have to kill him, and that would cast a shadow over all he had dreamed these past months in convalescence.

Hagen watched Trammel finish his conversation with that weasel reporter from the *Bugle*. His first order of business upon taking over the town would be to buy that damned paper and shut it down. But for the moment it served its purpose.

He watched Trammel lumber back toward the jail, which was right next door to the Clifford Hotel. Hagen did not have many regrets in life, but he regretted that he and the big man were no longer friends. Trammel abhorred his selling of laudanum at his saloon and the laudanum he allowed the Chinese to sell in a canvas tent next door.

But he had not regretted it enough to stop selling laudanum. In fact, laudanum played a key role in his plans for revenge.

He saw Trammel cast a quick glance up to his balcony and, upon seeing him, quickly looked away.

Hagen got out of his chair and went to the side railing as he called out, "Behold the return of the conquering hero! That was a mighty impressive sight to see, Buck. They complain about the new saloons on Main Street, but say nothing of the houses I'm building. They're a fickle bunch indeed. At least you turned them before they got themselves hurt. They wouldn't have received a warm reception in my saloon."

Trammel stopped walking and glowered up at him. Hagen had to admit the sheriff was a frightening sight to behold when he was angry.

"I've told you not to call me that," Trammel said. "We're not friends anymore, Hagen, so quit acting like we are."

"I'm still your friend," Hagen said, "even if you're not mine."

"If you mean that, then quit selling dope," Trammel said. "You've got half the men on your father's ranch using the stuff, and most of the coal miners. Quit rotting their brains and you and me can be friends again."

Adam appeared to think it over, though he had absolutely no intention of stopping the flow of laudanum into Blackstone. If anything, it was just the opposite. He decided to have a little fun with the sheriff. "A wise proposition. Why don't you come up here so we can talk about it instead of shouting at each other like this?"

"And look like I'm up there to kiss your ring?" Trammel shook his head. "No chance."

Hagen laughed. "You always see me in the worst light. Even after all we've been through together. I'm not your enemy, Buck. You saved my life, and I'll never be able to repay you for it."

"Don't thank me," Trammel said. "If I'd known what you'd turn into, I wouldn't have bothered."

"Yes, you would," Hagen told him. "You're a natural

hero, Sheriff Trammel, and this world needs heroes. It always has and always will."

Trammel looked like he was going to say something more but didn't. Instead, something in the distance captured his attention.

And when Hagen looked in the same direction, he understood why. Dr. Emily Downs was getting into her wagon.

Hagen imagined some might call her pretty. He had always thought of her as elegant, with an agile mind that made for pleasant company.

She had captured Trammel's heart from the moment they had arrived in Blackstone and, for a time, they had been a very happy couple.

But their relationship had soured after Trammel's run-in with the Pinkertons at Stone Gate. She had been a widow once and had no intention of becoming one again. She'd shut her heart to Trammel, and Hagen knew it had wounded the big man deeply. It had hardened him in a way that had made Hagen angry. She had given up Trammel because he could no sooner change who and what he was than Hagen could grow a new right arm. He had expected more from a woman of science, but as a widow, he could not fault her reasons.

Hagen watched Trammel forget the world around him as Emily released the break and snapped the reins, bringing her horse to a quick trot. He saw Trammel stand a little straighter and something of a smile appear on his face as she steered the wagon toward Main Street. Even the sight of her was enough to make him happy, and Hagen's heart ached for him.

She would pay for hurting him, and soon. But not that day.

She sat ramrod straight and made a point of keeping her eyes forward as she approached the Clifford Hotel. Hagen knew she could hear him as he called out, "And a blessed day to you, our fair Dr. Downs. Our humble town is grateful for you gracing us with your presence."

"Mr. Hagen," she said as she rode by, then added, "Sheriff Trammel."

Buck tipped his hat, entranced as she rode by without the slightest glance his way. "Nice to see you, Emily."

She said nothing more as she continued on her way.

Hagen pitied his former friend. He waited until she had passed out of earshot before saying, "Quite the peacock our Dr. Downs has become since throwing you over. I wonder how she'd fair if she lost her plumage."

Trammel slowly raised his head and looked at Hagen. "If you touch her, I'll kill you."

Hagen had no doubt he would and forced a laugh. "Why would I touch a hair on her head? I happen to like Emily. Besides, she has the virtue of being the only doctor in town. But cheer up, my friend. Fate is a great equalizer and, sooner or later, she'll regret having treated you so poorly."

Hagen watched Trammel's anger fade away before he turned to enter the jail. "Just leave her alone. And quit calling me 'friend.'"

Hagen decided he had given the sheriff a tough enough time already and let him go without another word. He went back to his chair and resumed squeezing the small bag of sand.

He cast an eye up the long hill to where King Charles Hagen's ranch house sat. It was a mighty place that lorded over all beneath it like a behemoth. It looked indestructible from here, but Adam knew nothing built by man would last forever. He looked forward to the day when he watched that house burn to the ground. No, he would not attack the house from the front. He would attack his father's empire at its foundation and watch it fall in on itself.

Yes, King Charles Hagen's end would come soon. But first, Buck Trammel would receive his reward, and sooner than he thought. And Emily Downs would learn what happened to those who displeased him.

He winced as he squeezed the bag of sand tighter as he looked at the Hagen ranch house on the hill and remembered a verse from the Bible. "Your glory, O Israel, lies slain on your heights. How the mighty have fallen!"

Look for THE INTRUDERS, on sale now!

Connect with  Us

Visit us online at
KensingtonBooks.com
to read more from your favorite authors, see books
by series, view reading group guides, and more.

Join us on social media

for sneak peeks, chances to win books and prize packs,
and to share your thoughts with other readers.

facebook.com/kensingtonpublishing
twitter.com/kensingtonbooks

Tell us what you think!

To share your thoughts, submit a review,
or sign up for our eNewsletters, please visit:
KensingtonBooks.com/TellUs.